# THE FOSSIL 3

JOSHUA T. CALVERT

# PROLOGUE

Hortat Junior inspected the little vial in his right hand and gently patted it with the other before slipping into the pocket inside his jacket and looking at himself in the mirror. Over the sink, his smooth bronze skin shimmered in the warm glow of the light strip. His big black eyes shone with moisture, which they very rarely did. But today, after all, was a day like no other.

"Sir?" He heard the voice of his personal assistant, who poked her head in the door to the men's toilets and regarded him indulgently. "It's time."

"I know," he said with a deep sigh, and looked away from his image before also taking his hands off the sink and smoothing his bespoke pinstripe suit. "Do you know what this mirror means?"

"That you are in love with yourself?" she asked with her typical expression of blended disdain and attention, crossing her arms under her breasts.

Hortat smiled and looked at the long row of sinks and mirrors, the last two of which were much higher, so that he could see himself without bending down. "It means, we have already accomplished more up front than what we've accomplished in this election."

"Don't downplay your victory, Hortat." His assistant shook her head. "It's not just the members of the media who have realized that this is a historic day. People are celebrating in the streets, not just in Johannesburg and in the SASAZ. You have accomplished this."

"No, it is those who have left their homes today to make their voices heard. They have done it."

She smiled. "I don't know anyone who is as devious, and at the same time, as naïve and altruistic as you are."

"Is that why you take your job so seriously?" he asked, smiling as he began to wash his hands. He inspected the patterns on his palms, watching as they grew deeper and more creased. Memories of seeing himself much older, in a mirror reflection on his ship under the red sands of Mars settled over him, making him shudder.

She dodged his question. "I know that look on your face. You're seeing him again. Am I right?"

"He is *me*," he corrected her.

"No, you are much more *he*. But even that is not true."

"No, it isn't."

"You have all his memories, but also those of all your male genetic ancestors. So, you are as much *them* as you are *he*. Meaning, you are just yourself, with far too much knowledge."

Hortat laughed. It was a deep bass sound that made the mirrors vibrate. However, the brief moment of cheer quickly faded when he realized how long ago he had last laughed so lightheartedly.

His assistant looked down at her old-fashioned wristwatch. "Not bad. That certainly lasted a good two seconds," she said with a shrug of her shoulders.

"I wish I had hired you because of your cynicism."

"That's precisely why you did it. That was your human side."

"You will never stop reproaching me for that, right?"

"You are not human, Hortat. Nor are you *Hortat*, as far as that goes."

"Why do you think we Builders choose our own names?" he replied, placing one hand after the other in the hot air dryer. He could not dry both hands together because the appliance was designed for human hands. All change took time.

"Because you were not born a blank slate," she said, waving dismissively. "For someone who not only does not forget his own experiences, but also doesn't forget those of his ancestors, you have a rather porous memory. We've had this conversation a few times."

"I'm as much a human being as you are a Builder, Agatha. You carry some of our DNA in you, or have you forgotten?"

"We are your descendants. Nevertheless, I see great differences. I can hardly compare myself to a chimpanzee, even though we are based on the almost identical genetic code."

"You are too hard on your own kind."

Again, she shrugged. "No, I just know us pretty well. Better than you do. That's probably why you hired me."

"You said I shouldn't enter the race. *And?* Where are we now?"

"Not where I... Well, that's another matter. I said you should do it like Luther Karlhammer, not like John F. Kennedy. And, I still think so."

"It's probably too late for that now. My speech is set."

"Yes. It *is* too late for that." Again she looked at her watch and raised an eyebrow in his direction as he slowly pushed his second hand as into the hot air dryer. "If you were a human being, I would believe that you were delaying putting off the inevitable."

"But I am not a human being, as you constantly remind me."

"No, you are what euphemists like to call humane, and that's why I'm here by your side—because humans like Karl-hammer and Amorosa cannot properly manage the most important legacy our species has ever received." She suddenly seemed to deflate, appearing depressed.

"It's not that simple," Hortat said softly.

"They reject you," she said with a bitter undertone in her voice. "That makes me, well, I just can't understand that. Above all, because—"

"I understand it."

His assistant merely snorted and rolled her eyes.

"They don't reject me, they reject the fact that I chose his name and thus made it public that Hortat had smuggled his DNA into Xinth's ten thousand descendants. He was a cunning rogue in the service of good," he reminded her. "That final move made them nervous, and I can understand that. I know it was his last act, but they don't. Their intentions are good."

"The opposite of good is good-intentioned."

"Why are you working for me?"

She seemed surprised by the question and tapped her index finger on her wristwatch. "We have to go."

"Answer this question first. Why?"

"Because I believe we must not give control over humans to any human."

"That's not the reason. That cannot be the reason, and you know why. Not after what we have seen."

"Yes, it is."

Hortat tilted his head in a very human gesture and looked down at her as he stepped in front of her.

She looked up and stood up under his gaze as few could, but said nothing.

"You hope that I can awaken in your fellow humans that which *you* need them to see, so as not to lose faith in them, and thus, in what you have started." He paused deliberately, and laid a hand on her shoulder. His hand was so big that it looked like he could crush her if he squeezed just a little too tightly. "That is very human. It is also human to believe that one is completely alone with one's opinions and one's convictions, but that is not the case. You will see. And now, I think we *do* have to go."

His assistant nodded and cleared her throat before going out and gesturing down the hallway. "This way, Mr. President."

Hortat nodded and followed her over the polished marble floor of the Crown Plaza Hotel. It was so quiet that the clattering of their hard heels echoed from the walls where the paintings of South African dignitaries of the last 200 years hung, highlighted by intricate frames of indigenous woodcraft. He liked the melancholy nature of human art, which reflected their fear of death in every form and function. Everything in their life was subject to the universal and relatively brief transience of all matter. He always felt something like a sting of longing when he saw their hands and thoughts creating things that translated this very knowledge—often unknowingly—into artistic expression. Ironically, many of those works had been meticulously cared for and preserved from decay over generations.

His assistant stopped in front of the large double door at

the end of the hallway and pointed at his forehead with her index finger. "There's a wrinkle."

Hortat smiled and relaxed, yielding himself to her as she straightened his shirt sleeves and smoothed his lapel like a mother would with a child on his first day of school.

"It will be all right," he said over the noise of murmuring voices coming from the other side of the door.

She finally nodded and knocked. His bodyguards on the other side immediately pulled the double doors open, setting off a storm of shouting and clicking cameras.

For a few seconds, he remained standing where he was, raised a hand to wave, and smiled broadly as his eyes tried to get used to the storm of photo flashes and his ears adjusted to the noise. Then he set off, following the cordoned-off corridor under escort by security personnel to the podium at the end of the room, like a boxer approaching the ring.

He shook hands that were stretched past the guards' broad shoulders, exchanged short words of kindness here and there, signed notebooks, fan cards, and forearms, and bowed slightly again and again. Here and there he stopped for journalist photos and waved kindly and modestly into the many lenses that stared at him like lifeless eyes before they came to life with brilliant flashes of light.

Chants of "Hortat! Hortat! Hortat!" broke out as soon as he reached the podium, and the hall's crystal chandeliers rattled as if they wanted to applaud.

He waved both arms as if trying to include all of the more than 500 dignitaries from politics, military and bureaucracy, celebrities, and media representatives before arriving at his lectern. He gestured to some aides to remove the inconspicuous teleprompters, which caused thunderous applause. His assistant made her way to the front row, seeming more excited than he.

The noise in the hall slowly subsided as he lowered his hands to the lectern and nodded patiently.

"My dear friends, I am proud to stand before you today as the president-elect of the South African Special Administrative Zone—a place that is regarded the world over as a symbol of Africa's spirit of struggle and resistance and a future of overcoming racial conflict. I am proud to have convinced you to support a program of reconciliation and cooperation rather than relying on division and fear.

"I am proud to say, 'I am a South African!' Two thousand years ago, the proudest sentence a person could say was, 'I am a Roman citizen.' Today, the proudest sentence anyone in the free world can say is, 'I am a South African.' Even though my physical time on this wonderful planet has been short thus far, I carry the memories of hundreds of generations within me and know how hard the fight for progress has been, and how hard the fight must be fought again and again.

"I proudly bow before all those South Africans before me, and before all of us, dear friends, who fought for decades against oppression, prejudice, and hatred, against Apartheid and torture. But those great men and women fought not only *against* something, but above all *for* something: for equality before the law and for dignity, for a policy that does not care about the color of one's skin, nor sexual orientation, nor political conviction."

He paused and emphatically pulled on the sleeves of his shirt, which accentuated the contrast with his bronze-colored skin.

"I would like to pay my respects to those personalities by reaching out to my political opponents. I am ready to forget everything that has been said, for the sake of standing together for this troubled country, and showing the world that there is also a different path than the path of differences. I see blacks and whites, men and women, old and young in the audience. So much seems to divide us, and yet we all think and feel, and you need only open your hearts for one moment to realize that so much more unites us.

"There are people who say that the Humans First movement is the wave of the future. To them, I say, 'Come to South Africa.' And there are others in China and other parts of the world who claim that they can work with the Human movement. Let them come to South Africa. And there are also a few who say that it is true that this movement pursues an evil purpose, but also say that it is, nonetheless, committed to the freedom and future of humanity. Let them also come to South Africa!

"A life of freedom and confidence is not easy, and our future will not be perfect. But we will never need to build a wall to keep our people here with us, to prevent them from going elsewhere. We give their voice feeling. I would like to tell you, on behalf of all those who lived before me, that they would be proud to experience this moment. Not because I was elected, but because a country that had already been written off has shown the world that there is another way, that walls can be torn down where they once surrounded and divided us.

"The election campaign behind us is the most egregious and strongest demonstration of the failure of the Human movement. The whole world sees this admission of failure in our victory over fear.

"'I have learned that courage is not the absence of fear, but the triumph over it. The courageous man is not one who is not afraid, but the one who overcomes fear,' said one of the greatest South Africans. He was someone who could not fall back on tens of thousands of years of memories and knowledge, and in that, he also sent us a sign—everyone here in this chamber, and everyone here in this beautiful land of hope, carries wisdom in their hearts—in good hearts that we just need to listen to in order to find the best, and right, answers.

"I know that we are only at the beginning, but I also know that what goes for South Africa goes for the whole world. What it takes is a positive example, and that is what we want to offer to those who believe in us and place their hopes in us. But we also want to offer it compassionately to all those who hate and despise us, because they, too, can overcome their fear of the unknown.

"Beginning today, you all now live on a protected island of freedom and compassion, of cooperation. But your life is also inseparable from life outside our borders, so I urge you to look beyond the triumph of today to the hope of tomorrow, from the freedom of this young nation with old roots to those who have met and will meet you with hatred. Forgive them, for they know not what they do. Forgive them because you know what you do.

"Focus your gaze on the advance of diversity and fraternity, across the walls of skin color, race, or species, on this day of new beginnings. Freedom is indivisible, and if even one is enslaved, no one is truly free. But the day is coming when everyone will have freedom, and our country and our planet will be united, when people and Builders come together as part of a globe of peace and the highest hopes.

"Then, when that day has come, we can say with satisfaction that it was South Africa and its diverse population that kindled the light of the future. All free people and Builders, wherever they may live, whatever they are going through, are citizens of this South Africa, and that is why, as a free man, I am proud to say, 'I am a South African!' And soon this place will be a visible symbol of the commencement of a new era—a symbol clearly visible to the eyes of the whole world."

Hortat stepped back from the podium and waved once more as the applause began and swelled to a veritable storm of jubilation. He bowed a few times and then walked down from the podium, where he was immediately surrounded by a cordon of his bodyguards—two Builders and six humans who watched with vigilant eyes, examining everything and everyone in the room. His assistant, whom he had seen leaving the front row during the speech, had since returned, and the bodyguards—after he had given them a sign—let her enter his small protective bubble as they slowly fought their way to the exit.

"John F. Kennedy. Not bad," she said when she'd reached his side, nodding appreciatively and, as always, with a mocking undertone.

"He was an inspiring personality, even for me. You co-wrote the speech."

"Because you didn't want to be dissuaded from it. JFK was controversial as president. The cult around him only arose after his assassination."

Hortat smiled but did not answer.

"You spoke of the future," she said, suddenly changing the subject after he had shaken some hands that had made it between the broad-shouldered security personnel. "It can't ever become perfect."

"You don't think it's an apt term for what we're going to do? We have won an absolute majority, so we will also be able to change the voting law. A good step toward a good future."

"The mills of politics grind slowly."

"Politics will not be the problem here, but technology, and this problem has been solved."

"Has it?"

"Yes. You'll see. Tomorrow the work begins."

"You are the winner of the election, but you are not yet sworn in. For me, it will begin, and I don't even know what it will look like. Or how I'm going to get through it."

"Reconciliation is best started immediately, and it takes paths that we often understand only in hindsight. If you can go down this path, it will reveal itself to you." He searched for her gaze, and their eyes lingered on each other for a while before she took a deep breath and nodded.

When they reached the exit and stepped out into the cool night air of Johannesburg, the convoy of vehicles was already awaiting them: a heavily armored limousine and four SUVs, with bodyguards standing at the open doors. The convoy was, in turn, surrounded by a police escort twice as large. The road had been cordoned off at his request, so there was no crowd to cheer him. Together with his assistant, he entered the back of the limousine, and when one of the bodyguards had slammed the door, complete silence enveloped them.

"Did you bring what I asked you to?"

She hesitated briefly and then nodded, laid the handbag beside her, and grabbed the door handle. "I wish I could come with you."

"No." He shook his head and smiled calmly. "Your path is a different one."

"I am proud of you," Agatha said seriously.

Again, their eyes met for a long moment. His driver was already impatiently looking back at them. He noticed that it was not Sabo but one of his substitute drivers, the one who had driven him to a campaign event a few months ago. The man seemed nervous in his new role—after all, his boss was no longer an outsider candidate, but president-elect of the South African Special Administrative Zone.

Eventually, his assistant opened the door and stepped out into the night. Without looking around, she climbed the stairs to the hotel. When she disappeared, Hortat's gaze remained focused on her after-image on his retina, her fading silhouette in the night.

"We can go," he said, picking up the handbag. His driver did not start the vehicle, and instead had begun to turn around when a powerful explosion shredded the sedan. The short-lived fireball lit up the street and soon subsided when a cold, heavy rain quickly set in.

# 1

## PANO

**Eight hours after the attack**

Pano looked down at his hand terminal and sighed. He reached into his jacket pocket and pulled out the small inhaler, which he'd found himself fidgeting with off and on for the past hour. After inhaling a blast, he sighed again, this time in relief.

"Fear of flying?" asked his seat neighbor, smiling mildly.

"No. Asthma."

"I understand that. I have struggled with it myself. But then I attended a seminar that my family booked for my birthday—or rather prescribed!" The older lady with the gray curls chuckled with her hand in front of her mouth and winked at him maternally. "I can tell you that back then, sweat would break out on my forehead at the very idea of flying."

"I don't have any fear of flying, Ma'am," he emphasized, and was unable to keep his eyes from rolling.

"It was the same for me. I thought that if I denied it, it didn't exist. That's how it was—"

"Listen, Ma'am," he interrupted, and cleared his throat before looking directly at her. "My forehead isn't perspiring, and I'm not afraid of crashing. If it helps you talk about your own fear of flying, then you're welcome to do so, but please: I have a headache and don't like having to take this trip."

"Ahem." His neighbor straightened up and smoothed her old-fashioned skirt. "Sorry, young man. I didn't mean to disturb you."

Pano sighed. "I'm sorry, I didn't want to be rude. I'm just having a bad day, that's all."

"I understand. We all have since that horrible thing," she said in a conciliatory tone. "My son lives not two blocks from the site of the attack."

"Yes, terrible," he muttered.

"He was the hope of an entire generation, you know? You're European, aren't you? Italian?"

"No!" Pano huffed, then quickly calmed his voice. "I'm South Tyrolean." He looked down at his pointed-toe faux leather boots and shrugged his shoulders. "I just have good taste."

"South Tyrol?" The lady looked as if she were wracking her brain. "I don't know where that is."

"We speak German, eat German food, and are rather more like Austrians. We work harder and—"

"But that's part of Italy?"

"Yes, but..." He sighed again and gave a dismissive wave. "Doesn't matter."

"What are you doing in Johannesburg, if I may ask?"

Pano lifted his hand terminal and held the display so that she could read the sum on his account app.

Her eyes widened. "Oh."

"Yes." He turned it back and once again looked at the seven-digit number. It was as if it were a complex image that contained many larger and smaller puzzles that he could not make out, however hard he concentrated. Of course, they were just digits, but there was so much more behind them.

Why was he being paid so much money? That was, of course, the most obvious question—one yet unanswered. But the second and much more important matter was why he had accepted after so little internal debate. For the umpteenth time, he opened the short message, which he had stared at so many times that it seemed to have burned into his retina: *I need your help. Come to Johannesburg immediately.* And then this strange countdown, which had since started in a separate app.

"So, you're traveling on business?"

"Yes." He nodded and stuck his hand terminal away.

"You don't seem like a business traveler to me."

"No?"

"Well, if you have so much money, you would certainly fly in business class and not back here in economy."

"I was offered a private jet which I refused, and there were no business class tickets left on the first scheduled airliner. But I don't care. The flight takes only a few hours."

"*Refused?* Why should you do that?"

"Because my business partner is an asshole—pardon—and I don't want any handouts from him."

"But you took his money anyway? This amount comes from this business partner, I assume?" she asked.

A fist balled in his stomach. "Yes," he growled. "And, I ask myself why."

"Do you know him?"

*Yes, I saved the world and the Builders together with him. He was happy to help, by the way,* he thought, and at the same time unclenched his features.

"Yes, I know him a bit. You'd recognize him, too." Pano looked out of the 'window,' an oval cutout in the cabin wall that had neither edge nor contour, pulled out his hand terminal, and opened the airline's app. "Wait a moment. I'll make the window bigger."

He tapped his way through the menu and searched for control of the window assigned to him so that he could command sensors to project real-time images from outside to the interior wall.

"It's really amazing that these old devices are still supported at all," commented the lady, who, despite rejuvenation, was apparently much older than himself. "May I?"

Pano gave up in frustration and threw the terminal into the small pocket in the seat in front of him. His neighbor smiled and opened her left palm, where dense STE tattoos were woven in the upper layers of her skin. Symbols appeared, and she tapped around on them with the fingers of her other hand. A short time later, the entire section of fuselage beside Pano became seemingly transparent. Some lonely clouds flew by, and in the east, the lights of Johannesburg could already be seen, stretching like a shining carpet under the deepening dusk amidst a monotonous, hilly landscape as far as the eye could see.

The city stood out with its many skyscrapers, some of which reached up to 1,000 meters high. They held no comparison to those new ones in Asia, some of which were two or three times higher, but for Pano, they were nevertheless an unfamiliar sight for an African country. But that was not what made his breath catch: it was the pitch-black pyramid that floated motionlessly in the air like a gigantic mirage directly above the scene. It covered the entire city center and cast a dense shadow on it, which was only breached by the many spotlights that lit the object's underside.

"You know, when I saw it on the news, I thought it was a hoax," his seat neighbor said in a thickened voice. "But it's absolutely real. That pyramid, I mean."

"Mm-hmm."

"What do you think it could be?"

"I don't know, Ma'am," he admitted, unable to turn his gaze away from the object. The peaks of the skyscrapers reached almost to the base of the pyramid. Its height was roughly the same as its distance from the streets of Johannesburg. He could not see any exact contours, although the shell, if it was one, did not appear entirely smooth.

"How can it just float there as if there were no gravity?"

"Builders," he muttered.

"Pardon?"

"Builder technology. I've seen things you wouldn't believe. They're kind of behind it."

"It cannot be a coincidence that this pyramid appeared only a few minutes after Hortat's death," she agreed, gazing outside, captivated. The electric supersonic jet went into a tight right turn and then braked noticeably.

"Ladies and gentlemen, the control software has initiated our final approach. We ask you to stop using the restrooms and remain belted in your seats, fold up your tables, and bring your seat backs to an upright position," the voice of one of the flight attendants sounded from the loudspeakers. They began to lose height.

The approach curve produced a strange effect, as if the pyramid were rotating around its longitudinal axis, which was, of course, merely a sensory illusion caused by the light reflecting from its black sides and edges.

Now another pyramid came into view: the new head-quarters of the Human Foundation, which was still under construction. In contrast to the mysterious object hovering above the city, over which the whole world had been shaking its head for days, the prestigious project—conceived as a stunning symbol of the foundation's power and influence—was downright puny, even though it was huge. Its shimmering golden façades and glass construction repre-sented the most astonishing thing that human architecture was capable of achieving.

But it was only that—human architecture. If there was any need for evidence that their species not only ranked some leagues below their bronze-colored predecessors from the Cretaceous period, that it was not even playing the same sport, the dark pyramid provided such evidence on several levels. Not only was it much larger and more massive, but it also floated, and its gloomy simplicity seemed to say, 'I do not need pomp or ostentation. I have no need to underline my superiority.'

*Decadent!*

"What do you mean by that?" the lady asked.

"Pardon?" He shook his head in confusion and broke free from his grumbling thoughts.

"You just said 'decadent.'"

"Oh. I was just thinking. My destination is the pyramid. The smaller one."

"You work for the Human Foundation?"

"No!" he replied a little too quickly and harshly. "What I should've said is that I haven't agreed to, yet."

"But you got a lot of money. Isn't that what the amount you showed me is about?"

"Only to get me to come here and listen to whatever crap they want to tell me."

"You really don't seem to like the Foundation. May I ask why? I know that many people in Europe and North America demonize them as too Builder-friendly, but surely an educated man like yourself would not believe such nonsense?"

"It's... complicated." He began to turn the gold ring on his right hand and sighed deeply.

"Are you married?"

"I was."

"So, you're divorced?"

"No, I—"

Her ebony forehead furrowed, and her wrinkled mouth grimaced as if in shame. "I'm sorry," the lady apologized. "I didn't want to upset you, Sir."

"It's all right." Pano waved and sighed. "It's been a long time."

"So, is that why you're here? Because of your wife?"

"No. Yes." He paused. "Maybe. I don't know."

"Does she live in Johannesburg?"

"Uh-huh." He nodded, too. "She joined the Human Foundation a long time ago."

"Oh. But you didn't?"

"No. I had finished with our old life, and she seemed to have done so as well until the clones were resettled from Siberia and were granted civil rights, and all the problems in the world began."

"So, you think the Builders are to blame?"

"No."

"The Human Foundation?"

"Yes. They pre-screened and laid claim to all the technologies that have flooded us over the last twenty years. These STE tattoos, rejuvenations, all that. We weren't ready for it, and we still aren't."

His seat neighbor wanted to know. "And your wife disagreed?"

"She felt that we ought not to simply leave things to others and rest on our former laurels. She believed we should act to protect the Builders from our hyena-like species. So, she underwent a rejuvenation, even though we had decided, together, not to do it."

"Is this the reason why you still use such an old-fashioned hand terminal?"

"Yes. I don't want to artificially augment my body with things I don't need to be happy. Comfort is the death of happiness, you know?"

"But you are obviously rejuvenated."

"Yes," he whispered and turned away to look at the approaching lights of Johannesburg. A scene in the Alps played out before his mind's eye. He was standing with Agatha in front of the glass door of their balcony, through which they could see the entire valley with its beautiful green slopes and meadows. Her wrinkled, aged face was marked with anger. Not as in other people, with contracted brows, narrowed lips, and quivering cheeks. No, it was Agatha's very personal way of expressing anger—without any emotion, her facial expressions as tranquil as a mountain lake, her eyes cold.

She held the flyer of a Human Foundation rejuvenation clinic in one hand and her hand terminal in the other. He could not see what was going on, but knew it was a news app reporting the latest horror stories from major European cities: new anti-Builder riots, another attack on branch offices of the Human Foundation, extreme police violence in some places, violent clashes between demonstrators and counterdemonstrators in others.

Her lips moved—she spoke, but in this memory, he

could not hear her. He did not need to because he would never forget what she had said. She wanted to get back into the action, not look away. She was ashamed, not of herself or him, but of her entire species, which seemed to wound her deeply. He saw himself taking the flyer out of her hand and trying to appease her. The next moment he was sitting on the balcony and watching her drive away in her car. A lonely tear fell onto the glossy paper, landing on the friendly smiling face of Luther Karlhammer and some publicity about all the good his foundation did.

Angry, he'd crumpled the brochure in his fist.

In another memory, he stood in front of a Vienna clinic, with the Human Foundation's logo emblazoned above it. He wanted to turn around, but eventually took a step toward the entrance.

Just as he shook himself free from the inner images of his memory, they landed. The aircraft AI eased the stream-lined jet onto the paved runway and braked so gently that there was no real jerk. The glittering lights of the elongated terminal passed by until they turned onto the taxiway and headed toward one of the gangways. As soon as the plane came to a stop and the 'Fasten Seatbelt' signs were extinguished, Pano nodded to the old lady.

She put a hand on his shoulder. "Johannesburg brings happiness, did you know? Don't worry too much."

"Thank you."

Together with the other passengers, he left the Lufthansa aircraft and lined up at passport control, only to be approached by two men in pinstripe suits.

"Herr Hofer?" one of them asked, in a voice that hit Pano's ears as accent-free German.

"And you are?"

"We are here to take you to headquarters. My name is Schmidt, that's Mr. Obanayo. Please follow us."

Pano shrugged and trotted after them to the counter for diplomats. There was no queue, and the officer there paid them no attention as he ushered them through with a bored wave.

"The shining South African Special Administrative Zone," he snorted. "Where corruption and xenophobia are a thing of the past."

"Our car is waiting in front of the terminal," said Mr. Schmidt, the larger of the two, without emotion.

Pano quickly noticed the conspicuous police presence. Dozens of fully equipped officers stood between the food stalls and travel agencies, which were opposite the exits from the gates, and kept a watchful eye on the hordes of bustling travelers. A family was stopped by police officers and had to open their bags, which led to everything being ransacked into disorder before the intimidated parents repacked in front of countless pairs of eyes—an undignified procedure that did not seem to bother bystanders.

Yet it seemed more as though everyone was embarrassed but pretending not to notice. There was an atmosphere of fear and tension that Pano could almost touch, as if he had been shoved into a straitjacket that was too tight and from which he could not free himself.

Outside the glass doors, where an astonishingly cold night greeted him, a large SUV with tinted windows and open doors awaited. At the rear door stood a dark-skinned woman in a black trouser suit, smiling pleasantly at him and pointing into the vehicle. Shortly before he got in, he noticed the two other cars parked one in front of and the other behind the SUV.

"A whole convoy, just for me?" he remarked pointedly.

The lady smiled neutrally, waited until he was comfortably seated, and then followed him inside. "My name is Eluise Poyogami," she introduced herself, and a bluish shimmer lay over her eyes as she regarded him.

Pano covered his face and stretched out uncomfortably on his luxurious seat of sinfully expensive faux leather. There was even a minibar between the front seats, where Schmidt and Obanayo had made themselves comfortable. The car, of course, was self-driving, and in apparently perfect synchronicity with the two accompanying vehicles.

"We are very happy to welcome you to Johannesburg, Mr. Hofer," she continued in immaculate English. The glimmer in her eyes was gone, but she made some entries on the STE tattoo on her left hand. The lines and colors of tech moved back and forth like tiny snakes, reacting to every touch. "The journey will take about two hours, which we apologize for."

"Two hours?" he asked in surprise.

"Yes." She nodded. "Unfortunately, the situation in the city is very tense at the moment. The president has declared a state of emergency after the attack on President Hortat and completely sealed off some parts of the city. Due to protests and scattered uprisings within the city limits, delays are currently unavoidable."

"That's why the escort?"

Poyogami nodded. "You needn't worry. Our premium-class vehicles are equipped with extensive defensive measures."

"I thought this was the Promised Land," he replied grumpily. "Living in harmony instead of discord."

"The attack has changed everything. President Muyabe is trying to keep himself in power with emergency laws. Hortat would have been sworn into office in only a month, so the loser of the election still sees himself as the legitimate head of government. Muyabe does not accept Hortat's vice-president Judy Jones as his successor. At least not yet."

"That's why people have taken to the streets, I presume."

"Yes, but they have no support among the country's powerful politicians because they are all afraid of being detained—or immediately made to disappear—by Muyabe's police units under the emergency laws."

"Sounds like a dictator, if you ask me."

"That's why people are taking to the streets, even though they are only permitted to travel to work and return home."

The uneasy feeling in Pano's stomach spread and gained in intensity as he looked out of the armored windowpane at the city that passed by. Most of the houses surrounding the airport were multi-story concrete blocks, which had presumably been erected in a hurry in the last century to cope with the exploding population. Johannesburg, to his knowledge, had always been a criminal behemoth, even though the country's second-largest city had experienced a minor renaissance since the early 2000s, and the number of murder victims—often exceeding those of road deaths—had declined.

Then, of course, there was the 2051 reactor disaster, when the entire area north of the city had been declared a restricted zone until the Human Foundation had also redressed this condition with 'fairy dust,' as the inhabitants called it. Of course, everyone knew that it was the Builders from whom they had once again unlocked a secret. It was only thanks to this circumstance that the public mood in South Africa toward the young giants had turned from angry hostility into almost blind adoration, and that made it possible less than 20 years later for a Builder to be elected president.

"He thus uses the attack to present himself as a strong man who merely wants to maintain order and clear up the murder," Pano summed up, without turning to his neighbor. "Classic."

They passed a burned-out terraced house at an intersection and then raced at breakneck speed under a large inner-city bridge onto a main road that was sealed off to the north by 100 police officers with helmets and batons. Two large, six-legged riotbots stood behind them. Their front arms bore weapon attachments waving threateningly over the heads of the crowd that was surging against the security force's shields.

Five minutes later, they saw an entire street burst into flames, and flashes of large-caliber weapons strobed in the darkness. A helicopter squadron chased over them, and their AI-controlled mini-convoy veered sharply when a truck raced into a barrier and crashed onto its side, blocking the road in front of them.

"My goodness! It's quite the paradise they're always raving about. Really."

"You may regard the situation cynically, but for us South Africans and the Human Foundation, it is a disaster. We were well on the way to making the future more peaceful and tolerant until..." Poyogami shook his head. "Let's just say, this country needs to discover who was behind the attack, and rapidly."

"That's why I'm here, isn't it?"

"I am not authorized to have that kind of conversation."

"Sounds more like I'm dealing with the CIA, not an aid organization."

"You will soon be able to ask all your questions, Detective Hofer."

"Detective?" He snorted. "For a CIA agent, that's pretty sloppy research."

Poyogami frowned, perhaps irritated, perhaps unsettled by his brusque manner.

They remained silent the rest of the trip. He noticed that they made a wide detour around the city center, where flickering lights flared like red fog between the skyscrapers and hinted at more street fights. The pyramid of the Human Foundation, presently under construction, would become its new headquarters when completed. It was located on a small hill that had been leveled at an apparently specified height so the complex would tower over the city. The imposing structure's base looked almost finished with its golden façades and pitch-black glass windows, which alternated evenly in layers much like the rings of a tree. Its appearance above the base, however, created a very different impression.

"Looks a lot like the half-finished Death Star," Pano commented, waving at the skeletal appearance of the structure in the upper half of the pyramid, where about a dozen cranes were situated. Some of them could be seen rotating in the glow of the countless construction lights. *This work must be going on around the clock.*

"Death Star?"

"Well, it's certainly not a moon."

"I'm afraid I can't quite follow you, Mister."

"You are *not* the only one," he muttered into his beard. Their escort vehicles turned off as they approached the security fence surrounding the site and were checked by armed personnel at a barrier. Then they drove up a gravel road to the main entrance, which looked like the glass-constructed dream of a luxury hotel.

An old-fashioned revolving door reached out to the forecourt, where concrete-cast shapes indicated that fountains were planned there. There was no additional security, although he supposed that somewhere nearby there was a novel sensor strip that could absorb pretty much any spectrum of electromagnetic radiation and acoustic signals.

Poyogami gave her colleagues a sign and nodded to Pano before her gaze became absent. He shrugged and got out of the car along with Schmidt and Obanayo, who flanked him once outside and pointed toward the entrance. Once through the revolving door, they were in a large foyer with a long counter reminiscent of the console fittings of the Starship Enterprise thanks to its unobtrusive lights and gleaming white surfaces.

He felt like he was in one of the new robot clinics that had sprouted from the ground all over Europe, and at the same time, the silence reminded him of a museum. Apart from a simulacrum behind the counter—obviously a hologram—there were no people present. Pano saw the projection rail on the ceiling, and the blonde female with the unrealistically good looks flickered a few times as she smiled at them.

"Welcome to the headquarters of the Human Foundation. I am Xinthia, virtual assistant. How can I help you?"

Schmidt and Obanayo led him wordlessly past the counter to the elevators. The ten elevator cars indicated the extent of the mammoth structure.

They rode downward, contrary to his expectations, which caused him to raise a brow. His two shadows did not seem to notice, or else opted to ignore it. After several moments, they stepped out into a large open area the size of several football fields, which had been transformed into a labyrinth by innumerable small glass partitions.

To Pano's surprise, he oriented himself quite easily, as

most of the glass dividers had a slightly different tint than the rest. Behind them, hundreds of people and even some Builders worked at desks and in AR collectives, which he recognized by the seating circles and the empty gazes of their occupants.

"Construction site, my ass," he said as they stepped into a conference room where awaited Luther Karlhammer and a woman in a pantsuit. The woman paid him no attention. She seemed a little lost at the end of the expansive table, which housed all sorts of buttons and extendable displays. In the middle, a round plate indicated a holo projector.

"I'm happy to see you, too, Pano," said the founder of the Human Foundation, standing up to extend a hand. Pano pretended not to notice and looked around appreciatively as he walked toward the chair pulled out beside the most powerful man in the world.

"Let me guess. You can assure me that this Death Star is fully operational."

"Umm, how's that?" Karlhammer exchanged a confused look with his secretary—at least Pano assumed that was her role, as she appeared to be typing relentlessly on a virtual keyboard.

"No one has any taste in videos anymore," Pano murmured almost inaudibly.

"We moved into our headquarters a few weeks ago, but without the knowledge of the public. Developments in recent years have forced us to be more circumspect."

Pano recalled the images of the attack on the Human Tower in Cape Town early last year. A hijacked suborbital rocket had hit it. Although it only shredded the top of the skyscraper, it devastated an entire street in the city center, causing great concern among the civilian population.

"Are the rumors that it was the CIA true?" Pano asked.

Karlhammer made a dismissive hand gesture. "It is no secret that the United States is not sympathetic to us. They want control of Builder technology and don't value us as gatekeepers. However, they are not alone in this. You as a European know that all too well. Politics is always the same game—everyone wants an advantage over others to force them into things that only augment that advantage and lead to the detriment of those others."

"And you don't?"

"We do what is for the common benefit of humans and Builders. We create a balance."

"And you filter which technologies are good for us and which are not."

"Yes," admitted Karlhammer. "Unchecked technological progress quickly leads to dead ends. Just think of the invention of the Internet. The inventors had it in mind as a network that would enable faster data exchange and increased availability of knowledge, access to education, and all those things. Soon after, almost half of the world's data traffic consisted of pornography. Later, the entertainment streams took up a good part of the rest of the cake. Productivity also steadily decreased, largely due to smartphones, which relieved our brains of work.

"Hardly anyone had to remember anything anymore. Information was always only one app away. What was the result? A generation of know-it-alls who were no longer even able to conduct a conversation without constantly checking facts on their phones—or rather, looking for evidence that they were right about their own opinions. And we are not even talking about the spread of fake news through social media and the formation of increasingly fragmented fringe groups."

"And you would have prevented that?"

"Yes." Karlhammer nodded emphatically and sat down as Pano finally took his seat.

"So, you decide for people what's good for them and what's not. Like a dictator. Perhaps you would fit in well in the United States or Europe."

"I see my work as a service to humanity. The Human Foundation makes no profit, invests all proceeds in aid projects and research. Our rejuvenation treatments are extremely inexpensive, and even those who live off basic financial security have access to them through lottery. In the meantime, we can guarantee a profit after three years at the latest. Isn't that progress?"

Pano swallowed when he heard the word rejuvenation and straightened up in his armchair. "Why am I here?"

"I owe you a lot, Pano. Not least of all, my life. What you did for me in Antarctica back then—"

"—I would have done it for anyone. Besides, it was Agatha that I..." Pano hesitated.

"I'll show you why you're here." Karlhammer's eyes brightened a little. Then a display rose from the tabletop in front of Pano. "You have retinal implants, don't you?"

"No."

"Well, then, we have to make do with the visual data." The South African pointed to the display, which presented a razor-sharp shot showing the entrance of the Crown Plaza Hotel in the city of Johannesburg. Pano knew the street inside and out from the news, which had been reporting on nothing else. Hortat's limousine was located just below the stairway to the entrance. Before and behind it stood armored escort and police vehicles. There were no passers-by, as a large area around the vehicles had been cordoned off.

The door to the hotel opened, and the bodyguards in

their pinstripe suits were moving as the Builder stepped into the night air with Agatha at his side. She looked like she was in her late 20s, with full blond hair and the strict facial features that lent her an elvish air, while at the same time a distinctly aristocratic one. It was *his* Agatha, and yet he hardly recognized her. If he were honest, he missed her wrinkles and crow's feet and the narrow mouth that had always frightened him a little.

Pano swallowed, but did not yet notice anything. He waited, watching as they got into the limousine. Shortly afterward, the door to the limo's rear seats opened again, and Agatha went back into the hotel. Then, what he had seen so many times on television happened—the vehicle exploded in a bluish fireball that shredded the heavily armored vehicle and shattered the surrounding window-panes. Security guards and police officers jumped out of their cars and swarmed like bees whose hive had just been torn open.

The image froze.

"Why are you showing me this? It isn't as if the whole world hasn't seen what happened," Pano asked, thin-lipped with impatience.

"Did you notice anything?" Karlhammer asked without answering his question.

"Her handbag. When she came out of the hotel, she had it with her, but apparently left it in the car because she came out without it," Pano said, gesturing a question with his palms turned up.

The chairman of the Human Foundation looked at his secretary and smiled knowingly.

"What? I was an investigator for over twenty years, and it surprises you that I notice something like this? Nevertheless,

I do not know why you are transferring two million euros to me so that I can look at it."

"I'll show you something else." Karlhammer pointed back to his display, and the image of a glass flask, which was held between two metal blocks, appeared on it. It was obviously a technical drawing, as lines and arrows pointed at individual components and at links indicating further information. "This is an experimental liquid explosive that we have developed as a cost-effective product for open-pit mining in Africa and poor regions in South America and Asia. Twenty hours before the attack, a prototype was stolen from our laboratories."

Again, Karlhammer pointed to the display when Pano looked at him inquiringly. A number was highlighted and enlarged in the same image, which had previously been so small and illegible that he had not noticed it: 1,234.3 grams.

"And?"

"Our net jockeys have looked at the security sensors of the door system from the Crown Plaza. We looked at the data regarding Agatha, and we noticed something. The sensors not only perceive the entire electromagnetic spectrum and scan through bones and soft tissues alike, but there is also a weight scale integrated into the floor."

"Theft protection?"

"Protection from augmented people."

Pano twisted his face in disgust. "Understood."

"Here's the data when Agatha checked in several hours before the attack: she weighed 121.765 kilograms. With her handbag."

Pano flew over the security file and nodded. Then another figure appeared with a new timestamp, and he watched a small cutout as she came out the door with Hortat to go to the limousine: 122.994 kilograms.

Karlhammer twitched his fingers, and a new file showed the data as Agatha left the car and stepped back through the security area. *Without* a handbag.

"That can't be," Pano breathed. "You believe that Agatha stole your prototype and blew up Hortat, the new Messiah of humanity?"

"The contents of her handbag—which she had apparently accidentally left in Hortat's car—weighed pretty much what our stolen prototype weighed. That cannot be a coincidence."

"But... Agatha would never do such a thing. She adored Hortat!"

"I know, but she obviously did, and I want to know why." Karlhammer's face turned into a tortured mask. "This is a disaster for all of us, Pano. The country is sinking into chaos, and if we do not find answers soon, there will be a conflagration that we can no longer contain. Our civilization has been at a crossroads for years, dancing on a blade, and I fear that your wife may have brought us down."

Then with the most serious of expressions, "I have to know why!"

## 2

## AGATHA

**Seventy-two hours before the attack**

"That's a shitty plan!" Agatha shouted.

"Ahh," Hortat replied, and his wide mouth grew even wider as he grinned. "So, this is the old Agatha of whom I've heard so much."

"Yes, and if you suggest more such nonsense, you'll get to know her much better."

"You will understand why it is a good plan."

She growled in lieu of an answer and looked out the window at the streets of Paris, where the European Security Council meeting had just ended. Traffic was not particularly dense, and the autonomous vehicles coordinated by the traffic control system propelled themselves across the tarmac at precise intervals and with no confusion. At inter-sections, digitally orchestrated order reigned, even without traffic lights.

*Fits their system of government,* she thought, and sighed to herself. It was not particularly difficult to lose hope considering the last two decades of humanity, but she had become determined not to remain on the sidelines and watch everything she had fought for go down the drain.

When absolute chaos erupted after the fossil was found on Mars, ensuring that the descendants of Xinth could grow up safely in Siberia, it resulted in many casualties. At that time, the public had been softened by the speeches delivered by Xinth and Hortat and people were proud that humanity had granted asylum to aliens—as the Builders were still regarded. But, as so often in history, those feelings faded as quickly as they had appeared, giving way to everyday life, which, as always, was about one's self-interest and convenience.

After a few years, hardly anyone was interested in hearing news about the little bronze babies being raised under large dome tents somewhere in the middle of the nowhere that is Siberia. Many had probably believed that the cuddly-looking gentle giants would react to their human caregivers like children to their parents, which of course did not happen. Builders did not need rearing because they remembered everything their ancestors knew and experienced. This fact remained a concept with which the human mind could not quite come to terms.

In any case, at some point they were glad that these strange creatures were somewhere in Russia and not on their own doorstep, until they realized that the Russians had not only been kind enough to donate their endless expanses as a kind of reserve, but had also made sure to secure reconstruction aid from the United Nations. The former tsarist empire had faced many setbacks in the middle of the century, including a collapsed economy, two uprisings, and the nuclear disaster in the Arctic Sea. The former superpower in the heart of the Soviet Union had become one of the world's poorhouses, left behind by other nations.

When, after five years, United Nations financial aid was suspended under pressure from the United States and the European Union, the Russians wanted to get rid of their bronze pupils quickly, and with them the Human Foundation staff and their UN consultants and inspectors. Only South Africa had agreed to take in a large number of Builders as refugees, along with Japan and the EU, which had almost collapsed under political pressure from the right, even though only 2,000 asylum seekers were at issue.

Currently, much of the EU was ruled by autocratic or paternalist regimes that consolidated their power by demonizing the Builders, who had since been driven underground and were promoted by many as humankind's enemy. After the massacre in Zurich, the former ancestors of humanity had been forced to armed resistance, which led to the founding of the Dark Tongue, the first terrorist Builder group, which, as so often happens, many regarded as freedom fighters. It had taken only a handful of attacks to bring the EU back to the brink of collapse, but in the end, the democratic forces had failed in their efforts to liberalize, and autocratic structures had become even stronger.

"They didn't even listen to you properly. In fact, they were only concerned with convincing the public that they had interrogated you like they would any company boss who paid too little in taxes."

"Maybe. Maybe not. Who knows what goes on in the minds of these politicians?" Hortat tilted his head. "We also got what we wanted—airtime on TV, live, without cutting away. If some viewers understood my message, it was worth it."

"They will have heard you, but not understood," she said.

"You trust your own kind too little, Agatha."

"Really? Most people spend their time in better-than-life VRs and use their rejuvenation treatments for exuberant sex parties. We are just wasting all the technological advances that we owe to you."

"That doesn't surprise me. Evolution is an essentially wasteful process."

"No, it's efficient. That is why it will also sort us out as a failure once we succeed in doing away with ourselves," she countered.

"Oh, on the contrary. Evolution is extremely wasteful. Many animal species prefer males and females with extraordinarily selected characteristics that provide no survival advantage. A peacock has a much harder time moving, fleeing predators, or going undetected than other bird species because its beautiful feather adornment has established itself as a mating advantage. Peahens consider such males to be particularly strong, and therefore suitable for mating precisely because they can afford this disadvantage.

"There are hundreds of such examples in the animal kingdom. Some crab and ant species consume more calories when moving around because they have excessively pronounced useless body parts that are attractive to females. The antlers of a deer are also an example. Oh, this male can afford to be inefficient. What a magnificent fellow," Hortat explained calmly, his eyes on a motorcycle passing by.

"Even the human brain is evidence of the waste of evolution. Twenty-five percent of your caloric consumption is claimed by your thinking organ. How much of this constant stream of thoughts is really efficient and purposeful? Ninety-six percent of all thought processes are pure repetitions of unimportant information. Each of you suffers from it, so don't be too hard on your species. Or with evolution. It doesn't care anyway."

Again, they were overtaken by a motorcycle.

"Shouldn't the road be cordoned off?" she asked, her forehead furrowed, letting her right hand wander to her left breast.

"Plainclothes police, I'm sure."

"I would like to have your confidence in our species," Agatha sighed.

"You have it. That's why you entered my service. Isn't that so?"

"I've worked on acquiring it. And now I'm working to keep it, despite everything."

"What bothers you so much about them?" Hortat wanted to know.

Agatha regarded his soft, even expression to look for signs of ridicule or cynicism, but, as so often, she found nothing. She could discover nothing but a genuine interest in his big eyes, and knew once again that she was right where she needed to be, despite everything she'd had to leave behind.

"Humans are violent and greedy, have no relation to their environment, and do everything for the sake of more comfort and less effort. We are a species that has gotten lost, Hortat. Lost in a web of convenience, simple answers to complex questions, and the unbridled urge to seek a shortcut for each solution."

"Do you know why you have never discovered extraterrestrials?"

"Pardon?" she asked, bewildered.

"Why have you never discovered aliens? You have been

listening to the heavens for more than a century. Why have you never received an answer?"

"Because most civilizations must have lived before us, if one takes the age of most of the central stars in the Milky Way as an indication of conditions conducive to life," Agatha replied with a shrug. "Or so I've heard."

"False."

"Do you want to rub my nose once more in the fact that you have found out much more, but do not wish to share this knowledge with us? Because then—"

"No." He shook his head very humanely. "You have always assumed that the will to progress is something intrinsic to any forward-looking culture. But there are not very many indications of that. Here on Earth, in the case of Homo sapiens, it has been the case that the most expansive and aggressive culture—the European one—has conquered the globe."

"I think the Chinese and Japanese would disagree."

"But they too have adopted the system of capitalism and compulsive technological progress that was spread by the ships of European explorers and inundated the world. They, too, are counting on ever-increasing growth, on benefits from innovation, and on rising monetization. The indigenous peoples of North and South America never did so. They optimized their lives in harmony with nature, yes, but they lived for centuries and millennia without ever developing firearms, the steam engine, the printing press, or anything like that. They lived according to their traditions and were satisfied with it as long as there were enough wild animals to hunt and berries to pick.

"Gunpowder was invented by the Chinese long before the Europeans, but the Chinese did not come up with the idea of using it to kill people. Instead, they turned it into fireworks and enjoyed them on festive cultural occasions. Only the chronically divided Europeans saw this path as obvious, thus changing the world.

"Ancient Japan was very traditional and stuck in its way of life until, here too, Europeans and their descendants changed everything, first with trade, then with violence, as was the case with the opium wars in China. There were always locals who could be infected with their way of thinking, if you want to put it that way. Once the virus of progress, growth, and ownership was transmitted, it spread rapidly everywhere, and today we have the globalized market economy, which was just able to avoid environmental collapse."

"That's only been postponed," Agatha grumbled and then sighed. "Well, I understand your argument. Most of our cultures have been involved in conflict with each other and were, at the same time, not overly expansionist or technophilic. It could be the same out there, and only a few percent of intelligent species choose this path."

"Yes. There is no evolutionary compulsion that would inevitably have to move in that direction, and so it is for your kind even now. What you need is just an alternative that is worth living—a positive example. That's what we're working on."

"The problem is that no one believes you, because you have become so wealthy yourself, thanks to this unfettered market economy."

"Ahh." He waggled his fingers, as he always did when he half-heartedly tried to dismiss something. "I've just revealed the potential of asteroid mining."

"And not only made South Africa rich, but yourself as well," she remarked.

"I could have gone the way of the civil rights activist, but they just get shot."

"That's not funny." Agatha's eyes followed another motorcycle rushing past them. "Those guys are starting to make me nervous."

"Europeans will not dare let something happen to me on their territory. The blame for it would be far too obvious considering our political enmity," he assured her, yet he too was gazing out through the heavily armored window, when it abruptly fell dark.

"Shit!" cursed Agatha, and in an instant, she had her pistol in her hand. Her retinal implants automatically switched to infrared vision, and immediately Hortat lit up like a flame next to her. The two bodyguards in front also glowed—albeit much weaker. "What's going on? Why is it dark outside? It's the middle of the day!"

"The Dark Tongue," the Builder muttered, and all at once, the air in the car seemed to have become much thinner. Suddenly, crash and thunder erupted outside. A red flicker awoke to life for a fraction of a second and was immediately gone again. Agatha's retina altered her infrared data in real-time, converting it into comprehensible silhouettes and faces that seemed unreal in their false colors and distortions, but had greater relevance to reality than the various grays and bright red sources of heat.

"Get out of here!" Agatha roared as a volley of large-caliber projectiles crashed into the car's body.

"No!" replied Sid, the driver. "Outside, we'd serve ourselves on a silver platter!"

"That's just what we're doing here," she disagreed. "Whoever is out there, they know they're attacking an armored convoy."

Agatha ripped open her door and grabbed Hortat by the shoulder, clawed her hand into the fabric of his suit, and tore at him, knowing that she would not move him one bit if he resisted. But he followed her out of the vehicle into the complete darkness that was repeatedly illuminated by infrared flashes. In front of and behind them, the fires of the destroyed police escort flickered. Several vehicles were destroyed, even though they heard sirens and the screams of men and women over the crackle of fires.

She thought of Nadja Amar's number and was connected to her in an instant.

"Ms. Devenworth?"

"Attack on Hortat's convoy! Builder-Tech employed! Rue de Gaulle at house numbers 250-300." She ended the conversation, ducked, and shoved Hortat down behind the open door just as something struck it with such force that the armored glass splintered. A figure appeared in front of them—a man who had just gotten off a motorcycle and raised a submachine gun. Agatha did not hesitate, shooting him twice in the chest and once in the head.

She then took advantage of the brief instant of reprieve to get an overview: the road was usually four-lane, with two lanes in each direction, but had been cordoned off for the convoy. A view over the roof of the car showed her indistinct outlines in the windows of the terraced houses, but she did not dare to look longer and ducked down when a shining lance of light emerged over the wrecks. At first, she believed that their limousine had been hit, but it was only the after-images on her retinal implant, which could not keep pace with the demands on its filtering program. Somewhere further up front, an explosion roared, followed by a deep red fireball and truncated screams from burning police officers.

Agatha did not wait for more to happen and began looking for an escape route on the side of the road facing them.

"We should—" Hortat began.

"Flee. Yes!" she cut him off and pointed to a small alley between two of the Art Nouveau houses lining the road. Behind some of the windows, heat sources intermittently appeared. They identified as human outlines, but they appeared so briefly that they had to be frightened residents. She held Hortat close, loudly whispering, "Keep your head down!" as they ran toward the alley. Two shots whizzed past them, so close that she heard their hisses resonate in her ears. Behind her, someone screamed, something fell to the ground.

An instant later, they were in the alley, surrounded by stone house walls and a pleasant coolness that replaced the heat of the destroyed convoy.

"Move on!" she pushed her charge, steering him toward a small courtyard where several garbage cans stood, where she found an old-fashioned combustion-engine car, a Mercedes sedan. Only now did Agatha realize that she could see normally again and that the darkness had disappeared, as if she had stepped out from a bubble and back into reality. A glance over her shoulder showed her the convoy in flames, or at least the section of it she could see through the entrance to the alley.

"Get in!" she ordered curtly, yanking open the vehicle's door, which was fortunately unlocked. She could not find a key, but it had to be somewhere in the vehicle because a push on the start button switched the engine on. Hortat forced himself onto the passenger seat and pulled his head and knees to his chest as they exited the other end of the alley on squealing tires and maneuvered through the traffic. Far away, countless sirens were blaring, and vector thrust machines roared, along with swarms of security drones, over the rooftops of Paris toward the site of the attack.

"That policeman," Hortat said, "on the motorcycle."

"Yes, I saw him too."

"It's going to be a problem."

"We've got another problem, and that's your survival. We'll deal with everything else when the time comes."

"The police escort. They attacked the police escort."

"The Dark Tongue?"

Hortat nodded. "I know the technology they were using, and I don't like it."

"They destroyed the escort because they wanted to outsmart us," Agatha growled, pounding on the steering wheel as she obediently stopped at a traffic light and merged with traffic to avoid attracting attention. It was not so easy, as she had to imitate the way a car controlled by the traffic control system drove before it was detected as a foreign object and an alarm was triggered—which would happen sooner or later anyway. "And this car—how amazingly fortunate that it was unlocked and ready to drive. They wanted to save your ass."

"I am not a friend of the Dark Tongue."

"You are the enemy of their enemy. That much is obvious." Agatha turned west and initiated another phone call in her head. It was not until she got the answer she wanted to hear that she changed her route and turned her attention back to the Builder.

"I know you don't like it, and I know the Dark Tongue always asks a price, but we have to live with that if we are to survive. Agreed?"

"Get us out of here," he answered.

"Already on the way."

Agatha drove to a garage belonging to Earth Wing, a kind of human intelligence agency that maintained offices and shelters in every country of the world, mainly to provide security to refugees and informants, and secret departures from dangerous areas. Officially, of course, Earth Wing did not exist, but Agatha was now much more closely involved with Karlhammer's organization than her official duties suggested.

The garage was in one of the suburbs shunned by the police—unless they were ordered in, but then they would come with tanks and transports—making it a perfect place for a secret, private garage where they could disappear and get rid of the car.

They were taken to another car, which took them outside the city to a maintenance hangar for air taxis. The owner, in whose company Hortat had heavily invested a few years ago, flew them unseen in one of his taxis to the airport in Bordeaux, where they finally officially checked in. It was not long before the media got wind of it all and caught sight of them on camera everywhere. So, there was no way for the French authorities to get hold of them without provoking an international incident.

They were safe, but of course, only until the next incident occurred.

# 3

## PANO

"Are you trying to tell me that my ex-wife murdered Hortat? May I remind you that this makes absolutely no sense?"

"You may. And I fully agree with you, Pano." Luther Karlhammer sighed and seemed to slump in his armchair as if all his strength had left him. He dragged his fingers through his full black hair, in which there was no trace of the gray Pano remembered from their last meeting two years ago. "That's why I really need you here, to lead our independent investigation."

"Independent? Since when have you been independent?"

"The Human Foundation is not subject to any state authority or controlling body. I would say that this makes us quite independent."

Pano chuckled and waved in dismissal.

"What?"

"You are dependent on yourselves."

"Could you elaborate?"

"I can. You have maneuvered yourself into an ideological impasse from which you cannot so easily escape. All hopes

47

for the future have been placed in the Builders under your protection and in their technologies, for which your foundation acts as a filter before any of it reaches the masses. This has made you many enemies, especially the state kind, but also a lot of friends.

"If anyone overregulates you, they risk being cut off from technological progress. If they don't, you remain, in effect, the most powerful entity in the world. This should give you a lot of leeway, but it doesn't."

Pano shook his head and folded his hands on his lap, hoping it would appear to be a gesture of relaxation, while he would have preferred to rip the display foil off the wall and shred it. *Agatha, a murderer?*

"I don't feel especially limited in my room for maneuver," the most powerful man in the world replied with a shrug. "Apart from that, I'm not the Human Foundation. There is also the board, if I may remind you."

"Oh, come on. You can employ a lot of resources, and you certainly still have some aces up your sleeve, but all these possibilities are only leading in one direction."

"And that would be?"

"To everything that is well-disposed to Builders and fanatically progressive. Anything else would be implausible and would weaken your position. So, you depend on the fact that it was racists, insurgents, dictators, unjust states in the West, or greedy corporations that blew up Hortat Junior. But based on the sensor images that exist, it looks as if one of his ardent followers..."

Pano paused. He had to clear his throat because of the lump that had formed there. "...as if one of his ardent followers killed him. What questions will this raise in public if Hortat's closest confidant decided that he had to die?"

Karlhammer was about to say something, but Pano fore-stalled him.

"What could she know that prompted her to do that? Was he a con man who had to be stopped at the last minute? Was he plotting something that compelled a former CTD agent to such a drastic act?" He leaned toward the South African. "You have to prove that it wasn't her, but one of your enemies. Otherwise the pro-Builder campaign will suffer potentially irreparable damage. Am I right?"

"Yes," said Karlhammer without hesitation, surprising Pano with his display of openness. "Agatha is a hero, just as you are. Ever since the VRs filled with documentaries detailing the discovery of Xinth, Hortat, and the Builders, everyone knows your names. Everyone knows that it was you both who discovered our excavation in Antarctica. Everyone knows that you are the ones with whom everyone can identify, and that you were the ones who ensured that the Human Foundation came to be perceived not as a global conspirator, but as what it is: an instrument for saving the future."

"Wait." Pano rubbed his ears. "I just had to knock the shit out of my ears. Are you done with the commercial now?"

Karlhammer's secretary visibly stiffened, and her cheeks grew so red that he expected her to explode in a tantrum right then. But the Human Foundation chairman gave her a barely noticeable shake of his head, and she relaxed a bit. "When did you become so bitter? I remember you as extremely friendly, sometimes even as humous and charming."

"Of course, you do. After all, I saved your ass when that possessed man had your mind under his control."

Karlhammer smiled indulgently. "What do you want?

Another 'thank you?' You and Agatha have led a very good life, I think. What else do you need?"

"The better question is probably what I *don't* need," Pano muttered.

"I don't understand. Twenty years ago, you both completely withdrew, rejecting any advisory post, no matter how good the pay we offered you. You didn't want anything to do with anything. Then Agatha suddenly appears in the news as personal assistant to the greatest star among the Builders—Hortat, who has risen from the dead without ever being dead. But you remained in seclusion." His counterpart pointed at him before pouring himself a coffee and crossing one leg over the other. "Seems to have done you good. You look refreshed. Youthful, even."

Pano twisted his face in torment. "Are you done? Or am I just here to justify myself for something that is none of your business?"

"I need you. You must find Agatha and bring her to me so that the Foundation can protect her."

"Protect her from *what*? To protect your beloved foundation from losing its reputation because it has sponsored someone who could now be exposed as a terrorist?" Pano snorted contemptuously and leaned back. His armchair creaked quietly. Contrary to the external calm he tried to radiate, he was more emotionally agitated than he had been for a long time. Agatha a terrorist? Impossible! Whatever had taken hold of her, it had to be a mistake. Or...

"Pano? Are you still listening to me?"

Pano shook his head like a diver who had been underwater for a long time and had to get used to light and loud noises. "What was that?"

"I said, if you help us, we will double your fee."

"What if *he* is back?"

"What? Who?" Karlhammer seemed confused.

"Agatha is neither a murderer nor a terrorist. She worked for the Counter-Terrorist Directive for nearly thirty years, and I don't know anyone who was as right-wing and strict on moral issues as she was."

"It's nice that we agree."

"But based on what you've shown me, I must say quite clearly, as a former police chief-inspector, that all the evidence suggests that it was she who blew up Hortat's limousine."

"Which immediately raises several questions."

"If she did it, why so clumsily? She must have known how it would appear. And how can it be that someone as intelligent and powerful as Hortat's son..."

"Clone." Karlhammer corrected him. "It's his grown clone."

"How can it be that his *grown clone* could be so easily duped by her?" He swallowed before adding, "It doesn't make sense, unless she wasn't herself."

The South African slightly stiffened and straightened in his chair.

*So, he's already considered that possibility, that it might have happened again,* Pano thought. Another agent with the ability to control the thoughts and actions of others as if they were nothing but puppets in his hands.

"Those are dangerous speculations," Karlhammer said calmly, closing his eyes for a moment.

"The agent was acting on Hortat's behalf at the time."

"An evil tool in the hands of the good, one might think."

"A soldier like any other." Pano waved his remark aside. "Our once so morally arrogant Western democracies often sent armed men and women to foreign countries to bring peace and justice while securing natural resources such as oil and water. Incidentally, of course, because they only wanted to protect a source of income for the local economy. Hortat fought for the survival of his species and used the tools he had at his disposal."

"When I think back to his coercion, my hands still sweat."

*Mine too,* Pano thought, and said aloud, "He might have done it again."

"Why should he? He has been working since he was ten to improve relations between humans and Builders and has always advocated unity between species. That doesn't fit."

"Who knows what goes on in the head of such an ancient being?"

"Agatha," Karlhammer replied, as if he had been just waiting for this question, and leaned with his elbows on the expensive tabletop to fix his counterpart with a forceful gaze. "That's why I need you, Pano. You have to find Agatha. No one knows her as well as you do."

"That's what I thought," he replied indignantly.

"What's happened between you?"

"I don't know my way around here. Not in Johannesburg and not in South Africa. I may know a few things about Agatha, but here I am just as effective as a fly that has fallen into the sea and is now supposed to find a very specific fish that once swallowed it and then spit it out a long time ago."

"I'm aware of that," Karlhammer agreed. "That's why you'll have a partner who grew up here and knows the ins and outs. You may also be able to understand Agatha, but certainly not Hortat Junior. I doubt any human being can."

Pano restlessly fidgeted in his chair. The surface of his seat squeaked from the friction. "What are you saying?"

"I'm saying that you'll have a partner at your side."

"A watchdog, you mean."

"Come on, Pano. Do we really need to have this clichéd discussion?"

"Just admit that the Human Foundation is as much of a power-hungry mega-conglomerate as the big corporations. Then at least we can talk to each other on some level of honesty."

"Your partner is not a watchdog," Karlhammer disagreed, giving his secretary a wink.

She closed her eyes for a few seconds.

A moment later, the tinted glass door opened and a Builder stepped in. Although the doorway was quite large, he had to tilt his head down a little, and his powerful muscles stretched the white shirt he wore as he pulled his shoulders forward and in to avoid bumping them on the frame. His face was as perfect as that of a porcelain doll, and although his bronze skin was wrinkle-free and youthful, his eyes radiated the serene superiority that was characteristic of every Builder.

Pano once again wondered what it must be like to be born with so much knowledge. Were they able to access it as infants even before they had acquired the ability to speak? How did it feel to have multiple lives in one mind? Countless lives? Was this knowledge even known as such, or was it as natural as breathing was for humans? Did one even think about it? Or did it simply function?

He imagined it as something overwhelming to recognize and know all those things that one had not experienced oneself. Or was he wrong? Did it seem like one single life for Builders, punctuated only by recurring deaths that seemed like a night's sleep seemed to people? A mere interruption in an endless continuum?

He did not know, and would probably never know, any more than he would ever experience being a dolphin or a chimpanzee. It was clear that he always felt like a child in the presence of Builders. Ignorant and inferior in all respects. It was not only that they existed in entirely different spheres in a spiritual sense, but they were also physically superior in every respect. This male who joined them now would probably not require any particular effort to tear him in half.

"Hello. My name is Ixlath." The Builder politely greeted him in a deep bass and hinted at a slight bow before walking around the table and sitting right next to Pano, a mountain of muscles that towered over him.

"Ixlath?" asked Pano, waving in contradiction. "Rollo."

"That would be fine for me, should it be easier for your tongue."

"Well, I can't even provoke him." He looked accusingly at Karlhammer, who seemed somehow anxious. Why? "It's not that bad," he continued, addressing the Builder. "Rollo was a—"

"—Norwegian Viking. According to the sagas, a very violent, but also a courageous and brave warrior," Rollo said.

"Oh, a history fan."

"Ixlath," Karlhammer emphasized, "is very interested in human history, which is also the reason why I asked him to pursue the investigation together with you. He grew up here in Johannesburg, under my direct care. He has a good instinct for us humans and our idiosyncrasies, but is also well connected in the local Builder community."

"Builder community?" asked Pano in bewilderment.

"There are now more than four thousand of us living in Johannesburg," Rollo explained.

"Four thousand?"

"Yes."

"But that makes—"

"Forty percent of us Builders, yes."

"That number is far too low, if you ask me," Karlhammer said. "Considering that this is the only country that welcomed them with open arms."

"Still. I heard that the president agreed to accept them only because of public pressure."

"Which makes it all the more important that you and Ixlath together prove that it was not Agatha Devenworth who killed Hortat Junior."

"Suppose I would agree to this here," Pano said, gesturing vaguely at everyone sitting around the table. "How do you imagine that we are to accomplish this? You don't have police powers, do you?"

"Our security personnel are allowed to carry weapons at all times, anywhere. You sign an employment contract, and then you are issued a service weapon that you can carry and use anywhere, if the security—"

"Forget that!" he interrupted the Foundation founder. "I will not become a member of your foundation."

Karlhammer looked as if he had punched him in the face. "But—"

"No!" insisted Pano. "I will participate, but only as a private person."

"But for your fee, we have to—"

"And keep your money, too. I do this for Agatha's sake, not for your world-betterment drivel."

Relief took over Karlhammer's face and he breathed deeply. "Well, then. Thank you." The ever-so-confident entrepreneur was apparently no longer as self-assured and calm as Pano remembered him.

The head of the Human Foundation stood, rubbed his hands, and nodded to them. "I am flying to Cape Town. Dorothee here will answer all your questions and provide you with all the resources that the Foundation can acquire. Ixlath, Pano, goodbye."

With that, Luther Karlhammer buttoned his jacket as he turned and walked out, leaving them alone.

For a while, the humming from the lights above the table was the only sound. Dorothee seemed to have withdrawn, her gaze directed straight in front of her, but empty. She was apparently engaged in an overlay calculation or something like that.

Rollo just sat there, the definition of serenity.

"So? Any idea where to start?" Pano finally asked.

"The pyramid," the Builder answered without hesitation. "It appeared shortly after the attack, and its geometric center is right above the place where the bomb exploded. That cannot be coincidence."

"And something so huge does not build itself."

"Well, technologically, it would be possible, but even then, the material for it would have to come from somewhere. It must be delivered and processed."

"So, there have to be co-conspirators. Participants. Witnesses." Pano nodded. "I know that the public is in the dark about this pyramid. I saw everything on the news. The whole city is completely beside itself. The whole world, one might think."

"If you think I know anything, I'll have to disappoint you."

"But you are a—"

"—Builder?" Rollo tilted his head a little to the side, the equivalent of a nod. "Do you know who made the plane over the Bering Strait disappear a few years ago?"

"What does this have to do with anything?"

"You also don't know everything your species or individual representatives are doing and not doing just because you're swimming in the same gene pool."

"So, you don't know more than everyone else?"

"No."

"What about conjecture?"

Rollo cast a questioning glance at him.

"Do you have any conjectures? I'm sure you can at least guess at more, figure out more than the likes of us." Pano clarified his question, and focused his own concentration because his thoughts kept circling Agatha and the video recordings of her. She looked good. Young and vital, he had to admit.

"Pyramids had great significance for our culture. Long ago, they were our temples and places of residence for the priesthood. Later, they evolved from religious pilgrimage sites into retreats that were meant to promise security and stability. My ancestors were never involved in their construction, so there will be others who can answer these questions better. You—we—may be able to determine what function it has based on the exact lengths of its edges. Provided, of course, that Hortat has adhered to past convention."

"It could be like leaving a message?"

"Yes. We will see," the Builder's voice rolled through the room like an avalanche.

"It won't be easy," Pano said, tapping the tabletop with the index finger of his right hand. "On the way here, I saw what was going on in the city. How, in the first place, are we supposed to conduct a proper investigation?"

"I think current events will give us enough cover to operate freely. The police are busy enforcing the emergency laws and pacifying an angry population. They will not care about two people asking questions in the midst of all this."

"From your lips to God's ear." Pano smacked the tabletop

with both hands and was about to get up when the Builder put one of his huge paws on his forearm. Pano's gaze descended on the shimmering hand and then looked up at the big face.

"You don't like working with me. Why not?"

"I..." Pano said, thinking back to Agatha. *I hate feeling inferior. And I have a problem with not understanding what I'm dealing with.* He added loudly, "I am not a racist, if that's what you're thinking."

Rollo leaned his head to one side. The sight gave the impression of the top of a mountain massif beginning to tilt over. "But it makes you uncomfortable."

"That's part of every good buddy movie, isn't it?"

"Buddy movie?"

"Yes, like 'Lethal Weapon' for example. The unreasonable white man gets assigned a wise and experienced black partner, and from fire and water they combine to make firewater that can compare with tequila and Essacher Luft."

"I'm afraid I don't follow you."

"Just forget it. Where do we start? At the scene of the attack?"

"We can't do that. The city police have cordoned off everything. We—"

"The scene of the attack, then. You drive."

# 4

## AGATHA

Agatha exhaled with relief after the flight attendants managed to push the onlookers and autograph seekers out of business class. Immediately after take-off, after having had to wait ten minutes for the excited passengers to sit down and buckle in, and when they were finally in the air to start their flight to South Africa, the whole plane had apparently just waited for the 'Fasten Seatbelt' signs to switch off to leave their seats and see Hortat in the flesh.

Everyone here had seen his speech to the United Nations, as a child, a teenager, or adult, and everyone had their own memories of it. There was no one who did not know exactly where they had been when the alien had spoken to the UN. No one understood that Hortat Junior was a clone and a descendant, not *the* Hortat, so they did what people always did when they did not understand something: either they fought against it, or they interpreted it in a way they could understand.

So it was that her employer had many enemies among the world population, as well as many passionate fans. There were those who adhered to conspiracy theories claiming that he was a reptile from the planet Tunga, which had been influencing humanity's fortunes from the shadows for millennia. They were mostly the same people who were convinced that humankind had coexisted with the dinosaurs six millennia ago.

Creationists, right-wing radicals, esoterics, and fundamentalists of all world religions agreed that Hortat was a con man and seducer who must be stopped at all costs, only too happy to view his wealth as a forward-looking investor as proof of his cunning. Others believed the opposite, that he was a kind of redeemer for all of them, a breathing symbol of hope, a superior bringer of salvation in all respects, which humanity needed to boldly move forward into the dark uncertainty of the future.

Paradoxically, it was precisely because of this global polarization that both streams of thought turned out to be correct, in a way. The Dark Tongue had emerged from it, as more and more Builders faced hostility and public restriction. After an international distribution conference two years ago, which convened because Russia had terminated the contracts for housing and rearing the Builders, the first 500 Builders, who were now 18 years old, had been taken in by Europe. Then followed 1,500 more, which meant that the EU had taken in the most refugees after South Africa.

Six months later, 500 of them disappeared without a trace and went down in history as the 500 that led to the foundation of the Dark Tongue. It was known that they were radicalized Builders. From where they operated, and where they developed and produced their increasingly prevalent high technology, however, remained a mystery that no secret agency in the world had yet been able to unravel, although it was an open secret that they were all going after the weapons used in previous attacks.

No matter how many billions China, the United States, or the European Union invested in their special forces and intelligence agencies, they did not produce results—at least none that became public, and since the fronts had not shifted in the cold war between China and the West, it was very likely that nothing had been found that would have made a difference.

How a relatively few dozen Builders were able to operate under the radar for so long and launch attacks that hit the affected countries so hard remained a mystery that could only be answered for the time being by the fact that it was the technology at their disposal that was so far superior to all human tech that it bordered on magic. Agatha thought this was conceivable, perhaps even probable, after everything she had seen and experienced in the early days of the fossil crisis.

"My pleasure," Hortat said, returning an autographed on-board tablet to a business class guest who thanked him kindly and, despite his obviously advanced age, seemed to rejoice like a small child. The Builder settled into his wide armchair next to Agatha and he looked like an adult in a child's seat. His private jet had been specially converted to accommodate his size, and Agatha had always felt like a dwarf in it, so she knew only too well how strange he had to feel. But, as always, he did not betray any sign of discomfort.

"What is it?" he asked, noticing her gaze and squinting at her from half-closed eyes, his hands crossed behind his bald head.

"It's strange to see a twenty-year-old giving autographs to old people."

"I am conspicuous for my obvious maturity," he joked.

"You're conspicuous because you're cheating."

Hortat winked at her. "It's genetics, stupid!"

She changed the subject, lowering her voice. "Why do you think they spared us?" His bodyguards occupied the seats in front of them so that there should be no direct eavesdroppers, but she still did not feel secure with the whole situation.

"The Dark Tongue?" The Builder's thoughtful hum sounded as if a deep bass was rolling over her.

"Shh!"

"I honestly don't know." Hortat seemed concerned, if such an emotion could even be read from his still, strange face.

Agatha had been with him for more than five years—since he was 15 years old and first entitled to conduct financial transactions in South Africa. Even then, he had looked young and yet ancient, with his calm manner and those huge, profound eyes behind which an entire universe of thoughts seemed to play—a universe whose rules of play she could not even hope to understand.

Today a heavy shadow had been cast over them, as if he were constantly worrying. She had to read him, and she kept believing she knew him until he once again said or did something that proved her wrong. But it was a nice thought, flying close to the sun and not burning her wings, so she liked to hold on to it.

"They have no reason to protect me. I spend a lot of money trying to find them, and not with the intention of congratulating them. I have never made a secret of my opposition to them," the Builder continued.

"You saw the policeman I shot?" she asked, and he nodded sadly.

"Yes. It seems that the French government, perhaps even the EU Commission, has seen and seized an opportunity to get rid of me."

"Uh-huh. Did the Dark Tongue know about it and get us out at the last moment?"

"Possibly. However, things are seldom as they seem. Someone wanted us to survive and escape in a getaway car that wasn't even bugged. If the terrorists are pursuing a hidden agenda in which I can only play a central role if I'm alive, then they would have a motive. But that is speculation.

"If the police got wind of the Dark Tongue attack plan in advance, it may just as well be that they wanted to make it look as if the attackers had wanted to spare me. This gives French politicians, and especially their current president, the opportunity to associate me with terrorists and feed more citizens with fear and anger, without me having to die and thus initiate conflict between South Africa and the European Union."

"I don't like either scenario," Agatha muttered. "Police officers who intentionally allow an attack to happen?"

"Often it is those who have sworn to protect us who do the wrong thing for the right reasons. The cosmos is extremely complex, and so are the potential deterministic branchings. It is easy to choose a path that has less to do with morality and more with efficiency."

"Are we still talking about the police officers?"

"Maybe." Hortat raised a palm with the inner side up, the Builder's equivalent of a nod. "Let's see how everything develops."

She wanted to reply, to scold him for dealing so thoughtlessly with such a disaster as today's, but what would she achieve except to appear ridiculous? Certainly, things were going on in his head that she could not even begin to comprehend, and who was she to presume to know more than someone who had the memories of someone who had gone to the stars and lived millions of years?

Hortat slept through the rest of the flight. The cabin lights were switched off half an hour after their generous meal, and only a few reading lights formed small islands of warm yellow in the otherwise dark cabin. Hortat's chest rose and fell evenly after just a few minutes, but Agatha simply could not find sleep. The influence of the adrenaline she had been under today was still too strong.

She repeatedly reviewed her memories of the attack; the eerie darkness, the motorcycles that had raced past them beforehand, the policeman who got off his bike and raised his gun in her direction, the bullets with which she had put him down. Was he the one to kill Hortat? Or was it one of those clichéd film scenes in which the apparent killer shot someone behind them, saving their lives? No, it was not, because she had gotten away alive.

And what about Hortat? Why had he stood around and done nothing? Although she had never seen him use violence, it was clear that he was more dangerous with his bare hands than any man, even one armed to the teeth. But he had remained so passive, almost as if he knew that he would suffer no harm. She was unable to put all this together in her head to form a coherent overall picture, except that the last word had not yet been spoken on this matter nor the last bullet yet fired.

So she stayed awake the whole time with one eye open and on the small number of other passengers in business class and made sure that the other four bodyguards alternated their sleep and two remained attentive at all times.

Two hours before landing, she had drunk so much coffee that she could no longer be sure if she couldn't sleep because of the amount of caffeine in her circulation, or because she had to frequently use the restroom, which gave her plenty of opportunities to scan the other sleeping passengers for signs of danger or evil intent.

She was back in her seat now and played the latest news from the plane feed, which her retinal implants projected directly into her optical screen. Once again, it was about the drug epidemics in Europe, North America, and China. Junkies were shown to be dependent on a substance that appeared a few months ago, colloquially called 'almond dust,' because it permanently altered the amygdala of an addict and caused the person to slowly waste away. They looked like zombies, with their bloodstained and empty eyes, and could only be admitted to psychiatric facilities— or, as in the case of China, simply disappeared.

There were reports of health systems in the West facing collapse because they were no longer able to cope with the tide of addicts destroyed by the substance. The autocratic governments in Washington and Brussels reacted, as they had so often done recently, using public fear to justify heightened surveillance and increased police presence in their inner cities.

Search results for the origin of the drug or more extensive finds of deliveries were not available. But some 'experts,' who spoke in line with the state media, said that tough measures were needed to ensure that this drug pandemic did not lead to more victims. Other articles reported on the wall between Mexico and the United States, where several thousand refugees south of Juarez had been stopped by the authorities, who were now searching hard for tunnels under the border.

The Horizon Orbital received a new missile defense system, and the two Chinese space stations, Lotus and Mao, welcomed their first permanent residents—allegedly private individuals with the necessary pocket money, even though everyone knew they were intelligence or military personnel.

In the south of England, there were riots over a proposed law on the equality of Builders and the granting of civil rights based on South African models, resulting in 80 people killed and 400 more arrested. The vote on the bill in the House of Commons had been postponed by a month.

Agatha continued scrolling until she came across a report from South Tyrol, and she debated whether to open it or not. She inhaled deeply and closed her eyes for a moment.

Before she could decide what to do, the cabin lights came on, and the plane braked gently. She felt the beginning of the descent in her stomach, as if her organs were gently pressed against her ribs. Hortat opened his eyes, looking awake as ever, brought his seat upright, and wished her a good morning.

During the approach, Agatha noticed a large column of pitch-black smoke wafting into the sky east of Pretoria, the northernmost part of the Johannesburg megaplex. She also noticed the brief expression of concern cross Hortat's face, like a flash that she saw only as an after-image. But since he did not say anything, she decided not to disturb him and focused on her job, which was not really hers—his safety.

After they landed, she gestured to the other business class passengers to precede them and stood between her seat and the back of the seat in front to block access to Hortat and shoo away those who wanted to get an autograph, or to quickly take a photo with him. Luckily, he did not call her off and seemed too engrossed in thought to tell her that these were good people for whom he might do a favor.

In the terminal, she immediately noticed that something

terrible must have happened. The police presence was enormous. At every corner, heavily armed officers in combat gear and closed helmets stood, scanning every passenger with their feeler-like sensors. In addition to electronic passport controls, they were herded through additional security zones where scanner corridors searched for additional hazards.

There was a gloomy mood of worry and fear that lay like a heavy blanket over everything. The numerous restaurants, bars, and shops were all closed, and their mesh shutters were lowered, as on the occasion of the nuclear disaster in Gaborone, the former Botswana, which had been contained by Hortat and Karlhammer only after a month—with still-unknown Builder technology.

"What happened?" she asked an airport police officer who had just taken off his helmet and wiped the sweaty strands of hair from his face. Hortat was still in the hose-like scanner, and she watched him and the immediate environment with one eye.

"Attack on a train," the policeman mumbled, looking reverently at the Builder.

"The Dark Tongue?"

"Nah. I heard that no alien tech was used."

*Alien tech,* she repeated to herself and decided not to comment on that. "Who, then?"

"No idea, Ma'am," he replied with the typical South African accent, which sounded a little choppy. "It happened just over an hour ago, and I don't have time to watch the news. I was actually headed out on holiday."

"Understood." Agatha nodded to him, but he pulled on his helmet and shooed away two of his subordinates who were about to take a break.

"Attack on a train," she muttered to Hortat as they

walked together toward their convoy of cars, staying inside a cocoon of a dozen bodyguards that had been waiting for them at the terminal.

"Does anyone know anything?"

"No." She shook her head. "I'll make a few calls right away and try to find out something."

"I have to prepare a speech for the media. However, my secretaries can put together the necessary information for me. I think they've been around long enough."

"Don't you need my—"

"No. I want you to go to the scene of the attack and look around yourself." Hortat nodded to their driver, who held open the door to the rear of the large electric SUV, and climbed inside.

Agatha followed him and greeted Simon, the head of Hortat's security team, who sat in front and turned to them. "It's nice that you're back, Boss. And you too, Agatha."

"Please put together a team from the campaign office to travel with her to the site of the train attack." The Builder seemed unusually brash. "They should be ready when we arrive."

"Clear, Boss."

"What's going on?" she asked Hortat.

"I'm not sure." The Builder paused and rubbed his chin. "But I want you to investigate the matter."

"Of course."

They remained quiet for the rest of the trip as Hortat's gaze grew empty. He was going over a newsfeed or the first parts of the speech his secretaries had prepared for him.

Agatha did the same and filtered the results for references to Johannesburg, which resulted in her receiving exclusive multimedia live tickers for the attack on a freight train northeast of Pretoria. From what she read, saw, and heard, it turned out that most of the cars had belonged to Heavy Chemicals Pretoria and had been severely fire-damaged.

After some brief research, she learned that this company was developing efficient mining explosives but did not yet have a product on the market. There had been three rounds of investments, and the last one had been made by none other than the Human Foundation, which secured a majority of 60 percent of the unlisted shares, thus creating a lot of confidence in the start-up's research and development. With a market capitalization of just 60,000,000 rands, it was no more than a footnote to the South African economy.

There was no trace of the attackers nor any other evidence, as the attack had taken place on an untraveled section behind a scrapyard that had not been under surveillance by sensory drones. How this could have been the case was still as unclear as the possible motivation for the act, which even the tabloid outlets with their incredible imaginations had not been able to invent. No fatalities had yet been reported, although it was expected that there would be none, as it was a fully autonomous-drive train. Therefore the damage was relatively minor, although repairs to the section of the line would take some time. Even so, public interest was huge, and the column of smoke was visible everywhere in the city.

The country's presumably most important election since the establishment of the Special Administrative Zone, which encompassed the entire southern half of Africa, was imminent. It represented a turning point not only for the young country and its eventful history, but for the entire world. All countries were looking toward the 'Dark Continent' and what was going to happen there in two days, and that made everyone in the city and across the country nervous.

As soon as something unexpected happened, people grew uncertain and feared the worst—something that could still prevent the election and stand in the way of a better future. It was almost as if the South Africans themselves could not believe what they might soon experience—the first swearing-in of a Builder as holder of the highest office of one of the most important countries on Earth.

Expectations were as high as the historical significance of the whole affair—eternal life, the end of all wars, money for all and triumph over poverty, new technologies, the exploration of space, contact with alien civilizations, and the list went on. No dream seemed too unrealistic or too high for the country's citizens. This was what worried Agatha the most, because Hortat could not live up to expectations that constantly rose to ever-more-dizzying heights, and the nervousness of the city was just another expression of the problem.

Hortat, who stood as a non-partisan, independent candidate in a runoff against incumbent President Anders Muyabe, had located his campaign office in Linden, a neighborhood northwest of the city center. The streets in this place were lined by unadorned townhouses that had been built in a very short time, after the founding of the Special Administrative Zone by UN troops, and contributed significantly to the ugliness of the city. When crowds of refugees from the countries shattered by crisis—Botswana, Namibia, and Zimbabwe—had streamed south, housing had to be built quickly. Superstorm Katchenka had ended any thought of rebuilding the ruined cities in these northern-border neighboring countries.

South Africa had been able to incorporate its neighbors, under the UN-recognized term Special Administrative Zone, mainly because it had allowed the international community to avoid opening its collective wallets— without losing face. So, the aspiring nation of South Africa was welcome to assume responsibility since it had not, after all, annexed those countries, but merely administered them.

For some, therefore, the houses in Linden were a symbol of shame, for others one of hope, because over time it had become apparent that the new, artificial state worked surprisingly well. Agatha reckoned that, since the Builders' arrival, this was because it no longer mattered whether someone was black or white, or what passport one held, but which species one belonged to. The differences in skin color or language faded when faced with humanoid giants that seemed superior in all respects.

A small, unobtrusive car was already waiting for Agatha at the door of the campaign office, which stretched upward over six floors and included, in addition to the security drones Hortat's team had deployed, a dozen police officers on the street who ensured that no one approached the entrance if they did not belong there. Over her retinal implants, she switched on the Augmented City, a kind of virtual overlay to actual reality. A ribbon of red light appeared, marking the security area with running ribbons indicating that it was a restricted zone, while Hortat's election campaign logo rotated above the roof: two strands of DNA interwoven into a larger double helix.

Agatha got into the car and entered her destination, a scrapyard north of Pretoria, which was reportedly very close to the site of the attack. The pilot software connected to the traffic control system, started the electric motor, and set off for the next junction, where it merged with the constant stream of vehicles carrying their passengers through the megacity.

Typical of South Africa, the traffic volume was significantly higher than in Europe or North America. Although its traffic system was AI-controlled, it was still one of the earlier systems purchased from the Japanese. It worked via camera surveillance and a networked system that evaluated all data. Based on that data, it made real-time adjustments to routes to avoid congestion and even allowed the presence of manually controlled cars, since each vehicle was captured by the data system. At some point, it would be replaced by a satellite model, but the South Africans were still reluctant to give up owning their own means of transport in favor of ordering seats instead.

So she rode leisurely but efficiently through the streets, passing a large rally of thousands of Hortat sympathizers who held up banners in the Randjespark and flooded the Augmented City with Emoticon Snaps and personal links. She also saw individual Builders among them, towering among the much smaller crowd but joining in the enthusiasm. It was strange to see representatives of this ancient species behaving so emotionally, since all the Builders she had met had been remarkably calm and sober characters, always appearing so thoughtful and superior. The prospect of the first elected leader of their species, supported by humans, seemed to have changed all that.

It took 40 minutes to reach the scrapyard, which was located about seven kilometers beyond the storm walls of the megacity. On a dusty lot stretching over several hectares, the compacted remains of countless internal combustion cars and motorcycles were piled up, hardly recognizable as vehicles. Like a relic from a long-forgotten time, which paradoxically was not so very long ago, the landscape of rust and metal passed by until her vehicle reached a dusty road to the west, just past the north side of the property. It led into a small stretch of forest, which had apparently not recovered from the last superstorm and consisted mostly of withered tree corpses.

At a warning sign that had faded to illegibility, but in the Augmented City carried the inscription 'Forestry Traffic Only,' a police cordon awaited her. Two bored, grim-looking officers had blocked off further access by stretching fluttering tape between two trees. There, a small troop of journalists had gathered, wildly calling to the two officers.

Agatha parked to the left of the road in a fallow field, got out, and with her hands in the pockets of her armored trench coat, walked toward the scene. She then circumvented the crowd to the left over a small dried-up creek.

One of the police officers noticed her and glared as she was about to pass by the tree with the fluttering ribbon knot. "Hey, Lady! You're not allowed through there."

"No?" she asked, turning to him. The officer, a short man with drooping cheeks and a watery gaze, looked at her with a furrowed brow and then seemed to recognize her.

His partner grumbled something impatiently, but the first officer made a reassuring gesture in his direction and then approached Agatha. "Unfortunately, you are not allowed to enter the area here, Ms. Devenworth," he said softly, glaring at the protesting journalists.

"I know. Hortat wants to know what has happened here and how he can help."

The policeman's eyes began to gleam when he heard the Builder's name, and she also noticed the helix symbol on his earrings. Others might not have noticed, but Agatha knew what to watch for.

"I heard about Paris. Is he...? I mean—"

"He is unharmed and secure in Linden," she assured him curtly, forcing a friendly smile.

"All right, go on through. If possible, try to talk to the captain right away. He won't throw you out, you understand. He's wearing a red hat."

"Thank you."

"And please win, the day after tomorrow, yes?"

"We will," she assured him, setting off down the forest path toward a clearing where she saw police cars parked with blue lights flashing.

"Hey, what are you doing?" she heard the other officials protesting behind her.

"She had a permit. I checked."

Agatha paid no more attention to their voices and slowly continued toward the sandy area at the end of the path. Behind the two patrol cars, the artificial blue lights of which somehow seeming out of place, stood two uniformed women gazing absently, their fingers flying over invisible buttons. Further to the left was an area bare of trees that was a little rockier—apparently the top of a slope. The captain's red hat immediately caught her eye, even though he was out of the norm anyway due to his size and stature.

At first glance, she could have thought he was a youthful Builder. Three other officers—a man, a woman, and a Builder—stood around him, gesticulating wildly enough that Agatha was sure they were working via their retinal implants.

"Sir?" she said calmly as she approached within a few meters.

"No journalists. Just keep them away from here," the captain replied without turning around.

Agatha cleared her throat, and only now did he turn his

head. His eyes grew wide. "Hey! Who let you in? I swear to you if—"

"Peace, Captain. My name is Agatha Devenworth, personal assistant to Hortat Junior."

"Ms. Devenworth?" His eyes grew even larger, and now the other police officers turned around, and it was her turn to blink in disbelief. The Builder was not only a rare sight, because only 50 of them worked for the police forces of the Special Administrative Zone, but this one was also a female, recognizable by the slanted, almond-shaped eyes and the hint of a nose in contrast to the two inconspicuous holes typical of male Builders. She had a soft expression on her face and regarded Agatha with interest, while her human colleagues wore expressions displaying a mixture of confusion and dislike.

*We can't expect change overnight,* she recalled from what Hortat had told her when she had been annoyed a few days ago by an article, dripping with clichés and lies, written by Muyabe supporters.

"Yes. I'm sorry to tell you—"

"You must not be here," said the policeman standing next to the captain. "This is a crime scene, and the captain told you that—"

"The *captain* can speak for himself," the captain interrupted him, looking down at his subordinates. "Take Gina and go to help the others with the barrier so that this doesn't happen again, right?"

"But, Sir—"

"No buts!" The huge man chased the two away and told the Builder to stay when she also attempted to leave. It was not until the three were alone that he shook his head. "Sorry, Ms. Devenworth. This election has divided not only families and friends, but our police precincts as well."

"I understand. It will take time for Hortat to prove to them that, despite their rejection, they mean something to him and that he is serious about governing for all South Africans. And please, call me Agatha."

The captain nodded and put a hand on the Builder's arm. She was only one head taller than he.

"I'm Walter. This is Herxmin, who will hopefully inherit my position after the election."

"Thank you, Captain," she boomed, slightly tilting her head. "Should we really talk to a civilian about the investigation?"

"She was with the CIA for thirty years!"

"CTD," Agatha corrected him casually, but he did not seem to notice, or at least pretended to have not heard.

"I understand." Herxmin bowed her head again and gave Agatha a cautious smile." Pleased to meet you."

Agatha shook hands with both of them and nodded in a businesslike manner. She would have preferred peppering Herxmin with 100 questions at once, so rarely did one meet any of these rare female Builders—not to mention that her kind rarely took on normal jobs like this. But Agatha reminded herself that she was here because Hortat had assigned her a task, and time was pressing.

"My boss wants to know if he can help, and whether the Dark Tongue may have carried out the attack."

"We heard about what happened in Paris," Walter said as he shook his head sadly, his black lips narrowing a bit. "These damn Europeans probably wanted to get rid of him once and for all."

Herxmin's voice rolled over them both. "The attack was carried out by the Dark Tongue."

"Here?" Agatha was surprised.

"No, the one in Paris. This one was obviously not perpetrated by them." The Builder looked at the captain, who nodded in confirmation, before she waved Agatha closer to the edge of the drop-off near where they were standing.

Below them, rugged rock led down into a ravine and ascended again on the other side. In the gorge itself, which might once have been home to a small river, lay the railway tracks. The burned-out train cars were wedged into each other like an accordion. Some were still burning. An entire army of forensics personnel in white chemical-protection suits wandered about among them, directing sensor drones and small snifferbots through wreckage and debris. In Augmented City, on the other hand, the entire valley was empty and designated with a flashing 'Restricted Zone' header.

"We have found cartridges of Chinese-made hypersonic weapons, remnants of trip mines, and human DNA traces, here on this hill and on the other side. The investigation is not yet complete, but forensics are likely to indicate that it is unregistered DNA," the captain explained, hooking his thumbs in his belt.

"Humans, then." Agatha watched the throng about 100 meters below them and frowned. "Or, the Dark Tongue did not want the attack attributed to them."

"Not their modus operandi." Herxmin angled her head slightly. "They profit from the fear they spread among people, not from the actual damage they cause. They are the mosquito in the elephant's ear that provokes it to stampede through the porcelain shop. Besides, due to their high volume of respiration, it is hardly possible for them to leave no traces of DNA." The Builder shook her head in a very human manner. "No, this was not the Dark Tongue."

"There is also no motive," the captain said. "A freight train on its way to Cairo transporting the simplest chemicals in raw quantities and fifty thousand tons of real wood. Why would you blow it up?"

"I looked at the route on the way here." Agatha pointed to the exit from the smoke-filled ravine a few kilometers north. "There is an old railway switching station, and the track divides. One leads to Cairo and one to Marrakech. Coincidence?"

"Sharp," Walter said, nodding thoughtfully. "In fact, the train's route was entered into the system as the Pretoria-Cairo line. We have already found the black box housing the pilot software. But something switched the tracks to Marrakech, and the train's AI knew it, but did not pass on any error message to the rail control system."

"So, someone manipulated the system?" Agatha thought aloud. "Or the pilot software?"

"Both," Herxmin was sure, raising two fingers. It was amazing how graceful her small gestures appeared, even though she was so big and strong. "The control AI did not report an error, and the control system did not protest when the train sent the request to change its route."

"That would mean that someone had access to the loco-motive and a contact in the Ministry of Transport, in advance."

"Someone might have hacked the pilot software."

"From the outside?" asked Agatha incredulously. "There are hardly any AR nodes out here to provide the transmission capacity sufficient to launch such a massive attack."

"That's true, but we've already discussed whether someone was on the train and hacked in there," said the captain.

"Wait. The tracks were sabotaged. Blown up, I'd guess?"

The policeman nodded.

"Changing the route of the train is also an act of sabo-tage. So, was it double-sabotaged?" Agatha pointed to the slope below and in front of them on the other side of the ravine. "First the route, then the attack right before the track switches? That makes no sense."

Herxmin leaned her head to one side and exchanged a long look with her superior, who gave her a barely perceptible nod.

"You are very astute, Agent Devenworth," the Builder said approvingly.

"As an agent, yes." Agatha snorted and then closed her eyes for a moment before continuing. "Who had access to the train? I'm not an expert, but aren't containers now loaded in a fully robotized terminal at the freight yard? Only maintenance engineers have access there, right?"

"That's correct," said the captain. "Heavy Chemicals Pretoria leased a total of twenty-three cars for the journey. Among the wrecks, however, we found only twenty-two that the station AI assigned to the company."

"An extra car not included in the cargo files," Agatha muttered. "Did HCP report a loss?"

"No," Herxmin's answer rolled through the dusk. "Also, a query at the holding company that operates the station has revealed that they have now discovered that a hacker attack was made on all autonomous systems at the train station."

"This significantly reduces the list of potential perpetrators. Apart from the large intelligence services and a few mega-corporations, I can hardly think of anyone with the means and experience to infiltrate such a system, *and* remain undetected for an hour or more." Agatha's face darkened. "But why would anyone be interested in a chemical start-up company that doesn't even have a finished product?"

The captain shrugged. "Your guess is as good as mine.

We do not know, but the investigation is only just beginning. Under normal circumstances, I would say that a competitor has paid a few roving gangs to blow up things here and there. But HCP has no competition because they don't even produce anything. They're just conducting research."

"That's not quite accurate," Herxmin said. "They make some simple chemical compounds used in heavy industry that generate some revenue. But they are such a small fish that it is unlikely to matter."

*It sounds like I should visit this company just to check if there were any irregularities,* Agatha thought, gazing at the ravine below with a sigh. The white figures of the forensic team seemed to glow in the dwindling daylight. The effect was compounded by the irregular flickering from fires that were still not wholly extinguished, although a steady stream of aerial firefighting drones had come from the city and were spewing dense streams of the foamy mixture from their tanks over most of the cars.

She estimated that only certain wrecked container cars could be safely unloaded, while others were being scanned by snifferbots. In a few hours, the police would know precisely what weapons and explosives had been used and from where the attackers had opened fire, but they would not answer the question they had not yet asked out loud: Why had projectiles been fired in the first place? Trains ran autonomously, and freight trains had no passenger compartments. The destruction of the tracks should have been sufficient to destroy the train, so people must have been targeted. But the captain had not mentioned this, so Agatha assumed that no bodies had been found—not even the hacker who had somehow gotten on board.

"We should go by Heavy Chemicals Pretoria and take a look, ask around a bit," Walter said, verbalizing Agatha's own thoughts. Then he addressed her directly, "Do you want to accompany us?"

"Is it permissible for me to do that?"

"Well, as a private individual, you can do or not do anything you want as long as you don't do anything illegal or obstruct our investigation. Since we currently regarded HCP as the victim of an attack, we will not have a search warrant and will therefore politely knock and ask."

"Sir, I think..." Herxmin said as if to raise a cautious objection—a comic image, as if an adult was trying to show humble deference to a child—but Walter did not let her continue and made a dismissive gesture.

"Oh, come now, Herxmin. Just two more nights' sleep and she'll be the national security advisor or minister of the interior."

"I don't want to cause any trouble," Agatha said cautiously, knowing that she had already won. How would she have reacted in the past? Life before her rejuvenation seemed so far away to her, so strange.

"Not at all!" The captain patted her shoulder and the Builder's as well, and then pointed toward one of the patrol cars. "A former CIA agent, a good old police captain, and a Builder. It sounds like the beginning of an adventure!"

*CTD agent,* Agatha thought, and smiled instead of rolling her eyes.

"A successful investigation, I mean, of course!" Walter added when he saw Herxmin's face. "Well, on to HCP!"

# 5

# PANO

The drive to the scene of the attack in front of the Crown Plaza Hotel seemed like running a gantlet. The heavily armored electric SUV could not drive autonomously because of too much rubbish and debris on the roads, which overwhelmed the city traffic control system. At almost every intersection, cars had simply come to a halt between overturned shopping carts, burned-out vehicles, and overturned dumpsters, many of which were still burning.

"It's not so easy to find people who still know how to drive, is it?" he asked Rollo, who towered next to him in the back seat like a colossus, pointing to their chauffeur, who routinely steered them around every obstacle.

"That's probably true. About half of the population is under forty and has never obtained a driver's license. They know nothing *but* autonomous driving."

"Can you drive?" Pano raised a hand before the Builder could answer. "Of course you can. After all, you can do anything."

"Then Hortat would still be alive." Rollo turned away.

Pano caught a glimpse of a face twisted in agony. "His death has shaken all of you, hasn't it?"

"Yes. We did not always agree, and I am not one of the Johannesburg group he led, but he was a brilliant and wise Builder to whom we owe a great deal."

"Because he has improved your image?"

"No. I knew him for several millennia—at least his work. In the times of my ancestors, death was just another stage in the cycle of life, as you experience the seasons: trees lose their leaves, appear dead, and grow new ones in the spring."

"A strange form of immortality. You inherit the memories of your respective male or female ancestors, but you are not *them* when you're born, are you?" asked Pano, looking through a window.

He was watching a group of rioters devastating a pawn shop at the moment two police cars stopped, tires squealing, and spewed out multiple officers who immediately went to work with shock rods and rubber bullets. In the glow of the burning debris on the sidewalk, they looked like cartoon figures cast with black paint. However, the bizarre shadows they cast on the walls of the houses were more like those from a horror film.

"It is not immortality," the Builder agreed. "It's just a continuity of experiences that are different every time. We are clones of one parent, but also half from the other parent, although we have a well-defined gender."

"So, you're not a real clone at all."

"Yes, clones, but not copies."

"Isn't that the definition of a clone?"

"Yes, from your point of view. But it's more complicated. If each one of us were to clone ourselves exactly, problems with genetic diversification would quickly arise. I am a descendant of my father and my mother. I have many similarities with my father and all his memories and those of the male line before him, which I experienced through his body as if it were me, and yet there is a certain distance to it because it was not me."

"That sounds complicated," Pano commented. "Hortat, in any case, has no offspring, does he?"

"That is correct. Our way of reproducing ourselves is extremely... complex, and requires special facilities, which in turn are equally complex."

"We live in a complex world, don't we?"

"I can't confirm that."

"Of course not," Pano sighed, shaking his head.

It took them just over an hour to get into the city, and that was good time. They'd only achieved it because the driver had opted for the city expressway where traffic was still regulated. The three lanes in each direction consisted of two levels, the lower one more like a tunnel, its entrances and exits meticulously guarded by armed police drones. The incumbent president had apparently declared the main traffic arteries exclusion zones—lucky for them in this situation, and at the same time, something that disgusted him. That measure meant the rich, once again, received priority protection. After all, these were roads that charged their own tolls, which were not exactly inexpensive, as he now knew.

"Shouldn't we exchange commlink frequencies so that we can talk via transducers?" Pano suggested at one point.

"You have a transducer? I wouldn't have expected that," Rollo replied.

"As if you and your people didn't scan every organ in my body when I came through the door."

The Builder smiled and sent him a file.

'*Test,*' he heard the digitized voice in his head say. "I hear you," Pano answered without moving his lips.

The Crown Plaza was an old-fashioned colonial building that, just two decades ago, would have been regarded as an affront to the majority black population. These days, however, it could be interpreted more as a sign of the increased self-confidence of the Special Administrative Zone. The people were no longer interested in skin color, but in the Builders, in their newfound wealth, and proud of the world's interest in one of the few places that still had real economic growth.

He recalled the words of Hortat Junior, "I am a South African." Pano had seen the Builder's victory speech on a live stream. Of course, that sentence had taken flight on the net and spread like wildfire, especially after the subsequent death of that vessel of so many hopes. Ironically, it was the martyrs who reaped even greater fame after their deaths. Apparently, it was necessary to die before people realized one's true worth. Many considered it a given, not that Pano embraced that kind of thinking.

The whole street was still cordoned off, and, contrary to expectations, there were no onlookers here because the zone secured by the police was so extensive that the entire block resembled a ghost town. It was as if they were driving onto an island of silence in the midst of chaos, the eye of a hurricane in which nothing moved while nature's violence raged unchecked all around them. The sky above them whirred with the sound of police drones, clearly visible against murky clouds from which rain began to fall.

Their driver showed his papers at the first barrier and linked up with the on-duty officer for a few seconds.

"Bribery," Pano snorted. "Wow. It's really evolved a lot, this South Africa."

Rollo looked at him and raised his palms upward. "The current president does not stand for change. He wants to bring back the past, for whatever reason."

"You think that's news to me? I'm from Europe."

"My condolences."

Pano pursed his lips and then relaxed as they were let through—until they reached the next barrier, where two huge riotbots stood on their man-thick spider legs, with multiple weapon attachments springing from their compact hulls like leafless forests. The occupants of the SUV were scanned, and then checked again by one of the countless officials who were there, covered in plastic ponchos against the rain. There was a brief discussion between their driver and the man in uniform, which took place in Afrikaans, so Pano could not understand a word they were saying.

"It's obviously getting expensive."

"We have money," Rollo commented succinctly.

"My bank account is in total agreement."

As if frozen in time, the president-elect's convoy of vehicles was still parked in front of the hotel. The burned-out limousine was nothing more than a skeleton of black soot and bits of peeled varnish that fluttered in the breeze like remnants of gray paper. The SUVs and police cars behind the limo had not been touched and were marked off with yellow and black warning tape. Shards and car parts were lying around everywhere, although it looked nowhere near as chaotic as he'd imagined.

The photos in the news had been taken by drones outside the airspace cordon and had therefore revealed little. Small markers with red numbers were placed on some bits of the debris. Two women, in long coats that looked as if the fabric was waxed, stood under the canopy of the hotel entrance talking to each other—until one of them pointed

JOSHUA T. CALVERT

out the approaching car to the other, and then both
followed the arrival with watchful eyes.

"Who are they?"

"I don't know," said Rollo, closing his jacket and donning
a wide-brimmed hat.

"Did you bring one of those for me?"

"No," the Builder said as he exited the vehicle.

The sound of rain immediately increased, giving Pano a
taste of what awaited him. "Well, that's just great." He
opened the door and pulled his jacket collar up around his
neck before rushing to join the two women under the
curved roof.

*'Where are you going?'* Rollo asked over the transducer.
He was moving toward the destroyed limousine. *'We're here
to find out something, not to wait out the rain with the detectives.'*

*'You, maybe. But I don't have a hat,'* he responded in kind,
nodding to the two women, *'and it's wet!'* Then he vocally
greeted the two policewomen. "Hello, ladies. My name is
Pano Hofer."

One stood a few centimeters taller than his height in his
boots, and she had skin as dark as night. The other woman
was slightly shorter and lighter-skinned. The two took a
quick look at each other and then assessed him.

The smaller one crushed out a cigarette on the stairs and
folded her arms across her chest. "Hello, Pano Hofer," she
said. "May I ask what you are doing here? This is a restricted
crime scene."

*'That is why we should ignore them!'*

"I know," Pano told the woman. "We bribed one of
your people to let us through. Twice, to be honest." He
gave her a smirky little grin, as if he were very
embarrassed.

"That damned Montu!" the tall woman cursed and

smacked one fist into the opposite palm. "I'm calling the service supervisor!"

"One request." Pano pointed to the cigarette butt. "Give me the time it takes to smoke one cigarette. Then you may report me, and your colleague. And mine, too."

*'What are you doing?'* Rollo wanted to know.

The two women glanced at each other once again, as if in silent communication. He figured they were talking to each other over transducers.

"A cigarette, hmm?" The shorter one pulled the box out of her coat pocket and opened the flap with her thumb so that he could pull one out and light it. "Just one puff doesn't count, mind you. So, what are you supposed to look for here?"

"The Human Foundation engaged me to find the assassin," he said quite frankly.

*'I warn you!'* Even in digitized form, Rollo sounded angry. Pano did not know that Builders could become so emotional —not to this degree. *'This is no joke.'*

"This is no joke," he continued, borrowing Rollo's words. "Luther Karlhammer is an old acquaintance."

He did not need any imagination to interpret the subsequent glances between the two women. They loosened up a bit, not acting so tense anymore. *Ahh, yes,* he thought.

"Wait a moment... Pano Hofer?" asked the shorter one, right after he had inhaled lightly on the cigarette. He was barely able to suppress a coughing fit.

He sent her a copy of his digital passport.

"It was you who, with Agent Devenworth, found Xinth's pyramid in Antarctica and saved him from Hortat's killer."

"Guilty as charged," he said, pretending that they could now arrest him by placing his wrists together in front of his belly.

"I'm Special Agent Deena Myers, and this is Special Agent Gloria T'Sbu," she said introducing herself and her taller, dark-skinned colleague. "I didn't know that the Human Foundation would send someone like you."

"But you knew that they were going to send someone," Pano said with a smile, raising the cigarette and an eyebrow. Agent Myers shrugged carelessly, and he dropped it in disgust and stamped it out.

"Of course. The whole city basically belongs to them," the agent grumbled. "I just wish that they would use their power to depose that criminal."

"Deena!" T'Sbu hissed.

"What? Nothing gets in or out of here. You know that yourself. There are so many scramblers on the roofs all around that my ears are buzzing."

"I know I shouldn't be here, and that I'm putting a strain on your sense of honor just standing here. But I prefer putting all my cards on the table." Pano swallowed and sighed as sadly as he could. "You know why."

The two agents suddenly began fidgeting as if they were itching all over their bodies.

"Have you found out anything about my wife?" In his thoughts, he corrected himself—*ex-wife*.

"I'm very sorry, Sir," Myers said. "We don't have any explanation for that yet, but so far, unfortunately, everything indicates that Agent Devenworth was the one who placed the explosive in the sedan and then disappeared shortly before it detonated. We found her DNA in several places in the hotel that provided a strange lead."

"*Strange?*"

"Come along."

T'Sbu's face darkened. "Deena! We can't just lead him around here and pretend he's one of us."

"What's wrong?" Myers paused and put her hands in her hips. "He's a cop himself, or have you forgotten? If we cops no longer stick together, just because another country is printed on our passport, who is to keep Hortat's dream alive?"

"He doesn't have jurisdiction here, and the investigation is still ongoing. If we involve someone who is unauthorized, the director will fire us."

"You know what? I don't care. That pig has the whole city by the throat and is using these emergency laws as an excuse for not giving up power. That's what is going on here, and we are his underpaid lackeys. You're from Botswana. You know yourself how this kind of thing works. Do you want that here?" Myers aggressively glared at her colleague.

T'Sbu did not seem interested in an argument and just shook her head. "It's only fifteen minutes before the forensic photographers come back from their break."

"That's enough for us," Myers assured her, giving Pano a sign to follow her.

They entered the hotel, where rubbish and broken glass were still strewn around like scraps of a story manuscript. Playing out before his inner eye, Pano sees several groups of party guests celebrating Hortat's victory and sneaking out of the stuffy and densely packed hall behind the wooden double doors to grab some air and talk to each other over glasses of champagne, praising their candidate. Then a loud bang. The windowpanes vibrate violently.

Everyone flinches, knowing immediately that something is wrong, while a few of them still maintain the appearance of normality, so as not to appear needlessly alarmed or stupid-looking in the event someone in the kitchen merely dropped something, or a construction crane collapsed nearby. Then the first individuals begin running; security, storming out of the doors with drawn weapons; fire flickering outside the windows. Someone opens the entrance door and starts screaming. The awareness of an attack spreads. And right in the middle of it is Agatha, emotionless, with that look of cool professionalism that had once frightened him before he had found it highly erotic.

"Mr. Hofer?" Myers was staring at him with a furrowed brow. "Is everything all right?"

"Yes." He gestured for her to proceed, and she led him through a small side door, where an area next to the door handle was marked with spray paint.

"Switch to AR-City."

"Won't work."

"Why not? Do you have a defect?"

"I don't have retinal implants, and I don't have any of those new neural things. The only thing I have at my disposal is an internal commlink and a transducer so that I can make phone calls when someone is boring me."

The agent nodded in understanding. "Ahh, a 'natural.'"

"Not anymore, unfortunately."

"In any case, those are her fingerprints. And, behind here," she opened the door and walked into a wide hallway, "the president-elect's staff waited until his speech. PR assistants, bodyguard reinforcements, make-up artists, people like that."

Pano nodded and looked at the floor, the empty junk food bags, abandoned makeup cases, and lots of shoes.

"She must have gone through here, and then took that door there." Myers pointed to the end of the hallway and walked to the door. Beyond it was a small courtyard fenced in by the towering walls of densely packed housing units. Two large trash cans with foot levers stood to the right. Puddles were already forming between piles of rubbish that had not found their way into the containers. A broken ladder stood to the left. The agent walked down the few steps to the crunching surface of loose gravel and dirt and pointed between the trash cans.

"Her DNA is here, everywhere—on the wall and on the ground."

Pano inspected the crushed garbage bags and bricks, stretched out a hand as if he wanted to feel the wall, but paused about a centimeter in front of it and clenched his hand into a fist. "Strange, isn't it?" he said. "She blows up the most famous man in the world and then has nothing better to do but to wallow in rubbish?"

"You tell me. You're her husband."

"*Ex*-husband," he corrected her absently without turning away from the wall. He imagined Agatha squatting here, hiding and desperately looking around. Then, as she loaded her weapon with her typical calm, she waited and then overpowered a bodyguard or policeman coming through the door.

"Hmm."

"She wasn't here alone," Myers said. "We found rubber shoe scuff-marks that coincide in time with her DNA traces. Someone was here with her, but there is no evidence of it from forensics, apart from the rubber abrasions."

"No DNA?" he asked, irritated.

"No, nothing. Either someone cleaned up damn well, or that second person was completely sealed."

"Like in a chemical protection suit, do you think?"

"Maybe."

"He didn't use the ladder, I assume?"

"No, but if we go by the traces left here, she hasn't used anything here either, and she is still sitting between these two damned trash cans. I think we agree that this is not the case, yes?"

"She was always talented, but not *that* talented."

Myers frowned. "So how did she get out of here?"

"The second person helped her. If he didn't leave any DNA behind, he might have brought something to enable Agatha to exit with leaving a trail," Pano thought aloud. "That would mean that she had at least one accomplice, and the whole thing was well planned. But a plan to attack a Builder has to be perfect for it to succeed. Especially on one like Hortat."

"Can you tell us something we *don't* know?"

When he looked at the agent, her forehead was deeply creased.

She raised her hands defensively. "Listen, I don't want to sound rude, but we have nothing so far, except for a woman with no motive... but, to whom all the circumstantial evidence points. A woman who was regarded as an ardent follower of her employer and, on the night of his great triumph, changed her mind and decided that everything was different and that she had to kill him. Why? What are we overlooking?"

"She didn't change her mind," he assured her. "Whatever her motive was—and I don't know what it was—she didn't conceive it on the night of the crime. Agatha is a woman who firmly believes in her values and beliefs, and acts strategically. Always. Nothing she does is on a whim."

"That is, she also knew exactly how high the pressure on the investigation would be."

"Of course, and that you would comb everything for DNA. However, choosing to have a partner is unusual. Even way back in the fossil crisis, she hated me being assigned to her. She is a loner, so I suggest that you focus on her accomplice. That will be her weak point, if you ask me. What about the recordings from the hall just before Hortat went to his car?"

"That's a little more complicated. Come along."

Myers led him back to the lobby and pointed to a large display above the empty counter. She then made a gesture as if throwing an imaginary stone onto the screen, and it came to life. It was strange to suddenly see the recording of a packed hall, with finely dressed guests crowding close to each other. The podium with Hortat could not be seen on the monitor, so the camera must have been at his back and directed at the audience.

"See them?"

Pano squinted his eyes, and pulled his glasses out of his jacket pocket. He put them on and ignored the brief sense of shame that haunted him.

It was as if he were searching through a hidden object drawing, as he did when he was a child. His mother could calm him for hours with one of those. It takes him only a short time to see Agatha standing at the door, which was on the opposite side of the podium. She is standing in front of two gorillas in suits who have just nodded at her. He immediately notices that she is carrying the brown Louis LeTerrier handbag, which he'd given her for their first wedding anniversary. The sight makes him feel like someone is pushing a stake directly through his heart.

She goes into the crowd and pushes herself sideways into the middle of the guests. Watching her causes him yet another stab of pain, this one even worse than in Karlhammer's conference room when he had seen her on the hotel entrance camera. The pictures then provided brief impressions that had only revealed her face in the still frames, like the many photos he still had of them both.

But now he had a real-life, not at all abstract Agatha in front of him, standing there with a serious face and heavy expression in her eyes, apparently muttering excuses as she made her way through the audience. She looks good. Young, of course. Her blonde hair is full and radiant, and she is wearing it loose, no longer braided or tied into a severe ponytail. There is nothing left of the wrinkles around her mouth and the crow's feet around her eyes that he had known so intimately.

*Of course not,* he thought, sighing.

"There!" Myers interrupted his thoughts and froze the picture. With a red dot jumping up and down over Agatha's head like a bouncing ball, she marked the neckline and then pointed to a figure next to her. You could hardly see anything, just a slight glimmer of bronze.

"Hmm. Whoever that is, he knew exactly where to stand in order not to be seen."

"Exactly. Afterward and before, there are shots, but only from behind. He's a Builder, but he does not appear on the DNA list of guests. Three of them were registered, and there are corresponding DNA traces of all of them. But this one here," Myers snapped her fingers, "is like a ghost."

"And how is that possible? I mean, in this technological world, everything is recorded and analyzed."

"Yes, which brings us to the problem outside in the backyard. I forgot that you're such a dinosaur. So, as in any other building with a digitized security system, there is an AI in the hotel that handles all security-related data. These include data from the DNA sniffer, which stores all genetic traces, distinguishes them, and compares them with the lists of registered hotel guests. The owner of the hotel and, of course, authorized personnel such as the on-duty net jockey, the management, and the police may have access to this data as soon as the owner releases the appropriate access code. He is obliged to do so."

"And you got this access code?"

"No." Myers shook his head. "The hotel belongs to Hortat, and Hortat is dead. The registered security manager and member of the management board is—"

"—Agatha." Pano nodded. "What about the net jockey?"

"We've tried to get hold of him, but he has informed us that he can only cooperate on the instructions of the board. The corresponding instruction was then quickly given. After all, this is an investigation that the whole world is watching."

"*Tried* to get hold of him? So, he's gone into hiding?"

"Yes. On our second call, there was no contact at all."

"Sounds guilty."

"Yes." Myers let the recording continue, spooling forward from time to time, until Agatha stepped out of the crowd and was allowed into Hortat's security zone. They chatted briefly and then headed toward the exit, which seemed to take an eternity. He knew what would happen next.

"Stop," said Pano, as the view of his ex-wife became clear for a second because two of the bodyguards stood so that the camera had a straight line of sight to her. "Can you make it bigger? Zoom in?"

"On Agent Devenworth?"

He nodded.

"Of course." The agent enlarged the frame without him seeing how, and then they had a complete picture of her, which quickly grew sharper on the display until it was crystal clear.

"That handbag in her hand," Pano said. "I gave it to her on our first wedding anniversary. Louis LeTerrier—some French luxury brand. It was intended as a joke, because

Agatha always hated luxury items. Waste, a portable vagina, Britney accessory."

Myers chuckled. "Portable *vagina?*"

"She could be quite creative in expressing her dislike. In any case, I gave her a trip to Paris, which she had always wanted, because her job never brought her to Europe and, like all Americans, she thought that Paris was the center of the continent. I always told her that we have cities that are much more beautiful—Rome, Prague, Vienna—but she really wanted to go to Paris. Even the fact that it is the fashion capital, and that the people there pay great attention to their appearance, could not deter her. So, I allowed myself a joke and packed the plane tickets to Paris in this handbag to tease her a little."

"*And?* How did she react?"

Pano's grimaced. "She hated the thing."

Myers laughed. "Great gift."

"The story is not over yet. In any event, she did not realize that it was a clever knock-off I got from a flea market. I guess I wanted to make something clear to her."

"Things only have the value that we attach to them?" The agent shook her head. "Come on. Kitchen-table psychology?"

"I wanted to show her that she often reacts with a strong opinion where things are not so clear. It was two days after the initial prototype of a retinal implant was unveiled by the Human Foundation to allow blind people to see again. I thought it was great, but she was concerned about the consequences that such a technology would have if it were forced on the mass market."

"You?"

Pano shrugged. "Times change. People, too. But hand-bags don't."

"What do you mean?"

"That bag is not the fake—it's an original. It's not her handbag."

"Okay, good." Myers combed her fingers through her long blonde hair and then scratched her head in a less charming gesture. "So, the handbag had a sentimental value for her, and she bought a new one. But this time an original."

"She wouldn't do that."

"Well, according to my documents, she has had not only a retinal implant installed but also neural chips, improved neural stimulation, an adrenaline pump, sequential muscle toning, and a synthacardium. Not to mention the military hardware, with which—so the rumors say—she is fully equipped. From what you have told me so far, she would not do so."

"I have proof that she wouldn't do it," he countered.

"Really?"

"The bag I gave her was nothing but a fake. It was exceptional, considering it cost only fifty euros. I knew she wouldn't believe it was a fake, so I helped and had a tailor build in a flaw. On the zipper is a small leather label, which, in addition to an alleged proof of genuine leather, also bears the designer's initials—after all, the ladies supposedly go off on that. I had the initials changed."

Pano pointed to the small label the size of a cigarette box that hung motionless under Agatha's elbow in the cross-section. The letters LLT were so intertwined that they might have been meant to depict a flowerbed or deer antlers.

"How?"

"I'll show you. Can you keep the still image and split the screen in half?"

"Of course. What do you want to see on the other side?"

"The clip from the beginning, please."

Myers frowned but did as she was asked, and next to the frozen image of Agatha, the camera video began from the beginning. She stood at the double door with the two body-guards. They nodded to her, and then she made her way into the crowd and disappeared into it. Shortly before, she turned so that the camera caught her from the side, and with it, her handbag.

"Stop!" he said sharply, and everything stopped. "Can you please do the same as with the other? Big and sharp?"

"Sure."

The zoom took two seconds, then Agatha filled the entire frame. The sharpening went much faster, and he saw every pore on her skin and every detail of the bag.

"Look at the two labels, Agent Myers," he said, pointing to the leather label, on which the initials looked a little cruder, and the curved ends resembled lines rather than waves. It took a few glances to see the differences, but once you saw it, they were evident.

"Actually... The... This is not the same handbag." The agent rubbed her chin and blinked a few times as if she did not trust her eyes. "I had not noticed that."

"How can you notice it if you don't know what you're looking for?" he comforted her in her apparent frustration. "Even then, you might not have noticed it until you compared them a dozen times. She still has the handbag."

"How's that, please?"

"No matter." Pano cleared his throat. "So, here we have something. She disappears into the crowd and comes out without her original handbag, but with another one that is almost identical."

"So, she switched them. It is impossible to figure out how or with whom she made an exchange amidst all those guests," said Myers. "It must have been the Builder who did not appear in the system."

"If he's not a false trail."

"In order to replace a handbag, she must halt at least briefly. There has to be a hand-to-hand exchange."

"Or she puts one down next to another and then picks up the other one instead of the one she had. That is less conspicuous and would not catch anyone's attention. After all, she went to the Builder and stood with him, our mysterious phantom, until the speech was over. So, I'm betting on a swap on the floor."

"Well, then she gave him the fake handbag and got an original in exchange? That's a good deal, I'd say. I'm not sure how that will help us. We do know that this person also gave her the contents of the bag that she left in the car at the end, which went boom!" Myers ground her teeth and sighed. "Shit, I wish he were still here."

"Hortat?"

"Yes. You do not know how much hope we all invested in his election."

"I have some idea."

"No, you don't."

"Because I'm European?"

"Yes. But that's not so important now." She waved dismissively. "How do you think this helps us?"

"The bag was more important to her than I thought. So, she wouldn't just give it away unless it was crucial."

"You mean, she not only got something but also gave up something important?" Myers nodded. "That might make sense. I don't know what that is yet, but we should keep that in mind."

"We have much more than that." Pano approached the

display, circled the counter, and tapped his finger on the original on the right. "This is an original Louis LeTerrier."

"How do you know that? You yourself said that you could hardly tell the counterfeit from the real product back then."

"Right. But this model is very old, and I'm tempted to bet that it's no longer produced. However, most manufacturers still keep old collections in stock and sell them to aficionados at horrendous prices, long after they've been taken off the market, even long after they've disappeared from the stocks of online sellers."

"How do you know all this?"

Pano pointed to his crocodile leather boots with their slightly rounded toes. "Seriously?"

Myers raised an eyebrow in his direction. "I forgot that you are Italian."

"I'm not an Ital—" he growled, but cut himself off with an ill-tempered grunt. "It doesn't matter. Anyway, I know."

"And how do we know it's not a fake and that someone didn't just mess with the initials?"

"Counterfeits last a maximum of one or two years, sometimes three. When a product is no longer en vogue, no one fakes it anymore, because the fakes only pay for themselves when they can be sold in high volumes."

"So, no one fakes such a handbag anymore?"

"No. Not this model. Not for at least fifteen years. And that," he smiled broadly, "is a good sign, for I will tell you how it all happened."

"Really?"

Pano went into a long explanation. "Agatha and our Person X talk about the exchange. Agatha says they need to get an exact copy of her handbag. It's the only way to get an item of Size Y—our suspected bomb—into the sedan without causing suspicion.

"Person X then says, 'Hey, we just buy two of the same handbags, and you leave yours home.'

"Agatha, meticulous as she is, says, 'No, they would immediately notice that once the investigation begins. I have a much better idea that no one will ever suspect.'

"Person X then decides to get a twenty-year-old original directly from Louis LeTerrier and calls Paris. The employee is friendly and charming, with his or her French accent, and tells him there are still ten in stock, but the price is very high. He agrees and orders one.

"South Africa's delivery should take two days unless it is sent by Super Express with a courier in a private jet. But if you have the money for an original, twenty-year-old Louis LeTerrier model, you can also afford that kind of transport if necessary. Then it would take the duration of a suborbital flight, in effect, an hour plus the drive.

"Now, ask me how many people have called Louis LeTer-rier in the last few days, or even weeks, to order an original, "Julie Fontaine" handbag, from twenty years ago—and paid to have it shipped to South Africa?"

Instead, Myers looked like she wanted to stick out her tongue at him. She pulled out her cigarette pack, extracted one out with her lips, and lit it. "That's good," she then said in an animated voice, exhaling a white cloud as punctuation.

"Who still smokes today?" he muttered, shaking his head in a vain attempt to evade the smoke. "If *you* had committed this crime, the investigators wouldn't have to call Paris first, they could simply look for who was the last person to buy cigarettes in Johannesburg."

"Very funny. We are not in Europe," she replied brusquely. "Here, you can still decide for yourself how to grow your cancer." She followed the last bit by rolling her eyes, dropping her cigarette, and crushing it out with her boot. "Satisfied?"

"Yes, thanks. And? Do I get a star?"

"That was good work."

"Thank you. Actually, it was just luck, because I know Agatha, and she will not have reckoned with that vulnerability."

"Why not?"

"Because she wouldn't have bet a single cent on me coming to South Africa. Especially not because of *her*."

"Then why did you do it?"

"Because I got a lot of money for it," he lied. "Life as a 'natural' is not particularly lucrative, you know?"

"Is it as bad as they always say in the media?"

"Yes. They get virtually no access to statutory health insurance without a vitality monitor and blood probe. They are, per se, considered at-risk patients for pretty much everything. You can also forget jobs, especially with the police. Even a teenager with level 1 muscle toning can knock a 'natural' down with a snap of the fingers."

"Bitter, hmm?"

Pano did not respond.

"Come along, Capitano Hofer. That's what they call you, right?"

"Hauptkommissar in my native German. I'm not an Italian!"

"Howt-ko-me-saar? What a tongue-twister."

"Chief Inspector to you, but I stopped being one."

"I have a job for you."

"Let me guess. I am your miracle weapon for reviewing hours of video footage?"

"No, you can be my secret weapon for everything. I'll involve you in my investigation," Myers said. "Don't look like I've just invited you to a funeral. We have a good lead now, and I owe it to you. I am not vain, I'm pragmatic. I also have a few questions about those 'olden times' of yours."

"Of course. You remind me of someone."

"Yes?"

"Yes, of the person we want to find. I don't know if that's an advantage."

"We'll see. So, come along."

"I have to talk to my partner first."

Myers' expression went blank, as if several emotions were fighting for supremacy in her. "With Karlhammer's Builder?"

"Yes. Rollo."

"*Rollo?*"

Pano shrugged. "Couldn't pronounce his name."

"Whatever. Take care of it, and I'll talk to my partner. She's a bit old-fashioned, but she won't mind."

"Good." He went out with her and saw Rollo, still tinkering around the wreckage. The Builder held a large flashlight in his hand and seemed to be taking a close look at every detail of the burned-out vehicle. However, Pano immediately realized that the Builder had also been watching the entrance and had noticed Myers and him at once.

'*Where were you?*'

'*Inside. We watched a few film clips.*'

'*How nice. And?*'

'*Saw some interesting things.*'

'*May I remind you that you work for us and not for the Johannesburg Police?*'

'*You may. But Luther's chief concern is that we find Agatha*' *and not that we rack our brains about how we do that, am I right?'* he asked back via transducer.

'*Can you at least tell me that it has done some good?*' Rollo asked him.

'*It has. We have a lead. But to track it down, we need to work with the two agents who've kindly agreed to involve us.*'

'*That's not possible!*' the Builder replied surprisingly quickly.

'*No? Why not?*'

'*I have to talk to Karlhammer first.*'

'*Do that. I'll be waiting in their car.*' Pano took a blast from his asthma inhaler and exhaled in relief.

# 6

## AGATHA

"Thank you for bringing me with you," Agatha said, addressing the captain she knew as Walter. To tell from his uniform badge, his surname was Breekens. She sat in the back seat of the large police wagon, its windows barred, reminding her that the times in South Africa had not always been as positive as they currently were.

The leap the country had made since the fossil crisis, when she had last been here and before Hortat had hired her, was enormous. At that time she'd still felt like she was in an industrialized nation that had come to the party too late. Everyone else had already gotten drunk on the many new technologies that filtered the air, cleaned the water, and made living together ever more strenuous by simplifying everything. She remembered how she and Pano had searched for traces of Ron Jackson, the missing archaeologist who'd discovered Xinth.

"Hey, everything all right?" Walter asked, and only now did she notice that he had turned the driver's seat around to face her and had probably been talking to her for some time.

*I'm getting soft and sloppy,* she scolded herself. *Concentrate!*

"Yes, I was just visiting some memories." She wiped away the distraction. "Excuse me. What did you say?"

"I said I read your biography. The one by Martha Welles with your picture on the cover."

Agatha had to force herself not to make a *just bit into a lemon* face, and smiled. "Ahh."

"One thing I always wanted to ask you—is it true that you are so unromantic and despise kitsch?" the captain continued, appearing to take her smile as an invitation to continue talking about the topic. "I mean, the saying you came up with is... Man! I laughed to tears when I read that."

He tapped Herxmin, who sat next to him like Mount Everest next to K2, scrolling through old-fashioned documents on a tablet. "Do you know what her motto was?"

"No, Sir."

"I don't exactly remember the whole thing anymore, but part of it was, 'your voice in my ears is like wet toilet paper stained with diarrhea, your charm affects my heart like scratching my crotch without anyone noticing, and your love is like a fart during a first date,'" Walter quoted, gleefully. "Is that really true?"

Agatha shrugged, hoping that would put an end to the subject, but the captain seemed to believe that she only wanted to keep him in the dark. He pointed outstretched index fingers at her and laughed as if they had just created a new insider joke. She very much hoped that his investigative work was better than his ability to read other people. Memories of her wedding to Pano rose within her and caused an unpleasant stab near her heart.

"You're not like your biography portrays you."

"How should I be?"

"Gruff, humorless, purposeful without regard for losses. I guess Martha Welles didn't know you as well as she thought."

"Oh, she did. I hated that biography and did not authorize it, but today I have to admit with some distance that my anger was caused rather by the fact that a stranger had managed, by and large, to accurately describe me and categorize me," she explained, looking out the window at the many lights and holo-advertisements of the city passing by like a dream of light and shadow. "My rejuvenation, my collaboration with Karlhammer, and then my work with Hortat changed me in a way that I would not have thought possible."

"For the better?" the captain asked in earnest.

"I don't know. I hope so."

"That's not for me." He gestured dismissively. "Not because of the supposed growth pains caused by cell rejuvenation, but because it feels wrong to me. No offense."

"None taken. I knew someone else who thought the same way."

"I don't think we're made for immortality, nor for the kind of genetic memory that Builders carry with them. Herxmin here can possibly process it all because it is natural for her, but *me?* Seeing the lives of my ancestors?" Walter raised both hands as if in surrender. "No, thank you. They experienced apartheid, the first and second world wars in Europe, several flights as refugees, and a terrible colonial era."

"But rejuvenation doesn't change your DNA and doesn't give you any memories. It only repairs the chromosome ends," Agatha said.

"I know, but these treatments are just the first step on the way to a new humanity, an improved one. How long will it take for people to demand the next step—to become like them?" He pointed to Herxmin. "Isn't that how it started with you?"

"That's correct," the Builder confirmed. "At least research into rejuvenation treatment came before the development of genetic memory clusters."

"See?" He turned to Agatha again, shaking his head energetically. "No, thank you. Most people have been living far too long without all this. Everyone says, 'Life is so short!' No, it's too long! Everyone talks all the time, but no one has anything to say—small talk, film marathons, VR games, boredom. If life were too short, none of that would exist. In addition, everyone looks forward to retirement when they no longer have to work for someone else from nine to five and are finally free to do what they want. That can feel like an eternity, such a life. How long will it take until—"

"—the state raises the retirement age even further so that we remain in the labor market for eighty years instead of sixty?" she interrupted, concluding his sentence.

"Exactly! Then we have the very same situation as before, just much longer!"

"My... ex-husband said the same things."

"He didn't let himself get rejuvenated?"

"Yes, but..." Agatha paused and cleared her throat. "It's a long story." She pointed out the window, turned on the Augmented City, and marked a point off the city expressway that she shared with him on the local node. "Is that HCP's company building?"

The captain was surprised by the sudden change of topic and turned to look through his window to find her marker. "Uh, yes. Looks like it."

At the same moment, their car veered off the highway and joined the heavier city traffic. Out here in the Tsakane

Industrial Park, there were many private vehicles conveying commuters who wanted to return to the city for its wild nightlife and lavish parties that had been going on every-where for weeks, celebrating what they believed to be Hortat's inevitable victory in the coming run-off.

Heavy Chemicals Pretoria's headquarters was located between a former cement factory half-fallen into ruin and one of the relatively new sewer canals. These canals were extended, gigantic concrete basins, spreading like furrows through the city and the surrounding area. Not a particu-larly appealing place, but the start-up did not have much flash, and everyone started small, didn't they?

"Pretty good security for such a small shop," she said, looking at the sentinel drone that was racing like a bullish beetle along a rail laid atop the perimeter wall, which was about three meters high. At regular intervals, sensor bundles were embedded in the concrete, and at least three surveillance drones suspended from black balloons hovered over the site.

"Heavy Chemicals has special safety requirements," explained Herxmin. "In recent years, there have been repeated attacks on chemical producers because many of their secondary by-products can be used for cooking street drugs—for example, phenylacetone for making meth-amphetamine. Such company premises can only be oper-ated by those who meet the corresponding requirements imposed by the state to safeguard their production or, in this case, *research* facilities against theft."

"Understood." Agatha did not know what reminded her once again that she was no longer an agent, but an assistant. In recent years, she had hardly had time to think about this fact, because she had been too busy scrutinizing Hortat's bodyguards and adapting security concepts.

At the same time, she'd had to make sure that he found his way around the human world. He might eventually be able to draw on millennia of memories, but at present he had about as little experience with humans as his actual biological age would indicate. Now, traveling in the company of these two police officers, some of her old life had come back to her. The idea electrified her. She had not realized how much she'd become another person who not only thought differently but also behaved differently.

"Then, let's knock on the door," Walter said, stopping the car in front of the gate, an electrified stretch of mesh that rolled to the side when their vehicle automatically identified itself. Two riotbots, their weathered appearance saying they'd been in service for at least a decade, flanked the driveway like insectoid shadows with their antenna-like shock weapons at the ready. Agatha's retinal implant reported an unapproved scan, which she accepted before her defender routines could initiate a small data battle.

On the premises around the company's unadorned, two-story, corrugated steel building, which had space enough to house several airliners, scores of pallets and autonomous fork-lifts were scattered around as if a child had been playing here and walked away without cleaning up. Half a dozen vans were exiting a gate on the west side and driving off at a brisk speed.

"They probably have to rush some goods off to Cairo as fast as possible," the captain joked, getting out as soon as the car had parked in front of the entrance to the building. Two people in civilian clothes waited outside an unassuming door bracketed by a DNA scanner and a sensor strip.

When Agatha and Herxmin had also exited the car, one of the waiting pair, a man with a youthful appearance except for gray-peppered temples, approached them. Because of his smooth cocoa-colored skin, it was difficult to tell how many times he had been rejuvenated or how old he might be. His jeans and turtleneck sweater were not recognizable brands at first glance but were still obviously expensive and designed to make a statement.

"Good morning, officers, and, oh!" The stranger's eyes widened when he saw Agatha, "Ms. Devenworth? To what do we owe the honor of welcoming Hortat's right hand to our humble premises?"

"We would like to help," she said, keeping her intentions concealed.

"And you are?" Walter asked with a sigh.

"Excuse me for my rudeness. My name is Winnie Makeba. I am chief operations officer of Heavy Chemicals Pretoria," he introduced himself. He pointed to his companion, who was still standing by the door. "This is my assistant, Gondo. Come in. Do you want to talk about the attack on the freight train?"

When he turned around, Herxmin had just come around the car, and the expression in the COO's eyes changed in a flash as if slamming a door. But, Agatha had to admit to herself, he had his face surprisingly well under control. What was it? Racism? Was he a supporter of President Muyabe? Or just an opponent of Hortat, which was not always the same thing?

"Oh," Makeba said, showing an apparently forced smile. Agatha, at least, could easily discern the pretense.

Walter introduced the Builder. "That's my colleague, Lieutenant Herxmin, and I am Captain Breekens." His facial expression darkened. "You don't have a problem with her being here, right?"

"No, no," Makeba assured him a little too quickly,

looking back at his assistant, who seemed at least as perturbed, but less in control.

"Wonderful!" The captain clapped his hands. "Well, you just invited us in. That's very friendly of you."

"Uh," the COO hesitated before nodding, "of course. Let me just talk to my people briefly to get you chemical protective suits. As our plant is a laboratory where volatile substances are processed, we are unfortunately obliged to take appropriate safety measures."

"Do you not have an office we could go to?" Agatha suggested.

"Sorry, Ma'am. No. Unfortunately, a crisis meeting with our customer from Cairo is currently taking place there. As you can certainly understand, damage limitation is a top priority."

"But of course," she replied with deliberately excessive friendliness, which briefly disabled his control and his frozen smile slipped for an instant.

"Well, I'll personally take care that the suits are brought here quickly, *yes?*" Makeba looked toward Herxmin with a head tilt. "Unfortunately, we don't have anything in your size. Would it be okay if only the two of you entered our laboratory?"

Walter and Herxmin changed glances. Then the captain nodded. "All right."

"Wonderful!" The manager clapped his hands and signed them to follow him.

"I'll also stay outside," Agatha decided spontaneously, reaping questioning glances from all present. "I'll keep Herxmin company."

"Are you sure?" asked Walter, astonished.

"Absolutely. You ask the better questions anyway, and we

want to clear up this misfortune for Mr. Makeba as soon as possible, without wasting anyone's time."

"Good. As you wish."

Makeba, his assistant, and the captain went to the door, which automatically unlocked, and they disappeared into the unassuming company building. Silence quickly returned to the cool night between the police car and the lonely lamp above the entrance.

Agatha finally broke the silence when the Builder turned to go back to the car. "May I ask you something personal?"

Herxmin turned, leaned her broad back against the driver's door, and calmly regarded Agatha before glancing at the sensors above the company's entrance. "Okay, but over a private channel, of course."

"Okay."

Agatha saw an incoming request for a private transducer channel on her retinal display. She raised an eyebrow in amazement when she saw the complex encryption, for which even her high-end hardware predicted an hour or more to crack.

Herxmin came straight to the point. *'What do you want to know?'* Agatha's implants translated the Builder's deep bass voice into her brain directly and with astonishing precision.

*'There is something wrong here,'* she answered from her own mind. After several years of living with neural implants, Agatha no longer found it difficult to overcome her natural inclination to move her lips. *'I know that there are still some in this city who yearn for the old days and hate Builders just as much as whites hated blacks at the time of apartheid, but I watched this Makeba closely. He was afraid of you.'*

*'A lot of people are. My size and what they know about us are intimidating to some people.'*

'That's not it. And then there's the thing about not having a suit for you. What do you think?'

'That is quite possible. It is most likely that no Builders work here.'

'And that's why he invented that excuse about the offices. For a crisis meeting with their customer in Cairo, a few people speaking via VR conference are enough. How are we supposed to disturb them?'

Herxmin inquired, 'Well then, what do you think?'

'They are hiding something from us here.'

'Hiding what?'

'I don't know, but either they didn't expect us to arrive here so quickly, or they were lagging behind their schedule. Believe me, I know when something stinks of shit.'

'That sounds more like the Agatha Devenworth from the Welles biography.'

Agatha twisted her mouth into an ironic smirk. 'And I always thought Builders didn't have a sense of humor.'

'We don't.' A short pause, then, 'I appreciate your suspicions, but there is nothing we can do except wait for Captain Breekens. I am in contact with him. He says he is looking at a rather boring lab through a large glass pane in the front room.'

'Why didn't they want you to go inside?' Agatha asked, looking around at the grounds littered with abandoned pallets and at the forklifts scattered over the tarmac.

'Well, unless they are the first people to develop, or steal, Builder technologies—which even the major intelligence agencies haven't done, then we can assume that it's actually just personal aversion.'

'Builder technology? What does that have to do with it?'

'Didn't Hortat ever tell you?'

'Tell me what?' Agatha looked up at Herxmin in irritation.

'There is a basic technology that we have had since the second age. Even if a hundred CIA agents were standing in front of a battle tank—not that we would construct something like that— they would not be able to see it. They would have to bump against it, and even then, the effect would not be what they would expect.'

'Does this mean that only Builders can see Builder technology?'

'If we wish, yes. At least as long as there is enough energy available, which is quite difficult these days.'

Agatha remained silent for a while and thought about what she'd heard. It made sense. After all, she knew only too well that agents who were endowed with a clear mandate and plenty of resources had been able to uncover every lead, so they should have landed at least one lucky hit by now.

'What are you doing?' Herxmin wanted to know, as Agatha walked to the left along the façade of the company building.

'If I had disturbed you at something and you needed to play for time, why might you need to do that?' she responded without stopping, feeling a tickle on the nape of her neck as the Builder followed her.

'To hide something.'

'Or to do away with something.'

'Or both. However, I must remind you that we do not have a search warrant and that HCP is officially the victim of an attack and not a suspect in this case.'

'I know. But I'm not a policewoman.'

'However, you have a reputation to lose! Your employer's. Hortat can change the world the day after tomorrow, and a scandal will not help his chances in the election.'

'Just follow me. You can pretend you want to stop me,' Agatha replied.

'Where are you going?' The Builder then thundered, "Stay

still, Ms. Devenworth. These are company premises, and we have no authority to enter the premises on our own initiative."

*'Did you see the vans that were rushing off when we arrived? The gate they exited from was on the west side. We're on the south side, and you can see there is also a gate. There was none on the east side because the canal is located there.'*

'But, behind the building is a large, abandoned parking lot,' Herxmin continued her thoughts, *'and you are extremely astute for a human being.'*

Agatha growled a sarcastic, *'Thank you,'* and accelerated her pace, knowing that they had just been spotted by the company's net jockeys. She imagined them now showing signs of nervousness and telling someone to hurry up and stop the two of them.

She started to run, and Herxmin's heavy steps splashed in a puddle behind her. As they went around the corner—at the very moment—a floodlight attached there to illuminate the surrounding area went out.

*What a coincidence,* Agatha thought when the residual light amplification of her retinal implants switched on, and she was able to dodge a stack of pallets that she had over-looked in the brief moment of confusion.

"Stop right there, Ms. Devenworth!" the Builder's voice rumbled behind her. *'We need to hurry!'*

*'Precisely what I was thinking. Turn off your implants for a moment.'*

*'Excuse me?'*

*'Just do it.'*

*'All right.'*

Agatha activated her ECM augment, which sat over her diaphragm. This was not only illegal military tech, but also so sinfully expensive that she was one of perhaps a handful of people in South Africa who owned one. It had been one of the conditions she had required of Hortat when she accepted the job. She felt a slight tickling around her stomach, and then her retinal implant reported that no electronic signatures could be detected within a 100-meter radius.

'*What did you do?*' Herxmin asked when she was back online and the two of them had almost left the west side of the building behind.

'*Unimportant. We are no longer being watched.*' Even as Agatha said this, new symbols gradually awoke in her retinal display. '*Shit!*'

'*What is it?*'

'*They're coming online again. No idea how they're doing it!*'

As they rushed around the corner, she came to a skidding halt and instinctively took cover behind a forklift. There was another gate in the fence here, open in the direction of the parking lot, which lay under the abandoned expressway behind the company. Thick bundles of cables climbed from the roof to the roadway's railing and down to the east across the canal. Loud shouts and the high-pitched hum of heavy electric transporters could be heard.

'*What a coincidence! Just when we show up, they're in a huge hurry to get deliveries out.*'

'*The train was sabotaged. It makes sense if they are under time pressure from their customer,*' Herxmin said, having stopped beside her.

Several cameras and sensor bundles were back online, but the light was still off. Passing the forklift, which had no cockpit, she searched the façade, finding a small entrance below an emergency exit sign that flickered at regular intervals, a framed fire ladder to the roof, and several garbage containers. A total of four trucks without headlights, presumably fully autonomous, roared into the darkness. A fifth peeled straight out from under the roller door as she nudged the Builder with her elbow and ran off—first to the wall, to which she pressed her back, then across to the roller door, which was already closing again.

*'What did you use back there?'* the Builder wanted to know.

*'It's unimportant,'* Agatha responded curtly, instead of truthfully saying *it's illegal* before she resumed. *'But it's likely to keep their net jockeys busy for a while, even if we're obviously dealing with military-grade hardware here. Let's go in!'*

*'No!'*

*'Are you crazy? You can see for yourself that there is well-founded suspicion here and that you do not need a search warrant!'*

The roller door was already half-closed again and continued to slowly descend, like sand running through an hourglass.

*'I haven't seen any legal violation,'* Herxmin insisted.

Agatha growled in frustration. If the policewoman did not go along with this, she herself could not sneak in, because the Builder would then arrest her—of that she had no doubt.

"Great. I'm on a mission with a fucking Judge Dredd," she grumbled, forcing herself to breathe evenly and let go of the rage that she had sworn off a long time ago. *Stay calm,* she exhorted herself. *That's not you anymore.*

She turned her head to the right and looked through the still open gap between the rubber strip at the bottom of the roller door—still one-third open—and the dusty concrete floor. Surprised, she frowned when she saw nothing but a white wall where there should have been room for several trucks.

*'I don't understand this!'*

*'What?'*

'*See for yourself.*'

'*I told you, I—*'

'*You are allowed to look through a window, aren't you?*' Agatha interrupted, impatiently pointing down at a spot beside herself as she made room.

The Builder hesitated, but then tilted her head and stepped where Agatha indicated before leaning to one side to look, while the roller still left a narrow gap open.

'*Get out of here!*' said Herxmin with sudden excitement in her digitized voice.

Agatha was still agent enough not to respond to something like that with What? or Why? and thus waste crucial time. She reacted immediately to the change of tone, turning and sprinting to the fire ladder she had seen. Her neural implants had just reported the receipt of a file from Herxmin that was automatically placed into one of her memory caches when a loud noise sounded, and the connection broke off.

She did not turn around. Instead, powered by her automatically activated adrenaline injector, she leapt onto the bottom rung and quickly climbed to the roof. Only now did she allow herself a side glance toward the roller door where she saw the Builder's body lying on one side like a sleeping giant. Herxmin had no head left—the remains lay scattered in a funnel-shaped pool on the concrete. The Builder's death gave Agatha a stab of deep regret. It was a loss that could never be recouped.

She regarded each of the bronze giants as a rare and valuable being, but here and now she could afford neither anger nor even sorrow. She could already hear the drumming of boots and the buzzing of rotor drones approaching from the night.

She switched all her implants to passive mode to make

locating her more difficult and went directly into a crouch when she scrambled onto the roof. She noticed two large circles in the center. She would swear that these were retractable towers with weapons attachments, as she had often seen this very type, including at Dalton Air Force Base the previous year.

Calls echoed toward her, and a red, target capture warning appeared in her retinal display.

"Shit!" she cursed, self-correcting to a less offensive, "Crap," as she ducked and grabbed onto the bundle of cables that led east across the canal. She took off her jacket, pulled out her service weapon, and fired at a drone that was flying from the north under the highway. It had glittered for a moment from a reflection on its matte black paint. She missed it, but made sure the fighting machine had to dodge and took advantage of the short advantage to drop her pistol, swing her jacket over the cables, and grab both ends.

Then, without slowing down, she ran to and over the edge of the roof. Hanging from her jacket, she glided over the wall. The Sentinel drone headed toward her and began firing. The projectiles hissed just past her, but she took no risk and immediately let go of the jacket as soon as she was over the thick broth that rolled down the wide canal basin toward the Indian Ocean.

The sickly-sweet stench of feces and chemicals battered her during her brief fall and was replaced by an unlocaliz-able feeling of absolute disgust when she was swallowed by the brown soup and carried south. Sharp smacking noises told her that she was still being fired upon, but she kept her mouth, nose, and eyes closed and waited, then let herself sink and be carried away.

To distract herself from the impossibility of taking air into her lungs and the urge to breathe, she opened the file that Herxmin had sent her shortly before the Builder's death. In it, she found a simple line of text, which explained the low transmission time of one millisecond. It displayed coordinates. With quick thoughts she called up a map of Johannesburg into her black retinal display and found the corresponding red marker in Marshalltown, the center of the city's wealthy.

It indicated #12, Eloff Street.

# 7

## PANO

"You're right," Myers said.

Pano sat in the back seat of the police SUV with Rollo, while the agent and her partner T'Sbu were in the front seats engaged in wild gesturing. He found this way of working in an augmented reality very silly-looking, but he was probably the only person far and wide who thought so. After all, one quickly got used to the 'new normal' when everyone was engaged working on tables, diagrams, and images that were invisible to others. He could well remember how, when he was a student, people telephoned with Bluetooth headsets and he regularly had to ask himself if passers-by had gone mad and were talking to themselves or were just speaking on their phones.

"What do you have?" he asked.

"A handbag was ordered. The lady in Paris was not particularly cooperative, but a call from the president's office seems to have been convincing enough."

"Who ordered it?"

"Some invented name. I've been chasing everything through our registers. The interesting thing is that it was only ordered and delivered yesterday—by courier on the suborbital plane," Myers explained.

"Well, who'd have believed it?" asked Pano laconically.

"But the delivery address was a post office in Roodeport."

"I understand."

The two agents exchanged looks.

"I quickly forget that you are not from Johannesburg. Tsakane is not exactly the neighborhood where those who can afford such handbags live—or order them."

"A commercial zone," explained Rollo, "with mainly small and medium-sized enterprises."

"Some are currently striving to grow, and others are on the way down. But none of the big players would risk their reputations by setting up business there," Agent T'Sbu said.

"But," continued Myers, "there is a company that hit the headlines the day before the election."

"And that would be?" Pano asked.

"You certainly heard about the attack on a freight train north of the city?"

"The world loves bad news, especially when it involves explosions. The feeds were full of them."

"The main casualty was Heavy Chemicals Pretoria, a start-up in which the Human Foundation has invested, which is supposed to help poor regions dependent on mining with an easy-to-mix explosive. The police stormed the company headquarters the night before the election."

"What does this have to do with the handbag?"

"It was ordered there—at the HCP headquarters in Tsakane." Myers nodded as Pano frowned. "Remarkable, isn't it?"

"What do we know about the courier? Is he back in France?"

"No. All suborbital flights were canceled due to the increased risk of attack."

"He could have taken a normal scheduled flight."

"But he didn't. He's in a hotel in Melville."

"And *that's?*"

"Downtown. The city center."

"Ahh," Pano said. "I guess that will be our first port of call?"

"Yes. We want to ask him a few questions about the delivery."

Since their car had been in motion the whole time anyway, there was no obvious change. No sharp U-turn, no acceleration, and they did not turn on the blue light that would have automatically prioritized them in the traffic control system.

Pano leaned his head against the window and tried to relax. His gaze tracked upward, as if under its own control, to where the pyramid's black base obscured the sky. From this perspective, it looked as if they were living inside a large box, and he was looking up at the lid. He imagined the skyscrapers as towers that grew ever higher to poke open the lid.

A primal fear spread through him and solidified in his stomach. It was the fear of being crushed by that massive structure if it suddenly obeyed gravity and crashed to the ground. He was sure it would flatten the whole city. After all, the authorities had already established that it was not a hologram or anything like that.

"Do you know what it is?" he asked, without turning his gaze away from the mysterious object.

"No," said Rollo, and his deep voice somehow matched the sheer size of the thing Pano was looking up at, a few kilometers above sea level.

"But it's Builder technology."

"Yes, that much is certain. In the past, pyramids stood for us as places of refuge, temples of the priesthood."

"Sounds richly anarchic for such an advanced civilization."

"We were always a spiritually-oriented civilization," the Builder calmly clarified. "Later, the pyramids were more like places of meditation and retreat, and no longer left to the priests."

"And they're always floating?"

"No, but there were some aerial habitats in pyramid form. This has something to do with the technology used by the machine singers. But I'm not one of them."

"What were you, then? Your genetic ancestors, I mean?" Pano truly wanted to know, and he looked at Rollo when the Builder did not immediately respond. Something in Rollo's facial expression suddenly seemed melancholy.

"We were... It's hard to translate into your language. Guardians would be an apt term, but also Parents or Herders. Our task was raising clones."

"I thought that every Builder grew up with all the memories—and thus all the knowledge—of one's ancestors. How much sense does education make?"

"You think it's like filling a glass of water."

"Yes."

"It's not like that. Access to genetic memory proceeds gradually and quite slowly. A brain must develop, establish links, and achieve a chemical balance before it is fully functional. Infants need closeness and emotional warmth to develop properly, to establish contact in a healthy way with what their ancestors experienced. Imagine a two-year-old who carries the experiences of his four-hundred-year-old father who died in an accident in great pain. He would be traumatized."

"So you would fill the glass slowly and gently." Pano nodded. "Then you were an educator?"

"That's not quite it, but it comes close enough, yes."

"We have a lot of those in Europe, one of the few jobs that hasn't been robotized yet." He immediately noticed that the corners of the Builder's mouth had twitched when he had said Europe. Rarely had he seen one of them betray an apparently uncalculated emotional reaction to something. They always seemed the personification of composure.

"You've been to Europe before, haven't you?"

"Yes."

"Then you must have been one of the five hundred that the Commission took in," said Pano, then stiffened. "I don't know if it makes a difference to you, but I'm sorry."

"It's not your fault," Rollo replied with a thick voice. Even Myers and T'Sbu reduced the volume of their discussion in the front seat. A depressed Builder. They probably had not experienced anything like that any more often than Pano had. "The memories of the camps in which we were shuttled back and forth in Serbia and Kosovo are not pleasant. We lived between barbed wire and stun guns, and every time we tried to flee, we were rounded up by police units and bots and attacked with tear gas and shock grenades. Today I know how the footage of it was cut together in such a way that we could be portrayed to the population as violent aliens. Those people didn't know any better."

"Don't try to excuse us," Pano urged him. "We don't deserve that. People always need someone to hate to make them feel better."

"You are not as bad as you think."

"But bad enough."

"Your species is young and full of contradictions. I have long tried to understand what causes the discrepancies in your behavior. I wanted to understand how a young woman who runs a shelter for rescued pets and is enraptured in her work to help distressed animals could eat steak from the flesh of a calf in the evening, without experiencing any contradiction, or drink the milk from a cow that has been locked between bars for its whole life, bred and fed just to maximize milk production but it can hardly stand on its own feet and legs.

"I wanted to understand why actors in movies kiss their film partners, which is fine, but are plunged into a life crisis by their spouse when the spouse does so with another stranger off-camera. The social-cultural context seems to determine everything, not the act itself. You are full of charity and at the same time full of disgust for strange things or for those you do not understand. You can go to your churches on Sundays, then watch the evening news and curse about us 'damned refugees,' without feeling that there is a contradiction.

"We have experienced everything—locals who have cared for us privately, aid workers who have spent their last drop of energy making our lives as pleasant as possible after we'd been deported to the camp, but also those who have tried to set fire to our tents and..." The Builder closed his eyes as if he were seeing a film running.

Eventually he cocked his head. "It was a very humiliating experience that I'll never forget and that changed my life. We were the masters of this planet, and it is hard to open our eyes and find ourselves lost in this homeland after tens of millions of years, just because another species is now in control. One like yours—I intend no offense. We have given you technologies to improve your life, but it hasn't accomplished much."

"We were on the right track as a species, you know?" said Pano.

"Until we came, you mean?"

"Yes. Most of us are somehow aware that we have no chance of enduring once the Builders multiply. To be blunt, most people know that it will take no more than ten thousand of you to wipe out us primates. That scares them."

"Them, or you?" asked Rollo.

"I admit that I have certain reservations, but I also had few points of contact, except on television, and that no longer enjoys a very high reputation, as you probably know." Pano felt as if the interior of the car was closing in and he cleared his throat before continuing. "When I hear what you've just said, I wonder you haven't developed a hatred of us. I don't know if I could say the same of myself."

"Do you have siblings, Mr. Hofer?"

"A sister, yes."

"Younger or older?"

"Younger."

"If your little sister were in need and required money, what would you do?"

"I would give it to her, of course."

"Of course. And if you were in need yourself, and your sister wanted to give you money?" asked the Builder.

"No!" Pano replied immediately. "I won't take charity from my little sister."

"Because you would feel needy? Inferior? Because a big brother must not need rescue by the little sister, but only vice versa?"

"Something like that, yes."

"But you would insist, in reverse circumstance, that she accept your help. Am I right?"

"Yes. Another contradiction you have identified in us, I assume?"

"No, a universal observation that I, too, had to learn, many, many generations ago. Generosity is easy, Mr. Hofer. Humility, on the other hand, is tough to master, if you understand what I mean."

Pano looked closely at the Builder. Their eyes met long enough that he thought he could spy deep melancholy in the big almond eyes, from which so many lives stared back that he could barely comprehend it.

"I understand, Ixlath," he said, swallowing to eliminate the dry feeling in his throat. *I called him Rollo. Pretty shitty of me!*

Ixlath just nodded, and that was enough. That one nod expressed more than a score of sentences might have covered.

"We'll be at the hotel in ten minutes," Myers announced from the front.

"Which hotel is it?" the Builder inquired.

"The Amorosa Inn."

"It had to be," Pano sighed, looking out and shaking his head.

"Not a very good hotel," T'Sbu added. "At least not for a deluxe courier who travels by suborbital plane. What is he doing in such a dump?"

"Either to lay low and not cause a stir, or the exact opposite," Ixlath said.

"Which means he's probably not a professional, and has seen too many movies. If he really wanted to get our attention, he would have called. But since no one was likely to notice the handbag discrepancy, it is quite unlikely that he'll think he has anything to fear," Myers said.

"Unless he saw or heard something that he should not have seen or heard," Pano said, without removing his forehead from the windowpane. His warm breath fogged the treated glass, leaving a white mist so fleeting he might have imagined it. The others kept talking, but he ceased listening, and instead did what he had always done during his time as an investigator—he repeatedly went through everything he had known and understood, took the information apart like pieces in a mental puzzle, reassembled it over and over to look for missing parts.

"... always been to Melville," T'Sbu said just as Pano interrupted her.

"This raid on Heavy Chemicals Pretoria. That's weird, isn't it?"

The two agents in the front seats briefly glanced at each other and seemed annoyed at the interruption, then irritated by the question.

"I mean, an attack outside the city destroyed a lot of their goods, and then there's a raid on the victims of that same attack. Why?"

"Two police officers, including a captain, the head of the Pretoria district police station, had routine questions about the incident, according to the reports, and wanted to question the company management. According to their vehicle's GPS data, they also reached their destination, but have since disappeared somewhere in the vicinity. Their car was found in an adjacent canal, but not the officers. One of them was a Builder named Herxmin, who meant a lot to all of us here. She was the first goldskin who—"

"Deena!" hissed T'Sbu, tipping her head in Ixlath's direction.

"It's all right," said the Builder calmly.

"Sorry," the agent said, appearing unrepentant. "In any case, their disappearance caused a great deal of concern, and the Deputy Director launched a raid on HCP."

"And? What happened?"

"Nothing. No trace of Captain Breekens or Herxmin."

"Was there any sufficient reasonable suspicion?" Pano asked.

"In the opinion of the director, no. He dismissed his deputy immediately, along with his entire advisory staff."

"Extremely tidy—and very quick."

"Yes," Myers growled in agreement.

"Was there still a report on the raid?"

"Yes. I can send you the file if you want."

"Deena!" T'Sbu sounded indignant.

"What? It's not like it's a top-secret document."

"I should make a phone call," Ixlath said abruptly. "Could you turn off your scrambler? I'm not getting a connection."

"Do it. Two minutes." T'Sbu waved casually toward the Builder and gave her colleague a dark glare. "We've discussed the fact that—"

Pano nipped the incipient argument in the bud. "Can you send it to my hand terminal?"

"Hand terminal?" both agents asked simultaneously, seeming honestly confused as he pulled his antiquated device out of his pocket.

"You're a real dinosaur! Wait a moment." Myers said with an abstracted gaze.

Pano's hand terminal beeped and displayed an internal police report, which was not accompanied by any non-disclosure notices. He flew over the details. A special task force composed of 50 officers had been involved in the search. No shots fired, no resistance from the four HCP security guards, no DNA traces of Captain Breekens or Sergeant Herxmin, although a sniffer drone deployed there had detected something "inconclusive."

There were stock lists for indoor and outdoor inventory, each about as exciting to read as a weather report. Not a damn thing that could have pointed to any illegal activity or the whereabouts of the two police officers. In the entire 20-page document he flew through, he found only one violation of applicable law that had been ignored—a truck parked outside had contained some of a supplier's chemical, shipped in small containers. There were no freight documents for these chemicals, but this was apparently due to a programming error in the logistics software. In accordance with the protocol, the truck bed had been scanned and fitted with a sensor pack to investigate the infringement and to determine the ridiculously low fine assessed in the subsequent court proceeding.

"Well, well," he muttered. Only after he looked up did he notice that the others were staring at him inquiringly. "Oh, it's probably nothing. Hours after the raid, one of the trucks from a supplier company was missing a unit of guanidine nitrate that was still present during the search. Whatever that is."

"And?"

"Well, there were thirty thousand small units on the truck. But why would anyone steal precisely one of them when the police were investigating a minor crime—one count of missing documentation for one load of a delivery that's made all the time—and when the truck was under observation? There will be nothing, I guess, but it surprises me," Pano exclaimed.

He shrugged and searched the net for the supplier

company and its product, a simple reactant for chemical mining explosives. It was sold in large quantities, but also in very small units, such as in this truck, bottled in protected containers the size of a half-liter soft-drink bottle. "Ahh, it belongs to the Human Foundation. Oh, what a surprise."

"We're there," Myers informed them as the car began to slow. The Amorosa Inn was located on the outskirts of Melville, a district divided into upper and lower towns. The lower town, which contained the hotel's long, sprawling concrete structure, had been overbuilt by highways and new buildings at some point when South Africa had reformed the building law, and 'land' had also been sold above the ground. So, the more prosperous strata had simply begun to build their houses on massive pillars high enough to over-shadow the landowners underneath. As a result, it was pretty dark where they were, and it felt as if they had arrived at the filming location for some gangster movie.

"Can you get a look at the hotel's occupancy online? Pano asked, inspecting the two cars that were standing in front of the entrance. "I can do that even with my hand terminal, I think," The rest of the street was clear, except for a few pedestrians who walked with their heads hanging as if purposefully trying to see nothing and no one. One of the vehicles was a black van, the other a run-down hatchback.

"You can." Myers followed his gaze and nodded earnestly. A moment later, she cursed. "They currently have only one guest."

"I thought so. No wonder, given the current situation in the city. The only question is, who owns these two vehicles. Can I have a gun?"

T'Sbu spat a curse and pulled out her service pistol. Myers did the same, and both rushed out their doors and toward the hotel entrance. When Pano attempted to follow them, Ixlath held him back by the arm.

"What are you trying to do?"

"I'm making a contribution."

"That's not a good idea. We have no official authority here, and we can only get them into trouble."

Pano broke free from the Builder and opened the door. "Or save their asses."

The air outside smelled of ozone and waste, olfactory testaments of the bad climate beneath the level of the wealthy upper class that had risen above the old Melville. After only a few breaths, he felt as though there was sand between his teeth. He circled the SUV and briefly looked at the hotel. It was a rectangular slab building with three floors, standing against the background of the mighty columns supporting an overhead expressway that flooded the area with constant noise.

"How practical," he muttered, looking to the left, where the front lawn of now-withered grass ended in a wire mesh fence. A wide driveway full of dumpsters separated the hotel from the building next door, a brick hovel infested with black mold. Pano ran toward the brick building and accelerated his steps when he heard a brief, loud argument from one of the upper hotel floors.

He took advantage of a hole in the wire mesh, loped over the dead lawn, rushed to the scarred wall of the house, and then headed around the corner to the back. Except for the noise of the expressway, it was quiet—apart from the usual background noise of a megacity, which he might never get used to. How Agatha had been able to exchange her house in the Alps for a place like this would remain forever a mystery to him.

Behind the hotel was a short gravel lot that led to another man-high wire mesh fence. The open space between the pillars of the expressway behind it was full of old car wrecks, and among them he could see the flickering of burning garbage barrels, where shadowy figures warmed their hands.

Suddenly, he noticed two movements and ducked back behind the corner. With one eye, he looked carefully around it and spotted a small group of shadows that disappeared behind the hotel on the other side as he heard, "Halt! Police!" He guessed it was Agent Myers, but because the person was shouting and her voice resonated, he could not tell for sure.

Somewhere window glass rattled, followed by a loud noise, and someone crashed through the remains of a door onto the unkempt gravel lot. The figure held something in one hand that could have been anything. But Pano was unarmed and decided to play it safe when he thought they were turning in his direction. He retreated behind the corner of the house, where he pressed himself against the cold bricks, counted to three, and then turned again so that he could see.

The unknown figure—man or woman—had just crashed against the wire mesh fence and began to climb awkwardly as Myers and T'Sbu sprinted across the lot, their steps crunching on the gravel. T'Sbu was faster, grabbing the shadow by the hips to pull it down as it tried to hurry over the fence, managing rather badly. Myers had pulled her service weapon and shouted something in Afrikaans that he couldn't understand when the figure raised the object it was holding.

Beside him the barrel of a pistol appeared out of nowhere, and Pano instinctively slapped it upward when a shot was fired that clapped like thunder. Ixlath stood next to him like a giant from a monster-movie giant incarnate. Myers and T'Sbu were startled by the bang and instinctively leveled their weapons at the Builder, at which point their prey tried to flee again and they had to return their attention to their task.

"What did you think you were doing?" Pano shouted at his partner.

"I thought he was going to shoot Agent Myers."

"They had him under control. Since when have you been so impulsive? And how did you manage to appear from nowhere, right here next to me? Damn, I almost pissed my pants!" It was only now that he noticed how familiarly he now treated the Builder.

"Excuse me. I did not want to scare you." Ixlath put the gun back in his jacket.

"We want to interrogate the guy, or did you forget?"

"I just wanted to protect the two ladies."

"Let's have a look, gunslinger." Pano walked across the gravel with his hands in his pockets and approached the two agents and a man with the ageless face of the freshly rejuvenated. His eyes were wide open in fright, and he was breathing heavily. The steel-fisted police grip T'Sbu employed on him was probably the cause of his anxiety. She was also at least a head taller than the man.

Somewhere nearby they heard squealing tires and the roar of gunning engines.

"That's probably the kidnapping team," Pano commented on the noise, looking back over his shoulder. "Good timing, I'd say."

"Who was that?" Myers asked the courier. "And what did they want from you?"

"No idea!" the man whimpered. "They showed up just before you and hacked the AI reception computer in the lobby."

"And why did you take off so quickly. Hmm?"

"I wanted to call a taxi, and the house AI didn't react, so I thought something was wrong, and—"

"Nonsense!" T'Sbu hissed. "Nobody calls an autonomous drive taxi via a house AI!"

"Don't bullshit us," Myers growled. "Otherwise we'll gut you right here, like a shitty Christmas goose."

"But, but... You can't do that. I have rights!"

"You're here in South Africa, or have you forgotten? We regulate things differently here than you do in green Europe."

The courier's eyes widened with fear and seemed about to emerge from their sockets.

*Good bluff,* Pano had to admit, watching the action.

"I'm going to count backward from two because I can't count to three," Myers continued, impatiently loading her pistol. "Two, one—"

"Stop, stop, stop!" The terrified man waved his hands as if they could protect him from a gunshot. "What do you want to know? My Lord! I have nothing to hide!"

"Of course, that's why you're staying in this shit hole," T'Sbu sneered.

"I just made a simple delivery, okay?"

The tall agent with the ebony skin pulled a credit chip from his jacket pocket. "And what is this?"

"That's the payment for the job."

"Nonsense. That's done online."

"It... was a tip," stammered the courier.

"I'll start again at two, I think," Myers said casually, and the bloodlust in her gaze looked so real that Pano had to wonder how much of it was feigned. That, or she was just really good.

"No, no, okay! I earned a... a little extra."

"And that would be? I am quickly losing my patience."

"Nothing big, really. I only—"

"Stole something?" asked Pano, pulling out his hand terminal. He scrolled through the last called-up files with his thumb and showed him one of the transparent containers with the reactant that had been stolen from the truck on the HCP site.

"It's hard to say. These things all look the same, and..." The courier squeaked in horror when Myers put the barrel of her pistol against his knee. "Yes, yes! All right, that's it!"

The agent gave Pano an appreciative look and then an encouraging nod.

"You put it in your handbag and gave it to someone, am I right? That's how I would do it. Your DNA is not registered here in the SASAZ, so someone would find out that something has been stolen, but there are no traces. They could probably get to the bottom of it with great effort, but who would do that much work if only one of thirty thousand units disappeared, right?"

"Sir, I—"

Pano interrupted the man whose accent suggested he was from Scandinavia. Sweden maybe, or Norway. "You will tell us how the handover went down. What and whom you saw, and where it all took place."

"But there's hardly anything to tell!"

"Then it won't take long, and you won't have a hard time remembering every detail." Pano looked out of the corners of his eyes to Myers, who noticed it and clicked back the gun's hammer. The courier's eyes became even more restless and jumped back and forth between his two interrogators so quickly that Pano was worried that they might actually pop out.

"Okay, okay! I got a call from the customer who promised me a very generous tip—besides telling me that no one would ever know. He gave me the truck's code, so I could get in and also one for the sensor and alarm systems. So, I grabbed a flask and took it to the AI taxi."

"Company?"

"Uh, MyDrive, I think." As Pano's eyebrows gathered like clouds of thunderstorms, the man raised his hands defensively. "All right! I'm sure! The window opened, and I gave him the stupid thing."

"Front or rear?"

"What?"

"Which window? The front or the rear?"

"It was very dark and... Uh... Rear. Yes, certainly at the back!"

"And the payment?"

The courier put on a tentative smile. "So, the payment, well, you know what it's like. All network transactions always take their time with all those authentication measures and... oh!"

He fell silent as Myers let her gun wander from his knee into his lap, putting on a facial expression that even made Pano fear she might do something stupid.

"Yes, down to the last cent!" the Scandinavian assured her. "You can have it all. Really!"

"Did you see anything else?" T'Sbu asked. "Something particular that could save your life?"

"No, it was really very dark."

"Shit, I think he's lying to us." Agent Myers sounded

angry, her voice vibrating with emotion. "What a little shithead!"

"Deena!"

"No, leave me alone! This jerk comes from his filthy Europe and rakes in a fat wad of rands committing a theft here that's somehow related to Hortat's assassination? That's just too much!"

"Hortat? Assassination?" the courier sounded honestly horrified. "What?"

"Who sent you, hmm?" the agent asked, snarling. She seemed on the verge of losing control.

Pano was surprised and alarmed at the same time, since he had underestimated just how emotional the officer was over the death of a Builder who had held a Messiah-like status in large parts of the world.

The agent pressed. "Were you to help the killers get away with it? Was that the job?"

"W-w-what?"

"Hey, Deena," T'Sbu carefully placed herself between them and pointed her hands in the direction of the pistol, which her partner held in now trembling hands, pressed against the courier's chest. "Calm down now, okay?"

Myer's voice broke as if nothing could keep her anger in check. "You saw something, you pig!"

"I—"

"If you didn't see anything, we don't need you anymore."

Pano saw something in the agent's eyes that he had seen many times with drug suspects when they were tripping and suddenly thought something completely insane was a good idea. You could see a switch turning on in their head, and you just had the amount of time they were slowed by the drugs to protect yourself from some colossal act of stupidity.

"Don't!" he cried, and, just like T'Sbu, wanted to reach

for his absent weapon when the courier howled, his eyes wide open in panic, like a shying horse. "Th... there was a shadow, a... a... a shape! It was big. Maybe a... a... bil... Builder, or something. But I can't say for sure!"

"Well now, that wasn't so hard," Myers said, and just like that she went calm, holstering her pistol and nodding contentedly.

"He pissed himself!" T'Sbu said accusingly in her partner's direction, pointing to the trembling courier, who cringed in torment and looked as if he wanted to dissolve into thin air.

"Man, you even made me believe that you are totally insane!" Pano sighed and ruffled his hair. "The poor guy almost had a heart attack."

The agent shrugged. "He was paid pretty well, wasn't he?" Addressing the courier, she said, "You can go."

"*What?*" the man and T'Sbu asked at the same time.

"Whoever was here before us obviously knows what trail we are on and wanted to grab him before we could. The best thing for him would be to make himself disappear. We could take him into protective custody, but for how long? He has confessed to a petty theft that we cannot even prove. If he is remanded into custody, they will find some way to eliminate him."

"She's right," Pano agreed. "And then we can get on with it. We now know that it was a MyDrive taxi, so with your help, we can tap into the sensor data from around the HCP headquarters and find out the license plate and the transponder code. Then we'll know which taxi it was."

"You really are a dinosaur, aren't you? I mean, really!"

He looked at the smaller agent, furrowing his forehead. "What?"

"It's an *AI* taxi. Companies like MyDrive have a single

license plate and a single transponder code for all vehicles in the fleet."

"What? But that makes no sense. What if one of the things causes an accident?"

"Damage generalization. That is the legal basis for autonomous taxis. If one causes or provokes an accident, then the company is liable for it, not any individual owner. A robotaxi does not race away from the police, but immediately switches to stand-by if it is involved in any problem."

"That makes it the perfect vehicle for the persons we're looking for," T'Sbu added, giving the courier a nod to run away.

Ixlath now spoke for the first time and looked thoughtfully after the fugitive as he slipped through a hole in the wire mesh fence and disappeared between the abandoned cars under the highway. "After all, we now know that a Builder was probably in the taxi—our Person X, who exchanged handbags with Agatha, I'd guess?"

"Looks like it." Pano shook his head. "But without a license plate, I don't think that will help us."

"We should still talk to MyDrive. There may be something that can help us," Myers said.

"All right. Let's go."

All eyes turned toward him.

"What?"

"To a robotaxi company? We can only contact them on the net," T'Sbu explained, making no effort to hide her disbelief at his ignorance.

"Well, I can't very well come along without neural implants."

"No."

"I'm going to use the time anyway. I want to visit someone."

"I'm coming with you," said Ixlath, while the two agents simultaneously asked, "Who?"

"No, I'm going alone." When the Builder wanted to protest, Pano raised a hand to nip his objection in the bud. "Could be a waste of time, but if not, your presence would be a problem."

"Then I have to make a phone call," replied the Builder, turning around.

## 8

## AGATHA

Agatha crawled from the sludge, like the first evolutionary fish making its way onto land, when she was almost unconscious from lack of oxygen. She crept up to the top of the canal's rough concrete bank, saw the spotlights of drones further north, searching the horrendous stream of feces, sewage, chemicals, and garbage that had pulled her away from the HCP compound. They were getting closer—quite rapidly—so she reluctantly activated her panic beacon as she wiped the stinking brew from her eyes, nose, and mouth. She gagged several times before she finally vomited. When she could force herself to continue, she scurried along in a crouch and slipped a few times while trying to hurry along the bank with her head ducked.

*So many drones looking for me,* she thought, looking at the many lights hovering above the canal. They were approaching fast and would soon reach her. Whatever they had discovered at Heavy Chemicals Pretoria—or rather, whatever Herxmin had discovered—it was tantamount to breaking open a hornet's nest. A small company like HCP

JOSHUA T. CALVERT

could not have had so much hardware, so her instincts had not failed her this time.

Now she just had to make it out of here. The counting time display at the bottom right of her retinal display indicated 78 seconds as she reached the small wall separating the canal from the adjacent industrial park. She rolled over the wall and crashed into a wide strip of greenery, which inflicted more than a few painful cuts and scratches. She imagined each break in her skin filling up with the slimy morass that was glued to her everywhere, and she felt like vomiting again, but the adrenaline boost whipped her on, inducing her to spring up and sprint across the street toward an opening between two office buildings. She heard a high-pitched whir followed by a slap.

She spun around and went to reach for her pistol, only to remember that she had dropped it on the roof of the HCP building, and saw a strip of silvery light at the moment a cold sting near her shoulder made her look down. A slender dart stuck out from below her collarbone. She yanked it out, but her neural implants sounded the alarm that her symbiosis was battling a military-grade neuro-dampener, and she only had about a minute left until she lost consciousness and fell into a coma.

She could still feel pleasure about that. After all, without her sinfully expensive implants, she would have gone straight to the ground and into a nirvana-like haze until her pursuers decided to wake her up in some dark place.

Two more drones shot across the canal wall and formed a semicircle with the one that had shot her. Agatha heard a dull noise, followed by a roar, and twisted her lips into a triumphant grin. "Goodbye, assholes."

Missiles hit all three drones simultaneously, turning them into short-lived explosions and clouds of debris. The heavily armored vector thruster crashed out of the low-hanging clouds and braked with engines swiveled downward, sending down long fire tails, vaporizing the remains of the destroyed machines while still in the air.

The elongated vehicle looked somewhat like a stretch limousine without windows, and with four pivotable nozzles instead of tires. A door slid sideways and spat out two combat paramedics in fully sealed armor, who rushed toward Agatha as she collapsed to her knees. Four other soldiers from the High Threat Response team jumped onto the tarmac and secured the abandoned area with rifles at the ready as she was laid onto a fold-out stretcher and lifted inside the aircraft. There, one infuser after another was applied to her neck before she was sprayed with a bitter-smelling solution.

The red light in the narrow cabin, along with her feverish thoughts, combined to present a strange, night-marish image. She was connected to a blood washer, which she associated with the pain in her feet and back of her hand, and the warmth she felt as the solution dispensed by medical nanobots flooded her system and devoured the neuro-dampener quickly brought back some clarity.

Her labored breathing grew lighter, made her feel as if she were flying, and she quickly regained control over her fingers and feet. A short time later she felt her arms and legs again, and when the infusion needles were pulled out of her veins, she already felt surprisingly good, less than five minutes after she had been retrieved.

She was stripped, cleaned and dried off, and dressed in a set of expensive civilian clothes bearing no conspicuous embellishment. As usual, the thoroughly disguised HTR soldiers did not speak a single word, even though she knew that they had reported every step of her extraction and treatment via their encrypted radio channel to supply the corresponding report to the Ministry of the Interior with evidence.

HTR teams of private security services—such as Alpha Extractions in this case—operated within a very narrow legal framework, and each case resulted in lengthy procedures that examined the legality of each step of the operation. Of course, not everything was conducted lawfully, which is why Alpha Extraction's largest department was its legal division. But companies that promised their customers safety against any threat and accident situation—demanding a seven-figure annual fee for their services—had to be able to afford such legal backup teams.

Her retinal implant displayed an incoming call icon. "Hello, Hortat."

"Agatha!" For the first time since she knew him, the Builder sounded almost upset. "Are you okay? Are you doing well?"

"Yes, I'm perfectly fine," she replied, admitting that she felt a little flattered by his concern.

"What was going on? Your vital data—"

She interrupted him and cleared her throat several times as a metallic, drug-induced taste spread across her tongue. "I'd rather not talk about it over the phone."

"The line is safe," he assured her.

"I know. Still, it's not a good place."

"I understand," Hortat said succinctly. "Should we meet?"

"Not yet. I'll get in touch as soon as I can."

"I trust you."

Agatha knew he meant it kindly but she felt the weight on her shoulders increase and shrugged. "Thank you."

She ended the connection and turned to one of the two paramedics. "Please let me out at Eloff, corner of Fox Street."

The figure, in dark blue armor fitted with chunky ceramic components and joint-assist servo motors, pointed its visor-less helmet at her and nodded. The whole team began cleanup, disposing of some of the used medical components and storing the rest in the aircraft's many wall mounts. During the short flight to the city she checked her news feed, scrolled through her messages, and to her surprise, found only a quick note about an Alpha Extraction operation in the industrial areas in the southern city outskirts—nothing about Heavy Chemicals Pretoria, which surprised her. The net jockey forums in the Augmented City only contained a smattering of chatter about strange events in that area.

*Either they bought the best net crawlers there are, or someone at the top is making sure that nothing goes public,* she thought. On one hand, she was amazed and alarmed, and on the other, relieved that she did not appear in the media and thus cause a scandal that would hurt Hortat so shortly before the run-off. The city was already in a high state of excitement, so it would not require much of a spark to set off the whole place. Or worse—to cause Hortat to stumble over something she had caused. *I assume I should be grateful.*

The vector thruster dropped her off in a nearby airpark, which lay diagonally opposite a monolithic skyscraper, the address that corresponded to the coordinates Herxmin had sent to her shortly before the Builder was killed. Most of the people on the crowded sidewalks were expensively dressed residents of downtown who were flocking to the area's numerous expensive pubs and dance clubs after work.

There were big election parties and creatively tailored menus for the two candidates in the run-off to take advantage of the magic that had focused the eyes of the whole world on South Africa. For a few weeks, it no longer felt merely like the Special Administrative Zone, an artificial state not even formally recognized by the UN and that was best known for its diverse populations and the 2051 reactor disaster.

A rapid technology transfer and a new start-up culture with low taxes and generous funds from the Human Foundation would not alone have triggered the magic that had come with the emergence of Hortat as an investor and the only prominent Builder who had settled here—and then even run as a presidential candidate.

Agatha pushed through the throngs on the sidewalk, joined a crowd in front of an Augmented City traffic light, which could only be seen with retinal implants, and then crossed the street, immersed in the faceless crowd of chatting passers-by who were shedding the stress of the hectic working day and anticipating a long, exciting weekend.

Across the street, she walked to the imposing entrance of the skyscraper, over which a large silver gleaming sign read, 'Johannesburg Police Headquarters.'

"Really now?" she muttered and stopped, knowing full well that hidden sensors had already taken notice since she was the only one to stop and look up the stairs to the dark doors. *What's going on, Herxmin?*

She tried to feel annoyed, but nothing could compete with the painful sense of regret over the Builder's death. She sighed deeply before walking up the stairs. She simply had to trust that the policewoman's last recorded thoughts had not been wasted, but that she had reason enough to bring her here.

*If I hadn't been dunked in feces, and shot, I wouldn't have been surprised at being where I am now,* she scolded herself.

She paused abruptly when an androgynous voice sounded, and her neural implants warned her of unauthorized scans that were automatically blocked. But Agatha enabled them manually, except for the subroutines that hid her military augments.

"Please remain where you are, citizen. If you would like to lodge a criminal complaint, please use our Augmented City access. If you need help filling out the form, please log in to the net."

"Lieutenant Herxmin sent me," Agatha replied succinctly, and it took less than 20 seconds for one of the six armored glass doors to hum and automatically open inward. Two seemingly inactive large bots and two police officers in uniform were waiting for her. The police officers waved her through a body scanner.

"Please follow me," said the dark-skinned policeman, an attractive young man who had the natural youthfulness of someone who had not yet undergone rejuvenation treatment.

"Okay," she replied, hiding her surprise. Their steps echoed on the polished old marble of the reception hall, which, before complete digitization, had undoubtedly been filled with hundreds of confused civilians. It now seemed as quiet as a cemetery. The light was sparse, and the counters that receptionists once occupied were abandoned.

She was led to the elevators, which took them to the penultimate story, the 87$^{th}$ floor. "Where are we going?"

"The Deputy Director wants to talk to you."

*The deputy chief of the police department?* she thought. *Why? I imagine he knows who I am and wants to know what I'm doing here.*

When the elevator doors opened after a long silent ride, they stepped out into a hallway, walked to the opposite end, and stopped in front of the only open door. Behind other milky glass doors she had seen the shadows of crowded offices and VR rigs where officers worked. Subdued conversation sounds reached them in the hall.

"Please," said the young policeman, signaling her to step through. He then folded his arms in front of his chest and waited. She went in and the door closed behind her.

The deputy director, a gray-haired man who must have been at least 90 years old, and apparently never rejuvenated, sat behind a huge cedar desk. A wide, tinted glass panel behind him rendered the city's lights into a washed-out pastel glow as if it were a hologram. All life seemed frozen out there and forced into an unnatural calm.

It was only at second glance that Agatha caught sight of a single Builder who emerged from the shadows next to the curtains and cocked his head slightly. He seemed a little thinner than Hortat or Herxmin and at least half a head shorter, which still made him a giant. The bronze skin looked matte, but that might have been an effect of the sparse lighting, which lent a touch of conspiracy to the ambiance.

"Deputy Director," she greeted the city's deputy police chief, then nodded to the Builder.

"Agent Devenworth. I am Deputy Director Lubanzi Mukoena." The old man got up and shook her hand before pointing to one of the two empty chairs in front of the desk.

"Ms. Devenworth," she corrected him.

"Ahh, yes," Mukoena said with a smile that seemed to conceal a whole world behind it and sat down again. His face became serious when he pointed to the Builder. "This is Hlarch. He is a special advisor to the department and the reason why you are here."

"I thought Herxmin was the reason. I am sorry to have to report the murder of your colleague," she said.

"We already know," Mukoena said, his mouth twisting into a thin grimace and his sagging cheeks tightening slightly, "and you must ensure that those responsible are held accountable."

"*I?*" Agatha blinked in surprise.

"Yes. Hlarch received a transmission from Herxmin shortly before her death. She wanted you to know the content or she wouldn't have sent you here, and I know what an excellent agent you are. Well, everyone knows that."

"But not everyone *wants* to know."

The old policeman nodded sadly, and his voice became a bit hoarse. "Yes, that's probably true. That's why you're with me and not with the director, who's in crisis mode right now because of the attack on the train at Pretoria."

*This man is a Hortat supporter. That's good,* she thought. "I understand," she said, keeping her manner neutral. "What exactly should I see?"

"Herxmin has conveyed something to me that you can assess better than we can," the Builder said in a voice that rumbled so profoundly that she thought her bones would begin to vibrate. He approached her and regarded her for a long moment. "She wanted you to see it."

"Conveyed? What do you mean by that?"

"There are ways in which my species communicate with each other that is less reliant on spatial distances than you might think."

"Telepathy?"

"You can call it that, even if it isn't exactly accurate. But that is irrelevant to this process. Please deactivate all camouflage routines that you have currently activated."

"I..." She wanted to say that she employed no such

programs, but both pairs of eyes left no doubt she would have embarrassed herself if she did. So, she acquiesced despite grave reluctance. "Of course."

"Thank you." Hlarch again tilted his head and closed his eyes. "You will see through Herxmin's eyes and share her last sensory impressions. Please stay calm. This can be a little disturbing to a human mind."

"I understand."

"Are you ready?"

Agatha straightened up and folded her hands in her lap. "Yes."

"Please close your eyes."

When she opened them again, they were no longer hers. She was overcome by a completely new corporeal sensation, brimming with strength and yet tamed, as if she were a huge dam holding back indescribable masses of water. So many things happened in her mind that she did not see any of it clearly, and yet it seemed somehow normal and at the same time so overpowering that she would have preferred burning to ash.

All her thoughts moved above a sea of voices and images, all of which existed simultaneously, yet took on an opaque hierarchy that did not follow a transparent pattern. She breathed a city's foul night air, which seemed to contain so much more than Agatha had known, and caught a glimpse of herself—Agatha—but she was *not* herself.

She saw swirling colors around the outline of the human woman, which she captured simultaneously as a pulsating work of art and as a material appearance that included every pore of her skin and every cell of her hair.

Then she turned to the side, peeking under the closing roller door into the interior of the HCP building. She saw a white wall that slowly dissolved, as if, by scanning something, she ended its existence. Behind it, a vast hall opened, from which organic-looking hoses grew downward into dense trees, reminiscent of bare, moist bundles of muscle.

At their ends hung the bodies of at least two dozen Builders, whose heads hung lifelessly on their chests, as if on hooks, while tiny needles stuck in the back of their necks led to the hoses. Other Builders and humans ran around between them, pulling out blue vials from machines at the base of each of the muscle-like hose trees, which were located just above the gray floor. The Builders were armed and were laying assault rifles and grenade launchers upon long tables, while two figures dragged away the body of Captain Breekens, and five of them sprinted toward the roller door—and her.

She saw every movement with unique clarity, including every lamp and pin in the large room, although the moment lasted as long as an inhaled breath. She caught a glimpse of the projectile that hit her as a golden flash. Then everything turned black.

And Agatha saw through her own eyes again, finding herself back in the deputy director's office and being overwhelmed by a wave of nausea. Powerless, she slumped from the chair and fell to the right onto her hands and knees. Her stomach cramped, causing her to vomit.

A miserable sound came from her mouth. She spat the last of the sour bile onto the floor and tried to stand up with trembling limbs. Her retinal implant displayed various warning messages triggered by her neural implants. Almost all areas of the brain were in a state of acute overactivity. Strong hands grabbed her and hoisted her back onto the chair. It was Hlarch. Opposite her sat the old police officer. She was in his office.

*I... Agatha,* she admonished herself. *I am myself.*

"I'm sorry you had to go through that. I experienced it, too, before you came here," Mukoena said. A cleaner bot came from a small charging station on the wall and began cleaning up Agatha's reeking vomit.

"'A *little* disturbing?'" She directed her question to the Builder. "That was probably the under-exaggeration of the century!"

"Your thoughts are not compatible with ours, but the two seconds of conveyance should not leave any lasting damage," Hlarch assured her. Stung by her unrelenting stare, he retreated from her and stood at the side of the desk.

"That was the Dark Tongue, wasn't it? What are they doing at a chemical start-up?"

"That's what we wanted to know from you, Mrs. Devenworth."

"Ms.," she muttered, and blinked to restore logical order to her thoughts. It was still exhausting and seemed unreal. "No idea. But I saw they were using human equipment. Why? And why should they have their hiding place in Johannesburg, at HCP—and work with them? Since when have they been working together with people at all?"

"This has never been the case before, as far as we know. But that's not very much, I have to admit," said the deputy director. "Did you see the big screen on the left wall, behind one of the hose trees?"

"Yes," Agatha nodded and tried to remember details. There had been a screen, but that was all.

"Well, Hlarch knows the details. There he saw the schematic drawing of a train and two names: Victor Dalio and Joseph Bellinger. Both are European citizens with diplomatic passports, as we have already discovered."

"The train?" Agatha looked back and forth between the Builder and the policeman. "The COO told us that they were here to discuss some crisis with customers in Cairo, but not with an armed team of Builders and humans in a laboratory housing hanged Builders!"

Again a wave of nausea rose within her, and she swallowed to squelch it. "Have you already inquired at the embassies? Dalio and Bellinger—they sound Italian and German."

"Not just that. On the rail line to which the train was to be diverted is a French military base in southern Angola just over the border from the Special Administrative Zone," Mukoena said.

"You think they are acting as EU agents?"

"Acted," he corrected her.

"Why should they hijack a train with HCP chemicals and divert them to one of their bases?" Agatha covered her face and answered her own question. "Because of what they're sucking out of the Builders."

"Yes." Hlarch's voice did not sound as firm as before.

"I thought the Dark Tongue was committed to the radical protection of the interests of Builders. So, either it was not the Dark Tongue in the company building, or the organization is not what we think it is."

Mukoena nodded gloomily.

"That's not all," Hlarch said. "I also saw a PIN code through Herxmin's eyes."

"PIN? How old-fashioned."

"Yes. It could mean anything... or nothing. I'll send it to your neural implants."

"Does the Human Foundation already know about this? After all, this is a disaster for them. They are the biggest investors."

"No. We want to understand what we are dealing with before we inform anyone." The deputy director leaned forward, lowering his elbows onto the tabletop along with his voice. "This is political dynamite for all the factions in this election, and we must not light the fuse."

"But we can't just let it rest!" she protested.

"No, we can't," he agreed. "That's why we are asking you for help."

"You can't use this evidence, right? Hlarch does not officially work for the police, and this..." Agatha swallowed. "...this method of telepathy is not to be made known. Am I right?"

Mukoena did not answer, but instead wove his fingers together before finally turning away from her stinging gaze, as if he were in pain.

"It's like this, Agent. The days before the election are fragile. We must not make mistakes, or at least not allow anything to become public that, in the eyes of our enemies, will be regarded as mistakes. They're just waiting for that. If we had two days, things would be very different, but we don't. We must clear up this matter now, even if the Chief would contradict me."

Agatha understood the indirect hint that she should keep this meeting to herself, and nodded in apparent sympathy.

"Have you already completely evaluated the train's black box?"

"No."

"I want to have access. On-site."

"You have it."

"And your backing. If not officially, then indirectly, as best you can."

Once again, the deputy director nodded, and Agatha stood up. "I agree."

"Find out what these shitholes are doing, Agent Devenworth. Take them down if you have to. We must not allow anyone to endanger the election or to kidnap Builders in our city's underground and... whatever they are doing."

"And hurry, Ms. Devenworth," Hlarch said. "These people at HCP, yours and mine alike, have prepared for something, and I have the feeling that they both have the same goal."

# 9

# PANO

The taxi had a spacious passenger cabin that could easily carry six people, and he had it all to himself. Thanks to the generous expense allotment from Karlhammer, the entire vehicle belonged to him and did not collect any other passengers on the way. The seat in which he reclined was comfortable and resembled an armchair. The black faux leather headrest bore the lettering 'MyDrive' embroidered in yellow.

He had made the call from the taxi to the person he was about to visit, using a prepaid hand terminal as a precaution. When he bought the unit at a small kiosk in Melville, the salesman had looked at him as if he knew very well that Pano was intending something illegal as part of a 'job.' The man even winked and grinned at him, but that did not bother him. Let the guy believe what he wanted.

"I want the car to gleam when we reach our destination. Please include a carwash on route," he asked the driver AI.

"There is no need to clean this vehicle," an androgynous voice answered. "At MyDrive, we only offer our services after professional cleaning of both body and interior."

"I'll pay twenty percent extra," he said, and authorized payment through his hand terminal.

"Thank you for your payment. The stopover is authorized. Please remember to get out before washing commences."

"Of course." Pano looked out the window as the lights of the many cars passed by like the surreal glow of distant stars. He imagined himself rushing past them as they trailed long streaks in the onsetting rain. This city was a strange cosmos that played by its own rules.

Of course, he had known this before he had boarded the plane. Even years ago in Cape Town, during his investigation into the Ron Jackson case with Agatha, South Africa had come as a big surprise to him. You never knew what was waiting around the next corner, or what cultural peculiarities would make you stumble.

But Johannesburg in the 2060s topped off the whole thing—an ugly behemoth with a few shining exceptions, such as the city center. Its radiance could even compete with Manhattan, and the plethora of adjacent neighborhoods that looked like a mixture of dystopia and industrial melancholy—monuments of human ugliness cast in concrete, and at the same time a testament to its ability to hope.

The fact that Hortat had chosen this place to proclaim his illusory dream of a better world without human flaws could well be regarded as a statement. At the same time, Pano was not surprised that the megacity had cost Hortat his life. Although less than two days had passed since, Johannesburg had changed forever. Not only the ubiquitous fires that blazed and flickered at every third alley along the gorges between tall buildings, but most of all, the pyramid above their heads seemed to say that there was no way back for this shining hell hole.

"We have arrived at the carwash," announced the taxi after a pleasant, three-tone chime, and it drove up a driveway to one of six washing bays fronted by square gates. The facility was once a hangar for rotor drones, the walls having been dismantled down to its skeleton of steel beams. Employees in shiny rain ponchos stood there in boredom, leaning against something that looked like a pump, while customers automatically paid, got out, and let their vehicles arrange the rest with the cleaning computers until they re-entered on the other side.

"Dear passenger, you have to leave the vehicle for your personal safety before washing begins," the taxi instructed him.

"I'll stay seated."

"I am sorry. This system prohibits allowing vehicles with their occupants in the cleaning zone. There is a significant risk to your health."

"Why?" he asked, smiling contentedly as he heard what he expected.

"Some of the procedures for deep cleaning of the body include electromagnetic fields that can destroy your implants."

Someone knocked on the left windshield, and Pano operated the electric window. "Good evening," he greeted the washing plant employee, who looked in at him disgruntledly. Water ran from the guy's plastic hood.

"Ya godda get out. Hav'n' you read the signs?"

"What signs?"

"The AR signs flashing all around the entrance to the washing bay!"

"I don't have implants."

The man looked at Pano as if he had lost his mind. "What?"

"I'll explain it to you." He took his hand terminal and released 500 rands, which he sent to the only Bluetooth connection nearby. After a confused blink, the employee clicked his tongue and shrugged his shoulders.

"Okay. Your risk."

Pano's account app showed a deficit of 500 rands, indicating that the amount would be offset with the corresponding amount in euros within four hours. He closed the window again and leaned back.

"Well, let's go, taxi."

"I have been given clearance. Please confirm that MyDrive has warned you of health hazards if you continue despite my warning."

"I understand. Don't worry. I'm not going to complain."

The car accelerated gently and steered into the washing bay. Huge brushes and high-pressure cleaners extended out of the robotic frame that moved back and forth while the taxi was being processed. It roared and pounded within as if he were in a rainstorm. Then the machines withdrew and nothing happened, if one ignored a slight tug Pano felt in his bowels. However, he estimated that the feeling was purely psychosomatic. He only realized that this was not the case when he could not operate his commlink nor his transducer, his only two implants. It was as if he were gasping for air.

He smiled contentedly as they rolled back onto the road and continued their way to his destination. According to his brief research on his hand terminal, Alberton was a district in the south of the megacity, a favored residential area that still offered something like town villas with small front yards. It was far enough away from the hustle and bustle of the city, and at the same time not so close to the massive

storm walls that it would make one feel like the occupant of a big prison.

The home of the former deputy director of the Johannesburg police was located on a wide street with manicured sidewalks behind a white slatted fence, and the house was built of burned brick. Pano had the taxi park opposite and deposited 150 digital rands so that it would wait an hour. He then opened the door and pulled his jacket over his head like a tarpaulin to protect himself from the rain.

As fast as he could, he crossed the wet road, rounded puddles, and jumped over a storm sewer grate before taking the paved path to the front door and shaking out his jacket under the roof. He looked into the dark sensor strip on the door frame and gave a laconic wave. It took an eternity for the face of a dark-skinned man with a gray, three-day beard to appear.

"Mr. Hofer?"

"Uh-huh."

"Come in," said Lubanzi Mukoena, pulling the door open wide.

"Thank you." Pano stepped into a wide hallway with creaking wooden planks and gave his host his soaked jacket. "I thought it wouldn't rain in Africa."

"A typical Westerner comment."

"That was a joke."

"Ahh." Mukoena nodded thoughtfully, pointing to a door leading into a dining room with a table and four chairs.

Pano felt as if he had traveled back 20 years in time when he saw an electric fireplace and an old 3D television on the wall.

"Sit down, please."

"I was in a carwash on the way here," Pano said. He acceded to the request, and nodded in gratitude as the fired deputy police chief served him a glass of fresh water. *Is it real and not recycled?*

"Everyone who wants to know already knows that you are here," Mukoena said, and sat down with him. His movements were halting, as if he were suffering from an arthritic disease or as if he were older than he looked. He was certainly rejuvenated, but not with the typical characteristics. The gray beard and the subtle crow's feet around the eyes painted a picture of experience and permanence, without suggesting fragility or senility. Smart, for a position like the one he'd recently held.

"I wish my ex-wife knew."

"I thought you were here because of her."

"Why else should I be here?"

The South African seemed surprised. "You probably weren't a fan of Hortat?"

"Not really. But that's not why I'm here, as we have already agreed." Pano looked around with interest. "Are you alone?"

Mukoena understood the question and nodded. "I have curious neighbors, but I have been with the police long enough to know that it is better to live on my own."

"Hmm. Quite an honor that you allow me into your esteemed solitude, just like that."

"I want you to find Agatha Devenworth."

"You're not the only one." They looked at each other for a while, neither of them speaking, until Pano spoke again. "You look rather worn-out, haggard even. What happened?"

"One of my officers was murdered."

"In the course of the HCP investigation, I assume?"

"Yes. It does not appear in any report because the information about it was obtained through an unauthorized procedure, but I have seen it myself," Mukoena grumbled, placing his hands on the table and clenching them into fists. At that moment he looked like a boy who could not decide whether to be angry or sad.

"You were there?"

"No. The Johannesburg police had three Builders in its service, one of them a sergeant in the mobile readiness unit. Her name was Herxmin. She was shot on the site of Heavy Chemicals Pretoria."

"So, then you gave the order to storm the company head-quarters. Without consulting your superior," Pano concluded.

"Yes. I had an eyewitness and felt safe enough. We could not tolerate that. You do not know how valuable Builders are to our work and to bringing our two species closer. We need more of them in law enforcement and security to gain their trust and make them part of the new normal. This goes far beyond policing. It has a political dimension."

"Agatha was your eyewitness?"

"Yes, but she was just suddenly gone, went into hiding, and then... then this attack." Mukoena looked like he had to gasp for air. His eyelids lowered. "It was right to fire me, you know?"

"You see yourself as complicit in the attack," he said. "Why?" Pano insisted, confused.

"Hlarch."

"Pardon?"

"Hlarch, one of my advisors."

"A Builder."

"Yes. Shortly before her murder, or just as she was murdered, he received a kind of telepathic transmission from Herxmin. Then I ordered the deployment. Heavy Chemicals Pretoria is involved in criminal activities and has killed a Builder. Probably one of my captains as well. I was convinced of that at the time."

"At the time? So, no longer?" asked Pano. "Why?"

"Hlarch has since disappeared."

"That makes sense, doesn't it? After all, he employed an unauthorized method for gathering evidence—which *you* authorized. Perhaps he simply wanted to avoid having to submit to disciplinary procedures."

"Oh, come on. What would have happened? I was fired because my actions would lead to a huge legal shitstorm. I was tricked and am now paying a high price for my blindness. But a Builder? No." Mukoena shook his head. "They would never have sacked him. Maybe a reprimand, but nothing else. It would be like breaking the only real gold prong off of a crown otherwise made only of sheet metal."

"Why would he then go into hiding?"

"I had hoped that you could help me with that question. Honestly, I would like to give you all my money and hire you to find your ex-wife and bring her to me so that I can personally strangle her for her double betrayal of me and Hortat. But I want to know one thing above all—the cause for which I lost my job, my reputation, and the person for whom I ordered the deployment."

"You thought you were protecting Hortat," Pano concluded, sighing. "Agatha was his right hand and asked for help."

"Yes," the former Deputy Director muttered. "She took advantage of me."

"She can be very... determined if she wants something."

"I know that you have personal connections with Luther Karlhammer. I've seen everything about you and your wife that was ever played in the streams. Did you really save his life? In Antarctica, I mean?"

Pano nodded.

"And this…" When Mukoena saw his facial expression, he took a deep breath. "Karlhammer has engaged you, I'm sure. He will be as shocked as I am and will do everything possible to find and hold your ex-wife accountable. He wanted to light fireworks in Hortat's honor, did you know? An orbital fireworks display. Today, it sounds like a bad joke."

"I saw the announcement on TV. It is fair to say that he is a great fan of the Builders and above all, of Hortat, as much as he supposedly supported him."

"You don't sound convinced."

"I haven't forgotten what he says about politics," Pano replied. "Basically, he has accused us Europeans of living only in sham democracies. More specifically, those with low levels of education. Have you read what he said about the need to link the right to vote to an intelligence and knowledge test?"

"He's not wrong, is he? Wasn't it mainly the reactionary, xenophobic portion of the population, those who no longer had jobs after robotization, that elected all those despots to power?" asked Mukoena.

"Probably yes, but that doesn't mean you have to condemn them all. Instead of excluding them, one should investigate the reasons why they have become as you describe them—which is because they feel exactly as they are—excluded and abandoned."

"Does the world have enough time?"

"I don't know, and that's not why I'm here. I want to find my ex-wife. She wouldn't be my ex-wife if we hadn't had our problems, but she's not a terrorist. Whatever has happened here, I have to figure out why. Since you accepted my call and have invited me here, I assume that you have something for me that could help me?"

The former deputy police chief leaned back carefully in his chair and regarded Pano a moment before reaching into his pocket and placing a small last-generation hand terminal on the table—one that had been produced before neural implants flooded the market. He pushed it into the middle of the table between them, and for a few moments, they both looked at it as if it were some miraculous object.

"Do what you need with it."

Pano reached out and put his hand on the terminal before pulling it to him and putting it in his pocket. "I saw it when I came in."

"In my pocket?"

Pano nodded.

"And?"

"I had thought about stealing it from you because it seemed rather strange that anyone here would still be using a hand terminal."

"You wanted to rob me?"

"No, I just played with the thought."

"You're a great investigator, as far as I can tell. After everything I saw in the streams, I would have thought—"

"The streams? Oh, come on. They needed heroes after the fossil crisis to distract from the fact that it was Hortat and Xinth who put everything in order. I was a good thief before I trained with the police. Why do you think I finally studied law?" Pano snorted. "I could steal almost anything from you without you noticing. I learned that in Bolzano's train station district. A good school, actually."

"Why are you telling me this?" asked Mukoena.

"I mean, you're not being very careful."

"I have nothing to lose."

"You already sound bitter, at least."

"By the way, I found out something else," said Mukoena, as Pano was just about to get up. "There was an attack on a man in Randfontein, right by the wall. He swears that a woman who fits Agatha's description assaulted him. Not that any of the officers on the ground would have seen the connection, but who knows what's really going on in these insane days?"

## 10

## AGATHA

"That's... disturbing," Hortat said with a serious expression, his likeness displayed in a large image she could hardly avoid noticing, overlaying the myriad colorful lights of Johannesburg that passed the robotaxi's windows.

"I know. Can you do anything about it?" she asked, dabbing her forehead with the sleeve of the jacket that Alpha Extractions had given her. Just telling him about the brief vision of Herxmin's final seconds had driven sweat from her pores. It had been one of the most miraculous and sublime experiences of her life, but at the same time, one of the most traumatic. The feeling that one's mind was filled and swollen with something that grew firmer with every second had been devastating. How could she ever look at a Builder again and not think about how many indescribable things were going on behind those big almond-shaped eyes?

"I'm not sure."

"What does that mean, you're not sure?"

"What you have described is, as I said, disturbing. Everything suggests that it was the Dark Tongue you saw, but they wouldn't work with humans. They think of you as oppressors, as you might if your lab rats were to start to push you around and racially lord it over you. For them, this is unimaginable and offensive."

"Which I can understand," Agatha had to admit.

"They use violence to enforce their point of view. This is not our way, nor is it necessary," Hortat explained. "There are other ways to set us apart and protect us."

"And why don't you?"

"That's what we are doing. But not all of us are patient, or so it would seem."

"What are all of you doing? What are *you* doing? Do you mean the election?"

Hortat hesitated. "Primarily, yes."

*Primarily?* she thought, forcing herself not to pursue it and waste valuable time.

"If they are kidnapping our own and abusing them for some type of experiment, it creates a precedent that we cannot ignore," the Builder continued, and his eyes seemed to be saying so much more than his words conveyed.

His digital image made her think that she could almost physically feel him moving an entire cosmos of thoughts and connections behind his forehead as if something that she would never understand were weighing on his shoulders—which was probably the case. If she had not been able to come to terms with this realization, she would never have been able to enter his service.

"Does that mean you agree to my plan?"

He seemed anxious as he regarded her. "It is dangerous."

"I know. But it is efficient. See it as a good return on investment for the insurance payments you've made. Moreover, if something happens, we will appear as victims, not as perpetrators."

"Because then all of you are the victims."

"We'll see. There has to be a reason why they did not use Builder technology there."

Hortat tilted his head to the side. "The Human Foundation."

"They have committed themselves to enforcing the ban on non-licensed Builder technology, at least within the limits of the Special Administrative Zone." Agatha nodded. "But is the Foundation so powerful that it can intimidate the Dark Tongue?"

"We have to assume that. Even I have little insight into the capacities and technological advantages of Luther's organization."

"Why?"

"Because of the Horizon Orbital, where all important decisions are made. My eyes don't reach there."

"Yours, or any Builder's?"

"Both. It has something to do with the vacuum. It's complicated."

"All right. Then you'll send me the team?"

"Yes. With your desired equipment. They will meet you at the scrapyard." Hortat looked directly into her eyes. "Agatha. Don't do anything reckless, okay?"

"Yes."

"Promise me."

She rolled her eyes. "Yes, Dad. I promise."

"If it becomes necessary, you call me."

"No. You must not be seen as connected with this matter."

"What good is the office of president if it is built on the corpses of those who are close to my heart?" he asked.

"I... I'll manage." She felt a warm feeling spreading in her. "Trust me. I survived that damn fossil crisis that you were to blame for."

"It was Xinth who—"

"Don't start that again! The connection is getting very bad right now."

Hortat smiled slightly and tilted his mighty head. "Good luck, Agatha."

"Thank you."

She disconnected and tried to relax a little while the taxi took her northward at more than 200 kilometers an hour on the expressway's priority lanes, thanks to her premium customer rating. She raced past the center of Pretoria, which the megacity had absorbed in the last few decades. The car slowed only after reaching the exit, which led her to a less used country road that she had already picked out on her previous trip there.

The night began to look particularly dark where the first meadows and smaller forests spread like waves crashing against the storm walls of the city. They were so tall with their 20-meter height that they shut out the city lights. Behind the trees loomed an all-encompassing glow that even reflected off the clouds and made them gleam red. It was a welcome relief for her eyes, and at the same time, she realized how strange it seemed not to be surrounded by all the flashing symbols of the new high technology.

She remembered long evenings with Pano on the balcony of their alpine house in South Tyrol, where they had enjoyed the silence and the darkness with a glass of wine apiece—simple pleasures. Did the valley still seem so out of touch with time? Or had the technology transfer initiated by the Human Foundation already reached it? And Pano? Was he still sitting there and believing that everything could stay as it was before? That the Earth did not have to rotate?

Agatha shook off her musings as, with the aid of residual

light enhancement, she caught sight of the scrapyard. As soon as she submitted her code, two pairs of headlights sprang to life next to one of the walls of crushed metal, and she received the appropriate confirmations. She ordered the taxi to stop and let her out so that the on-board sensors recorded just enough, but not too much in case of an investigation.

The air outside was fresh for this time of year, and she could even hear some nocturnal birds calling. She wished she could have stopped and listened to them a little while, but instead approached the two cars awaiting her in the form of four cones of light and got into the rear SUV.

"Pablo, Steve," she greeted the two public relations officials from Hortat's campaign team. Pablo was a twice-rejuvenated veteran of the business with a youthful grin and a movie star's charm that he knew how to use to make a flamboyant impression. Everyone who knew him liked him—one way or another. Steve was a man of mellower tones, and played the quiet, matter-of-fact uncle in concert with Pablo, complete with the right touch of gray at his temples and simple corduroy suits.

"Hello, Agatha!" Pablo said with a handclap. "Can you tell us why Hortat sent us here? Rather creepy out here."

"The AC connection here is really nasty," Steve added, looking around uneasily.

"Stop complaining. You'll be back in front of your cameras and web feeds soon enough. You don't have to do anything but run after me and talk to a few people when things get tough. You can do that, can't you?"

"And what are Julie and Marissa supposed to do?" Pablo pointed to the neighboring car, while Agatha opened the bag on the seat next to her and took out the armored clothing, made of programmable polymers, to exchange for the Alpha Extractions outfit she still wore.

"What's the matter with them?" she asked as she bemoaned the effort of changing her clothes as discreetly as possible and without attracting the looks of the two PR men.

"They are trained diplomats. They travel the world for Junior to shake hands with people in his name," Steve explained. "What in heaven's name are you planning to do with them at the site of a terrorist attack?"

"They're nice."

"Nice?"

Agatha shrugged. "Yes, it's nice to have them around you. They don't ask so many questions."

"Because they're in the other car!" Pablo turned to face forward and folded down the sun visor mirror above the driver's seat to primp his meticulously styled hair.

"No, they're just not as whiny and nervous as you," she said, smiling sweetly as the two turned to her and glowered. She waited until her figure-fitting armor had snuggled tightly to her body, and then got out to put on the coat that was also in the bag. The last thing in the bag was her spare pistol, which slipped into the holster hidden below her left breast. "Well, guys, are you coming?"

Reluctantly, they got out but quickly tried assuming the firm expressions of strong men, just as she had expected they would.

"Much better!" she praised the two, reaping sour looks for it. "Hello, Julie! Hello, Marissa!"

"Hi, Agatha!" The two attractive women who were Hortat's mouthpieces to the world—besides herself, of course—embodied the perfect blend of motherhood and alluring beauty that had already made many heads of state and corporate bosses look like rabbits confronted by a snake. Agatha liked that they knew this and were still extremely uncomplicated and astute.

"Julie? Marissa?" She hugged both fleetingly. "Do you think you can take care of our two scaredy-cats here while I take care of the reason for our being here?"

"Absolutely," Marissa assured her, winking at her knowingly as Pablo and Steve snorted. "What are we actually doing here? An investigation into the train crash? How exciting!"

"Something like that. Just keep a low profile. Follow me, and pretend you belong."

"Let's go. I wanted to get out of the campaign office anyway. They are all so excited that my hair's going gray just watching it all."

"We're going to win, don't worry." Agatha got serious. "What I'm going to do is dangerous, and you can't know anything about it because otherwise it won't work. I apologize for that now, but it is so important that we have no other options. If all goes well, we'll all come out of here alive, and possibly uncover something that will have far-reaching consequences for humans and Builders alike. At this point, you can still drop out if you want."

None of the four moved: Julie and Marissa, because they thought the whole thing was exciting fun; and Pablo and Steve—who repeatedly glanced at their female colleagues out of the corners of their eyes—out of a sense of honor or shame.

"Good. Then let's go. We'll drive your car to the barrier," she said to Julie.

In less than five minutes they were standing behind the small car that had brought her. This time they turned to the left and walked along the edge of the forest to the ravine entrance, which the police still had cordoned off. ECM jammers stood next to the rail track behind old-fashioned warning tape and emitted electronic noise that prevented flying drones from getting a look at the crime scene from the air, which is why not many of the flying sensor bundles were whirring over their heads.

"Hey, you can't go in there!" yelled one of the five police officers who guarded the 50-meter-wide access to the ravine. The officers had been standing in a small group before one of them noticed Agatha's group. From this perspective, on the bottom, the ravine's slope seemed much steeper than it had from the top, and the dry riverbed and rail track looked much narrower. The illumination from the construction lights set up around the attack site cast long shadows on the knotty clumps of grass and the wrecked cars in the distance.

"My name is Agatha Devenworth. I have an authorization code." She sent the file she had received from Deputy Director Mukoena to the person who approached her.

"Who issued this?" the officer asked.

"That doesn't matter. What is important is that I'm authorized."

"Let them go. The code is fine," said one of the others.

The first officer pointed to her companions. "And who are they?"

Julie stepped in with an adorable smile. "We are her assistants. We don't want to make any trouble, Sir, just make your work a little easier."

"And what kind of work is that?"

"Friends, we're all about making your job out here a little easier." Pablo patted himself on the jacket. "We were called in as private contractors to speed up forensic analysis."

"I haven't heard anything about—"

"You know how much time those lazy lab boys always take," Steve said with apparent regret. "It seems someone at the top wants to take care of you, so you don't have to go to the election parties tomorrow all worn out. We are paid by the hour, not for sitting around."

"It's about time," one of the police officers muttered with a grumpy look. "They've been scurrying around for eight hours or so, and we have to freeze our asses because those—"

"—those armchair farters have no friends they'd rather be with anyway," Pablo agreed, pretending the idea was worthy of outrage.

"Yes! What are they doing? Fiddling around with their earplugs and talking all the time."

"Well, that's why we're here. One hour, and we'll be gone, gentlemen." Marissa fluttered her eyelashes, and they were waved through.

"When you're there, tell the sarge that we don't have any coffee here!" demanded another policeman.

"Will do," Agatha promised him, raising the warning tape to let the others through before proceeding along the tracks to the wrecks. She saw almost no fire now, but dozens of workers in white chemical protective suits were searching the slopes to the right and left. She paid them no further attention and stopped at the cars, partly buried in earth and gravel. At two places the cars formed crumpled ramps on top of one another and others were, as was usual for a train wreck, compressed like the folds of an accordion.

"Your TV faces can be pretty useful," she remarked along the way, loud enough to be heard over the crunching of the railbed gravel under her shoes.

"They didn't even recognize us," Pablo complained, brushing a strand of hair out of his face like a polished fashion model. "How good can we be?"

"What is it like to be married to a mirror?" asked Marissa.

"Great. The guy inside doesn't make stupid comments."

"Yes, he does, but only the same ones as you."

"I'd rather see myself than the faces of fat politicians with rotten teeth."

"Are you finished?" Agatha interrupted. "I know you're excited or nervous, but this thing here isn't fun. Keep your heads down and stay with me. Clear?"

After waiting for each one to nod or mutter 'yes,' she went on past a group of white garbed forensic experts who were examining a seriously dented container. Farther ahead, they came to the rearmost car, which had thundered like a ram into the side of the one in front of it, almost cutting it in half. A man with an absorbed look was guiding a tennis ball-sized drone through a hole in the car wall with flying fingers and virtual hand gestures.

Now that they were on the site, no one seemed to pay special attention to them, as if one was assumed to belong there once on this side of the police barrier. Agatha took advantage of this freedom and went straight to the on-duty sergeant, whom she identified by the black hat with the red brim. He was standing next to one of the spotlights and was apparently on the phone as his lips were moving, but he was saying nothing audibly.

"Hello, Officer," she greeted him. "I'm Agatha Devenworth."

The sergeant—Dodunda, according to his nameplate—blinked a few times. Then his gaze cleared and he frowned. "Hi, what can I do for you? Wait a moment. *Devenworth?* You're Hortat's right-hand woman?"

*This moment will decide how easily things will go,* she thought, nodding in reply.

"Man, what a surprise!" His mouth transformed to a broad smile as he firmly shook her hand. "No one is listening, so I can probably say that." He lowered his voice and came a little closer. "I'll keep my fingers crossed for you tomorrow evening! Or rather, this evening. It's already after midnight."

"Thank you. That's very kind. My assistants and I are here on behalf of the executive floor at Eloff, corner of Fox Street. Can you give us the latest information?" She sent him the appropriate authorization code of the deputy director for security.

"Oh, hmm. Okay, of course. The locomotive is destroyed, but we have already read out the tachograph. I can send you the file. Chemicals were stored in most of the containers, nothing special, that's what the eggheads tell me—simplest raw materials for mining explosives. The stuff is produced cheaply here in South Africa and then sent to processing companies, such as Al Hachmin in Cairo, that make them into explosives for their mining customers, specifically adapted to suit their needs. Only a single car couldn't be opened."

"Didn't you get the unlock code from the train company? This is a special case," asked Julie, surprised.

"Yes, we did, Ma'am." He looked at Agatha, who nodded, before continuing. "But it didn't work on that car. That hasn't happened for a long time, but tomorrow morning special equipment is supposed to come and cut the thing open like a tin can. It's pointless if you ask me. We've seen three dozen of the cars including their contents, and just because a lock has a malfunction, the effort isn't worth it— not just to find more barrels with blue or red soup. Well, it's not my decision."

"Which car is it?"

"The third. You can't miss it. It really took a beating from large-caliber stuff."

"Thank you. We'll take a look." Agatha shook the sergeant's hand and, from the corners of her eyes, looked around the slopes and the rock ledge above, but all was still calm. They walked past the wrecks, some of which were still radiating heat, passing small groups of forensic investigators in their white hazmat suits that made them look—and move very awkwardly—like astronauts, until they finally reached the area around the front of the train.

The car they sought was indeed not difficult to recognize. It seemed as if it were standing perfectly on the rails, wedged between two cars that had dug themselves crosswise into the railbed like T-pieces, destroyed and nothing but smoking wrecks.

There was a side door, which was seriously warped from the wave-like deformatities inflicted upon the container still positioned on its massive carriage frame. A DNA sniffer and a keypad had been effectively destroyed. She scanned both with her retinal implants and saw that there was still a weak electronic signature. Using an infiltration routine that she loaded into the still-active node, she fed in the PIN that Hlarch had read from the screen at the HCP headquarters and nodded contentedly when a high-pitched click sounded.

She walked toward the door and tried to push it open, but despite her strong arms, she failed to get it more than a few centimeters wide because it was so deformed. A disgusting stench seemed to be coming from inside.

"Help me!" she ordered the others, who hesitantly came over to her and grasped awkwardly at the open gap to tug at the warm metal. It squeaked and groaned, and they made progress centimeter by centimeter until a soccer ball-width opening had been exposed and they encountered resistance that, despite their best combined efforts, would not yield.

"You stay out here."

Julie, Marissa, Pablo, and Steve stared wide-eyed when Agatha pulled out her pistol and began to squeeze through the opening. The stench was almost unbearable, and the inside of the car was so dark that she had to switch to residual light amplification to see anything. Pure chaos had reigned in the car. It was obviously not a transport container, because there were input consoles, AR terminals, and several displays on the walls, all of which were burned out and dead. There was only a weak energy signature, and it was not coming from them.

"An EMP?" she thought aloud, looking past a chair ripped from its fastenings and seeing a man's corpse. He had an ageless face and lacked an arm, which lay further back, half under an overturned toolbox, the contents of which were scattered everywhere. A corresponding bloodstain was on the ceiling. An older-looking man—head lowered to his chest—was leaning against an old server cabinet. At first glance, he looked unharmed and he was the source of the weak energy signature.

Agatha looked back at the corpse and then at the seated figure in front of whom she was squatting. She pressed the pistol under his chin and carefully lifted it, only to stare into alert eyes and almost fall over in terror.

"P-put an end to it," the stranger muttered, clearly in pain. He coughed weakly.

"That's not why I'm here. You must be Joseph Bellinger," she said.

He did not answer.

"I recognized you by your German accent. And him there?" Agatha pointed to the partially dismembered corpse behind them, at the end of the car. "Victor Dalio, I presume?"

The German remained silent.

"You work for the ESD, I suppose? Why is the European secret service diverting a train hauling such uninteresting cargo, hmm? Hack a train and the signal box, divert it toward a French military base. For what? Do you want to fly out chemicals on a large scale? You can talk to me now, or with the Dark Tongue when they arrive. What do you Europeans want here?"

Since the agent still did not respond, and did not appear as though he intended to, she began to search him, finding a vial containing blue liquid along with an infuser inside of his jacket. Her retinal implants were sure it was emitting the weak energy source she had registered.

"What is this?"

"I'm not talking, so don't get your hopes up," the German growled. Only his mouth moved, and his head wobbled weakly back and forth.

"Spinal cord severed high, I guess?" she replied, nodding understandingly. "I know you won't talk."

"Because you were one of us."

"Yes. I get it. I just want to know what happened here."

"If you do me a favor, I'll do you one, too," Bellinger suggested.

"I like favors. Where does the change of heart come from?"

"This matter is more important," he said. "Maybe you will do the right thing."

She received a file that her security routines immediately blocked. She tilted her head and looked at him.

"Isn't a daemon," he assured her feebly. "But you have to take the risk."

She did and opened a file with 22 Johannesburg addresses. "What is it?"

"What it looks like. Any of them will suffice. No matter which one."

*I don't understand,* she wanted to say, but Bellinger continued speaking, "There's a flap under the console next to Victor. What you find there will be important. Take it with you when you visit the addresses."

"I need more—"

"No, we have a deal. Now it's your turn," the paraplegic moaned weakly as an explosion sounded from outside, followed by shrill shouts and screams. "Go! Don't forget the infuser."

"The infuser?"

"Yes. In my jacket. Take it with you."

"What?"

"You'll understand. Go..." He coughed blood. "Now!"

Agatha raised her gun and pressed the barrel to his forehead. He gave a trace of a nod, and she pulled the trigger. She then rushed over to the flap he had described to her. She tore it open and staggered back when the container was hit by something and rocked violently. Dozens of vials, like the one she had secured, tumbled toward her.

"What in the—" She was interrupted by the rattle of automatic weapons and the roar of turbines. More explosions thundered outside in the night, echoing metallically inside the car. "That was quick."

"AGATHA!" she heard an excited voice scream from outside and she rushed to the small gap. She squeezed through, careful not to damage the vial in her breast pocket.

Julie, Marissa, and the campaign team's two PR consultants huddled on the railbed with their heads pulled in and hands over their ears. They could see numerous muzzle flashes at the top of the hillside, and a helicopter roared across the valley. With loud hisses, rockets detached from its stubby wings and raced downward before the helicopter turned away under fire.

"OUT!" she yelled, grabbing Marissa and Julie, then sprinting off, pulling the two forward so violently that they fell when the rockets hit the container railcar where they had just been. The pressure wave caught them in the middle of their fall and hurled them a good bit further forward toward the slope. The impact was painful, like a fist-thick boulder boring into her ribs, which would probably have broken without her armor.

Agatha looked up and made sure the others next to her were alive. They were already scrambling up again, but they were disoriented and in shock, their faces dirty, and their eyes a mix of empty and restless.

"That makes the next step a little easier," she muttered. She went into a crouch and fired at all four in quick succession. She hit them with precise shots in one shoulder each, grazing their left trapezoidal muscles—low blood loss, acceptable pain, rapid healing, no lasting damage. Julie and Pablo screamed, perhaps more from terror, but Marissa and Steve did not even seem to notice. Agatha grabbed the latter two by their collars and screamed in their faces, "Get up! Follow me! Let's go!"

She pulled them both to their feet, saw that Julie and Pablo were following her with their eyes wide open, and then ran back to the tracks, past the destroyed container with the bodies of the two European agents. The rattling of automatic weapons was now ubiquitous, like the pounding of heavy rain. Everywhere, blood-soaked forensics personnel lay along the ravaged ravine. The blood on their white suits formed an ugly contrast, like a symbol of their innocence as unarmed victims of the violence they had tried to expose.

Those who were not yet dead, or not so injured as to leave them whimpering for help or inarticulately screaming and holding severed limbs, ran around in panic, trying to find cover. The attackers had planned their approach well. From the entrance and exit to the rail cut, black-armored figures constantly fired, their aim more lethal with each step, while huge shadows on top of the ridges took down one officer after the other with targeted bursts of fire.

"Under the car! Go!" she roared over the noise of fighting and pushed her civilian colleagues roughly onto the tracks. They crawled under one of the two railcars that had drilled themselves like T-pieces into the secret service container that was still on fire. A salvo of bullets narrowly missed her, and gravel sprayed to her left. Adrenaline boiled in her veins, compelling her to a surging haste, as if she had to move faster than her arms and legs could possibly manage.

Grunting and breathing heavily, she helped make sure that her companions complied more quickly with her order, shoving and pushing, firing her pistol at the crest high above them with no hope of hitting anything with it. But it would be enough to force some of the attackers into cover.

Nevertheless, sporadic shots again narrowly missed her, eating their way with metallic screams into the already half-destroyed steel container. This time the projectiles hissed so close to her head that the whistle triggered a sustained high-pitched tone in her left ear, which she could hear over the loud pounding of her heart.

She waited no longer and went to her knees to find her own cover under the car. One of the gunmen hit her shoe and shredded a piece of its sole.

"Stay in the middle!" she commanded, crawling close to Marissa, who cried unrestrainedly.

She remembered something she had once said to Jaydon when he'd been shot by a Moroccan bomb-maker during a joint mission in Colorado. *Go ahead and cry. What you cry, you don't need to piss.* That had been over a year before the fossil crisis—before his death. Today, she was ashamed of the brusque manner in which she had pushed away her feelings so as not to allow any vulnerability. What she liked to euphemize as pragmatism, she today acknowledged as a weakness she had long refused to admit.

She secured her pistol and then wrapped the diplomat firmly in her arms. In the process, she called up the time onto her retinal display and grimaced fiercely in frustration. Only 15 seconds had elapsed.

The noise of the fight was already waning. "You're doing well," she assured the others, not even having to shout to be heard.

The one or two dozen patrol officers who'd cordoned off the crime scene hadn't had a chance. *Not against Builders,* she thought.

"What was that?" Julie exclaimed angrily. "You... You..."

"Just trust me!" Agatha turned her head and saw, between the bottom of the car and the railbed, several pairs of boots approaching from the south. Their marching pace immediately told her that they had to be former special forces, drilled as military.

"You shot us!" Pablo moaned, staring at his bloody hand in horror as he took it off his shoulder.

"Just trust me," she repeated, crawling to the side, toward the open space, toward the strip of light in which the boots of the approaching attackers emerged as nightmare figures.

"But—"

"Stay here and hide, is that clear? Hold on!"

"What do you have—"

"Quiet now!" Agatha climbed out from under the car, dropped her pistol, and with her hands raised, stepped a little further to the left in front of—or next to—the wrecks that were wedged into each other. She made sure not to step on the bodies of the forensics people and looked around alertly.

"I HAVE WHAT YOU'RE LOOKING FOR!" she cried out as loud as she could, and looked toward the black-clad figures, who accelerated their pace and came toward her. Even on the slopes, a few shadows came out from cover and approached her, and she did not have to look around to know that it was the same on the other side. Far above her in the night sky, a light pulsed regularly. She knew it was a scrambler drone that was cutting off all incoming and outgoing signals.

*Just gotta wonder how long it's been doing this and how expensive it was,* she thought and waited, while six of the figures that were coming from the south bore down on her, shooting wounded forensic experts in the head along the way as they tried to crawl to safety. Two of them were so large and massive that they had to be Builders, even though they were covered in full-body armor that bore no badges or other forms of recognition.

"Take it out of your jacket very slowly," shouted one over a larynx microphone as they stood in front of her in a loose semicircle. The smaller humans carried assault rifles that they trained on her. The Builders bore massive machine guns and mini cannons, which were usually seen mounted on vehicles.

Agatha stared into the barrels and raised her hands a little higher. "What is this?" she asked, consciously avoiding looking into the sky, knowing full well that the only thing that saved her from being punctured by bullets was the vial whose gentle pressure she felt against her left breast.

"Immediately!" barked the same voice. The shadows on the slopes had already covered half the ground in her direction.

"Builders working with humans," she said, snorting. "I don't know if I should rejoice at this new form of cooperative behavior between the species, or be frightened by it."

"Last warning!"

"Okay, okay, I'm doing it." She moved her right hand toward her lapel before pausing. "I need reassurance that you won't shoot me immediately after I give you the thing."

"I'll give you something better. If you don't, you're dead immediately."

Agatha did not need to think first to realize that she would die if she uttered another word. She reached slowly into her jacket and grasped the vial just as a thunderous crash sounded, followed by a high-pitched bang. The heads of the masked figures jerked back to stare into the night sky above them, to where the remnants of the scrambler drone rained down on them in glowing pieces of debris. Agatha slowly got down on her knees, retracted her hand, and placed it atop the other on her head.

"Do you know what's the best thing about going out with weak-assed coworkers who, despite their fragility, are essential for an enterprise?" she asked, as four vector thrusters, each bearing the red eagle of Alpha Extractions, peeled out of the night and raced down upon them with roaring engines swiveled downward. "One can afford a lot of security."

Humans and Builders shouted wildly, racing off in all directions while firing at the aircraft, the undersides of which sprouted automatic gun turrets. They fired systematically and with merciless cadence at anyone that was not a police officer, anyone that carried an unlicensed weapon or that merely seemed hostile. That included pretty much everyone who was still alive, except Agatha, of course. One body after another burst before her eyes, shredded by .50-caliber projectiles and bursting into red clouds.

When the vector thrusters were only ten meters above her and went into full brake thrust, the side doors opened, and HTR soldiers in servo armor jumped onto the gravel of the ravine. They carried long autocannons and used them to sweep the slopes and destroy everything that moved. Some of them were hit, jerking from the impacts, but firing mercilessly, ignoring two of their own who fell to the ground.

The paramedics offloaded next, as the machines descended, and they pulled Julie, Marissa, Pablo, and Steve out from under the railcar that had served as cover. Hortat's four employees seemed confused and frightened, throwing Agatha blank, sometimes-angry glances, and were hastily treated with medication injected into their necks with infusers. Although they half-heartedly resisted, they were strapped onto fold-out stretchers by the lobster-like paramedics and hastily loaded, each into a separate vector thruster.

"Can't you take me with you?" Agatha shouted over the roar of the engines, but one of the HTR soldiers stretched out a palm toward her, in which she saw a target-enable induction field.

"Stay behind, citizen. Remain calm until the extraction is complete!" she heard in a distorted voice through hidden suit speakers, then he stopped and fired at someone outside her field of vision, before walking backward with his teammates toward the open door of one of the fliers.

It took no more than a few seconds for the HTR teams to re-board, close the doors, and race off into the sky under full acceleration. Then things calmed down and Agatha struggled to her feet. As far as she could see, she could only identify corpses. White bodies next to black bodies, united in the blood mixed in sand and gravel.

*How telling.* She shook her head sadly and ran her fingers over the bulge on the chest of her jacket before running in a crouch toward the southern exit of the ravine, hoping that her car was still where she had left it.

# 11

# PANO

The district to which Pano's MyDrive taxi took him was called Randfontein. *An apt name,* he thought. Rand meant 'edge' or 'rim,' and the area indeed pushed up against the western storm wall and was thus as far away from the city center as possible. The tops of the towers of the wealthy upper-class and financial world, bright monoliths on the horizon, disappeared into clouds that seemed to glow from the inside. They reflected the lights of the megacity, appearing like reddish cotton batting pushing eastward from the sea into the interior, only to get hung up on and supported by the skyscrapers.

Out here on the trash-strewn streets, which had not been repaired for decades, if ever, it was difficult to imagine that Johannesburg was a sophisticated cosmopolis and home to some of the world's most important tech players. Even the golden pyramid of the Human Foundation on the horizon looked more like a mirage, much further away than reality.

Naturally, Pano had questions. Which was the 'real' South Africa—this nitty-gritty place, or the glow on the horizon? Was it this area, with its patchy power grid and appalling poverty, or was it the promise of a high-tech civilization exemplified by lives of luxury for all to see, while the inhabitants of Randfontein still could only view the spectacle from the fence, like fans who could not afford a ticket to the game?

The address Mukoena had given him was at the very end of one of those disheartening streets, forgotten by progress, right at the wall, a run-down shack that reminded Pano of a trip to Bosnia. At that time—it seemed to him like an eternity ago, a different life—he had been part of a training program to help less-developed regions of new EU members build up effective police forces. Since this program had taken place immediately after the Bosnian-Serbian conflict, the country had, of course, still been marked by war, but he had seen shanty towns like this everywhere—a journey through time to a less privileged past.

He remembered exactly how he had wondered at the many friendly faces and laughing children he had either met or passed. How can they be so happy, he had asked himself more than once? Later, while traveling to South Asia and South America, he had the same experience—destitute people living in squalor, smiling much more than where he lived and where all basic needs were met.

This phenomenon had occupied his mind ever since. Why did the people around him look more unhappy than those engaged in a daily fight for a viable future? Because their lives made sense? Because it was a fulfilling task for humans to provide food and protection and generate offspring in obedience to their basic genetic programming, while in the West, people pushed piles of paper from left to right eight hours a day? Was it this alienation from real life that caused depression rates to explode in the affluent West?

Alienation from oneself and from what makes humans what they are?

He would have liked to believe that this also applied to those who were living in these shacks and lean-to hovels that had grown together like a sea of garbage and non-existent craftsmanship. The little artificial light that fought against the night here made it hard to see if people were lurking in the shadows somewhere and looking at him. Did they look upon him kindly?

Pano's taxi stopped in front of the shack, its improvised door hanging so crookedly that it almost revealed more than it concealed. The interior consisted of a single room, which was such a confusing mess that it brought tears to his eyes. Between the rubbish and even more rubbish, a man with emaciated limbs clad in shorts and an undershirt sat on the floor with his arms wrapped around his knees. In rhythmic jactitation, he rocked back and forth like a psychiatric patient.

"And who are you? Skinny Pete?" Pano asked, but the man did not react, so he looked around and discovered something behind an empty shelf that might once have been a window. The pane was cracked and did not afford an outside view. On the wall behind a half-shredded sofa hung a flag that he did not know, and the music, which quietly whimpered a stupid bass sound from somewhere, also seemed bizarre to him. Yet, it was quiet enough so as not to bother any neighbors.

Eventually, he squatted in front of the hut's apparently sole occupant and tapped him on his bare shin. "Hey!"

Still no reaction, apart from the whisper that the man uttered in an endless litany between his cracked lips. Pano grumbled and looked around again.

*So, what do we have here?* Absolute chaos, no semblance

of order, a broken TV, probably destroyed by the occupant to tell from the fragmented screen. The guy is as thin as a herring, obviously no sensation of cold, the way he is dressed despite the draft in here. Malnourished but active. Jactitation indicates a psychological trauma, whether real or imagined. No puncture points in the crooks of his arms, but the typical neglect of simple hygiene and order—clearly a junkie.

"But what did Agatha want with an impoverished junkie at the edge of the city?" he thought aloud. "He's about as interesting as foot fungus. Hey, you! What do you take, hmm? Almond dust? Yes, it's almond dust, isn't it? The new cocaine of the poor. Heroin is out."

Suddenly, the junkie's head jerked up and he stared directly into Pano's face. His eyes were wide open, the pupils widened to the edge of the irises. "Got somethin'? Got somethin'?"

"Maybe."

"THEN GET OUT!"

Irritated by the sudden hostility, Pano jerked back before his counterpart fell back into his rocking and incomprehensible whispers.

"Where do you have it? The stuff?"

"No stuff, no stuff, no stuff. Why they take it? Why they take it?" the junkie howled and began to cry uncontrollably. Suddenly, however, the sobbing ended, and again his head jerked upward. This time, no grief showed in his eyes, but madness raged. "My head will explode. EXPLODE! Because that what they want up there! Is good they gone. Good, they gone. Or they explode, too."

Pano's forehead creased to deep folds. When the occupant of the house, torn between fear and anger, grabbed him by the wrists, he at first tried to break free, but resisted the impulse and listened instead.

"I seen it, ya! Seen!" The junkie let go and seemed to collapse. "Shouldn'a seen it, no. But now at least I know what's going on."

"What did you see? Did you see a woman? Blonde hair, serious face? A narrow mouth? Bright eyes that look like they want to kill you or even dissect you?"

Madness became fear in the man's eyes. They twitched to the door as he scrabbled backward surprisingly quickly, cutting a path through the ubiquitous rubbish before colliding with the sofa.

"She here?" he asked in a panic.

"No." Pano paused to consider, reassessed the situation. "She gave you something, didn't she?"

Instead of answering, the junkie began to cry unrestrainedly and shook with violent sobs.

"What did she give you?"

He did not get a reaction. Whatever this guy was afraid of, Pano had already questioned enough dealers and drug addicts to see when he was approaching a dead end, and the suspect was about to close up. In the world of narcotics, addicts could suddenly switch off completely when something invaded their existential terror and they feared it might get worse. So, he had to be careful.

"I see you're scared. I am too," Pano said calmly.

A quiet question arose between the sobs. "You see it too?"

"No, but I've heard about it. It's on everyone's lips. So, everyone talks about it. But I don't think many have seen what you've seen."

"They wouldn't understand."

"I think they wouldn't *stand* what you've had to take. Not

everyone is so strong, you know that." Pano put as much understanding in his voice as he could. "I can make sure that the evil woman doesn't come back, you know? That she will never come back. But for that, I need your help. Just once."

"What? And she really no come back? Never?"

"Promise."

"Don' matter anyway. Soon everything don' matter and is all over. For me, for us. Out here. Sh-shit!" The junkie ran his fingers through his hair and then sprang up so abruptly that Pano was terrified and, like a child, fell on his butt. The very thought that he had now touched the ground with something other than his shoes sparked a deep feeling of disgust in him.

"What she gave you. I can take it with me. Get rid of it. Do you hear?"

"They don' understand," the addict lamented, staring Pano in the eyes. For a moment, his gaze seemed to clear. "Is not our fault. I come home. Hello, Ma, the school was boring. Smack in the mouth from Dad. Father. Father more, ya. I don' want to sleep yet. My legs tremble. Bad, that. Sneak out in the morning, mouth smacked again, 'cause the crust still on the toast. I don' understand! I'm a kid, a shit kid! Now I must be taken away 'cause I such a fuckin' pig. I get the cane! CANE! But I don' want it. I don' want it, no. NOBODY ASKED ME!"

"I can help you," Pano assured him in a calm voice. "I can take it with me again, so you don't have to be afraid anymore."

"No!" the man shouted excitedly. "NO, NO, NO!" He held his ears and squeezed his eyelids so tightly that they trembled.

Pano had lost him, that much was clear, but just before he freaked out, the junkie had cast a fleeting, unconscious look behind him. At first, he thought it was the paranoia of a drug addict who looked for imagined danger everywhere.

He got up and looked at the flag behind the sofa, smelled a smoky note over the stench of unwashed clothes, sweat, and dirt, as if paper had burned. The closer he got to the flag, which clung to the wall like a poster, the stronger the smell became.

*Classic,* he thought, drew the flag to one side and looked at the surface of the storm wall to which the hut clung like an ugly parasite. At first glance he noticed nothing, but then he saw a square section that looked as if someone had marked it with a pencil. Two recesses on the right and left were just big enough for him to insert his fingers and pull out a thin block, the size of a human head, from the wall. Every junkie has his hiding place.

"And then it pouring down on us!" the junkie yelled behind him and sang a pathetic lament. "From above. Take everything from us! I suffered always. Now I finished again. 'Cause I had nothing."

Pano found a small compartment in the wall, which must have taken the occupant years to scratch out with a chisel or fission cutter. In it, in the middle of a small pile of ash surrounded by grayish balls, almost all of which were scorched, lay a charred device that looked something like a cross between a crack pipe and a manual nutcracker. Pano immediately realized that it involved almond dust.

He had just taken some of the crumbs between his fingers and wanted to take a closer look at them when he heard a sound that seemed so furtive that it immediately made his hair stand on end. It was a quiet rustling, like withered leaves blowing over asphalt, only there was no foliage here. He froze and then slowly turned around. The rustling became steps, unmistakably softened, as if someone wanted to hide his presence.

Pano looked around reflexively, searching for a way out. The broken window? He would just cut himself and make lots of noise—even if he could fit through. So, all that remained was to hope that they were just neighbors on their way home. He walked away from the sofa and moved to the wall on his left, breathing in and out quietly, waiting until someone violently ripped the door off the hook it hung from and hurled it into the night.

Two women came in, and for a fraction of a second, Pano's heart leapt when he thought they were Myers and T'Sbu. The joy lasted only as long as his neurons fired incorrectly. The ones he was dealing with here were tall and strong, with angular faces and chrome-plated augment eyes that looked as cold and dead as the jerky movements that hinted at military implants that enhanced their reflexes.

"Oh, shit," he muttered as they came in, calmly regarding him and the junkie. "I don't have any stuff. I have nothing, really."

Both pairs of chrome eyes were aimed at Pano. He considered running away but dismissed the idea as the ridiculous fantasy it was. His visitors' vibrating limbs left him in no doubt about their physical superiority, and he would certainly not make it even ten centimeters toward the door before they tossed him into the air like a piece of paper.

"Where is it?" one of them asked with a scratchy voice. He thought that she sounded more like a robot than a woman.

"What? The stuff?" Pano pointed to the flag. "Behind that!"

One of them walked toward the sofa while the other

came to him and grabbed the lapel of his jacket, squeezed it, and then lifted him effortlessly off his legs with one hand.

"Oh, shit," he stammered as his entire body weight lay on her fist under his neck, and he could barely get any air. His head felt like a blood-filled balloon that threatened to burst at any moment. "I c-can't brea... aahrg!"

Neither woman reacted unless one counted how the woman who had him by the collar almost imperceptibly tilted her head, staring at him like a predator from her dead chrome eyes. The other found the secret compartment, positioned her emotionless face right in front of it, and then stepped away before shaking her head toward her partner.

"Time to die."

Pano felt how the fist twisted under his chin, tightening his jacket collar like a vice, completely choking him. Adding to the onset of asphyxia was a stinging pain, as if a noose were digging into his skin. He wheezed and thought his eyes would jump out of their sockets. They bulged and swelled until they felt they would burst. Panic set in, and he kicked his legs, pounding his fists on the head and arms of the woman who was about to murder him so casually.

He could just as well have been pummeling a rock. She did not even seem to register his desperate attack and remained unperturbed. Pano felt like an animal that was being euthanized and had no more strength to fight back. First, stars danced before his eyes, then a black shadow arose all around him, beginning from the edge of his vision and contracting to the center. His hands went numb, fell powerlessly to his sides, and dangled uselessly in the air.

Only a tennis-ball-sized portion of life remained before he would die when the grip suddenly relented, and he fell to the ground like a wet sack. His face slapped upon a pile of moldy paper boxes. Unable to move, he saw a large figure break through the door like a force of nature, grab one of the two women, and hurl her through the roof. The burned corrugated steel shattered under the force of the impact and the night sky was exposed.

The other woman hammered her fists into the newcomer who towered over her, and she was lightning fast. For a brief moment, it looked as if the newcomer could be in real danger as he jerked back and stumbled from a blow. But he caught the next blow with one hand, held her fist, and turned it 180 degrees. An ugly cracking and crunching resounded, which somehow sounded metallic, and then the shadow hurled her through the brick wall, which collapsed on her.

"Pano?" The giant shadow suddenly squatted in front of him.

Pano noticed that saliva was running out of his mouth and he could not do anything to stop it.

"Pano? Are you okay?"

"Ixlath?" he croaked. His throat felt like someone had worked it with emery paper. Strong hands lifted him and leaned him against the shelf. The pressure on his throat was gone, and yet he felt that the pressure in his chest was getting worse.

"Yes, I'm here. Just in time, I believe."

"I... can't... get any..." Pano repeatedly pounded his chest and kept on until his breathing began to cramp. Ixlath grabbed his jacket and pulled the asthma inhaler out of the inner pocket, pushed the mouthpiece between his lips, and then pressed the trigger on top as Pano nodded weakly to him. The atomized cortisone instantly expanded his bronchial tubes by easing the cramping of the muscles in his lungs.

He inhaled in relief, although an ugly rattle still accompanied his breathing. His head felt like a stone and ached terribly, but the claws of death slowly released him.

"Couldn't you have come a little sooner?" he muttered weakly, wiping bloody saliva from his lips with the back of his hand.

"I'm sorry."

Ixlath gave him back his inhaler, and Pano sighed.

"You wanted to go on your own."

"Thank you. Really."

The Builder nodded earnestly. "We are partners, remember?"

"Sorry, but I wasn't sure if the man I intended to visit was a big fan of you and yours. Pure investigative caution."

"I understand." Ixlath sounded unconvinced. "In any case, you seem to have called on the wrong people."

"Obviously. Shit, what did those augment zombies want from a petty criminal junkie like this one?"

"One might ask what *you* wanted from him."

"Touché." Pano took another hit from his inhaler before putting it away. "How did you find me in the first place? Not that I'm complaining."

"Myers and T'Sbu are in the process of looking into MyDrive and have hired one of the police net jockeys to track down the data of the vehicle that was rented. I asked them to give me the data of your trip."

"You were spying on me."

"I was worried." The Builder looked around the destroyed hut. "Rightly so, it seems."

"Shit, I'm not going to complain if that's what you're implying."

"*And?* Have you found out anything?" Ixlath helped him to his feet and skillfully caught him when Pano began to fall. His legs still had no strength and were trembling violently.

"No, not really. The guy was afraid that someone would make his head explode. Those people up there," he snorted. "The classic illusions of paranoid junkies."

The Builder frowned and seemed to ponder something. "Why did you come here in the first place?"

"Mukoena suspected that Agatha might have been here, but whatever it was she was looking for is apparently no longer here. Even though it seems that I wasn't the only one looking for it, my timing really could have been better. Where are they, anyway?"

"I don't know. Those augment zombies are pretty tough, but I guess they have withdrawn. We should now return to Myers and T'Sbu."

"No, I want to make a little detour."

"Where to?"

"Heavy Chemicals Pretoria."

"You aren't serious, are you?"

"Yes. Trust me," Pano pleaded.

Ixlath did not seem to be looking forward to it. "At least tell me what you have in mind. And, I have to make a phone call."

## 12

---

## AGATHA

Agatha sat in the back seat of her small car and checked the functional status of her pistol, which she had almost left behind at the ruins of the train. Above her, the sky was full of blue lights that raced from the city like a swarm of fireflies. She was sure that the military had been involved, and would soon demarcate a large security area to make the crime scene inaccessible. On the ground, once she had passed the scrapyard, police cars approached her going toward the scene. She and her vehicle were scanned but not stopped.

She dialed Hortat's number while still going through the check routine on her handgun.

"Agatha? Are you all right?"

"Yes." She nodded to his likeness in the darkened windshield because she dared not power up all her implant functions. If spy drones were in the air, she did not want to provide any reason for further investigation. "There are a few colleagues who will hate me for a long time, but thanks to them, the plan worked."

"What have you found out?"

"In person would be—"

"You know my schedule," Hortat sighed, looking more tired than he had looked in a long time—an unusual sight. "My speechwriter hasn't left my side, and I've got four more appearances tonight. Four! Some advisors tell me to appear only virtually, and others say I have to show up in person. I'll be glad when all this is over, and we can begin to do the things for which we must be elected."

"I understand, but we should not risk anything, this affair—"

"The line is safe, Agatha. I also need to know the status in case—"

"—in case I get killed?" she asked a little too quickly.

"Listen, I didn't want—"

"It's okay." She took two deep breaths before looking at him again as she engaged the safety on her pistol and put it into her shoulder holster. "Sorry. This whole thing must have awakened the old Agatha in me."

"No, *I'm* sorry." Hortat lowered his head. "I would prefer you to abort and come to me."

"*But?*"

"But, I *know* you," he gently reminded her. "You are like a terrier who can't let its prey go once it's gotten its teeth into it, and I truly appreciate that trait in you. Besides your honesty, it was one of the reasons why I wanted you. Therefore, I will not order you to do anything that is against your convictions. I do not have that right."

"Thank you," she replied, and cleared her throat to fill the ensuing silence. "The European secret service is somehow involved in the matter. There is a substance here that they were transporting. We need to analyze it."

"You think the EU secret service sabotaged the train?"

"No. I think they wanted to get hold of its cargo and

divert the train so that they could steal it in Zimbabwe. The attack seems to have been carried out by HCP forces with the help of the Dark Tongue."

"That's hard to imagine." Hortat rubbed his eyes. "The Dark Tongue always avoids detection, certainly by humans. They do not work with them at all."

"I didn't see them myself."

"How, then?"

"It's a long story. I need something from you."

"And that would that be?"

"A chemical analysis. You must also contact Deputy Director Lubanzi Mukoena of the police and offer him your help. Tell him I was wounded and I'm not available at the time. But you can tell him that his fears have been confirmed and that he can raid the HCP subsidiary."

"That... I will see what I can do, Agatha."

"Thank you."

She disconnected, pulled the vial out of the inside pocket of her jacket, and regarded the thick blue liquid inside. Then she started looking for an opening. The ends of the transparent, finger-thick tube were encased in gray octagonal pieces of plastic, which could neither be twisted nor pulled off. Instead, she spotted a tiny marker below the edge of one of the plastic pieces.

"Well, well. A predetermined breaking point?" she muttered, turning the vial a few times in front of her eyes. The images of the suspended Builders flashed repeatedly through her mind. They had been connected to those strange cables that had looked like bundles of muscle. Should she try to open this one here and dip the chem sniffer on the little finger of her right hand into it to get a quick response from Hortat? What if that rendered the substance unusable?

She had only this single vial. The rest had been destroyed in the railcar in the ravine, just as the terrorists had apparently planned to do before they withdrew. Now, everyone who had been looking for answers there was dead, and there was no longer any sign the vials ever existed. Of course, the electronic trail remained—everything the officers had learned had long since been stored in the cloud storage facilities of the municipal police.

The electronic trail was a problem that could be solved with extremely talented net jockeys. She had no doubt that HCP, or whoever was behind it, would allocate the appropriate resources.

*I must warn Karlhammer,* she thought. *Presumably, he doesn't know about his foundation's relatively small investment in that start-up, but he'll soon get covered by shit if it hits the fan.* When *it hits the fan,* she corrected herself.

Mukoena would not wait long to storm HCP's principal subsidiary if he received the green light from his superior, the chief. But she also believed Mukoena capable of creating facts and moving forward before consulting his chief, and waiting to see what the fallout would be.

She rejected the idea of breaching the container for a chemical sample, thus possibly destroying the contents, and decided to go through the list of addresses that Bellinger had sent her. A quick check of the city map revealed that they were all in ordinary residential areas of the western section of the city, the former slum area, which today could be generously designated 'lower class.' No house number matched any particular address such as a business, a government authority, or anything like that.

"Except for you," she said, looking at the last address on the windshield. It was not in the west, but downtown, where the rich competed for status and prestige with their luxury villas. "You're what I call an outlier."

Agatha fished around in her memories and reached the pretty-sure conclusion that it was in a gated community complete with high walls, NATO wire, and private security. The prisoners of the $21^{st}$ century were the affluent, who, for fear of 'the criminals,' voluntarily imprisoned themselves— surrounded themselves with walls, bars, and hired guards— paradoxically, and in other circumstances, a reason for amusement. In this case, however, it was a reason for concern, since she would not be readily admitted. The residents there were chronically paranoid, so she chose the first address. After all, Bellinger had emphasized that it did not matter which one she checked out first.

Randfontein was a former mining town in western Johannesburg that 40 years ago still lay outside the city and had arisen during the gold rush at the end of the $19^{th}$ century. With the decline in profits that had never reached the hoped-for heights, investors gradually withdrew, and the residents became impoverished.

Even though this process hadn't begun until much later —at the turn of the millennium—there was nothing left of the past's goldrush ambiance. The old sandstone buildings of the wealthy bosses had fallen into disrepair and mutated into graffiti-smeared ruins because no one could pay for their maintenance. Those who had once valued the place had long since turned their backs on it by the time Johannesburg absorbed the small town.

Today, simple huts and shacks made of bricks and corrugated steel crowded close to each other right up to the storm wall, which loomed like a black rampart in the west, looking as if it were meant to protect the city's lights from the sea of darkness out there. The whole district was an ugly, disjointed witness to the fact that the Special Administrative Zone in general, and Johannesburg in particular, had not yet fulfilled all the hopes that South Africa, the entire continent, and now even the world saw in it.

There was still much to be done to combat poverty and crime, even though the megacity had developed rapidly. Today, the city center accommodated hundreds of globally active companies, which had gradually spread wealth to the residential areas around it and had created a middle class that had never existed before.

But Randfontein remained a spectator to change, an old-fashioned slum that Hortat would have to work on if elected. He had already told her in a personal conversation a few months ago, when they had developed his campaign program, that he planned to invest a significant portion of his multi-trillion rand private fortune right here, in educational institutions, social housing, parks, and health centers, to show how quickly redistributing unnecessary wealth could contribute to better education and the city's overall standard of living.

That idea alone electrified her—the idea that someone would come and do it differently than the unregulated market forces of recent decades, even though mega-corporations and governments had already realized some time ago that the planet needed salvation in order not to suffocate the Holy Grail of Growth with $CO_2$ in the truest sense of the word.

The traffic density, since the introduction of the traffic control system and comprehensive autonomy, was not as high as it had been when people had guided their cars with their own hands on the steering wheels. It decreased so massively in Randfontein that she soon saw hardly any other vehicles as she drew closer to the wall.

The address that her control software located was at the end of a road pocked with broken asphalt and littered with rubbish and scrap. The car repeatedly stopped, swerving right or left until it reached the next obstacle as if to remind her where the fusion of AI and cameras had its limits. So, she took the wheel herself and drove to the wall, where she got out and looked around in the darkness.

The houses mostly had connected walls, with the rare alley in between, and were partly built over each other. Power lines connected one shack to the next and ended in the middle of nowhere, presumably illegally tapping the city lines that led from the older Thorium reactors outside the city. There were hardly any lights, except for the sporadic flickering of fires or streetlights that someone had repaired out of a sense of community responsibility.

Agatha looked up at the massive, solid concrete wall and noted there was no gate, as if the designers had determined that there would never be through traffic in Randfontein, or had never imagined that the inhabitants would choose to escape their misery. The 20-meter height testified to the power of the superstorms, the first of which had been recorded 30 years ago and were probably due to the almost total loss of rainforests.

She had witnessed several superstorms, and even in the Silver Tower, Hortat's private residence in the heart of the city, she'd believed that the skyscraper would simply tip over from the force of the wind. Here it had to be catastrophic, and the wall probably only offered protection because it was so dense that the resulting lee reached far enough to create a zone of relative calm.

"All right. Bunyard 22," she said, walking past a ripped blue sack from which used junk food bags were spilling and, caught up in a wind swirl, scraped awkwardly across the tarmac. The hut was located directly on the wall. Its roof was of welded-together sheet metal slabs that sloped at an angle, and the door looked like it had been improvised from a car roof. Agatha knocked and looked over her shoulders. It was quiet, as quiet as it should be at this time just before sunrise.

She knocked again, listened, and heard something indistinguishable, like music maybe, but no one answered or opened the door. She reached into a sharp-edged hole where a handle should have been and carefully pulled. The rusty metal made an ugly screech as it scraped on the rough concrete, and the noise was so frighteningly loud that it made her jump, but that did not stop her. She slipped past the door into a large room so crammed that she had to blink until she could gradually make out what she was looking at.

Opposite the storm wall, which bore faded posters of old South Africa flags, stood a hole-riddled sofa on which a young man lay, staring into nothingness with a grin on his face. There was a rusty refrigerator, three stacked microwaves with ripped-up instant ramen packs in front of them, an old flat-screen TV with a shattered display, a collapsed table, a shelf full of things Agatha could not identify, and tons of garbage that surrounded it all like a kind of craggy carpet. Amid the stinking refuse, which smelled like a mixture of vinegar, sweat, and musty clothes, sat two children aged approximately two or three, who looked at her with wide eyes. They were so filthy that she could not even say whether they were boys or girls.

"Hello," she said and cleared her throat. "Is this your father?"

The two did not answer but followed each of her movements with attentive glances. Their hair was matted and their skin marred with patches of eczema. Nevertheless,

Agatha felt no disgust—there was no room for it—only compassion and anger.

"Can you speak?"

*Can they even do that at that age?* she thought, wishing once again that she felt less fear of contact with children.

As she again did not get an answer, she stalked over all the rubbish to the sofa and stood in front of the man. He wore a stained undershirt, and his dark skin shone with sweat, despite it being fairly cold in the house. His eyes moved incessantly, as if he were dreaming, even though they were open.

Agatha shook him by the shoulder. He began to laugh, but it was not an amused or even joyful laugh, but rather an insane cackle. Sighing, she went to the shelf and began to dig through the contents.

"A junkie usually has more stuff," she muttered, and after a short time found a rust-eaten metal can on which she could make out the black fist of the South African nationalists, who had only been re-elected to parliament last year. From there she drew a small bag of whitish crystals, a crack pipe, and a lighter. She crushed one of the crystals into the spherical end of the pipe and held the flame of the lighter underneath until the powder turned to smoke, and then stuffed the other end into the man's mouth. With his next breath, he forcibly inhaled it and began to cough wildly. She took a step back when he slapped himself and his eyes went wide.

"Kak! Waar is ek?" he roared, and the two children turned around lethargically as if to assess whether it was worth spending their little energy on fleeing. The man breathed heavily and stared at Agatha as if she were a ghost.

"What's your name?" she asked, in an effort to find out why she was there in the first place. What did all this mean?

Why was someone like this guy of interest to the European secret service? Of enough interest that one of its agents had even bothered to pass it on because he thought it was more important for her to find something than to fail entirely.

"What you do here?" he asked in broken English, gulping when he realized where he was and why she should not be there. He saw the crack pipe in her hand and wanted to reach for it. Anger flashed in his eyes as she withdrew it. Then the rage alternated with grief and sheer hatred at such short intervals that she could hardly follow them.

"Almond dust," she muttered. "You're on almond dust, aren't you?"

The man licked his cracked lips. "You give the pipe if I tell you?"

Agatha looked at the yellowed glass in her hand and then nodded in disgust.

"Ya. Almond dust. I take the almond dust, haha!" He laughed erratically and snatched the still smoking vessel from her, held it to his lips, and greedily sucked on it. "Aaah."

"Do you still have any of it?"

"What? NO!"

"I don't want to take it away from you."

"Of course you want that! You and these troggies!"

Agatha flinched when she heard the derogatory term for Builder and squinted at the South African flag over the sofa. A junkie and nationalist who was probably in some gang conspiring to hunt down Builders, even if they would never get close to one.

"You don't like Builders, huh?"

"What, hmm? What?"

"Builders. You don't like them."

"Of course not!" the junkie groused and spat somewhere into the sea of garbage.

Agatha had to consciously control herself to fight down her nausea.

"These Kak aliens are contaminating us! Have their fingers in everywhere! Check us! Always!" He leaned forward and giggled. "They in your filthy head now! Filthy head! Haha!"

"Why am I here?" she asked more to herself, her hands clenched into such tight fists that her gloves were crunching. *Control yourself!*

"Everybody here know this! Only you big bosses, no! Kak-bosses, that you! In bed with the troggie aliens! They want to get rid of us! Us humans! Yes!" Another pull on the crack pipe before he began to chuckle. "But South Africa will not be silent! No! We chasing these fuckers to hell, where they from! We starting with this Hortat!"

Agatha felt like beating him senseless, but pulled herself together and wondered once again why the ESD had collected these addresses. A flipped-out junkie in a hut in Randfontein? An almond dust addict and Builder hater— even in the Special Administrative Zone there were several million of them, albeit many orders of magnitude fewer than in Europe or North America. *Why this one?*

She followed her intuition and began searching the shelf, prompting the owner to an orgy of cursing. But he seemed too high to physically confront her and satisfied his anger by wildly waving his thin arms and issuing a stream of imaginative insults.

Agatha ripped open every can and box, and turned over everything that had two sides, but found nothing. She then searched the floor. There was nothing there either, so she stood in front of the sofa.

"Off," she ordered with a pointing hand gesture.

"What? No!" There was anger mixed with fear in the junkie's face. She could see it so plainly in his eyes, he might as well have advertised it with a sign. It did not require her many years of experience as an agent at the Counter-Terrorist Directive to see that his mood had turned.

She grabbed his wrists and ripped him off the sofa. He crashed into the rubbish next to the children and unleashed a tirade of insults at her as she threw aside the seat cushions —which was surprisingly easy. Underneath, she found a good deal of credit chips, two dozen or more, and dark gray pellets—pastilles—in plastic zipper bags.

"What do we have here?" she asked herself more than him.

"Hey!" he protested. "Is *mine!*"

"Almond dust." She held one of the packets against the light of the light bulb over her head and saw it diffract in the pastilles, lending them a bluish shimmer.

"I kill you!" the junkie raged, crawling around like a zombie in the garbage on the floor.

"You deal in almond dust," she continued, unmoved. "Why do you live in this shit hole?"

"Camouflage! Ha!" He giggled and stretched out his hand. "Give it to me. Come on!"

"You were a dealer. Now you have violated the most important rule of dealing and started taking it yourself." Agatha shook his head. "How long has it been?"

"One year? Two? What is time? GIVE IT TO ME!"

"No." She pulled the vial out of her jacket pocket and held it so that he could see it but was unable to reach it. He immediately fell silent, and his pupils grew even larger.

"You know what this is, don't you? What is it?"

"That... Where you get that? So much! Aaah!"

"What is it? You can have it if you answer me truthfully," she promised him, and he visibly sobered himself and seemed able to displace his incipient madness, at least for a short time.

"Almond dust!" he said. "I show you!"

"Forget it!"

"I get a bit of it, I show you, and then I can keep it. Deal?"

Agatha hesitated, but eventually held the vial out to him without letting go of it when he reached for it.

"If you fuck with me, you're dead," she lied, opening her jacket with her free hand so that he could see the gun in its holster.

"Yes!" He waved her warning away and took the vial as if it were a gem before crawling to the shelves. Wildly, he cleared an entire shelf and threw its contents to the floor before pulling out something like a nutcracker out of a metal case. It appeared to be battery-powered as several lights came on when he touched it.

"Is that biometrically secured?"

"Ya."

"How did you get such tech?" she asked.

"Shhh!" He cut a small hole in the plastic at one end of the vial with a laser cutter.

"Hey!"

"Shhh!" With his tongue hanging over his lower lip, he dripped some of the harsh blue liquid into the nutcracker and pressed around on it. Fine steam rose. Then he plucked a dirty plastic zipper bag from the garbage and held it under the bulbous top. Gradually bloating pastilles swelled from it, like popcorn from a hot pan, and fell into the bag.

"Aaah!" In the eyes of the dealer, greed shone. "Dis goed! Maak de papa ryk!"

Agatha grabbed the vial and searched the shelf for a roll

of duct tape she had seen before. She tore off a piece and taped over the small hole in the plastic end piece. A glance at the dealer told her that he was still following the process in his hands with his eyes, totally enthralled and probably calculating the digital rands it promised. He did not even notice that she was taking the packet of almond dust, which was still lying unattended in the ripped sofa.

When she turned to go and saw the two children, who were attentively following each of her steps, she hesitated and opened an encrypted connection to the police.

"Johannesburg Police Department, please state the nature of the emergency."

"I want to report a case of child abuse and neglect. There is an acute danger to the life and health of minors."

"What is the address, Ma'am?"

"Bunyard 22 in Randfontein."

"And your name?"

"I want to remain anonymous in accordance with my rights."

"All right, Ma'am. Thank you for your call."

"Hurry." Agatha disconnected, swallowed, and turned away.

"Hey! What about the rest?" the dealer angrily exclaimed as she reached the door, which was more like a metal crate.

"Be glad that I don't kill you," she growled. "Fifteen years ago, you would have been dead."

She left him behind and went to her car, scanning the environment with her implants for electronic signatures but detecting nothing in the vicinity that would have corresponded to a camera or even a sensor bundle.

Back in the car, she entered her next destination and then opened the dome of her right middle finger to expose the chem sniffer, a pointed sensor feeler that she inserted into the hole in the vial. She cleaned it and then held it into the bag of almond dust. She waited for the chemical analyses to appear as complex structural formulas in her digital display and then called Hortat.

"Agatha?"

"Yes. I'm sending you the chemical analyses now."

"I've been wondering why it was taking so long. Did you have any trouble?"

"No. Did you get the files?"

"Yes, they are just coming in," said the Builder. No one would have noticed that he was doing two things at the same time. "Interesting."

*Of course, he just needs to look at it and immediately knows what he is seeing,* she thought in frustration. How long would it have taken a chemistry professor to do this?

"The first thing you sent me could be an explosive. The molecules are volatile and reactive. With the right reactant substance, this would be an extremely efficient—"

"And the second?" she interrupted him.

"Almond dust. I saw that immediately. The corresponding structural formulae have been known to narcotics investigators for almost two years when it was first confiscated. Why did you send me this? You don't want to—"

"No, no," she assured him. "But this explosive you see is the primary material for creating almond dust."

"*What?*" Hortat seemed honestly surprised. "That's... strange."

"I have seen it for myself. I watched an almond dust dealer make the one out of the other, before my very eyes. And the explosive is a specimen I took from one of the agents in the container railcar." Agatha pondered whether it was wise to talk about this even over their encrypted connection, but she did not know how long it would take her to see him again. "HCP has reportedly developed a prototype for a highly efficient mining explosive."

"Yes. You think that's what the sample is all about?"

"Yes." She nodded. "Except that it's not a prototype. I saw many of these vials. I believe that HCP, even if it did not invent almond dust, produces and distributes it. At least in South Africa."

"The camouflage would be perfect. No one would suspect a small business that does not generate large revenues nor work in an industry that would interest anyone. Camouflage as an explosive is clever because explosives are highly regulated and officially chemically tested."

"Besides, the Human Foundation is a donor, and no one would suspect it of producing a drug that, according to many conspiracy theories, is extracted from the blood of Builders," she added.

"From the hypophysis," Hortat corrected her.

"What?"

"The pituitary gland. The cerebrospinal fluid is extracted from the pituitary gland. I've feared that for some time now."

Agatha thought of what she had seen through Herxmin's eyes. The Builders who had hung lifeless on the cable bundles, like pigs hung after slaughter. "I saw it," she breathed.

"What?"

"How it was extracted from them."

"How?" he asked, surprised.

"It's a long story." She dismissed the question. "But it looked like they'd done it voluntarily. I think it was members of the Dark Tongue who had the stuff extracted from themselves. But why would they do that?"

Hortat seemed thoughtful and remained silent for a while before he stirred. "I don't know, Agatha. But we have to be careful. We should follow the raid on the HCP facility."

"You said that, in case of doubt, you'd have resources with enough firepower to help you solve any problem, right?"

"Yes. Why do you ask?"

"I think now is the time."

"Tell me about your plan," he requested.

"In a moment. I have a question first. Have you ever taken almond dust?"

"No!" Hortat seemed outraged.

"Why are you so indignant?"

"Because the idea alone is tantamount to cannibalism."

"So, it is true that the drug gives access to the memories of you Builders?" Agatha pressed.

"It's... possible."

"Possible? I always thought that was just junkies spinning fantasies! A selling point to attract even more buyers! It was always said, even you've said it, that it caused dangerous hallucinations."

"And that is the truth," the Builder replied calmly. "These hallucinations are not authentic experiences of the users themselves, but foreign memories. Possibly. That fits the definition of hallucinations."

"You wanted to prevent other sections of the population —other than conspiracy theorists and Builder haters—from resorting to the drug."

"Yes. At the moment, its use is rampant among all those who know their enemy and want to find proof of the alleged malice of my kind. But even if they do—and there are black sheep among us, too—no one will believe them because they are all regarded as junkies and crackpots. Which they are, because the experiences they gain destroy their brains due to the incompatibility between our cognitive processing of sensory impressions."

"These vials that I saw," Agatha changed the subject. "They then contain a mixture of pituitary fluid and various chemicals that together produce an explosive."

"Assuming that there is a reactant for it."

"So, a substance that produces a bang in reaction to the mixture."

"Simply put... Yes."

"The German agent, Joseph Bellinger. Why did he have this one vial with him? What's so special about it?" she wondered, turning the vial in her hand, close to her eyes. She looked at the many small refractions of light in the blue liquid, which reminded her of star glitter. *What are they hiding?*

"I don't know. Nothing extraordinary emerges from the chemical analysis," Hortat replied.

"We need to go to the EU embassy and find out what Bellinger has reported to his superiors."

"No, Agatha."

"But—"

"No. The answer is no! You are not breaking into an embassy. That is not just illegal, but sets a dangerous precedent for the future of this country and diplomacy in general. I cannot and I will not allow that."

"Then there is only one alternative." She resealed the small hole at the top of the vial with the duct tape, put it away, and lifted the bag with the almond dust.

"No, Agatha. The risk is too high!"

## 13

---

## PANO

"Where did it go?" Pano asked.

He lay prone on the roof of a semiconductor manufacturing facility located opposite the Heavy Chemicals Pretoria plant that had been evacuated two weeks ago, according to the barrier tape. In an attempt to stay dry, he had dragged the cover of a trash container up the fire ladder, turned it over, and sprawled on the dry side. The rain had reduced to an ugly drizzle on the way here and apparently could not decide whether it wanted to become a fog or what, but the flat roof was covered by a thin layer of water that only slowly drained away. He held binoculars to his eyes, which he had bought on the way at a 24-hour vending machine.

From this position, he and Ixlath had an unobstructed view over the company's wall and across the extensive asphalted terrain crowded with barrels on pallets and massive containers waiting to be moved by forklifts the next day. Now in the early hours of the morning, long before sunrise, everything looked deserted. If a lone lamp had not shone above the staff entrance, he would have thought the company had disappeared just like the one on whose roof they were now perched.

"I don't know," Ixlath responded. "According to police records, the truck was to the right of the main entrance, there, next to the roller door by that stack of pallets." The Builder had stretched out one of his mighty hands and pointed across the wide road, beyond a stretch of the wall atop which a security drone raced past on its rail.

*I can forget about sneaking in,* he thought, gritting his teeth in frustration. "How can the thing suddenly be gone, just now, when we're coming?"

"The better question is, why was the truck there so long after the raid?"

"Because the police cordoned it off on account of suspected theft or false cargo papers."

"Do you seriously mean that?" asked Ixlath.

Pano raised a warning index finger in his direction as he turned his head to the Builder. "Don't give me that eyebrow!"

"What I want to say is this—a trivial matter such as one missing unit of a chemical agent among thirty thousand in a shipping contingent will not persuade a company to meekly accept the detention of an entire delivery. It is not only HCP that is affected, but the supplier as well. Their legal teams will have contacted the police last night and have obtained a suspension of the crime scene restriction due to negligible cause."

"That makes sense," Pano confessed, but shook his head again. "Why, then, would it have still been here until so recently?"

"There could be several reasons. Maybe the cordon was already lifted, but they had not yet moved the truck, or the city court with jurisdiction over the matter delayed approval of the injunction. Even such urgent procedures can drag on if someone in the administration wants it to. This probably occurs quite often in Italy."

"South Tyrol."

"South Tyrol," Ixlath sighed. "It's the same here, only worse, I suppose."

"Hmm. I'm going in."

"What was that?" the Builder asked in alarm.

"I'm going in there. Something just isn't right with all of this, and I have no desire to be led around by the nose."

"What do you mean?"

"That should be obvious," Pano muttered. "Someone is shadowing me or us. There's the courier, who happens to almost be kidnapped just before we arrive, then the two killer sisters who just happen to visit a small, insignificant dealer just when I am there, and now the truck disappears, just before we arrive to inspect it."

Ixlath carefully raised his gaze and nodded slowly.

"That place over there is involved in some shit, whether the attack on the train or some illegal business—after all, they're producing explosives. I go in there and 'fish for information,' as they say."

"I don't think that's a good idea," the Builder said.

"Oh no? And why not?"

"If someone is shadowing us, they certainly won't just stand by and watch while you search their business premises," the Builder said. "This is dangerous."

"I was married to Agatha," Pano muttered sourly. "So, I'm kind of used to living on a razor's edge. I am not afraid of them." He got up, brushed off the raindrops that had settled like a shiny carpet of parasites on the water-repellent fabric he wore, and handed the binoculars to his partner.

Ixlath began to get up. "Then I'm coming with you."

But Pano signed him to stay. "No. How are we supposed to invent a good story to explain why a Builder suddenly shows up at their door? You'll stick out like a fully decorated Christmas tree at a midsummer festival."

"Conspicuous."

"Precisely. You stay here and we stay in touch via transducer. If something happens, you can still pull me out."

"Are you aware of why I have to rely on a phone?" asked Ixlath.

"You mean the smart plug in your ear?"

"Yes."

"No."

"Because I can control your transducer over a kind of telepathic connection. I don't have implants."

"I've heard that you don't have electronics in your bodies. I like that," Pano replied.

"The range for this is quite limited."

"It'll be enough." He put his hands on the fire ladder and began to climb down. To his relief, his partner stayed where he was.

After a brief sprint across the forecourt of the deserted semiconductor company, he climbed over the barrier and pulled out his hand terminal to call Agent Myers.

"Hofer?" she asked before he heard a dial tone.

"Is the line secure?" he asked.

"Yes. Runs through our net jockey."

"Good. I am currently standing in front of HCP headquarters."

"Why?"

"I wanted to inspect the truck, where that one unit of the chemical stuff went missing."

"The reactant," said Myers.

Pano nodded. "Yes. It's gone."

"*Gone?*"

"Yes, gone. It must have happened before we came here, and not very long before. I also visited a junkie where Agatha might have been. That's when I was attacked."

"Someone is on your heels."

"Looks like it. That's why I wanted to warn you."

"But that's not the only reason you're calling, is it?" Myers asked, with her typical brief stress on each syllable, which sounded like she was hacking every word into its individual parts with a hatchet.

"No." He lowered his voice. "I visited the fired deputy director, and he gave me something. I have a question about that."

"You... Oh, doesn't matter. So, tell me. What did he give you?"

Pano pondered how far he could trust her, but decided to follow his intuition and instinct as an experienced investigator. "A hand terminal with some police code that I could have used to authorize my access to the truck."

"Ahh. On a hand terminal?"

"Is that strange?"

"Not necessarily." Myers hesitated. "There is backward compatibility, but when you use the thing, it is stored in the system at the headquarters—for the legal department."

"Isn't that the case with all the codes used? These are priority codes, aren't they?"

"Yes. With these, we can electronically open any house door lock installed since the 2030 Security Act, and no longer need to break the door down. This also applies to all vehicles, and to access to crime scenes—an efficient system. The problem is that your code will stand out immediately among the many hundreds that are used every day because it was transmitted via a hand terminal. Technically no problem, but it is not very inconspicuous."

"I understand." Pano looked along the deserted road from left to right as if to look for traffic as he crossed, and then walked on, avoiding the puddles, and stopped at the wire gate that had been inserted into the wall. "You're investigating the taxi company with your net jockey, aren't you?"

"Yes. Why?"

"I might need your help again."

"Sounds like something illegal."

"You just need to have it redirect calls from HCP to you. Is that a problem?"

"Why do I have the feeling I won't like it?" asked Myers.

"Trust me."

After disconnecting, he put the hand terminal back in his jacket pocket and went to the bell at the gate. A small rotor drone came flying in, probably scanning him, and then nothing happened for a long time until a security guard came round the corner and lit his face with a flashlight. "What do you want?"

"My name is Steven Erickson. I was appointed by the second chamber of the municipal court as an expert to determine the sum of the damage caused by yesterday's raid," Pano said.

"At this hour?" the security guard asked with a groan. "It's not even four o'clock in the morning."

"I don't need to explain to you why time is pressing, right? Didn't you notice that this city is a powder keg resting on sticks of dynamite?" He rolled his eyes as if talking to an unusually slow toddler.

The short man waved his flashlight over Pano's shoulder and searched the street. "And where's your car?"

"I parked around the corner. Your company was the

victim of a terrorist attack. I am happy about the hazard pay for this job, but I'm not anxious for the Dark Tongue to notice me. That's why I would very much like you to turn off your flashlight and let me in already."

"Do you have an ID or something?"

"Your superiors are listening, I suppose?" Pano looked into the sensor strip on the corner of the wall. "My implants are all offline. The court wants to deal with this with as little publicity as possible. There has already been enough negative press about you and the police. I'm sure that this is also in your interest. Please call there to have my legitimacy confirmed."

The security guard hesitated and wanted to say something, but Pano did not let him speak. "Uh-uh," he said, wagging his index finger in front of the man's face.

Shortly afterward, the guard's gaze became empty, and he finally stepped back as the wire gate electronically glided to one side.

Pano hoped that Ixlath was all Builder and had not become unnerved by the fact that he could not reach him via the transducer. "All right."

The security guard accompanied him to the small staff entrance next to a closed roller door, which led into the large square hall. Another sensor strip above the door illuminated him, then the door opened. A smiling man in jeans and a turtleneck sweater stood in the doorway and extended his hand. He was as tall as Pano, dark-skinned, handsome, and with gray-speckled temples despite his youthful appearance.

"Winnie Makeba," he introduced himself, and they shook hands. "I am the COO here at HCP. Come in."

"Thank you."

"Unusual time for your visit."

"Unusual working hours for a COO," Pano countered.

"Ahh, yes. Unusual *times*, I guess. This attack on our delivery hit us hard, as have the actions of that corrupt deputy director." Makeba shook his head, and the corners of his mouth turned down. "It's not just the city that's been in crisis mode ever since. We are as well."

"I can well understand. The director was furious when he heard about Mukoena's high-handedness. The judge, by the way, too."

"Ahh, I understand. Judge—"

"Sorry, I can't name the man who's handling the case. I don't want to be fired." Pano winked at the manager to make it clear that he had already done him a favor by revealing his gender, as this would probably make his guesses easier. *I am your ally,* he tried to express nonverbally.

"I understand." Makeba led him through a long unadorned aisle, where a few black-and-white photos of lab equipment hung in ultra-close-up. "As you will be aware, the case that our lawyers are conducting against the police is not about revenge, but about compensation."

Pano nodded. "The police torched my house in Alberton a year ago when they tried to take down an alleged almond dust ring. In Alberton! They wanted to portray this to the court as a case of collateral damage, including a reduction in the amount of compensation."

He put as much anger in his voice as he could without appearing unprofessional. "So, I understand all too well. The police have a mandate to uphold the law, not to harass innocent citizens—or businesses—just because someone pushing the right buttons is following an instinct. But I am only the expert. In the end, the judge has to decide."

"Based on your report," Makeba remarked, smiling in a way that made Pano sigh surreptitiously in relief. The tired-looking man had swallowed the bait and probably regarded him as something like a gift from heaven.

"Based on my report. First, I would like to see the damage caused where they broke in, then any equipment destroyed and the delivery with the stolen reactant."

"The delivery?" The COO seemed confused for a moment.

"Yes. I figure that you have rightly obtained an injunction to lift the detention of evidence on the grounds of negligible cause. That's how I would have done it. You have to keep the production and shipping going, especially after the loss of the cargo on the train," Pano explained, holding his breath for a moment until the manager nodded, the sign his risky move had paid off.

Seeing an objection emerging on the guard's face, he quickly added, "What you may have forgotten is the theft. That one minor matter allows the police to keep a foot in your door. They can still appeal against the injunction on the pretext of being obliged to investigate the theft. However, if, based on my observations here, I conclude that one of the officers broke into the truck during the raid, then the situation is quite different. After all, the preliminary search warrant did not apply to the property of the forwarding company, or your suppliers' products, but only to Heavy Chemicals Pretoria. That would be a clear violation that would stifle the further proceedings before it caught fire."

"Our lawyers had already indicated something like that."

"Your lawyers seem to understand their work."

Makeba led him past the main hall, which contained rows of laboratory tables with machines and complex instruments, and at which about 200 employees—presumably the night shift—were working in white protective suits.

The whole area was shielded by transparent windows with adhesive labels warning of chemical hazards.

On the right was a small office complex—almost a building in a building—and on the left a large storage area, from which materials were being conveyed to the laboratory on automated conveyor belts. The COO said goodbye after a short time and assigned him two watchdogs, which he presented as helpful assistants. They remained comfortably in the background and showed him where the heavily armed police officers had broken in.

The damage was significant, showing the extent of the powers that Mukoena had granted his officers. Pano recorded everything on his hand terminal, which caused a few strange glances, but his behavior did not seem to seriously surprise anyone for an expert from the court. The deputy director must have been wholly convinced by Agatha to have ordered it. Then he could well understand Mukoena's anger at her.

He was surprised that the man had given him something that enabled him to return to the scene, which in the worst case would be traced back to him. He did not know what drove him, but Pano did not care as long as he could continue his search for Agatha. Something told him that this theft at the periphery of this whole spectacle was a rock that he had to turn over.

In the end, they led him to a part of the storage area where the reactant was stored in a separate room, concealed behind a wall of security glass. His guards informed him that he could find all the information about the inventory and its condition on the terminal next to the locked door and refused him access, indicating the hazardous substances stored in it.

"Can you at least open the door so I can turn on the

chem sniffer? I have to prove that the delivered reactant is actually in there."

One of them phoned briefly and then nodded before opening the door and taking a step back. "But don't hold the terminal inside. In the event of unauthorized access, the security door will automatically close and must be unlocked by authorized personnel."

"I understand," said Pano, gazing at the vials of the reactant, which were contained in large storage chambers, shimmering with a bluish hue. He brought up his hand terminal and pretended to make some inputs and read data when he took out another—the one the deputy director had given him.

As soon as he was holding one in each hand, he feigned clumsiness and dropped his own. He bent over to pick it up and heard a loud "Don't!" as the door closed, and he dove forward as if he were trying to escape a guillotine. He suddenly found himself in the secured room with the reactants and saw the two guards, who looked horrified and were speaking excitedly.

Pano put on a panicked face and hammered his fists against the door. "Get me out of here!" he yelled.

One of the men ran out of the storage area while the other ran to the display next to the door and disappeared from view.

Pano made use of the brief, unobserved moment and turned around. After licking his lips and inspecting the containers in front of him, he pulled out one of the vials and fumbled around on its cap, which was intended for automated screw cap sealing. He had just managed to open it, after suffering a few scrapes and cuts to his fingers, when the door emitted a loud beep.

"Shit!" he cursed softly and thought frantically. He could

not take the sample with him without the system identifying it as missing. Then he came up with an idea. When the door opened, he had put it back and just turned around.

The two 'assistants' and the COO were standing there, the latter with a grim look on his face.

"Oh, thank God!" Pano whined, racing out of the secure storage area as if his life depended on it.

"Sir, I have to ask you, unfortunately—" said Makeba.

"Why didn't you warn me? I thought I would suffocate in there!" Pano shouted at one of the assistants, who looked at him first in surprise and then in anger. He attempted to leave, but the two strong men blocked his path in a way made to appear unintentional. The manager went to the display next to the door and apparently checked the inventory list because he turned around shortly and signaled his people with a barely noticeable nod and they let Pano through.

"Mr. Erickson, I have to ask you to leave now."

"But I..." Pano sighed and then nodded. "All right. I'm sorry, I didn't want to cause trouble with my clumsiness. Please do not file a complaint with the second chamber, okay?"

Makeba nodded, as impatient as he was noncommittal, and then Pano was politely but firmly led by to the gate his two watchdogs, where they waited until he disappeared.

Pano, meanwhile, patted his chest pocket with a smile and called Myers.

"And? How did it go?"

"Just fine," he said. "However, the second chamber of the City Court will soon start conducting a search for me, I fear."

"Well, then, it would be best to call your patron, Mr. Karlhammer."

"Did you make any progress with the taxi?"

"Yes, we found it. It was driven by the automatic maintenance system for some repair work at a contract repair shop," explained the agent.

"What a coincidence."

"We thought so, too. Shall we meet there?"

"Send me the address."

# 14

## AGATHA

At first, Agatha felt nothing. Then her palms grew a little damp and her heart began to race. The tightness in her chest became so unpleasant that she perspired even more. *Just an autonomic reflex,* she talked herself into believing, and forced herself to adopt a steady breathing rhythm.

However, these physiological reactions were the only effects she noticed and she looked quizzically at the packet in her hand, certainly worth a few thousand rands on the street. She'd sent her car on an unobtrusive course through the city, spiraling into and out of the city center so that the traffic control system did not register any suspicious deviations. The sun was already rising, and under the growing lapis lazuli hue of the morning sky, the first commuters were making their way to the metro shafts like lonely shadows.

Traffic was slowly increasing, the rows of anonymous taillights and dazzling headlights slowly growing thicker. The reflected light on their windshields made them impenetrable to the naked eye. But she did not need to see because she knew there was a story behind each of these anonymous vehicles.

Sometimes she had stood in Hortat's downtown Silver Tower for hours, looking down at the megacity's nocturnal hustle and bustle, the enormous columns of cars, the pedestrian crowds rolling across the sidewalks like ants. From that height, they had been no more than pinheads, one-dimensional dots in an infinite space, and yet so numerous that she had always wondered how so many things could coexist —so many microcosms.

Within each of these dots was a very personal story of love, anger, fear, hope, and a thousand thoughts, all of which were held as crucial because they meant everything to the person who owned them, every individual unavoidably the center of his or her own universe. And yet, these dots were as grains of dust among a multitude. An outsider perspective revealed the apparent insignificance of them all.

One only had to zoom out far enough to achieve distance from the serious gravity of thoughts obsessed with 'me, myself, and my problems.' How many of these points were men and women who had just had their hearts broken? How many worried about their health? How many had just fallen in love and were on their way to their beloveds? Who was hungry, who was crying? Everything happened at the same time and was so meaninglessly insignificant that it always rendered her speechless and made her feel very small.

*And what now, Agatha?* She let her head sink back against the headrest in frustration and closed her eyes for a moment to revisit everything she had experienced over the last 24 hours. The problem was, she could still see. She immediately realized that she had experienced what had just happened—from inside Herxmin's short memory.

Her perception was much sharper and so comprehensive that she saw, smelled, and felt everything simultaneously without being able to process it. It was almost as if she watched sand running through a sieve and she could recognize every single grain, only to lose each one so quickly that it became a mental echo.

She was herself and yet someone else.

Every second brought a new impression, a new time, a new physical sensation. She saw time passing by, looking down on bronze skin that was smooth and grew wrinkled as in time-lapse. She saw death, the eternal sleep, which was just a nap before everything started all over again and she was the same, and at the same time, someone... other.

There was nothing in her perceptions that could have tied this experience to her life, and so it was just as disturbing as events in a feverish dream. She loved and suffered, hoped and cared. She experienced discussions and arguments, stood on a lush green meadow under white sheep-like clouds, and gazed at tear-shaped spaceships rising from an endless plain and floating toward the sky as if gravity could have no effect. It was a majestic exodus to the stars that filled her with pride.

Afterward, she sat in a pyramid underground, pursuing the same work, day after day, on a smooth display console. Another life was lived in the same pyramid—at least she believed so—and led her into a large incubator with thousands of embryos, onto which she—for some reason—pinned her high hopes.

Agatha wanted to scream, to flail about so that it would end, but at the same time, she wished it would never end, because along with the feeling that her head could burst at any moment, another sense of grandeur and greatness came, as if she were filling the entire universe. Nothing could harm her, not even time. Her body was as strong as a monolith in the surf, giving her something that went far beyond self-confidence. It was indescribable, a beautiful pain.

The last thing she saw—and it seemed to her that she had seen everything and nothing, because the memories ran through her like water through cupped hands—was Luther Karlhammer, sitting with her at a table. On the left was a window through which she could see Earth as a blue sphere with white cloud bands and brown-green continents.

The sight seemed normal to her, nothing special, more like a thing of beauty she had seen countless times. One still enjoyed it without it making any particular impression. She saw a document lying between herself and Karlhammer—who looked as small and fragile as a child to her—on a transparent tablet. The South African nodded and pointed to the Earth beyond the viewing screen. An agreement had been reached. She understood that much without being able to follow the conversation.

She was too busy holding her mind together as it was bombarded by too many things at once. Agatha knew this was important, but how could she ever comprehend what was going on?

Suddenly, with her eyes ripped open, and breathing heavily, she found herself in her car, raising her hands in panic. They had the same smooth shape and white color as always—no bronze tone, but also no more grand sense of superiority.

"I am me," she said to herself. "I'm me. Not him. Not that." She emitted a guttural sound and then an unarticulated roar, simply to ground herself. She slapped her cheeks hard enough that they burned but did not hurt. Her thoughts slowly calmed, detaching from the impressions she felt sinking into herself like an alien virus that she would never get rid of again.

*Don't think about that. Think of what I saw! It was impor-
tant. But why? What was on the document? Where was I
sitting?* she wondered. An orbital station, that much was
certain. But Karlhammer? What was he doing on a space
station? The Human Foundation, along with three of
Africa's largest banks, owned shares in the Horizon Orbital,
but according to people behind the scenes, he was terrified
of space.

Agatha looked out through the windshield to see where
she was—she had not thought to call up her map program.
It had to be somewhere in Mayfair, judging by the houses.
They seemed to have decided they preferred, somewhere on
the way to becoming skyscrapers, to remain modest. She
shielded her eyes from the sunlight, which seemed strangely
weak above the city, as if a giant, invisible filter had been
thrown over the buildings.

Only now did it dawn on her that the central star was
almost at its zenith, no, it had already gone beyond it.

"Damn!" she cursed, and called up the time in her
retinal display: 3:23 p.m. *Crap! How is that possible?* she
wondered.

She went through her missed calls, saw a total of six
from Hortat and another 22 from one of his secretaries. The
polling stations were already open.

"No, no, no!" She hastily ordered the car's control software to drive to the campaign office, taking the fastest route.
Then she dialed the Builder's number.

His secretary Cindy took the call. "Hello?" As always she
had perfectly styled blonde hair, but she looked exhausted.
"Ahh, Agatha. There you are!"

"Where is he?"

"He just cast his vote in his Jeppestown constituency.
The media..."

JOSHUA T. CALVERT

Agatha let her head hang and sighed. *Oh no, I missed his poll appearance!*

"Cindy? I have to talk to him!"

"That's not possible. He's giving interviews. You can turn on Channel Nine. Then you'll see it in on live stream."

"Damn! Then tell him to call me back immediately, understood?"

"Yes, of course. What's going on?"

Agatha disconnected and switched Channel 9 to the windshield. Hortat was standing on the top steps of the entrance to an old sandstone building with a columned portico. In the background flew the flag of the South African Special Administrative Zone. Pen microphones poked like a forest out of the lower section of the picture, all pointed at the Builder who wore a flawlessly fitting suit of human production, in itself a statement of the times. Behind him stood Pablo and Steve, with no sign of their injuries and with their charming smiles, each in its own way still making an impression.

"... that's why it was important for me to come back here today," Hortat said with his typically accentuated flow of speech and deep voice. When Agatha saw him like that, she could not imagine how someone could not elect this Builder. He radiated a quiet, intelligent presence that was so paternal that one could quickly forget his young official age. And it was not only the magnetism of his imposing figure that made every human being feel inferior to a Builder, as a child would feel.

*I should be there now,* she thought sadly, frustrated.

"Today, every man and woman in the Special Administrative Zone has the chance to choose change. A change for yourself and the world, and thereby set a good example. We have a choice—fear and isolation, or openness and trust.

Many wonder whether strangers should be generally mistrusted, and trusted only when they have earned it. But is that the way we should view the world? With fear? Why not *trust* strangers until they give us reason not to? Isn't that way of living a happier life?

"We Builders are a proud species that have long since renounced the concept of country and race. There is always more that unites us than divides us. We all breathe the same air, have feelings and thoughts, fear an unfortunate fate, and seek love and recognition. I know that I demand a lot. We are, after all, only guests on this planet, even though it was our planet for a long time. Today, it is no longer.

"This is a fact that each of my sisters and each of my brothers will have to admit sooner or later, even if we are extremely proud and do not want to see it so. I want my term of office to be a bridge between you and us, and that soon there will be only one 'we.' I believe we can learn a lot from each other as long as we listen to each other. Today I ask you to place your trust in this vision of the future."

Hortat began to turn away, but a veritable storm of questions slammed into him. One of them stood out and made him pause. "What are you going to do if you lose?"

"I don't intend to lose," replied the Builder with a winning smile. "But if I do, I will support Mr. Muyabe and continue to dedicate myself to my goal of highlighting the similarities of our two species and tearing down the walls that would keep us captive."

"You still haven't appointed a vice-presidential candidate, an unprecedented event in the history of this country!" shouted a female journalist from outside the screen-view limits.

"The Special Administrative Zone is a very young nation, even if it is not one officially," he corrected the woman, sounding friendly and patient even now. "I will announce my deputy and vice-president after the election."

"Why so late?"

"I'm aware that not everyone likes my candidacy, especially some very influential states, and I don't want to place anyone in danger. If we win, I will announce it the day after the election. If not, her name will remain protected."

"So, it's a woman? A human?"

"Yes. A human and a woman." Hortat turned away then and was immediately surrounded by a whole host of bodyguards—all humans—who escorted him to the waiting vehicles through the crowd of journalists and screaming fans. It looked strange to see this gentle giant between the much smaller men shielding him from overzealous compatriots.

Agatha's heart pounded so hard in her chest that she could barely swallow.

"He... Shit! I should have been there! I should have been there, damn it! Shit!" she raged, hammering her fists against the steering wheel, which continued to rotate right and left in obedience to the control software that guided her gently around corners. "Shit, shit, shit!"

An incoming call from Hortat appeared in her retinal display. She accepted the call before actually thinking about it.

"Hello, Agatha. I'm glad that... What's going on?" he asked anxiously. He was probably sitting in the back of his limousine, which was about to leave the polling station.

"Oh, nothing... It's just... the old Agatha broke through briefly." She smiled embarrassedly and smoothed her features. "I... I'm sorry, Hortat."

"What? I was worried."

"I should have been there," she replied with a bitter undertone in her voice.

"No." He made a dismissive gesture and smiled warmly. "I knew you would have good reasons, and I just hoped nothing had happened to you. I apologize—I had your vital data displayed, once. It won't happen again."

"What? That's okay. I've figured something out and need your help. I'm on my way to the campaign office."

"What is it?"

"I took it, and I think I know why Bellinger wanted to steal that one vial."

"Really? You have..." Hortat paused for a moment. Then, "Agatha! That was dangerous!"

"I know, but it was only this one time. You have to look at it."

"No!" he said immediately, sounding outraged.

"Hortat, I've seen something that... It's important, you understand? For all of us, I think."

"Are lives in danger?"

*No,* she wanted to say, gulping. "Yes," she stated, and immediately felt terrible about it. But she had to follow her intuition now and would ask for forgiveness later.

Hortat sighed tensely and nodded slowly. "Come to the Silver Tower. Not to the campaign office. And tell me everything." When she seemed about to speak, he raised a hand. "When we're there."

"All right. I'm already on the way."

Hortat nodded and disconnected. Agatha spoke the address of his residence aloud, and her car immediately adapted its route.

*He will understand,* she thought hopefully, countered by a guilty conscience such as she had not felt for a long time.

*The last time was...* She thought of Pano and shook her head. *No, Agatha, don't go through that door. Do you understand?*

She had to control herself better. It was only because the almond dust trip had been so horrible, and at the same time, so sublime and euphoric that her head was still swirling, as if she had spent a day on a particularly wild roller coaster that had made her feel sick, and yet given her an almighty adrenaline rush. She wanted that feeling back, comprehending, observing, and seeing through everything.

She wanted to see the auras of humans again, those wild shimmers of color that had surrounded them and told her so many things. But even now, after a single trip, she realized that a second one would change her forever and cause irreparable damage to her mind—if that had not already happened. She pulled the infuser she had snatched from Bellinger out of her bag, and looked at it as if it were a big puzzle.

"Just what are you for, hmm?" she murmured.

The drive to the Silver Tower lasted half an hour. Seized by sudden lethargy, she spent the whole time just leaning her forehead against the side window and watching the traffic. She passed polling stations with long lines of voters, even though about 80 percent of those eligible had registered for digital voting. So, the city crowd could only mean that even the remaining 20 percent, which could confidently be called 'dinosaurs,' were determined to cast their ballots, and the turnout would be historic.

The street cafés in the city center were crowded to bursting, and she imagined the patrons all talking about the election that would change their future. As always, she saw hardly any Builders in public, even though there were more than 5,000 of them in the Special Administrative Zone, of whom more than 4,000 were reportedly present in Johannesburg. She had once questioned Hortat about them because she was sure that he was in contact with them—after all, he was something like their leader, even if he always denied it, at least half-heartedly.

When asked if he knew where they were, he once replied that they were working on the future and were worried about appearing in the open. She did not know if that was true of all of them, but she hardly believed it. You could see some of them here and there, clearly not so shy about participating in public life.

The Silver Tower sat at the eastern end of the city, a conical edifice made of construction polyp and glass. It was one of only three buildings in the city based mainly on Builder technology, and human architects and materials scientists still puzzled over it. The polyp was an organic composition that had grown from huge, white balls. It had taken no more than six months for the skyscraper to expand into the sky on its own, forming a skeleton in which only the gaps had to be filled—with glass panes that a local company had made and installed.

Today, the Silver Tower looked like a sword thrust into the sky, emitting a silvery gleam that had prompted its name, and possessing a restrained alienness in the face of an almost boring normality. There were no gimmicks in the façade, no particular architectural forms, and in general, there was hardly anything that would have encouraged tourists to take photos, except that it was one of the few buildings in the world that had grown out of construction polyp without a worker ever laying a hand to it.

Her car drove toward the underground auto park's entrance, where a sensor strip scanned her and the car and sent a code query. Agatha answered it with her digital fingerprint and was then allowed to proceed to the DNA sniffer in front of the armored roller door. She breathed into the small sensor that extended from the yellow marked box to her window and waited until the LED switched from red to green and the gate rolled leisurely upward. The control software found the parking space assigned to her by the house system, and she got out to go to the elevators.

The vial in her jacket, the infuser, and the packet of gray almond dust seemed so heavy that her shoulders hurt, even though it all could not have weighed even half a kilo. Only now did she wonder what would have happened if the Johannesburg Police Department had not decided to storm the HCP branch and force the terrorists to flee or fight. Presumably, she would never have arrived here safely, to ride in one of these posh elevators lined with polished mirrors and strange wooden ornaments, which supposedly came from the acme of Builder civilization in the Cretaceous period.

Agatha did not understand what she saw in the whole design, as she saw only intricate lines that did not seem to have any natural equivalent, nor did they seem particularly artistic to her, but rather mathematical.

In the elevator's augmented reality interface, she chose the top floor, Hortat's private quarters, and had to provide a further DNA sample to a sniffer that snaked out from a panel. She breathed on the sensor and waited until she got the green light in the AR. The doors then closed, and the elevator car made its long way up. The high speed created pressure in her ears, which she repeatedly compensated for by clenching her jaws or swallowing. Nevertheless, it took her almost two minutes to reach her destination and for the doors to reopen.

Hortat's private quarters consisted of a very large room that covered the entire floor, surrounded by glass, except for curved parts of the polyp façade that seemed to move like snakes, although it could only be an optical illusion. The elevator doors were right in the middle, in a central column, a building core that held the whole structure together. They opened into a recessed area with marble tiles and a small central fountain calmly splashing away.

Three steps led upward, where the floor was blanketed with white carpet and looked so cozy that she felt like laying down on it every time she visited. On the right stood a large piano, a custom-made version for Hortat, which Luther Karlhammer had given him on his 18th birthday two years ago. To the left was a bed with white linens and a lamp that spread above it into dozens of branches. At their ends, smaller lamps radiated a warm yellow light. Straight ahead, she looked upon a sofa landscape with upholstery that looked like cotton batting, and an empty desk.

Hortat stood by the piano, his mighty arms intertwined behind his back, looking through the window down at the city. Flying taxis and delivery drones flowed mostly below them and stretched like pearl chains between the skyscrapers. A beautiful sight, especially since the air above them was clear and the sky was blue. Since the first Dark Tongue attacks, Johannesburg, like most of the world's other metropolises, had blocked airspace over its major cities above a certain altitude, allowing residents of a megatower to have a clear view of the sky.

He turned to her and said warmly, "Hello, Agatha." He had swapped his pinstripe suit for a Builder-style white robe that flowed along his body in several strips, defining every muscle without losing any of its elegance.

"Hello, Boss."

He smiled softly. Hortat did not like her calling him that, which is why she addressed him that way as often as possible. By now it had become something resembling proof of a daughter's love—a kind of insider joke, she admitted. At some point she had become comfortable with the thought of wanting to please him, as if the need of her whole species to keep up with the Builders weighed on her shoulders.

"You look depressed."

Hortat nodded. "What you ask me for is something that I find problematic. You can't understand it."

"Just like you can't understand football?"

"Oh, I understand very well. It is the simulation of a warlike conflict between two parties in the guise of a game in which two sides identify with their communities and want to prevail over the other in order to—"

"As I said, you don't understand it." She grinned, and he smiled. More seriously, she added, "I don't understand the reason, but I see you, and I know you wouldn't be hesitant without cause. I respect that. But if you can do it, I think you would realize the importance." He nodded and turned back to the hustle and bustle of the city.

"Do you remember my favorite poem?" Hortat asked after a silent interlude. Agatha had wanted to fill the silence with something, felt the urgency all the way to her fingertips because she could not waste any time, but the calm his presence radiated gave her enough composure to remain silent.

"Yes. *To Hope* by John Keats. I gave you the original. Have you forgotten?"

"No. I haven't forgotten any of it." Without turning around, he began to quote:

When by my solitary hearth I sit,
    When no fair dreams before my "mind's eye" flit,
    And the bare heath of life presents no bloom;

Sweet Hope, ethereal balm upon me shed,
And wave thy silver pinions o'er my head.


Whene'er I wander, at the fall of night,
    Where woven boughs shut out the moon's bright ray,
    Should sad Despondency my musings fright,
    And frown, to drive fair Cheerfulness away,
    Peep with the moon-beams through the leafy roof,
    And keep that fiend Despondence far aloof.


Should Disappointment, parent of Despair,
    Strive for her son to seize my careless heart;
    When, like a cloud, he sits upon the air,
    Preparing on his spell-bound prey to dart:
    Chase him away, sweet Hope, with visage bright,
    And fright him as the morning frightens night!


Whene'er the fate of those I hold most dear
    Tells to my fearful breast a tale of sorrow,
    O bright-eyed Hope, my morbid fancy cheer;
    Let me awhile thy sweetest comforts borrow:
    Thy heaven-born radiance around me shed,
    And wave thy silver pinions o'er my head!


Should e'er unhappy love my bosom pain,
    From cruel parents, or relentless fair;
    O let me think it is not quite in vain
    To sigh out sonnets to the midnight air!
    Sweet Hope, ethereal balm upon me shed,

And wave thy silver pinions o'er my head!


In the long vista of the years to roll,
    Let me not see our country's honour fade:
    O let me see our land retain her soul,
    Her pride, her freedom; and not freedom's shade.
    From thy bright eyes unusual brightness shed—
    Beneath thy pinions canopy my head!


Let me not see the patriot's high bequest,
    Great Liberty! how great in plain attire!
    With the base purple of a court oppress'd,
    Bowing her head, and ready to expire:
    But let me see thee stoop from heaven on wings
    That fill the skies with silver glitterings!


And as, in sparkling majesty, a star
    Gilds the bright summit of some gloomy cloud;
    Brightening the half veil'd face of heaven afar:
    So, when dark thoughts my boding spirit shroud,
    Sweet Hope, celestial influence round me shed,
    Waving thy silver pinions o'er my head.


Agatha remained silent for a while, letting the words work on her, which once again sent a shiver down her back. She did not know whether it was due to Keats's romance, or the sublime depth that Hortat's voice and presence gave to what she heard. And, did it matter?

"It is rare to see you so melancholy," she finally said,

addressing his back. He tilted his head slightly without turning around.

"Today, the citizens of the Special Administrative Zone have a choice, my dear." Hortat gave a long sigh. "And I am sure that this day will be a turning point."

"A turning for the good?"

"I don't know. The omens are very uncertain and do not provide a picture clear enough to see through."

"You mean the opinion polls? Even if they're off by ten percentage points, you will still win easily."

"I don't mean that." Another long pause. "Do you know what Keats tried to express so eloquently?"

Agatha did not know. She had never been able to do much with poems because they were merely wordy descriptions instead of targeted communication. *Come to the point,* she always wanted to shout whenever she heard one. Even when the beauty of the descriptions touched her, she could never say why, which bothered her, quite apart from the fact that she did not like beating around the bush. "Don't give up hope, I guess?"

"He was only nineteen years old when he wrote it. His parents had died four years earlier. Death had thus already played a major role in his still young life. A much bigger one than it should ever have played. It is not his best work, and did not receive much attention compared with his later poems."

"Why is it your favorite poem? Do you see something in it that his fellow poets didn't?"

"A poem's worth lies only in the feelings it evokes in you. It is like knowledge that transcends something as static as the words from the poet to the one who receives them. That alone is fascinating. I feel Keats's words like this—when discouragement, hopelessness, and disappointment haunted him, he asked for hope. He always capitalized every mood, as if they occupied a special place. For him, hope was something born on wings, a kind of angelic figure, one might say. It's about melancholy, driven away by a mythical creature. Radiant hope that drives out sinister despair."

"That sounds very interesting," Agatha replied hesitantly, stepping next to him. She noticed that he was not watching the traffic beneath them between the shreds of clouds, but was staring into the sky above the city as if he recognized something there in the uniform blue that hid from her. "But I still don't quite understand what that has to do with the election. Sure, hope is your agenda, our campaign claim, and what you want for the future. But this poem sounds rather melancholic, as you said."

"He died of tuberculosis at the age of twenty-five. Far from home, in Rome, where he had gone only for the sake of his eternal love. Fanny was her name, and she did not reciprocate his love. Do you know what he wanted inscribed on his tombstone?"

"Here lies One Whose Name was writ in Water," she quoted.

"How can it be that a young man whose life ran its course under the wings of death, whose name has survived hundreds of years, wanted to know himself remembered as something fleeting?"

"Because his innermost longing was not fulfilled," she pondered. "He was enraptured by romance, but his own romantic love remained painfully unrequited."

"What does it count to conquer the hearts of those who are not desired? The anonymous readers? It was Fanny, the one who did not understand or appreciate his art, whose love he longed for." Hortat pursed his full lips and smiled sadly. "Thus, he died unfulfilled, without the recognition of the poets of his time, without the love of his life."

"Why are you telling me this? Where does this melancholy mood come from? You are on the verge of your election victory. As early as tonight, you can probably proclaim yourself the winner and next president of one of the most powerful countries in the world and lead us into a new future, make your dream come true. For all of us."

"A deep love binds me with this poet, Agatha," he explained. "Not because he was as he was, but because he taught me something that I have not understood for many lives."

"And that would be?" she asked incredulously.

"I have always fought for a better future, for others, for my beliefs, for the survival of my species. I still do that today. But I do it *not* because I expect a result, but because it is what I must do."

"Because you must?"

"Yes. It feels right and good, and it is what I want. Serving a good cause is the fulfillment that I have always sought, except that I no longer live it for its realization."

"The way is the goal? Or something like that?"

"It always depends on what you feel and do now, not what you want for a future that may never come. If you serve a noble purpose, it is the right thing now, not only once you have succeeded. Do you understand what I mean? Even if I were to lose today, or if I were struck by lightning, nothing would be lost."

Hortat turned away from the window and placed one of his plate-sized hands on her shoulder. It felt warm. The pressure was firm and gentle at the same time. "Do you understand what I mean?"

"No," she freely admitted, and was relieved when he

smiled warmly and pointed to the piano. "My favorite composer is Rachmaninoff. He was a very sober and realistic artist, contrary to the romantic glorification he meets in music criticism to this day."

"Doesn't sound at all like Keats."

"No. Everything has its time. Keats lived some time before Rachmaninoff, and both were important for the evolution of art, which is nothing more than a universal language for translating human feelings into things that are not as fleeting as feelings. Words, songs, pictures."

"It is the solidification of the temporary. Presumably, the desire for art also comes from the fear of death, of transience."

"A very baroque view," Hortat replied, and pointed to the sofa landscape on the other side of the window. Together they walked toward it. It seemed to take an eternity, so large and bare was the room.

"Are you worried about something?" she asked bluntly after they sat down and he had poured fresh water from a carafe into two glasses.

"There is no reason to worry," he assured her. "Everything will take its course. The course it must take to be good."

"I have no idea what that means, Hortat, but I'm going to make sure you succeed. I hope you know that." They looked at each other eye to eye for a long time, until she turned away and nodded so as not to get lost in the infinity of those large, black almond eyes.

"I know, Agatha. This is also one of the reasons why I am not afraid of what will happen."

"God, you sound like you're going to lose today!"

"We're not going to lose. So, you brought me something?"

"Yes." She nodded and unwrapped the packet of almond dust, the vials, and the infuser.

He looked at the last item with a frown, then picked it up. The ring on his right middle finger melted and slid like mercury onto the medical device which was the size of a very short pen. "Interesting." The fluid metal returned to his finger and became a ring again.

"What's in it?"

"Hmm. You should take it with you and keep it with you," he said, holding it out to her.

She took it and pointed to the almond dust. "I'm sorry, but I've seen something that I could never understand without the mind of a Builder."

"I know that you would not burden me with anything unless you could not accomplish it yourself." Hortat opened the packet and took out several pastilles. He looked at them suspiciously before tossing them in his mouth without hesitation and then looked at Agatha. "It will only take a few minutes."

"It lasted half a day for me."

"Because your brain couldn't process the stimuli and impulses it was exposed to. Imagine you're watching a movie at maximum play speed. Your brain throttles down the speed until the images make sense, and the film takes longer." Hortat leaned back and closed his eyes and immediately fell asleep.

Agatha could see his eyes moving behind his lids. For the first time since she'd come to know him, he looked utterly vulnerable and helpless, and as young as he really was.

## 15

---

## PANO

"That doesn't sound like a success to me," Ixlath said, his voice rolling even louder and more deeply through the cabin of their Human Foundation SUV. They had exchanged the taxi for their original vehicle after the Builder insisted on the larger space. In exchange, they were driving autonomously now because Pano did not want to have a driver with them.

Working with Myers and T'Sbu was awkward enough for the two agents, without the risk of trusting additional people with knowledge of their actions. Maybe it was nothing and he was overly worried, but it was always possible that something could happen that the presence of a witness would unnecessarily complicate, especially since such a situation might put the driver himself in an unpleasant position.

"Why? I now know that Mukoena was right to order the raid."

Ixlath threw him a scolding look. "And Agatha, you mean."

"Well, as far as that's concerned... *Maybe.* This does not

acquit her of her guilt for the attack, but facts are facts, and I tell you that HCP is hiding something. That COO was as guilty as a snake that just swallowed a rabbit and shook his head 'no' even as his prey slid down his throat." Pano held his hands to his throat. "I didn't eat anything! Honest!"

"And how are they supposed to be involved in the attack? After all, the raid discovered nothing."

"Pah! Agatha was there snooping around hours before the raid, giving her enough time to prepare."

"Nobody could have managed to remove all the evidence," Ixlath said.

"Not if you look closely. But apparently someone activated their contacts so fast that the police chief—busy with the attack on the train at the time—quickly intervened."

"What is your theory?"

"Was Agatha also at the scene of the attack on the train, north of Pretoria?"

Ixlath nodded.

"She got some of the explosives there that HCP was smuggling. There is no better place to steal anything and go unnoticed than at a crime scene that's on fire and in chaos," Pano said.

"Smuggled?"

"Eighty percent of the cargo belonged to HCP. The rest was some agricultural stuff, if I recall correctly. It may also be that I had forgotten that, it was so unimportant. So, if the Dark Tongue decided to carry out an attack so close to the city—even in a country that is pro-Builder, and thus fully on their side—then there was something rotten about the cargo. What if it contained not explosive components but the finished product?

"Agatha gets access, which shouldn't have been particularly difficult. She takes a specimen with her and somehow gets the reactant. Okay, she brings the specimen to Hortat, and she gets the reactant from the mysterious Builder she meets in the hall at Crown Plaza to exchange handbags. She goes into the car, leaves the reactant there—presumably with a timer and an atomizer—and boom!"

Ixlath twisted his face as if the mere idea caused him physical pain.

"But the theft of the specimen from the truck at the HCP site took place *after* the attack."

"No. It was *noticed* after the attack," Pano corrected him. "That's something different. What if Agatha's contact man, the Builder, stole it before? The truck may have already been loaded on the supplier's property. Most Builders in the city are involved with the Human Foundation in one way or another, right? It might not have been difficult for one of you to gain access without the loss of one of those vials making a big difference."

"That's a cliché, and it's unfortunately not true. Hortat had many followers among us, if not almost all of us. They have been working with him for four years. I would say nearly eighty percent."

"And where are they? Here in the city, you never see any."

"It's only a few thousand, and they've been lying very low ever since. Hardly any of them work for the city or any human companies. Exactly where they are is something I don't know, nor does Luther Karlhammer. But they seem to shun the public eye."

"Obviously."

Their car stopped when a traffic jam formed in front of them. Pano opened the window and stuck his head out to see what was going on and he pulled it back inside in horror. About 100 heavily armored police officers accompanied by two powerful riotbots ran past them. Shouting and chanting could be heard farther ahead, followed by bangs and the clatter of smashed windowpanes.

"This city just doesn't want to calm down," he sighed, looking up to the black pyramid above them—or rather, the black wall he saw there.

"That won't happen any time soon, either. President Muyabe will not let go of power so easily. He saw an opportunity and clutched at it—the proverbial straw. People will not accept that their country should sink into a dictatorship after what's happened." Ixlath sounded both distressed and frustrated at the same time.

"At least they can still protest," Pano muttered. "Can't we walk? It's not far away. And it doesn't look like much will be moving here soon—if the car isn't torched in the meantime."

"That should be possible. Twenty minutes if we hurry."

They got out and had to push themselves back against the vehicle as more police officers ran past—and almost over them. When the uniformed men had gone, they ducked into an alley at a slow jog, whereupon things became quieter. The horns and screams, the sounds of the street battle faded into surreal background noise.

A couple of bewildered almond dust addicts sat on an old mattress between two garbage containers, babbling incomprehensibly. Presumably, they were on a trip with a one-way ticket to insanity. Judging by their clothes they were not homeless, in a neighborhood where homelessness was the norm. It was unofficially a lower-class area south of the city center, effectively separated from the wealthier district by an expressway.

The walls of today looked different and were not allowed to be called such. However, they were still walls. The area under the expressway was cordoned off for 'safety reasons' and secured by traffic police drones. The expressway charged tolls. As a result, hardly any of Turffontein's residents had regular access to the glass palaces of the city center.

They walked west, crossed another traffic jam on a parallel road, and caught a glimpse of the violent protests further north before the on-ramp to one of the expressways. Judging by the fires and the repeated explosions, the situation had already escalated, and many car owners were fleeing on foot in the opposite direction.

"I think the city has reached a critical point," Ixlath said anxiously, looking up, where the base of the floating pyramid occluded the sky. "We don't have much time left to find your ex-wife. If Johannesburg explodes, we will not be able to move or track anyone down."

"Then we'd better hurry."

Through countless alleys between run-down townhouses and newer concrete buildings from the 2040s construction boom, they passed other smaller demonstrations, people holding up banners with Hortat's woodcut-style image, other people looting shops, and rioting groups of angry youths. They frequently saw burning cars, firefighters extinguishing house fronts, police drones containing minor outbreaks of violence with shock waves, and large numbers of frightened faces behind the apartment windows on the higher floors.

The workshop sat at the expressway's edge in a two-story brick building, which seemed exceptionally well maintained. He almost would have confused it with the hotel in Lower Melville because the location was surprisingly similar and had the same pitch-black artificial sky. Only that one was a superstructure erected by humans and the other constructed by Builders.

The streets were also empty, as if they were in a remote area and not right on the outskirts of the city center. Immediately beyond the raised expressway, the city's skyscrapers towered many floors above, as if they formed the basis for the pyramid. On the ground floor, in front of a double driveway of cast concrete, the workshop was identified by a clean, illuminated sign and two employees clad in blue overalls and light exoskeletons working around a car that stood in front of one of six garages.

"Where are Myers and T'Sbu?" Ixlath asked as they walked toward the door to the office.

Pano looked at his hand terminal and saw the live location of the two agents. "They'll be here in five minutes. Why don't we have a look at the car?" he suggested, and together they entered a small, sweltering office equipped with dehumidifiers. Above them, a black spot on the wall emitted an unpleasant, moldy odor.

"G'day," greeted a short, light-haired man with his impressive belly squeezed behind a simple desk sporting a large display screen that looked about a hundred years old. "Order number?"

"We're here because of the taxi," Pano said, and the man looked at him for the first time, apparently with a pointed comment on his lips, until he saw Ixlath, and his eyes almost burst with a mixture of terror and admiration.

"Oh," he said, rolling back in his chair. Where his legs should have been were metallic cyber prostheses without cladding, so one could see the many artificial tendons and small parts moving back and forth. "Well, I don't get a visit like this every day."

The nameplate on the man's chest identified him as 'Customer Friendly Wallheeks.' He was apparently the owner, seeing that the workshop bore his name. The man stood up and bent over the table to shake Ixlath's hand. He looked extremely nervous and licked his lips several times.

"All right?" asked Pano.

"Yes, uh, of course. As I said, we don't often have a bronze... Uhh, Builder with us. Hehe. I'm a big fan, really! I also voted for Hortat!" Wallheeks's face darkened. "Bad thing, that."

"The taxi," Ixlath politely reminded him.

"Ahh, yes. I had it parked in the back. Come along."

"In the back?" Pano took a quick look at his partner. "Why there?"

"Well, there was just so much going on in the front and... Ahh." Wallheeks waved dismissively and beckoned them to follow.

As Pano remembered, he had seen only two mechanics, and only one of six garages had been open. It did not look overcrowded, which would have surprised him with the current situation in the city.

"So much work during a state of emergency," he commented approvingly as the owner led them through a short hallway to the back lot, where a fair number of cars stood parked in huge heavy-duty shelves and piled up to two floors high. "I wouldn't have thought it."

"There is only one curfew for the city center. Well, at least it is only enforced there. The rest is under reduced civil rights," Wallheeks said with a shrug, pointing to a MyDrive taxi, which was the only vehicle standing on the old asphalt between the walls of parked cars.

"Haven't you done anything with it yet?" asked Ixlath.

"No. I, uh, had other priorities. But right after the Boolsey in front, where my two uninterested cousins are fumbling around, it's the taxi's turn. Promise." Wallheeks seemed to be waiting for something when the shrill of a phone could be heard from inside. "Ahh!" he said. "I'm going to answer that quickly. The car is unlocked. I'll be back with you right away."

"There's something wrong here," Ixlath said as the short man walked away on his cyber prostheses. With each step, they made a loud metallic click.

"Ask me what's *right* here. That man is nervous." Pano paused as he turned to the building and pointed to the uninterrupted concrete wall. "He parks the car here, in this back lot, where it obviously has no access to the garages and lifting platforms."

"A request from the police should have priority."

"Yes. Besides, there is absolutely nothing going on here."

"That's all true," said Ixlath, looking up to the expressway that towered over them like a long concrete bridge stretching from horizon to horizon. It started above the wall of cars in front of them, only much higher, about 10 or 15 meters above the building. "And the man did not ask us for IDs, and did not ask us why we are the ones here for the taxi, and the police are not."

An unpleasant feeling spread in Pano as if the blood in his veins was turning to ice. He thought of the kidnappers who had turned up at the Hotel in Melville shortly before them, then of the two augment zombies in the hut in Randfontein and the truck that had disappeared from the HCP site just before they arrived.

*Someone is always one step ahead of us,* he thought as he swallowed. *What if that man meant to lure us here into the back?*

He looked around in alarm and saw a barely noticeable movement from Ixlath's direction. When he looked at him, he noticed a tiny red dot on his forehead, which the Builder did not seem to notice. Without thinking, Pano threw himself at his partner as a loud shot whipped through the night. Blood splattered onto his face as they stumbled. It was as if he had tried to ram an obelisk—he made the Builder lose his balance, but Ixlath did not fall. It was only at the last moment that his resistance seemed to give way, and they both fell to the side. Pano hit the tarmac hard but ignored the pain and looked around as he wiped the blood from his face.

Ixlath blinked. His left ear and a piece of his scalp above it were shredded. He was bleeding, but Pano could not see any signs of cerebrospinal fluid at first glance, so it was only a graze.

"Back into the building!" Pano roared, and sprang into a crouch before running, still crouched, to the stacked cars. "SNIPER!"

The Builder seemed confused, perhaps in shock or affected by a concussion caused by the graze or his fall. At that moment, Myers and T'Sbu ran through the door into the yard with their pistols drawn. Pano wildly gestured to them to stay down and to pull Ixlath behind the taxi into cover. Since there was no second round of shots, he guessed the shooter had fired through a gap in the cars that had offered a clear shot at their upper bodies.

"At least one attacker, large caliber, somewhere under the expressway!" he shouted to the two agents, carefully peering over the hood he was leaning against. In the dark area under the road, he looked through a wire mesh fence and saw a stack of old cargo containers, which had probably been piled up there by the city to create both a barrier and functional storage space in an area not meant for traffic. He repeatedly popped up to search for something noticeable, ducked again, and changed his position so as not to end up with a bullet in his head.

"Do you see anything?" Myers shouted. She and her partner had hoisted the injured Builder behind the taxi and peered edgily in his direction.

"No, nothing. That's perfect cover over there."

"I'm coming over." The agent came in a crouch and pushed her back against the body of the rusty sedan beside him.

"You have a pretty good view over the hood. I'll try to lure the shooter out of cover."

"Too dangerous," she said with a shake of her head. "We're waiting for reinforcements."

"No. He'll be long gone by then. He'll wait a short time for a second try and then disappear."

"How do you know that?" she hissed.

"I've had to deal with snipers before," he growled, then ran to the right before slipping between the trunk of one car and the bumper of another to reach the wire mesh fence. Relieved that he had not yet been shot, he discovered an opening in the fence and slipped through it, found himself on a dusty lot again, in front of a stack of sea containers labeled 'Hamburg Süd.' They towered toward the center of the area under the road, forming striped shadows and rusty twilight. Then he looked down at himself and spotted a red dot at the height of his heart.

"Oh, shit," he muttered, still thinking how stupid he had been and what a strange last thought that was when a shot sounded, then another. He was already falling when he realized that he had not been hit and that someone else had fired.

"I see something!" cried Myers, firing again.

Pano's gaze zipped upward, and he caught sight of a blond-haired head between two of the upper containers about 50 meters away, just as it disappeared into the shadows. The sight was brief, so brief even that he almost thought his optic nerves were playing a prank on him.

"Hofer? HOFER!" He shook his head to free himself from the trance-like state he was in and blinked a few times before realizing that Myers was standing next to him with her gun raised and aiming toward the upper container. "Did you see the shooter? I have to pass the position on to my colleagues."

Again, the image of blond hair and shadowy figure went through his head.

"No," he breathed hoarsely. He felt like he'd been hit by a sledgehammer.

"Damn!" cursed the agent. "I noticed a reflection and just shot in the direction to force him into cover, but I couldn't see anything after that. I directed the drones to the other side."

"They won't find her," Pano muttered.

"What did you say?"

"Nothing. What about Ixlath?"

"Ear shot off, glancing shot caused a skull fracture, I think. It's a good thing that there are no Alpha Extractions client memberships for Builders. Otherwise things would have gotten very uncomfortable here pretty fast."

"It was really close. I saw the dot on his forehead and—"

"You're still soaked with blood," Myers interrupted him, wiping her sleeve over his face as she would a child. Pano did not mind. Shortly after, they returned to T'Sbu and Ixlath. The Builder sat like a fallen giant leaning against the taxi with a glassy look. Blood covered the entire left side of his body.

"Hey!"

"Hey," his partner moaned, sounding groggy. "Thank you."

"Oh." Pano waved it off. It was strange and frightening to see such a formidable figure so hurt and helpless. "I've always wanted to know if I could take one of you off your legs."

Ixlath smiled absently. "That was close."

"Yes." Pano swallowed, trying not to imagine what would have happened if he had reacted the smallest fraction of a second later. "Where is that Wallheeks?"

"Gone," Myers answered grimly. "A damned trap."

"Deena thought that Mukoena had given you something?" asked T'Sbu.

"He did." Pano pulled the hand terminal out of his jacket pocket and looked at it as if it were a bomb that could explode at any moment. "Do you think it's bugged?"

"How else could this here be explained?" Myers answered. "Someone wants to see Ixlath dead, for whatever reason. The former deputy director seems to be involved somehow."

"Or it's a coincidence. A false lead," Pano said.

"Didn't he want to be informed of your progress?" T'Sbu gazed intently at him. When he nodded, she added, "Then call him."

Pano pulled out his hand terminal and dialed Mukoena's number but did not get through.

"No one is answering. Damn!"

"Don't blame yourself," Myers said. "In this city these days, no one is who he claims to be. This attack has thrown the whole country into chaos, but Johannesburg in particular. Gloria?"

"I'll take care of it." Her colleague's gaze grew absent as armed police rotor drones with blue lights and sirens chased over them above the roof of the workshop. "It seems that he has disappeared from his house, but his commlink connection is still active."

"That could be an advantage for us," Myers said.

"What are you thinking?" Pano asked lamely. He still felt like someone had hit him on the head. He could not get the image of the blonde figure out of his thoughts. Added to that was the waning adrenaline in his veins, which made him aware that his hands were shaking.

"They set a trap for us," she said. "Now we should return the favor."

# 16

## AGATHA

When Hortat woke from his almond dust trip, it wasn't how Agatha expected. He did not startle in fright, or breathe frantically, or open his eyes wide like someone might when emerging from a nightmare. On the contrary, his eyelids opened almost reluctantly, as if he were exhausted. But his gaze was awake and alert, with a sad expression creeping in.

"Is... is everything all right?" she asked cautiously, taking hold of his left hand. "Hortat?"

"Yes. I'm all right," he answered thoughtfully. "However, I do not want to do that again. It was..." A sigh that sounded like the rustling of autumn foliage on a rain-soaked road escaped his mouth. He looked into the tidy void of his apartment for a few moments and seemed to recognize something that remained hidden from her before turning his gaze to her and squeezing her hand.

"But it was right of you to show me this, as much as I feel the need to cleanse myself within and vomit," Hortat continued.

"What have you seen?"

"I'll show you."

"Yes, okay," Agatha said immediately, only to lean away a little and spring to her feet. "No! I... I mean, a part of me wants to do it again right now, but no. I must not do it again. I think it would change me."

She thought back to the junkie who had fallen into madness in his hut in Randfontein—the expression in his eyes that reminded her of the shadow of a cloud that loomed over a field and leeched it of color, as if it had never nurtured life. That feeling of grandness she had experienced through the eyes and body of the Builder had been exhilarating, but she had paid for it dearly, and the fact that she had just now agreed so impulsively worried her.

"No, I can't. Not again. I'm sorry."

Hortat smiled and reached out to take her hands in his own, causing them to disappear between his fingers. "Agatha. I don't mean the almond dust," he reassured her, and it was astonishing how gentle a pressure his fingers could exert. "The conversation between Ixlath and Luther Karlhammer lasted about an hour. I can relive it with you—at normal speed."

"How?"

"It's like this. Our memories are compressed, if you like. It is a directed mutation in the structure of our brains that we received from our gene weavers tens of thousands of years before our decline. In order to store the sheer amount of experience that a genetic memory brings, a lot had to change physiologically. You can imagine it as a compression program for your neural clusters, except that unpacking is parallel to the experience and does not occur in series, one after the other. However, some of us are able to break down and control the process. So, I can take you with me into my memory of Ixlath—as an observer, if you will. Everything will happen in a normal time sequence."

"How?" she asked, irritated.

"It's complicated. Suffice it to say, I invite you into my thoughts."

"And how is this supposed to work? An entanglement of our implants?"

"I don't have implants, as you know."

"Exactly."

"No. Thoughts also exist as something that can be measured in the form of energy, as long as one knows the frequency and has a correspondingly sensitive sensor system. You have to relax to get into the right state. Then it will be easy," he explained patiently.

"Relax?" she asked, snorting. "I've *never* been able to do that, new Agatha or not. I'm always on alert. It's also Election Day, and in four hours we'll have the first projections that will probably let you declare yourself the winner. I can hardly jump on the meditation pillow and find my inner Buddha. Moreover, this matter with Heavy Chemicals Pretoria is still going on out there. By the way, what came of the raid? Has anyone contacted you? Do your eyes and ears in the city have any information about this? And what about the European secret service? And—"

"Agatha," he calmly interrupted her and smiled warmly, "we have enough time for important things. And this here is also important."

"Your campaign team is waiting downstairs, hopping up and down because you've barricaded yourself in your apartment."

"I am a Builder." He tilted his head and did not seem at all concerned. "They will say, 'Well, they're just *weird*.' But I'm not going to force you."

"No, it's all right," she assured him quickly, nodding.

"Good. Then sit back down and close your eyes. You should keep your back straight, relax and put your hands in your lap so you're loose, but not so relaxed that you fall asleep. Now, tune in on your breathing. Do not control it, do not change it. Just observe air flowing through your nose, how it feels, and how your abdomen rises. Then follow the air as it streams out of your mouth and your abdomen falls, and the cycle begins anew. It happens effortlessly and without your intervention. You do not respire—you are being respired."

At first Agatha wanted to analyze everything, wondering why her breath was so shallow. Then she thought of breathing a little deeper, because this was undoubtedly done in meditation, but gradually her thoughts calmed down. She gave up the urge to control everything, only to discover that her breathing did not require any control and happened on its own. She knew this, of course, but feeling it was a different experience—after all, she pretty much *never* thought about anything as commonplace as breathing.

The relaxation suddenly set in by itself, without her immediately noticing it. It was only when Hortat's voice calmly asked her to turn her attention to the utter silence between breaths that she noticed the serenity with which she followed his instruction. She fell into a pleasant void, like a leaf, almost weightless. For a fraction of an immeasurable amount of time she became frightened because she sensed the idea that she was losing the structure of her very *self*, but her fear quickly evaporated and gave way to a sustained nothingness.

When she opened her eyes, she was sitting on an uncomfortable chair that had not been built for Builders, looking down at an aluminum table, at a tablet that lay on it bearing a long document. Opposite her sat Luther Karlhammer. He was dressed neatly—though not in his usual Hugo Boss suit with his orange shirt and brown tie—in a futuristic, white, one-piece suit with bronze-colored hems on its sleeves and collar. On the tablet, Agatha saw the time and date. It was December 21, 2060, 10:04 p.m. *Two years ago.*

"The tricopherone is stable. We can start with the next phase," Karlhammer said.

"Of course it's stable," said Ixlath, through whose eyes Agatha gazed, and through whose mind she filtered everything. She respected the South African. This man had more foresight than most of his kind, and was endowed with an intelligence that made it almost seem like she was talking to a teenager rather than a toddler. "We developed it."

"We developed it together," Karlhammer corrected Ixlath, and Agatha shrugged.

"It's spread will take several years."

"The main thing is that we have reached a critical volume by the time of the 2062 presidential election. Go over it again and tell me if we have overlooked anything—a logic gap or something like that."

Agatha sighed and took the tablet into her bronze hands, which she could easily have used to crush the device to dust. Of course, the plan was perfect—after all, Karlhammer had conceived it, but she and the Dark Tongue perfected the plan and had transformed it into a technically feasible reality. The document reflected all this, committed them both to cooperation, and resulted in a common charter encompassing humans and Builders to save the future of the Earth.

She flew over the individual points and nodded at the bigger picture. Tricopherone would spread as a drug in the non-educated social strata, who were more dependent on escapism than those in the middle class, and who resorted to harmful drugs such as crystal meth or heroin, rather than the more prosperous who chose their LSD or cocaine.

"You don't think much of your own kind." Agatha directed the comment at the South African, who was looking down at Earth through the window. From the Horizon Orbital, she looked directly at the African continent. Its center was embraced by dense bands of clouds. It hurt her that a primitive successor species like humans had inherited the planet and had led it to the brink of ruin, while her direct ancestors had been among those who had dedicated their lives to species conservation in Gunth's flying habitats.

But that was the reality, and these humans would surely need some help to grow beyond their primitive condition. If she could help, it also helped her and her kind, who were so few that they had to do what was necessary to work out a way to co-exist with their new cohabitants. Added to this was the low oxygen content on Earth, which severely affected their bodies, despite the recent adjustments Xinth and Hortat had made to their embryos. Sooner or later, they would have to leave their former home world and look for a new one, but that took time, resources, and—she had to admit—the help of humans.

"I know my kind," Karlhammer corrected her with a sigh. "You can see how they reacted to your kind when you could no longer be locked away in large dome tents in distant Siberia as a kind of reality show attraction."

"You want to infect the poor with tricopherone and blow them away after Hortat's election," said Agatha, and although she was Ixlath, there was no difference between the two. They thought and talked as one being, and it did not feel like a memory, like a one-way street, but like a natural process, as if all this were happening in the present. "This seems a bit extreme even to me, and I am officially the leader of a terrorist organization."

"The Dark Tongue arose in reaction to the Europeans!" The head of the Human Foundation shook his head sadly. "They pushed you underground when they put you in a camp and wanted to deprive you of human rights."

"Well, we are not human beings."

"No, you are *more* than..."

Their eyes met over the unadorned table and the centrifugal force, which was a pleasant half-g, seemed to rise a fraction.

"And you are sure that you want to put the fate of the planet in our hands?"

"Yes. There is no alternative. Those who sow hatred and fear and are receptive to it are allowed to vote in the West. They are the ones who have too little education to comprehend the larger contexts and instead live from one Better Than Life simulation to the next, worried that someone might endanger their meaningless lives. They are the ones who have elected the new despots to power in Europe and North America and applaud their every lie, as if they do not understand that they are celebrating their own downfall."

Agatha tilted her head. "That is democracy."

"That is its fatal error, that everyone can turn their opinion into power. It is not common sense that matters, but who tells the best and loudest story. This *cannot* have a future. It *must not* have a future."

"What makes you believe that the Western bloc will change, and not simply become even stricter in its policy of isolation?"

"Because the heads of half your population have burst,

and most of them are your loyalists. There will be an uprising and the whole economy will collapse. That's where we come in."

"Ahh. The Human Foundation and its Builder friends."

"Yes. We take care of the survivors and show them what it feels like to be helpless and receive help from others. We'll show them how things can be better. What it is like not to reject others in need, but to instead give them a hand and set a good example."

"After we've removed the ax."

Karlhammer nodded sadly. "Yes," he breathed, looking down at his hands. "It's now the only idea left to me. The alternative would be the threatening nuclear war between the West and China and its vassals in the East, which looks inevitable should the ongoing cyber warfare continue to escalate. I prefer to preempt those warmongers and then put the scepter into your hands."

"And your own," Agatha added.

"The Human Foundation must remain as the mediator between our organizations."

"That's what it will do. We will respect our part of the agreement. We will not forget what you and humans did for us after the conflict between Xinth and Hortat. They could also have denied us a new life—and thus our survival—on Earth. No matter what happens now, we will respect that," Agatha said earnestly. "We have also thought about how best to get the reaction going, and decided to recommend fireworks."

"'Fireworks?'" Karlhammer raised his eyebrows in surprise. "What fireworks?"

"If, as promised, you ensure that Hortat is elected president, we will empower you to set up a celebration to honor him in the form of an orbital fireworks display. You launch the rockets from here, and the blooms of the fireworks will be visible all over the planet. This will intimidate your opponents and impress the citizens. Also, in this way, we can distribute the trigger substance for the tricopherone evenly and relatively simultaneously across the globe."

"But there is still a problem—all the survivors will blame me or Hortat—or both of us. But he must survive."

"Yes, we too want him as the leader of this new era," Agatha confirmed. "That's why the Dark Tongue and I will claim responsibility."

"No!" Karlhammer protested indignantly. "You are the ones to whom the survivors must owe everything. Together with me, you are the ones who will shape the change to make a future worth living in. You must not be pilloried for doing the right thing!"

"Most of us already have concrete plans for progeny. A new cloning program is expected to start in about two years. So, I will survive in a way and will continue to act in the background until then," she said. "Perhaps this might even be helpful. After all, we are not in a position to foresee every consequence of our project."

"That's a big sacrifice you're making. Thank you."

"No." Agatha shook her powerful head in a very human way and regarded the secret leader of humanity. She saw every pore in his skin, interpreted the expression of his eyes in hundreds of ways at once, and almost casually filtered out the most likely interpretations as a mosaic of possibilities. She saw his aura of colors that seemed to diffuse like gas from his skin. Most of it was a bluish serenity with a slightly yellowish glimmer that could mean nervousness or tension, but also a black sorrow in his heart, laboriously restrained by his emotional discipline, which ironically made it easier to read his aura.

Agatha had respect for him and what he was willing to burden his soul with for the sake of doing what he thought was right. She knew how insignificant a single life without continuity was, an endless series of emotional ups and downs and meaningless activities designed to kill time, and calling it happiness. Developing a genetic memory and interweaving it into human evolution would help them recognize this and always see a higher sense in their existence. But if there were no real break, they will have destroyed themselves long before this could be achieved. Hortat was a strong leader to whom the Builders owed everything—or at least very much—but he was too attached to his faith in human reason to see how great a risk he was taking.

"You are making the greatest sacrifice, Luther Karlhammer," she finally said, rising from the uncomfortable chair, which was far too small for her. She was not particularly looking forward to the flight back to Earth, as she could hardly believe the primitive technology required for her to survive a wild ride through the atmosphere. But what was one not willing to do for the hope of a better future? "I hope you won't be broken by it."

"Maybe I will." The entrepreneur straightened and seemed thoughtful and exhausted, as if the weight of the entire cosmos stood on his shoulders. "But then let it be so. Better me than the future."

Agatha was just turning to go, but Karlhammer reached her before she could walk through the automatic door. "One more thing."

She looked down at his hand on her arm, and he quickly

pulled it back. "How long will it take when you are in power? The necessary genetic changes, I mean?"

"Twenty to thirty years."

"Good." Karlhammer seemed to nod himself. "That's good. And, Ixlath?"

"Yes?"

"Don't underestimate the Western intelligence services. Our procedure over the next two years must be perfect."

Agatha smiled, and then her vision went briefly black before she saw Hortat opposite her again. The memory ran off her like beads of water, yet left her shivering as if wet and cold. She trembled all over her body, but it wasn't that strange sense of shock like she'd experienced upon emerging from the almond dust trip, which had felt as if all the neurons in her head had to rearrange themselves. This time it was because of what she had just heard and seen.

"That... That just cannot be," she stammered. "That's the plan behind the almond dust? Karlhammer is behind it?"

"Yes. And we don't have much time left," Hortat said with a degree of composure that made her angry.

"This is a disaster! He's in bed with the Dark Tongue!"

"They think they're doing the *right* thing. The *good* thing."

"But they aren't!"

"I don't think so," he agreed.

"You don't *think* so?" she questioned indignantly.

"They are right about one thing. We are at a crossroads, dancing on the edge of a blade. However, something good cannot build its foundation on something evil, so we must stop it."

"But that fireworks show. It will take place tonight when you win."

"I know. We need to act quickly, and for that, I have to

reveal a few things to you that I would have preferred to keep secret. Even from you."

Agatha swallowed.

"I have a descendant," he said, making a reassuring gesture when she recoiled.

"What?"

"A clone. I created it from my and Herxmin's heredity material."

"When you locked yourself up for a week in the summer because you were supposedly sick?" she suspected, thinking back to Herxmin. "I'm very sorry."

"Herxmin and I had no love affair." His eyes filled with tears. "However, in a certain way, I *valued* her, and maybe even *loved* her."

"But you were not allowed to show it, so that no one would suspect."

"Yes. The reproduction of my species follows stringent rules of genetic control, and there are good reasons for that, which I cannot go into now because we do not have much time. Herxmin will live on in our daughter, just as I will, even if my continuity is not maintained through her, as it was between me and Hortat, my father."

"But you can still produce a descendant?"

Hortat looked at her and smiled. The sad expression in his eyes remained and unsettled her. "Yes," he finally said. "In theory, I can still do that."

"In theory?" she inquired.

He ignored her question. "We have to proceed very quickly now, Agatha. The fireworks tonight must not take place. We must prevent that at all costs."

"I agree completely. But how?"

"I have a plan. But you will not like it."

"I don't even like how you *say* it."

"Do you trust me, Agatha?"

"More than anyone else. Otherwise I wouldn't be here. You know that."

"Yes." He nodded gratefully. "I will have to ask something of you that you will hate. Therefore, you have to trust me that you will only see the whole picture at the end, and it will exact great pain from you. Please trust me now."

## 17

---

## PANO

"Finally! Where were you?" Pano said into Mukoena's hand terminal.

"I had to move to another location. My house has as many bugs as an ox's ass," replied the former deputy director. "The damned director probably wants to make sure that I'm not pursuing the HCP matter. In addition, I have given you a code on the terminal that, with some bad luck, can be traced directly to me. And that's happened to me quite a lot, lately."

"I understand."

"So, do you have anything for me? Could you find out anything about that piece of shit?"

"Yes. She tried to shoot my partner."

Mukoena looked shocked. "Your partner?"

"Yes, a Builder named Ixlath, who was placed at my disposal by Luther Karlhammer to assist me. We had an appointment in a workshop in Doornfontein, and she somehow knew we were going to be there," Pano said, putting as much fury in his voice as he could. "I suspect that she has two federal police agents we were dealing with in her pocket. That's the only connection I can see."

"Did you shake off these agents?"

"Yes, at least for the moment."

"I'm glad you escaped again. What do you intend to do now?"

"My partner and I will revisit the address in Randfontein that you gave me. I'm sure I've overlooked something. The junkie there was overwrought and panicked about someone who fits Agatha's description. I think you were right that she was with him."

"Be careful. If what you say is true, then she will—"

"Don't worry. We'll wait until dawn, cut off all the network connections we have, and then set off," Pano assured him.

"And how do you think you'll do that? She has the best connections in all—"

"We'll keep that to ourselves," Pano cut in. "Sorry, Mr. Mukoena, but we cannot be too careful."

"I understand. Good luck. Call me if you have a lead. I still have a lot of friends in the department and I can mobilize them now that I have given myself the necessary maneuvering space."

"I'll do that." Pano disconnected and looked at Ixlath, who was sitting next to him in the back seat of their SUV.

"And? Did he swallow it?" the Builder wanted to know.

"Oh, yes. If he hasn't realized that we've smelled a rat, then he was the worst police officer in history."

"Good. Let us just hope that our theory is correct."

"He's cooperating with her," Pano was sure. "There is no other explanation."

"This would have far-reaching consequences."

"For example?"

The Builder carefully rubbed his mighty chin and pushed his lower lip back and forth in a bizarre way. "Agatha Devenworth was known everywhere as Hortat's right hand. She took care of everything for him and kept herself out of the public eye as best she could, but that only increased the media interest. For many, she was the darling behind the big man, the human factor, a sign that you too can get to the top, on equal footing with one of us. I don't think many of Big H's followers believe the narrative that she was behind the attack."

Ixlath pressed a finger against the window screen—an unnecessary gesture, since half the city was now on fire, violence escalating in every quarter. "Those protests out there are not just the result of frustration over Hortat's death. People are grieving for him, of course, but they are above all angry at the official accusations against Agatha Devenworth."

"They have to be," Pano muttered, nodding understandingly.

"Yes. Otherwise, their entire narrative of hope would collapse. If she was an establishment agent the whole time, conspiring to end Hortat's rise with a huge bang at the last moment, then the attack was also aimed at the hopes of billions of people who were counting on a better future. The ultimate betrayal, the knife in the back from one's own family, and the end of the dream. Worse still, it would be a sign that they have all been deceived."

"What do you think?"

"I'm convinced we will only learn the truth from her, and we must neither rashly condemn her nor acquit her of any guilt. There's more to this whole matter than black or white. I feel that," Ixlath answered thoughtfully, and Pano nodded again, satisfied with his partner's analysis.

"You're a good guy. I don't know how Luther managed to get you involved in his games."

"He is the best advocate of your species that I have found so far."

"Oh, really? And why? He's quite power-hungry and convinced of himself."

"No, he is convinced of his cause."

Pano waved in dismissal. "One and the same."

"It's not the same thing. He has the best in mind for you humans, and is an important filter for the technology transfer between Builders and people. Luther Karlhammer was already working for the future of the planet when our mere existence was still a mystery in the shadows."

"His ego would like to hear that now."

"I think you misunderstand him," Ixlath said. "Does he do things that are unpopular? Definitely. Does he do it publicly? No. He knows that it takes uncomfortable decisions for the greater good of all, but he must not reveal them to people. You human beings are quick to judge, but very slow to adopt a new perspective. Luther understands this."

"Do you have an autograph book?"

The Builder suddenly changed the subject. "Do you think we have a good plan?"

"No, but it's the best plan we have to react quickly. Mukoena will have been in contact with her for a long time. The fact that we activated his hand terminal will make him think that we are not working with the police, and that you haven't discovered the transmitter will cause him to think. I guess he thinks I don't trust you and will therefore keep the terminal secret from you. It's no great secret that I'm not a fan of the Human Foundation. "Nevertheless, we'll go immediately, instead of waiting, so he'll think that either I'm nervous or you're urging me on. That will also pressure

Agatha into making a quick decision without allowing her time to think. She's pretty clever."

"I've heard that," Ixlath said.

They raced along the east-west city highway. Their priority code gave them access to the fast lane going west, where the storm wall formed a pitch-black line under the midnight blue of the horizon, which seemed no brighter, maybe even a little darker. The city's lights flooded over them like a liquid mixture of anger, fear, and despair, the ingredients that had turned Johannesburg into a bubbling cauldron. They had only a few hours left until sunrise, and with it, the end of the countdown.

Now that they had come out from under the edge of the pyramid, Pano could see that the sky was starry, and they would probably even see the sun if it made it over the walls before the clouds came in from the sea. He felt nervousness rise in himself and, lost in thought, rubbed his chest as an unpleasant pressure built up within it. He had not seen Agatha for so long and had been wondering for years about what he would do and say when it was time. Now the time might come under very different circumstances than any fantasy could have led him to believe.

"Are you all right? Is it your asthma?" Ixlath asked, and the honest concern in his voice moved Pano more than he would have thought. It was easy to instinctively see this big creature with his aura of absolute superiority as a father figure and feel comfortable in his presence.

"No, it's okay. I'm just a little nervous."

"I think it's courageous of you to deny yourself the use of implants—except for your transducer and the commlink, of course."

"Hey, you wouldn't have let me go if I'd told you, would you?" he protested.

"Probably not."

"And it went well."

"Luckily. How does it feel with an unmodified body among all the rejuvenated and improved?"

Pano looked for ridicule in the Builder's face but found only curiosity. "I'm rejuvenated. One of my last attempts to adjust myself so as not to lose Agatha."

He shook his head. "Not my proudest moment. It's hard. I haven't done the second treatment and I'm paying the price. I look a little younger, but my chromosome ends wear out quite quickly. Hence asthma, foot fungus, problems falling asleep, and my right knee is starting to complain. Almost like a real sixty-two-year-old, you might think. A teenager like you wouldn't understand that."

To Pano's surprise—and then irritation—Ixlath laughed, a sound that sounded like a subwoofer out of control and giving thus off an intermittent hum.

"Stop that!"

"What?" the Builder chuckled.

"I've never heard any of you laugh."

"There is always a first time." Ixlath smiled, and Pano could no longer resist the rare moment of serenity. A smile stole fleetingly onto his features but soon passed again, as if the sun had just shone through a tiny hole in the cloud cover to show that it was still there.

They remained quiet for the rest of the trip, occupied with their thoughts. They raced along the empty city highway, high above the rooftops of the surrounding neighborhoods still waiting for the progress and construction boom of the Builder era that had already turned the city into a sci-fi version of Manhattan. Pano imagined these former suburbs of Johannesburg, which had over time become the city center, as a kind of queue to the future rendered in concrete and stone.

Randfontein did not have its own exit. The highway was high enough to cross the storm wall toward Cape Town, ignoring one of Johannesburg's last remaining slums as though it did not exist if you just took the trouble to overlook it. So, their car steered to the exit for Kagiso, a former township of Krugersdorp, which was now barely recognizable as such. There were as many illuminated construction cranes towering in the sky here just as there were in all other parts of the city that were slowly but surely making progress.

"The streets here are just as empty as in Randfontein," he remarked casually.

"It's only half-past five in the morning. Ordinary people are still sleeping."

"Sure." Pano turned demonstratively and looked through the back window toward the city center, flickering in hellish orange as if it were on fire. "I rather believe that half the city is on its feet to fight the police in the city."

"They hope that the pyramid will do something," Ixlath said, "because of the countdown."

"And what would that be?"

"I don't know," admitted the Builder.

Although Pano found it difficult to decipher his facial expressions, he seemed depressed by that fact. "Nothing? No idea at all?"

"No. I have said that from the beginning."

"I thought that was something that only applied to humans. Secrecy and so on."

"No," Ixlath replied earnestly. "That building raises many questions. It was apparently built while the no-fly zone existed—the danger posed by the Dark Tongue sufficed as a pretext, of course. The technology to hide it from all eyes is not particularly difficult to produce. It even explains several mysterious drone crashes in recent years. After all, invisible does not mean 'not there.' But the resources for this must have come from somewhere."

"Hortat's companies?"

"Possibly. But there is the question of those who built it. We know that, of the over four thousand of us registered in South Africa, only a fraction of us hold official positions or have normal jobs. The rest are virtually invisible. With such a small number, no wonder. Nevertheless, I wonder if they have been busy building on it and whether they are still inside."

"Are you angry because they used your technology without you knowing about it?"

"It's not an especially advanced technology or anything like that." Ixlath waved dismissively.

"That is a huge floating pyramid!"

"I think you still don't realize how far our lead over you is and what opportunities we have. We do not brag about it or show it off, so as not to scare you. But the very fact that I can breathe normally here and now, despite the low oxygen content in your atmosphere, is the result of a gene adjustment that Xinth made to our embryos—one that required mere moments. The fact that Hortat has gathered so many of us around him without me knowing about it is much worse than the use of technology to build this thing. It represents a break with our standing policy."

"It sounds like it's a terrible idea," Pano said.

"Perhaps." Ixlath sounded as if he did not want to go deeper into the subject, so Pano left him alone. Besides, they were already driving down the road toward the wall, and the junkie's shack at its end—or what remained of it. When they got there, he grabbed his partner by his forearm and gave him a serious look.

"Are you sure this is a good plan?"

"The best one that has occurred to me. Remember—the countdown ends in just under three hours. At least she can't use her sniper rifle here." Ixlath paused, reached into his jacket, pulled out a pistol of human fabrication. He offered Pano the grip. "Here."

"But—"

"Consider it a vote of confidence. Besides, we will not need it if all goes well."

"I hope you're right. I'm not looking forward to this." Pano made sure the gun was loaded and put it in his belt.

"We can trust bad guys to do bad things."

"That's what I mean."

They got out together. Pano stepped over a length of broken power pole and toward the ruins they had left behind on their last visit. They had not even reached the door when they heard a rustling all around them and the sound of guns being loaded.

"Shit!" Pano hissed, raising both hands as figures in black suits and full-visor helmets emerged from the alleys and other concealment and trained submachine guns on them. Their entire equipment array was burnished and fused with the darkness that was more welcome than light in Randfontein. "That happened even faster than I feared."

"At least we know that your theory about Mukoena is right," Ixlath muttered, raising his hands as well.

Soon they were surrounded by gunmen, and two armored cars with tinted windows rushed forward on squealing tires. From the rear vehicle, toward which the pointed rifle barrels were herding them, emerged first Mukoena and then Agatha. She looked older than the camera images, with deep creases on her forehead that counteracted her youthful appearance. Her hair seemed a little brittle, no longer shining as it had after her rejuvenation way back when. There were dense shadows under her eyes, and her gaze was as stormy as an ocean.

When she saw Pano, her mouth twitched slightly but hardened as soon as she saw Ixlath. Her eyes narrowed to slits, and she looked as if she wanted to kill him on the spot. "The code!" she said to the Builder. "Give us the code."

"You cannot destroy the orbital," Ixlath answered calmly.

"*Code?* What *code?*" asked Pano, confused, looking back and forth between the two. He lowered his arms and was reminded to lift them again by a sharp blow to the back.

"That's not what we want. Give it to us, or I swear I will take you down."

"The way you took down Hortat?" asked Ixlath.

Agatha's jaws began to grind, and her right hand twitched. Eventually she pulled her pistol so fast that Pano registered the movement only as a blur. Before she could fire a shot, however, the Builder had reacted with equal speed. One of his hands shot forward, opened, and was suddenly clothed in a kind of metallic glove. He clenched it into a fist, and as if by magic, all the weapons around them flew toward him, crashing against his metal fingers, and gathering around them as though they were magnets. When he opened his hand again, the firearms fell to the ground like scrap metal.

Some police officers held their broken hands screaming, while others pulled batons and rushed at the Builder, who had turned into an unstoppable fighting machine. If Pano had previously believed that his partner was a kind of superhuman, superior in all respects, but still a being of flesh and blood, his eyes were opened to another reality. The bronze giant was not an adult among children, but a creature of such great power that everything occurred like a mystical miracle of brute force before his eyes.

Ixlath struck mechanically and calculatedly, each blow smashing larynxes, knees, and even helmets, which splintered under the force and left only bloody masses. When two of the police officers stormed in from the right and left, he grabbed them and smashed them against each other before grabbing Mukoena, who, with sheer horror in his eyes, was reflexively reaching toward his now-empty holster when Ixlath ripped him in half.

Even before his blood and intestines splashed onto the ground, Pano fell to his knees and vomited, wheezing. His stomach felt as if it had been pushed inside out. When he looked up again, the fight was already over, and the Builder held Agatha's neck in one hand and gripped it like a screwclamp around a toothpick.

"DON'T!" cried Pano, looking up in horror at his ex-wife, whose eyes were already bulging. She did not struggle and she did not resist, knowing full well that she had no chance. Judging by the surprise in her gaze, she, too, did not know who or what she was dealing with.

"She killed Hortat," Ixlath growled.

"You..." she croaked, but the rest of the sentence was just a disjointed rattle.

"Let her go! Please!" pleaded Pano. "We've got her. You are not a murderer!" He looked at the many corpses lying around him and swallowed. "At least not one like those guys, anyway."

To his relief, the Builder loosened his grip and set Agatha onto the filthy tarmac.

"What is the countdown for? What happens when it ends?" Pano asked.

Agatha looked at him, their eyes met, and she seemed to scrutinize him just as she had done so many times before. What he had always feared—that piercing gaze in her eyes —he now bore calmly, allowed her to look for whatever she wanted to find. She was no longer the Agatha who had left him behind, and yet she was just the same.

"Don't look at him! He is the only one of you two who still knows that he is fighting for good!" Ixlath's bass roared through the night as he lifted her by the throat again. The passenger door of the front police car opened but immediately closed again when the Builder's gaze jerked in its direction. The occupants raced away.

When Ixlath turned back to Agatha, his grip had loosened again because she could be heard sucking in air. "I know that you would rather die than tell me anything. I could only assume so much of someone who not only murdered one of ours, but also tried to kill me. But you can't. I see it in your eyes."

Pano also saw it, too—the tormented expression in her gaze, surprised that his partner was also able to read it so well and relieved when he set her down again. Before letting her go, Ixlath stuck one of his paws into her jacket pocket, a move that at first looked like an indecent touch, but then he held up a vial of blue liquid in which something dark swam.

"How is this possible?" the Builder breathed with a mixture of surprise and horror. "This cannot be!"

"Oh yes," Agatha growled grimly, rubbing her reddened neck as she stared at her opponent with hate and then looked at Pano. "Do you know at all—"

"Take us to the entrance!" Ixlath cut her off. "Because that's what it's for, isn't it?"

# 18

## AGATHA

Agatha once again called up the election result in her retinal display and saw that Hortat Junior had secured 65.14 percent of the vote. There had never been such a clear result in South Africa's history, even accounting for the other states merged into the Special Administrative Zone. It put a smile on her lips, but it was a sad smile. She looked down at the old wristwatch Pano had given her for their second wedding anniversary and saw Steve at the other end of the long hallway at Crown Plaza, patting his left wrist with his right index finger.

Agatha nodded and opened the door to the men's lavatory without knocking. She knew that he would have been finished long ago, but still leaned into the small gap and saw Hortat standing by the sink for Builders, making the others look like ones designed for children.

"Sir?" she said. He turned his face to her. He seemed relaxed. "It's time."

"I know." A deep sigh rumbled the length of his throat, like distant thunder. He looked in the mirror one last time and then detached himself from the sink, which he had been leaning over like a speaker over his lectern. "Do you know what this mirror means?"

"That you are in love with yourself?" she asked mockingly, at the same time putting all the affection she felt for him into her voice. She constantly thought of his words during the drive here. *You have to be professional today, Agatha. Act as if everything is normal, behave toward me as they all expect from a personal assistant, even if we are alone. In the end, everything will be all right. I promise.*

"It means, we have already accomplished more up front than what we've accomplished in this election."

Agatha shook her head. "Don't downplay your victory, Hortat. It's not just the members of the media who have realized that this is a historic day. People are celebrating in the streets, not just in Johannesburg and in the SASAZ. You have accomplished this."

"No, it is those who have left their homes today to make their voices heard. They have done it."

"I don't know anyone who is as devious, and at the same time, as naïve and altruistic as you are."

"Is that why you take your job so seriously?" he asked, smiling and beginning to wash his hands.

She dodged his question. "I know that look on your face. You're seeing him again. Am I right?"

"He is *me*," he corrected her.

"No, you are much more *he*. But even that is not true."

"No, it isn't."

"You have all his memories, but also those of all your male genetic ancestors. So, you are as much *them* as you are *he*. Meaning, you are just yourself, with far too much knowledge."

Hortat laughed, a deep bass sound that made the mirrors vibrate. The brief moment of merriment quickly faded, however, when he realized how long ago he had last laughed so lightheartedly.

Agatha looked down at her old-fashioned wristwatch and shrugged her shoulders. "Not bad. That certainly lasted a good two seconds."

"I wish I had hired you because of your cynicism."

"That's precisely why you did it. That was your human side." She wished that this banter between them would transcend time and last forever.

"You will never stop reproaching me for that, right?"

"You are not human, Hortat. Nor are you *Hortat*, as far as that goes."

"Why do you think we Builders choose our own names?" he replied, placing one hand at a time in the hot air dryer, which hummed as loudly as a two-stroke engine, to Agatha's annoyance.

"Because you were not born a blank slate." She waved dismissively. "For someone who not only does not forget his own experiences, but also doesn't forget those of his ancestors, you have a rather porous memory. We've had this conversation a few times."

"I'm as much a human being as you are a Builder, Agatha. You carry some of our DNA in you, or have you forgotten?"

"We are your descendants. Nevertheless, I see great differences. I can hardly compare myself to a chimpanzee, even though we are based on the almost identical genetic code."

"You are too hard on your own kind," Hortat murmured.

Again, she shrugged. "No, I just know us pretty well. Better than you do. That's probably why you hired me."

"You said I shouldn't enter the race. And? Where are we now?"

"Not where I... Well, that's another matter. I said you should do it like Luther Karlhammer, not like John F. Kennedy. And, I still think so."

"It's probably too late for that now. My speech is set."

"Yes, it *is* too late for that." Again, she looked at her watch and raised an eyebrow in his direction as he slowly and emphatically slid his second hand back into the hot air dryer. "If you were a human being, I would believe that you were delaying putting off the inevitable."

"But I am not a human being, as you constantly remind me."

"No, you are what euphemists like to call humane, and that's why I'm here by your side—because humans like Karlhammer and Amorosa cannot properly manage the most important legacy our species has ever received." Agatha swallowed hard against a growing lump in her throat.

"It's not that simple," Hortat said softly.

"They reject you," Agatha replied with a bitter undertone in her voice. "That makes me, well, I just can't understand that. Above all, because—"

"I understand it."

Agatha merely snorted, and rolled her eyes.

"They don't reject me, they reject the fact that I chose his name and thus made it public that Hortat had smuggled his DNA into Xinth's ten thousand descendants. He was a cunning rogue in the service of good," he reminded her. "That final move made them nervous, and I can understand that. I know it was his last act, but they don't. Their intentions are good."

"The opposite of good is good-intentioned."

"Why are you working for me?"

She was surprised by the question, and sidestepped it by

tapping her index finger on her wristwatch, clearing her throat as if to prevent tears. "We have to go."

"Answer this question first. Why?"

"Because I believe we must not give control over humans to any human."

"That's not the reason. That cannot be the reason, and you know why. Not after what we have seen."

"Yes, it is."

Hortat tilted his head in a very human gesture and looked down at her as he stepped in front of her.

She looked up and held his gaze, but said nothing, enjoying their togetherness.

"You hope that I can awaken in your fellow humans that which *you* need them to see, so as not to lose faith in them, and thus, in what you have started." He paused deliberately, and laid a hand on her shoulder. "That is very human. It is also human to believe that one is completely alone with one's opinions and one's convictions, but that is not the case. You will see. And now, I think we *do* have to go."

Agatha nodded and cleared her throat before going out and gesturing down the hallway. "This way, Mr. President."

She went ahead and was chased by the clicking of her shoe heels as if the echo were a round of applause. Or a flurry of curses. Hortat walked silently behind her, the silence so overwhelming that she felt she could barely breathe.

Steve had already gone inside after he had seen them coming, presumably to introduce Hortat. She paused in front of the decorative double door with its indigenous wooden carvings and inspected her boss one last time from top to bottom. When she pointed at his forehead, he smiled, even before she said, "There's a wrinkle." She straightened his shirt sleeves so they sat perfectly and peeked out exactly two centimeters below the ends of his jacket sleeves.

"It will be all right," he assured her.

*Let's just remain standing here,* she thought, but nodded and knocked on the doors, which then swung open to both sides. Immediately, the clattering of cameras began, and a hurricane of shouts and questions slammed into them. Hortat stopped, as always the most powerful magnet in the whole hall, although he radiated the most incredible calm and displayed nothing sensational in his presence. He waved and smiled, then headed toward the podium on the other side of the room, where a single lectern was set up.

She remained by Marcus and Thor, his two bodyguards, who were the only ones of his security entourage left at the door, while her boss walked down a cleared path surrounded by a cordon of powerful bodyguards, shaking hands and signing autographs. The two nodded earnestly to her, which she returned before diving into the crowd and heading toward Hlarch. The Builder was harder to find than she expected because he had presumably gone down to his knees among all the human spectators to match their size. Not only would he have blocked the view of others, but he would also have been too noticeable in the pro-Builder flush of victory reigning in the hall.

As the frenetic "Hortat! Hortat! Hortat!" calls slowly ebbed and he began his speech, she finally spied a pale bronze shimmer and stepped toward Hlarch. All eyes were drawn to Hortat as if spellbound. That was good, and at the same time, it hurt her not to be able to live this historic moment as she should.

"Congratulations on the victory," Hlarch whispered as she arrived next to him and apologized to a woman she'd bumped against. The woman did not seem to have noticed.

"If it is one," Agatha quietly responded, and he nodded earnestly.

"It will be. Have faith."

"I didn't know you knew him."

"We all know each other. At least those of us here in Johannesburg."

"Why?" she inquired, and took her handbag off her shoulder to place it between them and right next to the other—identical looking—bag.

"We work together. For him, one might say," he explained. It wasn't easy to understand his whispering because of his deep voice. "What are you working on?"

"You'll see. This very night. It is too soon, but it will have to be enough, I think."

"Can you tell me why?"

"No. He asked me not to. For your protection," she said.

"That sounds like him." Hlarch smiled sadly. "Go now. You will understand everything when the time comes. Hortat makes no mistakes."

Agatha nodded and picked up the other handbag while the Builder made hers disappear into his jacket. In his hand, it looked like a wallet. Then he headed toward the hallway and the lavatories, and she listened to the rest of the speech before heading toward the podium, the handbag over her shoulder. It felt heavy, as though filled with lead.

He had managed, under thunderous applause, to return to the cocoon of his bodyguards, waving as he went. When he saw Agatha, he told them to let her through, and she wriggled like a tadpole to get into the secured space.

"John F. Kennedy. Not bad," she said at his side, nodding appreciatively and slightly mockingly, because it felt like everything was the same as always.

"He was an inspiring personality, even for me. You co-wrote the speech."

"Because you didn't want to be dissuaded from it. JFK was controversial as president. The cult around him only arose after his assassination."

Hortat smiled but did not answer.

"You spoke of the future," she said, abruptly changing the subject after he shook some hands that had made it through the security cocoon of broad backs. "It can't ever become perfect."

"You don't think it's an apt term for what we're going to do? We have won an absolute majority, so we will also be able to change the voting law. A good step toward a good future."

"The mills of politics grind slowly."

"Politics will not be the problem here, but technology, and this problem has been solved."

"Has it?"

"Yes. You'll see. Tomorrow the work begins."

"You are the winner of the election, but you are not yet sworn in. For me, it will begin, and I don't even know what it will look like. Or how I'm going to get through it."

"Reconciliation is best started immediately, and it takes paths that we often understand only in hindsight. If you can go down this path, it will reveal itself to you." He sought her gaze, and their eyes lingered on each other for a while before she took a deep breath and nodded.

When they reached the exit and stepped out into the cool night air of Johannesburg, the convoy of vehicles was already awaiting: a heavily armored limousine and four SUVs, with bodyguards standing at the open doors. The convoy was, in turn, surrounded by a police escort twice as large. The street had been cordoned off at his request, so there was no crowd to cheer him. They entered the back of the limousine together, and when one of the bodyguards had slammed the door, they were enveloped in silence.

"Did you bring what I asked you to?"

She hesitated briefly and then nodded, laid the handbag beside her, and grabbed the door handle. "I wish I could come with you."

"No." He shook his head and smiled calmly. "Your path is a different one."

"I am proud of you," Agatha said seriously. For a long time she had thought about what her words should be. These felt right.

Again, their eyes met for a long moment. His driver was already looking back at them impatiently. She noticed that it was not Sabo but one of the substitute drivers, the one who had driven him to a campaign event a few months ago. *A change of plan since last evening?*

Finally she opened the door and stepped out into the night. Without looking around, she climbed the stairs to the hotel. The lump in her throat was so big, so painful that she could barely breathe, but she presented the security guards at the door a perfect business smile, even though she wanted to scream to get rid of the weight on her chest. The urge to turn around was so strong that she felt as if she were torn between her discipline and her emotions.

She walked through the reception area to the left, into the hallway for campaign staff, and then through to the very back where the hotel's dirty laundry was usually picked up, and the fresh delivered. No one from the campaign team was in sight—they were all in the hall or on their way to the party in the Silver Tower.

As soon as she stumbled through the metal door into the back lot, she ripped open the top buttons of her blouse and, in the darkness between the dumpsters, she leaned against the cold masonry.

When a loud blast rolled like thunder, she breathed so loudly and violently that she could not even hear her own sobbing. She only noticed much later that she had collapsed when she came back to herself, trembling and whimpering between the garbage bags, and a mighty shadow appeared in front of her.

Hlarch, stone-faced, held a hand to her. "You have to get up now," he said, handing her a vial that looked almost the same as the tricopherone, except that the blue liquid clearly showed the outlines of a dark embryo.

"It's done, Agatha. Now you have to take the next step."

# 19

# PANO

"I came in response to a request for help," Pano grumbled.

"Oh, from your best friend, Karlhammer?" Agatha hissed. "What a great service to humanity. The last dinosaur reconciles with the one man whom he wants to blame for everything that goes badly."

"Not everything."

"Oh yes, I'm also on the list."

"You decided to completely rethink your life and just throw your values overboard."

"Me?" She snorted like a horse. "Just because I didn't want to watch from the sidelines while our countries die in the swamp of creeping autocratization?"

"The word doesn't even exist!"

"I don't care. Its impact certainly does. That's why you came here, right? You wanted to see what it feels like to be where the future shines brighter."

"No, I..." Pano swallowed the following words, watching her from the corners of his eyes as she sat next to him in the back seat. She was not restrained. Why bother? She, and Ixlath in the passenger seat, knew full well that even with a gun on her lap, she would have had no chance of overpowering the Builder. "I wanted to help Luther solve a crime."

"Congratulations! You've helped one of the most terrible criminals lead us into a dark future!" she said, glowering at him and miming applause.

"*He's* a terrible criminal? Says the one who blew up the elected president of the South African Special Administrative Zone!" he shot back.

"Do you even know who Ixlath is?"

"Yes, the one who saved my ass when your two female fighting machines tried to kill me at that junkie's place."

"What?" Agatha waved in dismissal. "What did you find, hmm? Were you sniffing after me?"

"Nothing. That's just it. What did you want with an insane almond dust addict in his shithole of a house?"

"To take some almond dust," she said laconically. "Does this fit into your picture of me?"

"No idea. I don't have one anymore, since when you decided to sell your soul."

"Are you going to start in on those implants again? I hope my worthy kidnapper terrorist holds his ears shut before blood begins running out of them."

"What is left of you?" asked Pano, his bitter undertone audible.

"At least not osteoarthritis. How does it feel always wanting to be absolutely right, hmm?" Agatha pointed to his arthritic knee. "Or is your 'oh so sacred world view' already creaking as much as your knee?"

"Not as much as your conscience."

"That's enough," the Builder rumbled from the front, turning just far enough to see them both in his peripheral vision before shaking his head.

They spent the rest of the journey in silence, racing

across the highway back toward the city center, where the glow of the still growing uprisings was reflected in the glass façades of the skyscrapers as if they were themselves on fire. The underside of the pyramid reflected nothing of it, as though it soaked up all the photons in its environment like a sponge, and gave none back.

They encountered the first roadblocks shortly after the exit to Melville, where an officer and three riotbots stopped them. Ixlath spoke to the officer through the window. They were not allowed to drive on but were at least permitted to proceed on foot. Pano did not know how much money had flowed, but judging by the following cars, which stopped at the roadblock and were rudely ordered to turn back, it must have been more than even the wealthier had. This suggested that the rules adopted for the night had been tightened and that there were few exceptions, even with the most corrupt police officers.

They walked on, staying close to the façades of the ever-higher-rising residential towers. They ducked into dark corners and narrow alleys when sirens and blue lights came too close, or riotbots and heavily armed police officers raced past them. Toward Marshalltown, the streets were no longer empty and were filling rapidly. At first, there were some marauding groups of protestors who engaged with isolated units of the police.

Downtown was jam-packed. Here, citizens of all stripes crowded into the canyons formed by high-rises, some holding banners with Hortat's image in black and white, others with banners displaying his most iconic quotes. Pano did not even want to imagine what this place looked like in Augmented City. Rising emoticons most likely flooded the night like a colorful rain flowing in the wrong direction.

Ixlath stayed behind them both—more precisely, behind

Agatha, following her and giving her a little push whenever she walked too slowly. The noise around them was deafening, and the crowd around them grew thicker.

"This is a trap, isn't it?" Pano whispered to the Builder as they passed on the leeward side of a parked minibus, which served to provide some relief from the noise.

"Of that much, I'm sure," Ixlath said thoughtfully. "But I think she has no choice. She has to be in a specific place when the countdown ends."

"But why?"

"I don't know, but I'm sure it's related to the pyramid."

"Aren't you worried?"

"No." Ixlath tilted his head to the side. "She is playing with things she doesn't understand, but I do. And I have a suspicion."

"It's about the vial that you took from her, right?"

"Yes."

"What is it?"

"A problem. But also, a chance to get rid of it."

"You couldn't be more cryptic," Pano muttered.

"You'll see. Just remain alert and *don't* take risks."

"He needs you alive," Agatha said from in front, without turning around. "It has to fit in with Luther's overall picture. A Builder and a man who will save the future of humanity."

"Isn't it what you and Hortat wanted?" he returned angrily. "Isn't that the reason you ran away?"

"I didn't *run away*, I ran *toward something!* There's a difference. You are the one who ran away."

"No, I was always there."

"Not moving is a way of running away."

They came out of the lee of the minibus and were again inundated with wild shouts and cries at full volume.

"Is that true?" he pitched the question toward his partner. "Karlhammer wants to use me for PR? That would be typical of him."

"He hired you to find Agatha, and you did," Ixlath said, continuing to glare at her. "He also believes that it helps both sides if you work together with us. I think we've set a good example of that, haven't we?"

"Sure," Pano nodded, "but I feel like I'm just along for the ride and wondering if I have any control at all."

"Now you know how I felt when you went to Mukoena without wanting to take me, or when you invaded HCP without telling me about the transducer defect."

"Touché."

Pano felt heavier with every step they took through the agitated crowd, as if he were gradually transforming into a figure cast from lead. Seeing Agatha had been a shock, a sense of disruption that had evaporated before he could fully feel it. Ixlath's outburst of violence, without which they would now presumably be sitting handcuffed in some basement, had turned everything upside down. Now it was disturbingly normal to be so close to her—their quarrels, her dark gaze when she looked at him, the many unspoken things that stood between them like an insurmountable wall of reproaches, injuries, and the small acts of disrespect that had congealed into solid concrete over the years.

Agatha led them resolutely through the crowd, which periodically broke out in loud shouts and cheering, while Ixlath simply walked through them as if he were something of a saint, simply because he was a Builder—another Hortat, a relative of the martyr, the bearer of hopes and symbol of a joint, shared future. Hands reached for him, trying to touch him. He smiled kindly but noncommittally and held Agatha's belt from behind so she could not slip away from him if the crowd grew too dense.

As if automatically, Pano stepped up next to Agatha to help force a path through the throng and make sure that the giant did not need to hurt anyone on their way to the city center. Their journey eventually led them close to Crown Plaza, where demonstrators formed a solid barrier in front of a police cordon. Six riotbots on their powerful spider legs formed an almost-insurmountable wall of steel, ceramics, and weapons attachments that swung menacingly over people's heads. Another wall underneath consisted of fully equipped police officers crouched behind large transparent shields and brandishing shock wands.

The protesters shouted wild curses at them, including accusations like criminals, traitors, or murderers. Pano saw a single Builder among them, who repeatedly fired up the crowd with a megaphone and turned directly to the police officers.

"Don't oppose your own people! Do the right thing! Muyabe is a despot! Freedom for Johannesburg! Free South Africa! You are one of us!" the Builder's powerful voice roared down the street, on which, about 200 meters away, was the Crown Plaza Hotel and the wrecked remains of Hortat's convoy.

"YOU ARE ONE OF US!" chanted the demonstrators. Their numbers in the city center must have grown to a million or more, Pano finally realized. It had taken almost three-quarters of an hour to get here, but they'd only managed to make any progress at all because the crowd made space for Ixlath.

Agatha wanted to direct them further to the left, but the Builder yelled, "No. We're going to him!"

Reluctantly, she let herself be pushed in the direction of the bronze figure, who rose from the sea of heads, until they were right behind him. At that moment, something happened among the police. The riotbots lowered their weapons and scrambled aside in their typically lurching yet swift manner, and took up position in front of the shop windows of the barricaded skyscrapers. The police officers also threw away their shields and gave way to the roaring cheers of the demonstrators who surged forward, celebrated the police officers, and flooded the cordoned-off street and the scene of Hortat's assassination.

Amid this raging river of energized bodies, Ixlath and the other Builder stood out, the latter turning around and staring at his fellow Builder with a mixture of surprise and contempt. He was thinner and a little smaller than the few other Builders Pano had met in his life, and without ever seeing him, he knew that it had to be the one Agatha had met in the large hall of Crown Plaza to exchange handbags.

"Ixlath," roared the slightly smaller Builder, unflinching despite being shoved by several of the demonstrators as they screamed frenetically and ran past them.

"Hello, Hlarch. I should have known it was you."

"You two know each other?" Pano asked, but was ignored.

"You will not triumph. It's over."

"It is over only when it is over." Ixlath pointed upward.

"Your feet will not tread the interior."

"Hlarch, we have to open it," Agatha interjected. Her voice sounded tormented, as if the realization were causing her physical pain. "We have no choice."

"You *always* have a choice."

"No! He wanted this. He will have known," she insisted.

Hlarch stared at Ixlath, a flurry of throaty words departing his lips, sounding both harsh and melodic, in what had to be a Builder language Pano had never heard before. A brief battle of words ensued, then they stared menacingly at each other, and he feared that they might erupt in violence as unrestrained as what he had seen in Randfontein. Pano worried about the many people around them, but eventually, Hlarch nodded reluctantly.

"We must trust him," said Agatha, putting a hand on his forearm as if to appease him.

"Let's go. The countdown is almost over," Ixlath urged them, pointing forward. One last look, then Agatha and Hlarch nodded and proceeded along with the crowd, whose wild shouts began to choke the street with their echo. They only made it to Hortat's burned-out vehicle because a cluster of people had automatically formed around the two Builders, whom they wildly celebrated.

Hlarch seemed uncomfortable. He was trying to present a kindly appearance to the crowd, while obviously occupied by an inner struggle against his worries and fears—an expression that Pano had never seen before on a Builder.

Ixlath, on the other hand, seemed to have no eyes for his surroundings and kept looking up to the pyramid. Then he climbed onto the wrecked skeleton of the limousine, which lay like a table of black steel amid ash and debris, a dark island in the sea of demonstrators.

"Come," he said, a hand outstretched to help Pano make his way over the sharp-edged remnant of the driver's door to join him on top.

"I don't understand," he responded, bewildered. "What are we doing here? What is it?"

"We are giving your kind the future it needs to survive." Ixlath pointed upward before his gaze darkened. "No!" His voice rolled over them like thunderbolts as Agatha and Hlarch set out to climb onto the wreckage as well.

"You can kill us if you want to stop us," Agatha hissed. "What will all the people here be thinking when you tell them afterward why you, and your *dog* here," Pano flinched, "and your boss did what you did. How credible do you think you'll be then?"

Ixlath hesitated, finally lowering the hand with which he had intended to hold them away. "You can't stop it anyway."

"An orbital fireworks display to celebrate the day? Because Hortat's death gift has finally opened?" Agatha retorted.

"It must be so," said the Builder, pulling the blue vial out of his jacket pocket. It almost disappeared into his hand, but Pano caught a glimpse of the black shadow within, in the shape of an embryo.

"You underestimate us humans!" Agatha cried desperately.

"And Hortat overestimated you."

*He's probably right,* Pano thought, freezing when he was bathed in a sudden and intense, bluish cone of light. An area three meters in diameter, the wrecked car at its center, was illuminated as bright as day. *The countdown has expired! The embryo must offer some sort of DNA access! But... how?*

The crowds around them first roared a long "Oooh," then the first "Hortat!" calls began and grew until they all ecstatically chanted the name of their Messiah, their martyr.

"HORTAT! HORTAT! HORTAT!"

Pano tilted his head back onto his neck, stared upward like a rabbit mesmerized by a snake, and saw that the source of the cone of light was sharply bordered at the exact center of the pyramid. Although he was so dazzled that he could not make it out, his inner eye saw the circular opening there, several kilometers high, from which the light pointed down at them in a focused beam.

Then, all at once, the whole world became lighter. Pano first felt it in his feet, where there was less pressure, then in his tingling fingers and itchy scalp, which felt as if thousands of ants were crawling over them. Eventually, he was raised from the vehicle, suddenly weightless, as if he were in a vacuum. A queasy feeling arose in his stomach, and he floated upward just like Ixlath, Agatha, and Hlarch, away from the people around them, who gradually became only faces staring up at them in disbelief, first, and then rapture, while the 'HORTAT' calls swirled around them like leaves in a windstorm, which sounded—oddly—as if it was raging far away.

None of them spoke. On Agatha's face, Pano saw the same sense of wonder and reverence that he felt himself. Ixlath and Hlarch, on the other hand, seemed to be engaged in a struggle conducted with their gazes and about issues for which they did not need words—at least no spoken ones.

The crowd outside Crown Plaza became a mix of moving colors, then just one of many streets where demonstrators thronged. The many blue lights and fires in the city swirled into a confusing picture, as even cars reduced to tiny dots and the city spread like a carpet under them, presenting wildly diverse scenes and impressions. They simply floated in the light, free and lost at the same time, and Pano almost surrendered himself when the astonishment gradually made way for other thoughts, and he realized that there was nothing under his feet.

At close range, the pyramid's underside looked like a continuous surface of pure blackness, in which smaller joints were gradually recognizable, suggesting assembled plates. The formation seemed threatening and massive, so unimaginably large that he instinctively felt minuscule and insignificant. The hole above their heads corresponded to the diameter of the light cone and turned out to be a kind of open mouth, the edges of which were thickened like lips, looking soft and yet rough and mechanical. It swallowed them into impenetrable darkness, letting them float over the opening, but did not draw them further inward.

Ixlath reacted first and stepped to one side out of the beam of light onto a formless nothingness on which—somehow—he could stand. Hlarch followed suit, then Agatha, and then last, Pano.

Light came on, and from one instant to the next they found themselves in a room that could hardly be described as such. It was entirely and endlessly white. Armchairs, small and large, placed opposite each other grew out of the floor, emerging from formless masses right in front of their eyes, hundreds of meters—no, thousands, in every direction.

In immaculately ordered rows, they stretched away on several levels. Either they were hovering free of gravity, or there were transparent ceilings invisible to Pano that formed floors for the upper levels. At the center of the pyramid glowed a small sun, bright yet inviting, and provided comfortable warmth. It took several moments before he realized that thousands of Builders were floating to the forming armchairs.

"What is this?" he breathed reverently, overwhelmed by the majesty of what he saw.

"This is Hortat's gift to humans," Agatha said sadly and rapturously at the same time.

"And this here was the entry code," Ixlath added, looking down at the embryo in the vial. "A descendant who should not exist."

"Do not dare!" growled Hlarch.

"It cannot be allowed to survive. It does not comply with our laws!"

"We established our laws before we came to coexist with the new Lords of the Earth."

"What are you talking about?" Pano asked.

"You don't know." Agatha looked at him as if she saw him for the first time. "You didn't see it!"

"See what?"

"Ixlath's and Luther's Plan! You were in Randfontein! Didn't you find the almond dust?"

Now Ixlath also looked at him, and his large, almond eyes narrowed.

"I don't take drugs," Pano dodged.

"Did you find anything?" the Builder insisted, suddenly no longer sounding like his good-natured partner.

"Are you now afraid that he has proof of your crime, evidence that you didn't know about? He's good at keeping things to himself," Agatha said.

"Speak, Pano!" Ixlath demanded.

"What are you going to do?"

"We will now liberate you from those humans who think only of themselves, the uneducated, reactionary, xenophobic, backward-looking people led by their hatred and emotions, of those who have elected and would re-elect governments like yours in Europe, even though by doing so, they surrender themselves to the servitude of autocracy. Of those who do not want a future, but only long for the past."

"What? I don't understand a word!"

"The almond dust, Pano," Agatha explained, sounding almost pitying. "It's the almond dust. They have made it the drug of the poor, lured by the fantastic experiences of Builders, driven to madness, only to get rid of them all in one night and create a new world order!"

"In which Builders and humans walk together into the future," Ixlath added. "Without destroying, annihilating yourselves. But we are not holding a discussion here."

The Builder pulled out a small device, and Agatha recoiled and grasped her ears. She was in obvious pain.

"What are you doing?" Pano asked, horrified.

"I am blocking her implants." Ixlath placed the device on the floor, and a hologram of Luther Karlhammer appeared among them.

"Are we ready?" the South African asked earnestly.

"Yes."

Pano's right hand slipped into his jacket pocket.

"Good. Everything is ready. Today we free the world from those who would prevent it from rotating on its axis. I know that we are making a difficult decision that we will have to live with. But it's the right one."

"I know. How long do you need to prepare?"

"The fireworks will take place in fifteen minutes. The launch tubes are currently loading."

Thoughts raced through Pano's head.

"Do you have the embryo?" Karlhammer asked.

"Yes. It must not survive."

"I know. It is a shame, but it must be so. We are at a crossroads, and there must be only one direction else we'll divide ourselves in two."

The hologram disappeared, and Pano pulled his hand out of his pocket again. In it, he held the gray beads of almond dust he had recovered from the dealer's wall hideout in Randfontein. He held them out to Ixlath.

"This is a kind of evidence, isn't it?" he asked. "It sounds like you had to make a difficult decision, and I've heard enough."

"You must not!" Agatha shouted, horrified. "Have you gone mad?"

Ixlath nodded gratefully, took the almond dust, and hid it in his jacket.

"That's the right decision," he said, nodding to him before lifting the vial. He apparently meant to toss it through the opening in front of them when Hlarch rushed forward and grabbed the Builder's arm. The fight quickly ended when Ixlath broke Hlarch's hand and gave him a push that sent him plunging through the opening into the depths. Agatha screamed desperately, but he was lost.

"It's over," the Builder said earnestly.

The sight of his ex-wife struck Pano so profoundly that his breathing began to race. He had never seen her so crushed, let alone so helpless. Agatha Devenworth always found a path and walked it relentlessly to the end—and when she reached it, she found a new one until it complied with her views and beliefs as to what something had to be.

He pulled out his inhaler, turned it, and then looked at Ixlath. "That's it." Then he pressed the button with his thumb and saw the surprised look on the Builder, who had been looking intently at the atomizer. Realization bloomed the moment the almond dust in his jacket reacted with the atomized aerosol reactant and exploded.

The explosion was not particularly powerful, but it tore a flesh wound on Ixlath's flank, and he was thrown off balance—perhaps more from disbelief and surprise. Pano took advantage of this one moment of advantage and exchanged glances with Agatha, who reacted quickly. In unison they kicked the hollows of the giant's knees, and Ixlath tipped forward and crashed through the hole.

To Pano's horror, Agatha sprang after him and grabbed the vial with Hortat's embryo. He dropped to grasp the shoulder of her jacket. He wanted to roar his relief when he got hold of it, but instead emitted a surprised groan when he tried to lift her incredibly heavy body, dangling high above the city like dead weight.

Then, out of nowhere, several bronze hands reached out and pulled Agatha back to safety.

"You..." She stared at Pano, and a storm of emotion seemed to fight for supremacy in her heart. It seemed like she wanted to hug him, and when she did not, he felt somewhat disappointed. But she put a hand on his cheek and smiled warmly, as she had not done for so long that he could barely remember it. "How?" she asked. "Since when?"

"Since you sent me the message. You thought I came here because of Luther?" He pulled the hand terminal out of his jacket. "It helps to be a dinosaur, by the way. I recorded his little conversation with Ixlath. Other signal frequency, I guess." He pressed a few buttons and sent the file to Myers and T'Sbu. "No fireworks today."

"I thought that—"

"—that I trusted Karlhammer? Or one of his minions?" Pano snorted. "No, you didn't think so. Otherwise you wouldn't have sent me that message. I would have thought that you'd rather die."

"Thank you," she said simply, and her words took him unexpectedly.

"Maybe..." He cleared his throat in embarrassment. "Maybe we can talk soon?"

"We will," she promised, turning with him to the Builders who had gathered around them. They all wore white one-pieces that, as was typical of Builder apparel, clung to their perfect physiques. The appearance was both supple and classic. "I've got it with me. Are you ready?"

"They can hear you. All of them," said one of them, and reverently received the vial with Hortat's and Herxmin's offspring.

"What's going on here?" asked Pano. His hands were still shaking from the adrenaline rush, and with his blood-splattered clothes, he felt like an unwelcome parasite in this pure, impressive environment that threatened to overwhelm his senses.

"You'll find out now. Together with Johannesburg and the rest of the world," Agatha assured him, and only now did he notice that she had taken his hand.

They turned to the hole. Beneath them, the city looked like a suppurating sore in contrast to the interior of the pyramid.

# EPILOGUE: AGATHA

"My fellow Earth People, because that is what we all are, because that is what unites us. When you hear these words, they will be my last, and it would bring relief to my heart if it were Agatha Devenworth who reads them to you.

"First of all, I would like to thank all my supporters for the faith and the confidence they have shown me. Even though I could not keep to what I promised, because my death prevented me, I want to make one thing clear. I chose to do this in order to pave a way forward. I took the name Hortat Junior, not only because my direct genetic ancestor was named Hortat, but because he did something that we all must do—he reconciled with his apparent enemy, Xinth, to ensure our survival. Differences are always only as strong as our unwillingness to compromise and be far-sighted. Today, Builders and humans stand for Hortat and Xinth, and we can all do what they did.

"I'm not going to make a big speech—that's what Hortat did before the UN at the end of the fossil crisis. I fear that my death could tear through society and cause precisely what I always wanted to prevent. So, I need to explain myself.

"There was a plan underway to kill all the almond dust addicts in the world during the celebration of my election victory, thereby achieving a kind of reboot of the political order. With only a few hours left to stop it, I chose the quickest and most radical way to prevent this, while at the same time revealing how this coup was to take place. I persuaded my personal assistant, Agatha Devenworth, against her express will, to carry out this plan by using the time afterward to act behind the scenes and stop the murderous events planned.

"If she is reading this, she has succeeded, and I am proud of her. Only she will be able to publish details of this, as this lies in a future without me. My entire estate passes to her, including my genetic descendant, who is in her possession in the form of an embryo. My will and testament is on its way at this moment to the three law firms that have represented me so far. When they hear or read this, they are asked to publish it on the net and make it accessible to everyone.

"You're probably wondering why a black pyramid is hovering above you. Let me explain. For years, I have been preparing something that I think is more important than any other technology transfer from us to you. Technical progress does not make us mature or wise. It can even be destructive and tear apart our way of life. To protect ourselves from this, we have developed genetic memory. With the memories of all our ancestors of each respective sex, we have gained the insights of hundreds of generations, and have thus also created a more far-sighted approach to the wonders of science, which has protected us from self-extinction and social decay.

"If you could remember everything your fathers and mothers have been through, you would look at life differently. We do not need to eliminate those who are cut off from education and wealth because they elect the wrong politicians. Their anger is short-sighted, yes, but for myopia —which is widespread, by the way—there are glasses. Our glasses are called genetic memory.

"The way to the future cannot involve amputating an injured leg and living with that forever. We are only as good as we deal with the weakest of us. Amputation is quick and easy, but it is not sustainable because the amputated leg will not regrow. Healing takes time and patience, but it offers the prospect of restored wholeness at the end of the process. The pyramid over Johannesburg was built over the years by my friends and contemporaries to pass on to you the gift of genetic memory.

"The appropriate treatment and conditioning of neurons requires about six months, and we can only treat five hundred thousand of you at one time, but we have created a beginning, one that the whole world can see. We have reserved the first places for the poorest citizens of South Africa, Europe, and North America. We will inform them this very night and will even pay for their travel. May the whole world watch what happens here and recognize my legacy for what it is—a new beginning, a healthy grassroots formation.

"Maybe you hate Builders... the alien... change. Maybe you're afraid, and you don't know how to put it into words. All this will change when you understand who—and what —came before you—when you see connections you haven't seen before. I want to ask the wealthy to exercise patience. All of this will be available to you as well. I have asked Agatha to commission more pyramids. Your suffering is no different from that of the less privileged, even if it does not seem as obvious.

"But you can actively participate in the change yourself by contributing your resources to accelerate change. Every death is the beginning of a new life, and so I hope that mine has just laid the foundation for a better way than the one we have taken so far. Do not give up hope."

Agatha stopped speaking, and ended the broadcast.

"That is…" Pano muttered after a few moments of silence, looking down at the city below them. It seemed to have become quieter down there, as if time were standing still.

"That's Hortat," she said and sniffled, deeply moved.

"You are his heir?"

"As it stands, yes. He didn't tell me, but I guessed it." A deep sigh escaped her throat.

"But that's… That includes countless companies and a fortune that—"

"I know. It won't be easy. I never wanted it, but he would have said that's why I'm the right person for it."

"Maybe you should set up a foundation to implement his will. The Hortat Foundation? Surely the abbreviation HF will soon be available," Pano replied, smiling tiredly. His mind did not know what to think about first, what to process first out of all that had happened. It was as if the world had shattered into its individual parts and then magically assembled again, all in a time far too short to comprehend everything.

"You would like that, wouldn't you?"

"Yes, somehow. And what are we going to do now?"

Agatha sat down at the edge of the hole and let her legs dangle through the opening. "I would say that we should go for a coffee and talk about your stubbornness, settle all our differences, rediscover our love and then ride together into the sunset, but..."

"Don't come back with wet toilet paper and diarrhea!" he protested with a chuckle.

"Don't worry. I'm afraid we're going to sit in front of a TV surrounded by lawyers and devour the news to see how the world is reacting while having to initiate legal actions and discussions with government authorities. There is also a president here who absolutely must resign. It's going to be quite stressful."

"And you are intolerable under stress."

"Thank you. Maybe you'll want to stick around a little bit to protect those around me from my worst tantrums?" she asked, turning her face in his direction. "It won't be easy, but at least we have some time."

"There are no flights at the moment," he said, and her smile was like balm on his soul—a fact he had not wanted to admit for a long time. Quietly, he asked, "Do you think that it'll all work out this time?"

"Yes," she whispered. "I think this time it will be really great."

# AFTERWORD

Since the end of the first two volumes of *The Fossil* duology, the question of how the integration of Builders into human society would actually work would not go away. The result is this standalone third installment, a slightly darker thriller that I really enjoyed writing and can be regarded as a supplement.

If you want to know what's next, you can already pre-order my next stand alone novel *The Wall: Eternal Night* on Amazon.

Visit www.joshuatcalvert.com to subscribe to my newsletter, to be informed of all upcoming releases!

Did you notice any errors or plot holes? Would you like to contact me with criticism or feedback—positive or negative? I am happy to answer every single e-mail! Please write to me at joshua@joshuatcalvert.com

*Yours sincerely, Joshua T. Calvert*

May 2021, La Palma

# CHARACTER INDEX

**Alberto (Angulo Camacho):** Treasure diver and engineer on the *Ocean's Bitch*.

**Alhy, Romain:** Captain of the *Ocean's Bitch*.

**Amorosa, Filio:** Member and sole survivor of the first Mars mission, *Mars One*, and crewmember on the *Ocean's Bitch*.

**Bateman, Jonathan:** Operator of the Human Foundation, stationed in the pyramid in Antarctica.

**Bergensen, Thomas:** Treasure diver aboard the *Ocean's Bitch*.

**Bordotta, Marcello:** Member of the *Mars Two* mission, xenobiologist.

**Brewster, Hannah:** Laboratory assistant in forensics at CTD.

**Brown, Barbara:** Wife of Bob Brown.

**Brown, Bob:** Republican U.S. Senator.

**Brown, Fred:** Captain of the security forces in the Antarctic pyramid.

**Burton, Audrey:** Member of the *Mars Two* mission, engineer.

**Chapati, Putram:** Member of the *Mars Two* mission, botanist.

**Cortez, Silvia:** Secretary of Homeland Security of the United States.

**Dalam, Workai:** legendary treasure diver, lost.

**Danatouth, Andrew:** U.S. Navy lieutenant, Navy SEAL member.

**Danes, Roger:** U.S. Senator, member of the Republican Party. A pronounced critic of the Human Foundation.

**Degeunes, Liza:** Secretary to Jenning Miller.

**Devenworth, Agatha:** Special agent at the Counter-Terrorist Directive (CTD), United States citizen.

**Dong Won, Jackie:** Pilot in the service of the Human Foundation.

**Dornwald, Mikwart:** "The man in the black suit."

**(The) Enemy:** Alien entity hypothesized by the Sons of Terra terrorist organization to be secretly pulling the strings of world affairs, and who has infiltrated national institutions worldwide.

**Engels, Jakob:** Hired bodyguard for Filio Amorosa.

**Gould, Peter:** Former CFO of the Human Foundation.

**Greulich, Alexander:** Chancellor of the Federal Republic of Germany.

**Greynert, Markus:** Major in the Security Forces of the Antarctic Brigade of the Human Foundation.

**Harris, Elisabeth:** President of the United States.

**Hofer, Pano:** Capitano in the Italian police, assigned to Europol. Comes from South Tyrol.

**Hortat:** Captain and Builder who became *The Enemy.*

**Hue Tao Xing:** Member of the *Mars Two* mission, medical doctor.

**Jackson, Ron:** Professor of Archaeology, Anthropology and Linguistics.

**Javier, Dr. Camarro:** Maintenance engineer on the *Mars One* mission. Presumed killed in the crash of 2040.

**Johnson, Betty:** Secretary to Jenning Miller.

**Jones, Hugh:** Director of SETEF (Space Exploration Training and Evaluation Facility) in Nevada.

**Kalashnikov, Tatyana:** Member of the *Mars Two* mission, chemist.

**Karlhammer, Luther:** South African engineer, inventor and technocrat, head of the Human Foundation.

**Knowles, Timothy:** Pilot of the *Mars One* mission. Presumed killed in the *Mars One* disaster of 2040.

**Longchamps, Michel:** Commander of the *Mars Two* mission.

**Marcello (Bonimba):** Receptionist at Cape House Green Hostel in Cape Town.

**Marks, Heinrich:** Geophysicist on the first Mars mission, *Mars One*. Presumed killed in the crash of 2040.

**Matthews, Sasha:** CTD agent.

**Meinhard, Geronnimus, Dr.:** senior physician in the Antarctic pyramid.

**Miller, Jenning:** Director of the Counter-Terrorist Directive (CTD).

**Mombatu, Mitchu:** Secretary-General of the United Nations.

**Moosbech, Petr:** Agent of the South African intelligence service.

**Morhaine, Cassidy, Dr.:** Test leader of Level T in the Antarctic pyramid, and co-pilot of the transport module. Physicist and chemist.

**Morris, Laura:** Assistant to Hugh Jones, Director of SETEF.

**Nikitu, Mayuka:** Japanese envoy to the United Nations.

**Patchuvi, Mitra:** Indian archaeologist and professor at the University of Delhi.

**Phelps, Montgomery:** President of the United States of America.

**Pickert, Dana:** Student at the Maximilian University of Munich.

**Richter, Nicole:** Former member of *Mars Two*, removed from the mission.

**Rietenbach, Manfred:** Director-General of ESA (the European Space Agency).

**Ross, James:** Doctor of Archaeology, assistant to Prof. Patchuvi.

**Sarandon, Jane:** Treasure diver and first officer on the *Ocean's Bitch.*

**Shapiro, Warren:** Deputy director of the CTD (Counter-Terrorist Directive).

**Shoke, Solly:** Former receptionist at Cape House Green Hostel in Cape Town.

**Spärling, Regina:** Secretary to ESA Director-General Manfred Rietenbach.

**Strickland, Ellen, Dr.:** Head of Research of the *Mars One* mission, presumed killed in the crash of 2040.**Sue Tse:** Lieutenant in the Security Forces of the Antarctic Brigade of the Human Foundation.

**Tombatu, Aluwi:** Agent of the South African Secret Service.

**Treuwald, Markus:** Employee of the mercenary company B12.

**Vlachenko, Dimitry:** "Dima," Commander of the *Mars One* mission, *Mars One*, presumed killed in the crash of 2040.

**Wayan, Cho:** Assistant to Luther Karlhammer.

**Wittman, James:** Member of the *Mars Two* mission, geophysicist.

**Xinth:** Builder.

# GLOSSARY

**Accelerator mass spectrometry:** Age determination of fossils and archaeological finds using a particle accelerator.

**Adrenaline:** Hormone released in response to stress, responsible for "fight or flight" response, a.k.a. epinephrine.

**Analgesic:** Painkiller.

**Andesite:** A volcanic rock

**Antarctic Treaty:** An international agreement that stipulates that uninhabited Antarctica between 60- and 90-degrees south latitude is reserved exclusively for peaceful use, especially for scientific research.

**AR glasses:** Augmented Reality Glasses.

**AR harness:** Exoskeleton that, in combination with Augmented Reality, can be used to perform work on an object remotely through a robot receiving the signals from the harness.

**B12:** Mercenary company with headquarters in Unterhaching, Germany.

**Basalt:** Form of igneous volcanic rock.

**BCD:** Buoyancy Control Device. Wearable buoyancy

compensator, i.e. a vest that a diver can inflate or deflate with buoyant gas at the touch of a button.

**Bio Suit:** see MMSS.

**Black Aces:** Elite brigades of the mercenary group B12.

**BND:** Bundesnachrichtendienst, Federal Intelligence Service. German foreign intelligence service.

**Breathing Earth One:** System of algae "carpets" constructed by the Human Foundation and located in the Pacific Ocean to filter $CO_2$ out of the atmosphere and convert it into oxygen.

**Breathing Earth Two:** System of algae "carpets" constructed by the Human Foundation and located in the Atlantic Ocean to filter $CO_2$ out of the atmosphere and convert it into oxygen.

**C-2 Moonhopper:** Business helicopter of Northrop Grumman's deluxe line.

**C-220 Albatross:** Military turboprop transport aircraft designed for heavy cargo or moving large troop contingents.

**Cape House Green:** Hostel in Cape Town, South Africa.

**Chin-Feng Battery:** Chinese air defense missile battery.

**Clean Ocean Project:** Human Foundation project designed to remove plastic waste from the oceans.

**Cleaning robots:** Robot that independently performs cleaning work indoors and outdoors.

**Cortisol:** Hormone released in response to anxiety/stress, affects blood pressure, metabolism, and other body functions. Sustained high levels are harmful.

**C-reactive Protein:** Inflammatory blood factor; high levels indicate inflammation from infection, injury, or some types of health conditions.

**CTD:** Counter-Terrorist Directive. Intelligence unit falling under the authority of the United States Department of Homeland Security.

**Dart rifle:** Rifle that shoots stun arrows.

**Data glasses:** Augmented Reality glasses with audio earbuds and a completely enclosed visual area.

**Desertec:** Solar project in the northwestern Sahara operated in collaboration between the EU and the Maghreb states.

**Perfuser:** Device for transporting substances between two membranes without an injection needle. Medical use.

**Drone ship:** Autonomous transport craft that automatically collects algae from sweeper ships and adds them to the algae carpets in the Pacific and the Atlantic.

**Earthling:** Colloquial name for a supporter of the Human Foundation and participant in the lottery system.

**EDI:** Ship's AI on the *Mars One*.

**Emergency capsule:** Rescue capsule on a spaceship.

**ESA:** European Space Agency, the space agency of the European Union.

**Evac capsule:** See emergency capsule.

**FHR Reactor:** Fluoride-salt-cooled High-temperature Reactor. A new liquid salt reactor (nuclear) concept that combines spherical graphite fuel elements, liquid salt as a coolant, safety systems consisting of sodium-cooled fast reactors, and the Brayton circuit process.

**Fission cutter:** Mono-bonded blade made of a single-molecule layer, capable of cutting even the hardest materials.

**Flettner Rotor:** A rotating cylinder exposed to an airflow that generates propulsive force perpendicular to the airflow utilizing the Magnus effect. It is the basis of a zero-emissions propulsion system first patented and used as a ship propulsion system by Anton Flettner.

**Furious Fifties:** Region of the Antarctic Circumpolar

Current (West Wind Drift) between 50 and 60° S latitude. Characterized by violent storms.

**G-8:** Gulfstream VIII, a business jet produced by Gulfstream Aerospace.

**Gloucester:** British-registered scrapper ship.

**GMC E-Falcon:** Electric SUV made by U.S. car manufacturer GMC.

**Iridium:** A chemical element, precious metal and a metal belonging to the platinum group. Known to be the most corrosion-resistant element.

**Jet:** A handheld device with a propeller system used by divers to move more quickly through the water.

**Joint Chiefs of Staff:** Military Chiefs of Staff for the four armed services of the United States (Army, Navy, Air Force and Marines).

**Leucocytes:** White blood cells, essential to the human immune system.

**Maglock:** Locking system that uses polarized magnets for closing and opening.

**Maglocksmith:** Device for used for picking maglocks.

**McMurdo:** Antarctic research station first operated by the United States (and later the Human Foundation).

**Medical cuff:** Autonomous medical device that can independently control analyses and medication infusion.

**Membrane perfuser:** See Perfuser.

**Microphage:** Immune cells that can absorb and transport foreign substances (e.g. bacteria). They can also envelop and devour foreign objects.

**MMR 3:** Mars Mission Reconnaissance 3. The third robotic mission to Mars sent to prepare for the human-crewed landings.

**MMSS:** Maximum Mobility Space Suit. Flexible spacesuit that works via contact pressure.

**Muon detector:** Detector system that uses cosmic rays to detect and locate subterranean cavities.

**Muon tomography:** A method for three-dimensional imaging of large-volume objects using muons found in cosmic rays.

**Nanonic:** Used to describe substances at the nano level manufactured by nanites.

**NASA:** National Aeronautics and Space Administration, the space agency of the United States of America.

**National Intelligence Service:** The South African domestic intelligence service.

**Neuro T5:** Liquid nerve venom that strongly sedates its victims.

*Ocean's Bitch:* Old scrapper ship under the command of Romain Alhy.

*Okamalé:* A ship belonging to the Coast Guard of the Maldive Islands.

**Paleocene:** Geological epoch of the Earth that began around 66 million years ago and ended about 56 million years ago.

**Paleogene:** A geological epoch of the Earth, lasting from approximately 66 million years ago until the start of the Neogene approximately 23.03 million years ago.

**Pleistocene:** Geological epoch of the Earth that began around 2.588 million years ago and ended about 12,000 years ago with the dawn of the modern era.

**Polymer:** Materials made of chained macromolecules.

**Programmable foam:** Nanonic foam, used for sealing holes (especially in spacesuits), automatically hardens but remains flexible.

**Project Blue Hole:** Research project exploring the mysterious "blue hole" in Antarctica, the location where the Antarctic ice sheet exhibited the phenomenon of melting from the inside out.

**Project Globe:** Human Foundation project to use microwaves to transmit energy from space-based solar power systems to earth.

**Project Heritage:** A top-secret Human Foundation project.

**Pyramid Mountain:** A 2,800-meter-high mountain in Antarctica, roughly pyramid-shaped.

**Radionuclide battery** (also radioisotope thermoelectric generator = RTG): Converts thermal energy from the spontaneous core decay of a radionuclide into electrical energy.

**Regolith:** Covering layer of loose material on top of an underlying source material, which formed on rocky planets in the solar system as the result of various geological processes.

**Roaring Forties:** Region of the Antarctic Circumpolar Current (West Wind Drift) between 40 and 50° S latitude. Characterized by violent storms.

**Roskosmos:** Space Agency of the Russian Federation.

**RTG:** See Radionuclide battery.

**Ruthenium:** A silver-white, hard and brittle platinum metal.

**Scrapper:** Term denoting a treasure hunter searching for wreckage from *Mars One* in the Indian Ocean.

**Seal patch:** Self-adhesive patch for sealing cracks and tears in spacesuits. Can be used to cover wounds.

**Self-driving software:** Artificial intelligence responsible for the control and safety of a vehicle, and capable of autonomous action.

**SETEF:** Space Exploration Training and Evaluation Facility. Astronaut training center located north of Reno, Nevada, in the United States.

**Sharkskin:** Skintight neoprene suit worn to protect divers from minor injuries.

**Solar Genesis:** Human Foundation project in its planning

phase to use giant solar sails in near-Earth orbit to supply the Earth with clean energy.

**Sons of Terra:** A terrorist organization the goals of which include warning humanity against an alien presence known as The Enemy, which they claim has taken control of the world powers.

**Space Dream:** Lottery operated by the Human Foundation promising the winner a place on a future Mars mission.

**Space Walker Suit:** Plastic spacesuit for Mars, developed by the Human Foundation.

**Sweeper:** Huge autonomous ship sweeping the world's oceans to collect plastic waste, which it then breaks down into carbon dioxide and hydrogen.

**Thrombocytes:** The smallest blood cells, responsible for blood clotting.

**Traffic control system:** AI-controlled road network connected to GPS satellites to control autonomous drive cars.

**Transducer net:** A mesh of electrodes that can be worn on the head and which measures and interprets brain waves to produce speech output through a computer system.

**TSA:** Transportation Security Administration. The American federal agency tasked with the security of the transportation sector.

**Universal connector:** The universal interface architecture that replaced the USB (Universal Serial Bus) system.

*USS Barack Obama:* Gerald R. Ford-class aircraft carrier of the U.S. Navy.

**Volkswagen E:** The best-selling electric car in the world.

**VR Compartment:** A distinct space with VR glasses, VR suit with feedback sensors, and a multidimensional treadmill to completely immerse a person in virtual reality.

**X-ray fluorescence analysis:** A method of material analysis based on X-ray fluorescence. It is one of the most commonly used methods for determining the qualitative and quantitative composition of a sample.

**Builders:**
**Aartan butterfly:** Primeval butterfly in the time of the Builders.
**Antuan:** Temple capital of the Builders.
**Astrogator:** Operator on a Builder spaceship. Responsible for the energy nodes and drive systems as well as all active external systems.
**Deka:** Time unit of the Builders.
**Follicle:** Inflammatory reaction medium for incubation processes.
**Geth:** Builders' Name for the pyramid in Antarctica.
**Goldan:** Mars.
**Controller:** Operator on a Builder spaceship. Responsible for the interior of the ship.
**Machine Weaver:** Engineer of the Builders.
**Mammarian:** Highly regarded caste of Builders who take care of the offspring.
**Monnbat:** Whale-like giant mammal that dominated the oceans in the era of the Builders.
**Navigator:** Ship navigator on a Builder spaceship.
**Pendum:** Time unit of the Builders.
**Photon manipulators:** Light sources of the Builders, which consist of artificial electromagnetic manipulators and do not have a physically visible source.
**Plasma rod:** Welding torch.
**Quantum singer:** Quantum researcher of the Builders.
**Quantum mirror:** Portal capable of transporting to an alternate reality.

**Sleep coffin:** Sleeping cabin of the Builders, which is equipped with all life support systems.

**Tangir:** Southern continent as it was 66 million BC.

**Technolog:** Builder researchers.

Editing: Stephen and Marcia Kwiecinski

English translation: Duane March

Cover: Cakamura Designs

First edition: 2021

Joshua Tree Limited

Skoutari 25, App. 73

8560 Peyia

Cyprus

www.joshuatcalvert.com

joshua@joshuatcalvert.com

Printed in Great Britain
by Amazon

56958280R00199